D0699164

The Sword of Medina

A Novel

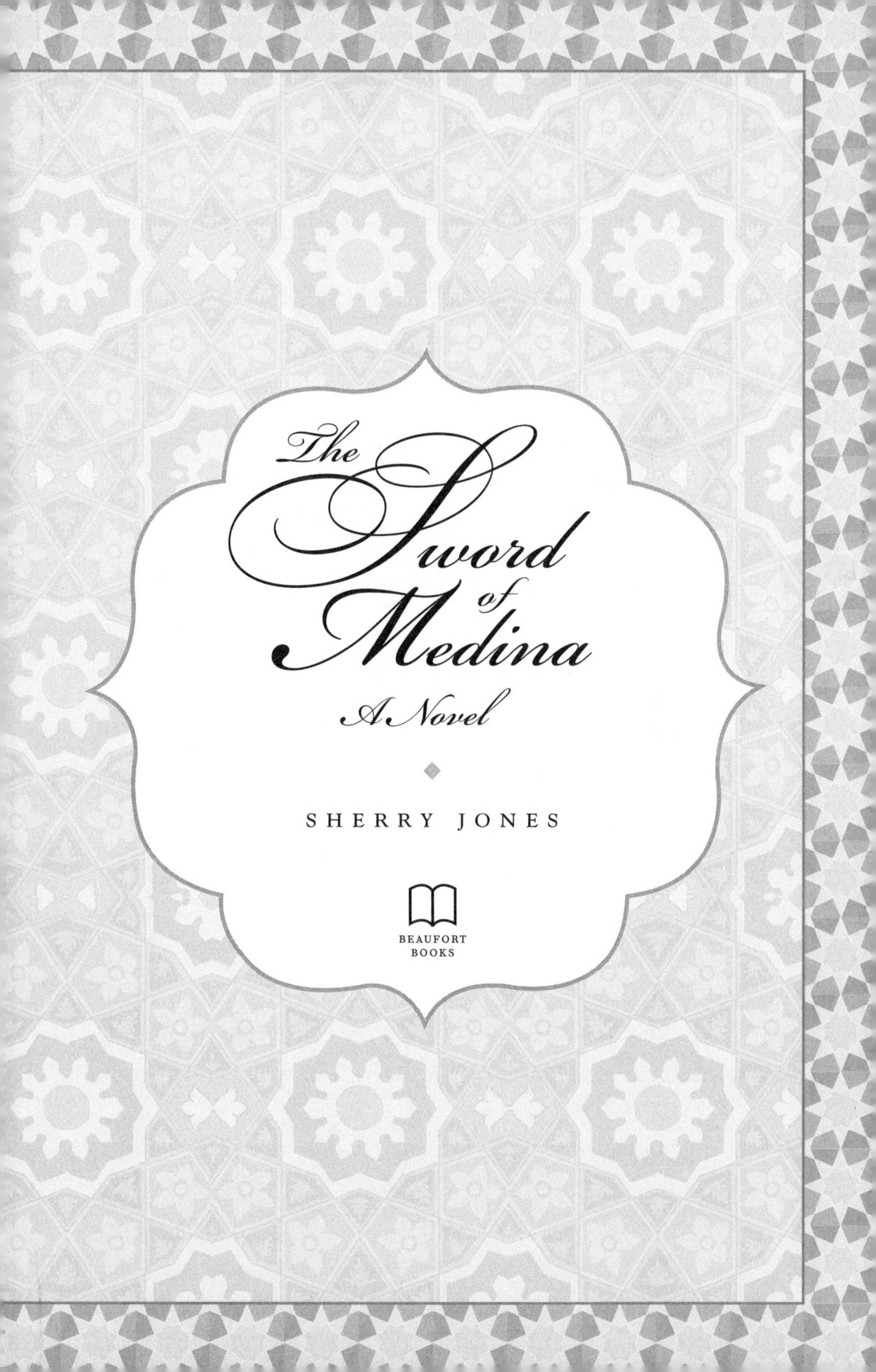

The Sword of Medina

A Novel

SHERRY JONES

BEAUFORT BOOKS

The Sword of Medina is a work of fiction. All characters, with the exception of well-known historical figures herein, and all dialogue, are products of the author's imagination.

FIRST EDITION

Cover Image: An Arab Girl holding a Sword, a Shield Behind her by Paul Desire Trouillebert (1829-1900) Private Collection/ Photo © Christie's Images/ The Bridgeman Art Library

Map: Kat Bennett, 360Geographics
Library of Congress Cataloging-in-Publication Data

Jones, Sherry, 1961-
The sword of Medina : a novel / Sherry Jones.
p. cm.
ISBN 978-0-8253-0520-7
1. 'A'ishah, ca. 614-678--Fiction. 2. 'Ali ibn Abi Talib, Caliph, 600 (ca.)-661--Fiction. 3. Muhammad, Prophet, d. 632--Fiction. 4. Muslims--History--Fiction. 5. Islam--History--Fiction. I. Title.
PS3610.O6285S96 2009
813'.6--dc22

2009016281

Published in the United States by Beaufort Books, New York
www.beaufortbooks.com

Distributed by Midpoint Trade Books, New York
www.midpointtrade.com

Printed in the United States of America

For Michael,
who reminds me every day
that love is a verb.

Acknowledgments

The author thanks Natasha Kern, literary agent extraordinaire and very dear friend, and my publishers, editors, and publicists around the world for their support during the most trying of times, especially Eric Kampmann and Erin Smith at Beaufort Books and publicist Michael Wright. Special thanks for editing help goes to Carol Craig and Trish Hoard, both of whom have helped make me a better writer, to Margot Atwell at Beaufort Books and Meike Frese at Pendo Verlag, who made this a better book, and to Richard Myers, Todd Mowbray, and the many other friends and fans who have encouraged me to persevere.

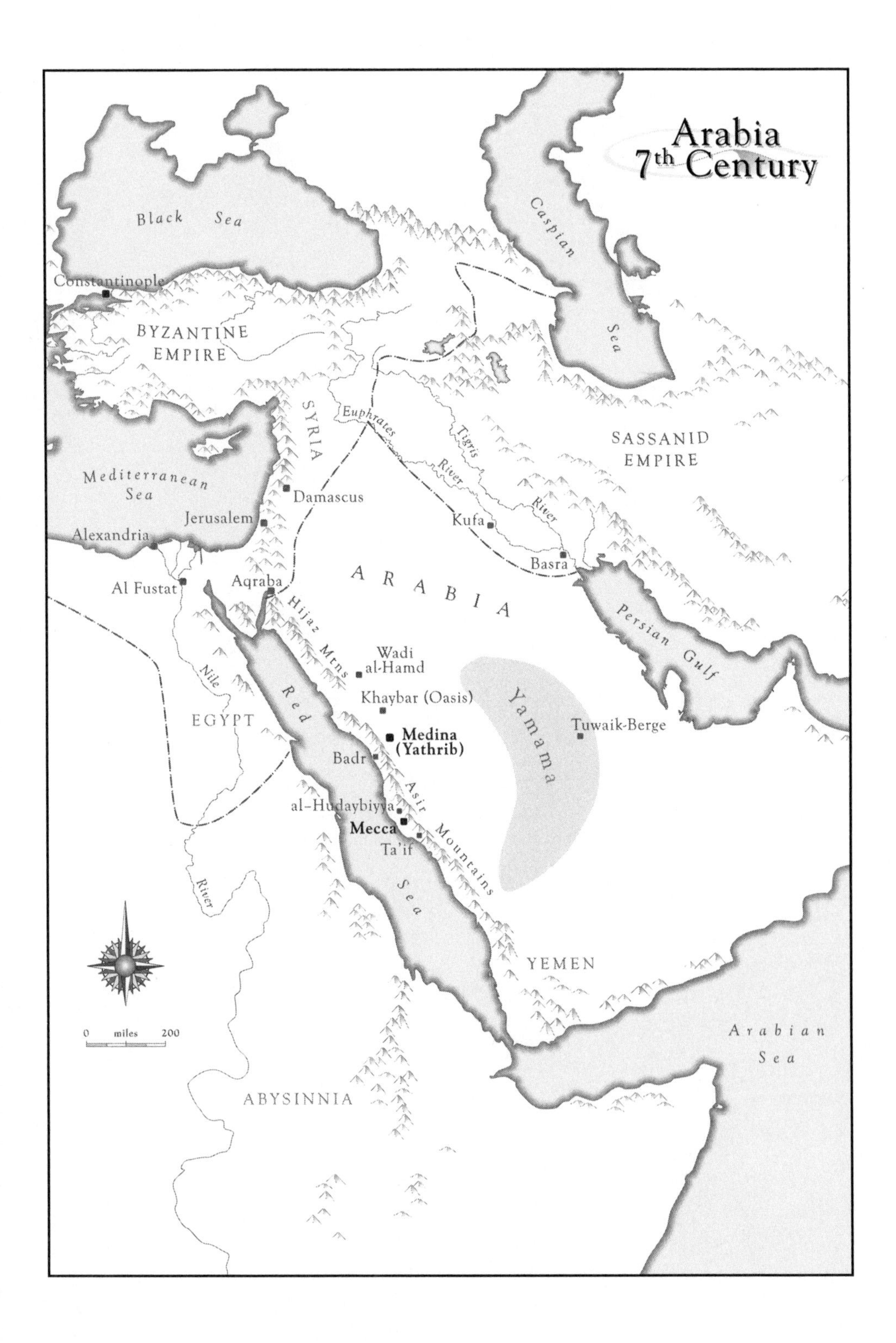
Arabia
7th Century
Black Sea
Caspian Sea
Constantinople
BYZANTINE EMPIRE
SYRIA
Euphrates
Tigris
River
River
SASSANID EMPIRE
Mediterranean Sea
Damascus
Jerusalem
Alexandria
Kufa
Basra
ARABIA
Al Fustat
Aqraba
Hijaz Mtns
Persian Gulf
Wadi al-Hamd
Nile
Khaybar (Oasis)
Yamama
Red
EGYPT
Medina (Yathrib)
Tuwaik-Berge
Badr
Asir
al-Hudaybiyya
Mecca
Ta'if
Mountains
River
Sea
YEMEN
0 miles 200
Arabian Sea
ABYSINNIA

THE FIRST RIGHTLY GUIDED CALIPH

◆

Abu Bakr

632–634 A.D.

A'isha

◆

Muhammad is dead.

In the heart-skip between waking and sleep, I remembered the awful truth. The long, slow exhale—my husband's final sigh—the evening before. His head pressed to my shuddering heart. His stiffened face, as if turned to stone, when I'd laid him in our bed. Now he lay beneath me, buried in my room, the fresh earth moistened by my tears. Exhausted after the long night, I'd fallen asleep atop his grave. Not even the call to morning prayer had roused me. Now a hand was shaking me awake, and Hafsa's voice, urgent. *A riot in the street. Your father. A'isha, you must come now.*

I could still hear the thunder and crash of my dreams. The images were already dissolving like mist burned away by the sun, but I vaguely recalled a splitting—was it the Ka'ba, our sacred temple, cracking in two? I sprang from my bed, my pulse fluttering, and shrugged off my nightmare, leaving it on the dirt floor. Holding our wrappers close about our faces, I and Hafsa ran into the small, cool mosque adjoining my hut, our bare feet kicking up dust, then out the mosque's front door and into Medina's main street. There a stampede of men brandished blades and cried, "*Yaa* Abu Bakr! *Yaa khalifa*! Praise to al-Lah for our new leader!" My heart's skitter slowed as I realized that *abi* wasn't in danger. The opposite was true: While I'd slept, my father, Abu Bakr, had won the heart of Medina.

Hours earlier, just after Muhammad's death, I'd gone to see *abi* in the town hall, where the men of Medina had gathered to choose the successor to my husband, the Prophet of al-Lah and the leader of our community. My father and his friends had learned of the meeting and hastened away to join it, leaving Muhammad's body unattended in my hut. I'd followed close behind, then returned to discover the terrible deed Muhammad's cousin Ali had committed, with his uncle urging him on.

I'd raced back to tell *abi*, who'd listened with his air of infinite calm as I'd described the digging of the grave in my bedroom floor while I'd listened outside the door; the washing of Muhammad's body while he was still clothed; the murmured assurances from al-Abbas, Ali's uncle, that this secret burial was necessary. If there were a public ceremony, he'd pointed out, my father, Muhammad's closest friend and advisor, would perform the prayer. *That would seal him once and for all as the Prophet's successor*, al-Abbas had said. Ali wanted the *khalifa* for himself. He and his uncle had hoped to keep my father from becoming the leader of Muslims. Today, I could see that their efforts had failed.

Men in white—Muhammad's color—and women whose wrappers sheltered their heads from the sun cheered and leaped and sang and whooped: "Come all, come! Pledge allegiance to the new *khalifa*, Abu Bakr al-Siddiq, the Truthful." After watching Muhammad's slow death from Medina fever I'd thought that my well was empty of tears, but now water flowed again at the sight of my father floating in the people's midst, carried aloft like a hero or king, his own eyes brimming, delaying his grief for the sake of the *umma*, the community of Believers.

I flattened myself against the building to avoid being trampled. But the torrent turned before it reached me and roiled into the mosque: Aws and Khazraj, the main tribes of Medina; emigrants from Mecca, our homeland, and elsewhere who'd come to Medina to escape persecution; and Bedouins of the desert, who'd loved Muhammad because he'd treated them as equals. Behind them marched Companions to Muhammad, including the stern Umar, his dark face forcing a heartsick smile, and Abu Ubaydah, whose eyes held worry even as he hoisted his sword and shouted *abi's* name.

Once they were all inside—by al-Lah, I never saw so many men squeeze into that tiny mosque!—I slipped in, also, made invisible by the wrapper I wore over my hair and face. The crowd set *abi* on the date-palm stump where Muhammad had stood countless times to lead our *umma* in prayer, with my elbow. "How could you steal the *khalifa* when it was given to you?" I said to him. "Al-Zubayr is only jealous."

"Does he want the position for himself?" My father shook his head. "Al-Zubayr is an ambitious man, but—to follow in Muhammad's footsteps?"

Talha grinned. "Al-Zubayr doesn't want the *khalifa*. He wants his cousin, Ali, in the position."

My laugh rang harsh. "Ali doesn't quit, does he?"

"Al-Zubayr and Ali say they'll die before they pledge allegiance to Abu Bakr," Talha said.

Umar hoisted his sword. "By al-Lah! I will be the one to fulfill their prophecy."

"Take heed, Umar," my father said. "I forbid you to carry a blade to the home of Ali."

The arm carrying Umar's sword fell limply to his side. He shook his head, mumbling. I held my breath, wondering if Umar would defy my father and undo everything the two of them had accomplished. Then, to my relief, Umar sheathed his blade.

"Hearing is obeying, *yaa khalifa*." With a gleam in his eye, he pulled a bullwhip from his belt.

"By al-Lah, here is all I need to do my work." His laugh cracked as he snapped the whip in my direction, making me flinch. "With this, I will have no trouble beating any rebels into submission—or strangling the defiance from their misguided throats."

◆

As Umar, Talha, and a growing mob from the mosque tramped down the street to Ali's house, I fled through winding alleys to my sister Asma's home—and found it empty. One of her sister-wives, a small woman with a frightened expression, shook her head when I asked where they'd gone. "Al-Zubayr dragged her away, and the boy Abdallah also. Al-Zubayr was shouting, 'I don't care if Abu Bakr is your father! You will not pledge allegiance to that traitor.'" I left her in a hurry, worry and fear clashing like swords about my head.

Asma and little Abdallah taken to Ali's! Al-Zubayr was using my sister. My father would never allow anyone to attack the house if he knew his eldest daughter and his only grandson were inside. Yet I'd heard Umar mention setting Ali's house on fire as he'd stormed away. Foreboding seized my chest as I fled back down the twisting path to the main road, thanking God for my father's ban on swords and daggers. *Please, al-Lah, keep my sister and nephew safe from harm.*

The crowd of men in front of Ali's home was as dense as if they were still hemmed in by the walls of the mosque. Shouts and threats punctured the air like the barks of dogs, and despite *abi's* prohibition I spied flashes of blade in the mid-morning sun. Wanting to avoid being seen by Umar—who would order me back to the mosque—I clambered over the courtyard wall and spied Asma through a rear window. She was huddled on the floor with Abdallah in her arms, holding him fast while he squirmed and protested that he wanted to join his *abi*.

Hearing my hiss, Asma leapt up and greeted me at the back door while Abdallah threw his arms around my knees. She beckoned me inside, then kissed my cheeks as I stepped into Ali's home. Looking around me, I felt my first twinges of compassion for the man I detested above all others.

His was a dark, barren house, more like a dwelling for hyenas than for humans. The kitchen, where I'd entered, offered one small window in a cramped room of mud brick whose walls needed whitewashing. A yeasty baby-smell tanged the air. A few tattered pillows of camel's hide lay on the dirt floor, which had no rug but only a crude woven mat of straw near the flat stone in one corner for grinding barley. There was no oven; Ali's wife, Fatima, baked her bread at the mosque. Often she and Ali would eat their daily meal with us there, Fatima joining the *harim* of sister-wives to gaze like a smitten puppy at Umm Salama and laugh wickedly when Zaynab insulted me. Fatima had always been jealous of Muhammad's love for me. How many times had I wondered why she didn't dine at home? Now, eyeing the squalid conditions here, I understood. We sister-wives lived ascetic lives, for Muhammad had always given all his possessions to the poor, but at least we had color and cheer—and windows—in our home.

We in the *harim* had time for weaving and dyeing cloth, and sewing cushions and curtains. There were eleven of us wives and concubines and only a few children, now adults, from previous marriages. Fatima, on the other hand, had three babies to care for. To feed her boys and infant girl, she worked as a laundress, a grueling job that stooped her back and left her hands red and raw. Where would she have found the time or energy for decorating? Ali had been so busy these past years fighting Quraysh and trying to sabotage my marriage that he probably didn't even notice the squalor.

As I embraced my sister and her sweet, hind-eyed little boy, a gurgling sound tugged at my ear. I peered in the dim lamplight and discovered Fatima in the shadows, sitting on the floor and shaking with sobs, uttering *abi, abi*. Mourning for Muhammad. She'd been his favorite daughter, the youngest of four and the very likeness, some said, of her mother, Khadija, Muhammad's only wife for twenty-five years. Fatima's baby girl, Zaynab, slept on the floor beside her. Her little boys, Ali al-Hassan and al-Hussein, patted her hair and back but she pushed them away. Once again, I felt the urge to abandon myself to grief—but my brother-in-law crashed into the room just then, drying my gathering tears with the force of his bluster.

When he saw me, his eyes widened and his nostrils flared.

"Praise al-Lah, my prayers are answered!" Al-Zubayr clamped his hand around my hair and dragged me into an adjoining room. My sister's shrieks, my shouts of outrage, Fatima's sobs, and her baby's cries filled the room. Anyone listening would have thought we'd hired the most dramatic wailing women in Hijaz.

Pain like one thousand and one needle pricks shot through my scalp each time al-Zubayr yanked my hair, stinging my eyes and making me too distraught to remember the dagger I'd sheathed under my left arm. Asma ran after us and leaped onto her husband's back. "Let my sister go," she cried, pummeling his back and arms. He released his hold on me and flung Asma to the floor, then kicked her in the stomach. As she doubled over, gasping for breath, I lunged toward al-Zubayr with a snarl, just as a sword whipped the air. I stopped mid-lunge to face a stern Ali.

"One should not interfere between a husband and his wife, *yaa* A'isha," he said. "As you told me many times during your marriage to Muhammad."

"How dare you speak Muhammad's name with the dirt from his illegitimate grave still under your fingernails?" I spat into his face. My spittle landed in his beard and stuck there.

With the back of his free hand, he wiped away my insult. "By al-Lah, it is not I who blasphemes the Prophet's memory, but your father. By seizing the *khalifa*, Abu Bakr mocks everything Muhammad achieved, and all he would have wanted."

"My father seized nothing." I lifted my chin. "He was chosen by the people."

"By the elites," al-Zubayr said. He lunged for me again but I whirled out of his reach.

"Al-Zubayr speaks the truth." For the first time I noticed al-Abbas, who sat behind me on a ragged cushion and cleaned his teeth with a *miswak* stick. He shook his head, sighing as if I were some poor, ignorant girl who needed to have the simplest of concepts explained. "The people never had a choice of *khalifa*. Abu Bakr and his rich Qurayshi friends snatched up the position before Muhammad's body had yet cooled. Ali was not even consulted."

"The people love Abu Bakr." I blinked back tears at the mention of Muhammad's body. *He is dead*. "They chose *abi* fairly and freely."

"Abu Bakr stole the *khalifa* in the night, like a thief!" al-Zubayr shouted through the window to the men outside. "And now, until he relinquishes his post and agrees to a fair election, his daughters will remain here. *Yaa* Talha! I have your beloved A'isha. Do you remember her? The girl you once wanted to marry? You will not see her again until Abu Bakr resigns."

His bragging didn't frighten me. As I knelt beside Asma, I looked up at al-Zubayr and saw not a fearsome warrior, as he had proved himself so many times, but a *majnun*, a crazed man. There was an emptiness in his eyes. I reminded myself to *think only, and cast aside your feelings*, as Muhammad had urged during my sword-fighting lessons. Al-Zubayr was not as clever as I. I had barely slept for three days, yet I still held the advantage.

"*Yaa* al-Zubayr, would you hide from Umar? That is most surprising." I smirked, stoking his rage.

"Al-Zubayr hides from no one!" he yelled, turning his head toward the window to be heard by Umar, Talha, and the rest. We could hear them talking again about setting fire to Ali's house.

"Making them burn you out would be an ignominious end to this rebellion," I said. "If I were you, I'd rush outside and run my sword through Umar's fat belly. He's one of those 'elites' you hate so much, isn't he?"

"Be quiet," Ali said to me. "Al-Zubayr, do not listen to her."

Al-Zubayr glared at me. "I will not fall for your trickery."

I shrugged. "Believe me, I wouldn't shed a tear if Umar met his end today." *I've never cared for men who beat their wives*, I could have added.

The baby's cries turned to screams. Al-Zubayr jerked his glance to Fatima, who was sobbing too hard to notice. Ali sheathed his sword and strode over to the child, then scooped it into his arms. I turned back to al-Zubayr.

"You're going to look quite foolish if you cower in here much longer," I said.

"Al-Zubayr does not care what you think," al-Abbas said. He tossed his *miswak* stick onto the floor.

"If you wanted a fight, though, you'd be disappointed," I said with a shrug. "None of those men has a weapon."

He cut his eyes at me. "No weapons? How can that be?"

"My father forbade it." I helped my sister to stand and, as she moved back into the kitchen, gave Ali a pointed look. "He wanted to make sure Ali didn't suffer any harm. Since Muhammad loved him so much."

Ali's expression softened. But al-Abbas snorted and said, "Abu Bakr is no idiot. He knows better than to gain Ali's allegiance at sword-point."

Al-Zubayr laughed. "You speak the truth, uncle. He will never gain my allegiance, either. As for the sword's point, let his messengers feel its sting!"

He threw open the door to his house and stepped over the threshold. Standing so close to him, I could have easily pulled out my dagger and knocked the sword from his hand. But I knew my father's admonition against weapons applied to me, also—and besides, I saw a better way. With a lift of my foot I tripped al-Zubayr, sending him and his sword clattering to the ground. In the next instant Umar stepped forward from the crowd, holding his whip aloft. With one flick he lashed it around al-Zubayr's neck and yanked him to his knees.

As Umar and his cohorts jostled al-Zubayr to the mosque, I went back inside and helped my sister and Abdallah walk back to their home. I settled her on her bed and gave a kiss to the child, who lay curled up beside her. He'd watched from the corner as his raging father attacked his mother. I caressed his brow and told him not to fret over what he'd seen, but to remember it.

"That way, you'll keep from ever harming the woman you love," I said.

The afternoon sun nearly struck me down with its own battering fist as

I headed home, my muscles aching with fatigue and my head throbbing. Soon I'd be in the privacy of my room, but one more obstacle stood in my way. When I arrived at my hut in the mosque courtyard, Talha awaited outside my green door.

"Invite me in," he said in a low voice. "We have urgent matters to discuss."

I felt myself droop like a plant in need of water, but I opened my door to him. Once we were inside, he gazed at me so intensely I felt my cheeks burn. How glad I was that my wrapper still hid my face! I pulled it more tightly and lowered my eyes to my bed, wishing he would leave so I could lie down.

"*Yaa* A'isha, what courage you exhibited today," he said. "Al-Zubayr would have attacked me or Umar with his sword. We might have been wounded or killed. I owe you a great debt—perhaps even my life."

I sighed and shook my head. Talha was exaggerating, as always. Life had never been exciting enough for him. That trait, more than his feelings for me, had once made him brag that, when Muhammad died, he would marry me. Unfortunately, his enthusiasm had sparked gossip in the *umma*, which caused Muhammad to declare that none of his wives could remarry. Because of that our futures now held loneliness and, with no husbands to provide for us, poverty, until we joined Muhammad in Paradise.

Of course, with my husband's body freshly buried in my room, I cared little about male companionship. Maybe that's why Talha's burning looks made me want to bury myself in the floor, also.

"I saw plenty of daggers and swords in the crowd around you and Umar," I said. "You were never in danger."

"Perhaps not," he said, "but *islam* faces a great threat." He stepped closer to me and placed his hands on my shoulders. How many times had he performed this gesture while giving me cousinly lectures? But now, with Muhammad's body lying under my feet, Talha's touch seemed wrong.

"*Yaa* Little Red, listen to me." Hearing Muhammad's nickname for me brought tears to my eyes again. "If Ali gains the *khalifa*, there won't be any future for you in *islam*, or for your father. In truth, Abu Bakr's entire clan—all of us—will lose everything, including our wealth and status. We can't let that happen, A'isha. Our family would suffer for generations."

Talha spoke the truth: Once a clan lost its status, getting it back was nearly impossible. But his words might as well have been the wind in my ears. After nursing Muhammad as he died, witnessing his secret burial, and seeing the *umma* so soon begin to tear itself apart, I felt numb to Talha's concerns.

I turned away, out of his reach.

"I don't know why you're telling me this. I'm a woman, remember?" Seeing my sister get kicked like a dog by one of the *umma's* top warriors—and seeing Ali do nothing to help her—told me this new *islam* offered little for women.

"You're a woman with a lot of influence." Talha stepped around to look me in the eyes again. "As Mother of the Believers and daughter of the *khalifa*, you have more power than most men, A'isha. You can protect our family's interests, if you desire."

But *did* I desire to play a part in these struggles? At the moment, the answer was "no." I wanted only to sleep and, when I awoke, resume my life of caring for the poor in the tent city, playing with my nephew Abdallah, cooking and gossiping with my sister-wives, and loving my husband.

But Muhammad was gone now. Everything was different.

I promised to think about Talha's words. Then I let him out and, at last, began to undress. As I untied my dagger's sheath from under my arm, my glance fell on the sword, lying on a shelf, that Muhammad had given me. My thoughts returned to his dying words: *Use it well in the* jihad *to come.*

"*Yaa* Muhammad," I said aloud, lying on the floor and pressing my body against his grave. "Here's another thing that's changed since your departure: I don't want to fight this battle, or any other. For the first time in my life, all I want is peace."

Ali

A'isha bint Abi Bakr was not a woman I would have chosen for myself, not with that fox-colored hair, not with that impertinent mouth. As I stood in the mosque with my sweet, humble wife and compared her to A'isha, I was reminded that Abu Bakr's youngest daughter had entered the world with the illusion that she was a queen, thanks to her doting father. And Muhammad, so wise in all other respects, had encouraged her erroneous belief.

When she had snapped her fingers, Muhammad had run to her side. When she defied him, he laughed. On the few occasions when she aroused his ire, she had only to flutter her eyelashes and he became as a man under a spell. By al-Lah! How I hated to see the Prophet of al-Lah display such weakness for a woman, especially one who valued herself so highly. I cringed doubly to stand in supplication to her now, as she sat beside Abu Bakr, the pretender to the *khalifa,* who held my family's fate in his hands and who listened to his daughter's every word as if they were gold dinars falling from her lips.

That her father suffered from the same malady as Muhammad was never more apparent than on the day my wife, Fatima, the epitome of womanhood, approached Abu Bakr in the mosque for her share of the property Muhammad had left behind. The income from even a tiny piece of his date-palm plantations would have provided us with so much that we needed: a wet-nurse for our little girl, Zaynab; a decent bed for us; a goat to supply our family with milk.

Anyone possessing a heart would have been moved by my poor wife's plea, uttered at that tyrant's feet while he perched like a monarch on the date-palm stump, profaning the place where a man so much better than he had exuded the very essence of al-Lah. Fatima entreated him with a voice as weak as the mewling of a newborn kitten, for in truth she was gravely ill with the fever that had struck her father down. We had told no one of her illness, for my wife was loath to see pity clouding the eyes of others. She had already endured solicitous comments and doleful glances too frequently, having lost her mother, two of her sisters, and her father.

"*Abi* would have wanted us to have this small inheritance," she said to Abu Bakr, keeping her eyes lowered modestly, as befitted a woman in her position. She did so in part because she did not wish her fever to be discovered, but I believed, watching her, that no one could fail to notice her trembling hands or her pale, perspiring brow.

Yet Abu Bakr was the foremost expert at seeing only what he desired to behold. I did not glimpse even the slightest turning down of his mouth at the sight of my poor Fatima begging him for what was rightfully hers—not even as he rejected her plea.

"Fatima, there is no doubt that your father loved you," he said in a voice like date syrup, a voice so thick that I thought—hoped—he might choke. "You were the favorite of all his daughters. Tell me, *yaa* A'isha. You knew the Prophet more intimately than anyone. Do I speak the truth?"

How I wanted to erase his smug smile with a single swipe of my blade! My muscles twitched to do so, for his self-satisfied air had inspired my dislike from the day of our first meeting. I was but a child then, with a child's perception, but I knew when Muhammad introduced us that Abu Bakr loved himself above all others, even more than he loved Muhammad, for whom, al-Lah willing, I would have given my life not once, but many times over.

On this day, Abu Bakr's love for himself and for his daughter was quite apparent. As A'isha nodded to confirm Muhammad's good opinion of Fatima, that goat-bearded pretender glowed as if his haughty daughter were a mirror reflecting the brightest of flames. Bile rose in my throat as my trusting wife stood with bowed head and the slightest of smiles upon her lips, certain that her request was about to be granted. But her expression withered like rose petals under the desert sun when Abu Bakr spoke again.

"My dear Fatima," he said, "I know you believe that Muhammad would have bequeathed you all of Hijaz, if it belonged to him. But let us examine the way things truly were, child. The Prophet gave you little while he lived, preferring to aid the poor. Do I speak the truth?"

Fatima could not bring herself to respond, so pitifully was she biting her lower lip in an effort not to humiliate herself further by shedding tears. I clenched my jaw, commanding myself not to speak, for she had asked that I remain beside her in silence while she presented her petition. *Your long-standing enmity with Abu Bakr may harm our cause*, she had said.

In truth, Fatima had not wanted me to accompany her today, but I had insisted on doing so. I was wary of the treatment she might receive from this man who had deceived so many with his seemingly benign charm that he was known as *al-Siddiq*, "The Truthful." It was a name that he proved, with his next words, to be erroneous.

"Fatima, I was present during your father's final hours of life," he said, tugging at the beard he had dyed red—to match his daughter's hair, no doubt. "And I distinctly heard him say, 'We do not have heirs. Whatever we leave is alms.'"

How my blood raged at this lie! In truth, I nearly bounded across the mosque floor to rip that sickly-sweet smile from his face, but Fatima stretched out her arm and halted me as effectively as if she wielded a sword.

"Forgive me, Abu Bakr," she said in a voice that shook like a leaf in the wind, "but truly you are mistaken. My father would not have said this."

"I assure you, he did," that liar said through those smiling lips.

"Perhaps, then, he was speaking of the dinars and dirhams he left in the treasury."

Abu Bakr shook his head. "Child, he left no coins in the treasury. He had given everything away."

"Then he must have been instructing you to give his camels, goats, and sheep to needy families," she said, her voice shrinking with each word until, at the end of her sentence, she sounded very far away. This was my Fatima: When she became angry, she never shouted or became shrill, but spoke more and more quietly, until her rage emerged as two red dots, one in the center of each pale cheek.

"*Afwan*, Fatima. I am sorry. The Prophet left no animals, only the oasis lands for which you ask. As you know, the proceeds from those farmlands have always supported the *umma's* poor, as well as the Prophet's household and yours. I believe he intended for that practice to continue. He certainly would not have wanted his wives or children to take the lands for themselves, and deprive those who depend on their income."

"You are lying," she rasped between teeth clenched like a fist. "My father never said it."

Abu Bakr's eyes popped open in surprise, a rare show of emotion from him in response to these words of disrespect from Fatima bint Muhammad, usually the perfect example of flowering womanhood. He turned to A'isha, the opposite of my beloved Fatima in every way, for confirmation of his falsehoods.

Her face held little color and her eyes softened as she gazed upon Fatima. For a moment, I thought she might disappoint him.

"Fatima and Ali are in need, *yaa abi*," she said, pricking my pride so that my face and neck burned. How humiliating to rely on this spoiled child's intercession! It was almost enough to send me reeling from the room.

"I've been in their home, and they have even less than me and my sister-wives," she said. "It was appalling, the crudeness of their furnishings, the lack of kitchen equipment, the dearth of food. The baby was lying on the floor for want of even an animal hide! I speak truly, *abi*: Ali's household is as poor as many in the tent city."

To hear her talk of our home in such condescending tones was excruciating. I imagined her standing in my house, casting supercilious glances at the ceiling, the walls, the floor, wrinkling her nose in disgust at what we lacked, touching with only her left hand—her bottom-wiping hand—the few items we did possess.

"But did you not hear the Prophet's request?" Abu Bakr pressed, his smile tight, his eyes boring like wood-eating worms into his daughter's hesitancy. "I am certain you must have heard it, for the Prophet's head rested against your chest as he spoke. Do you not remember how surprised I was to hear him say, 'We have no heirs, whatever we leave is alms'?"

A'isha's gaze darted from her father to Fatima and back again. She licked her lips and cleared her throat. Then at last—as I knew she would, for she is her father's daughter, after all—she nodded her head.

"Yes, *abi*, it's just as you say," that deceitful she-dog said. "I didn't remember it at first, probably because I was so grief-stricken at the time. But now I can hear Muhammad's voice clearly. It's as if he were here in the room with us."

Although I and Fatima did not touch, I could feel her body's shiver as if a cold wind had blown into the room. The time had come when I could no longer deny myself the urge to speak on her behalf—and, in truth, on my own behalf, for without the added income we would be relegated to struggle and squalor for the remainder of our lives. Fatima might have little time left in this world. I desired that, when she departed, she should know that her children would thrive.

"*Yaa* Abu Bakr," I said, ignoring Fatima's darting glance of alarm, "may I remind you that the Prophet enjoined us to care for the *ahl al-bayt*, the 'people of the house'? He left no sons, but two grandsons—Fatima's sons, and mine. Clearly, he would have wanted them to be provided for."

I addressed him in as controlled a tone as I could manage but, by al-Lah! I did so with a lifted chin. Even now, three months after Muhammad's death, I had not pledged allegiance to the man who stole the *khalifa* from me and my sons. I was not going to humble myself before him now, not for what was rightfully mine.

"Several times in the *qur'an* Muhammad establishes special considerations for the *ahl al-bayt*," I said. "He also granted to daughters the right to inherit money and property from their fathers. Would he have wanted to exclude his favorite offspring from these provisions that he himself made?"

"I do not know the answers to your questions," Abu Bakr said. "I only know what Muhammad said." He lifted his eyebrows at me in a consternation I knew to be feigned. "*Yaa* Ali, you were like a son to Muhammad, and I know you loved him well. Do you desire that his deathbed wishes be ignored for the sake of your own gain?"

That condescending tone; that supercilious gaze: Only a fool would have misconstrued his meaning, and Ali ibn Abi Talib is not a fool. Even A'isha's eyebrows jerked upward, so startled was she by his insinuations.

Unlike Fatima, I do not allow anger to consume my energy. For me, anger is a fiery spice sending heat through my blood and incensing my tongue. Although I had promised Fatima that I would remain calm today, Abu Bakr's insult acted as a fuel for that anger.

In an instant I had drawn my double-bladed sword and was pointing it at his eyes. A'isha gasped and leapt to her feet, then drew her own sword—*my* sword, al-Ma'thur, "The Legacy," bequeathed to me by my cousin along with all his weapons. A'isha claimed he had given it to her, but I knew she had coerced the bejeweled sword from Muhammad in his moment of ultimate weakness. Now she dared point it at me. His gaze still locked with mine, Abu Bakr admonished his errant daughter to sheath her blade and resume her seat.

"Do you think we relished this appearance before you, whom we already knew to be a man with the basest of scruples?" I cried. I paced the floor between him and Fatima, waving my sword.

Stopping before him I said, "In spite of your greedy behaviors of recent months, we approached you in the utmost humility—"

"You have shown perfect humility until this moment." Abu Bakr spoke as calmly as if he were discussing the sleep he had enjoyed the previous night.

"—knowing you would deny us, yet desiring to give you the opportunity to right past wrongs and redeem yourself," I continued, ignoring him. "Instead, you increase your sins by depriving the Prophet's daughter of her inheritance and accusing me of coveting it to enhance my status."

"You are known for your ambition," that scoundrel said. "Would you deny it, while you claim an inheritance that was never granted to you?"

"My inheritance has already been wrested from me," I raged. "This is Fatima's legacy we are discussing. And your hypocrisy reaches new levels, *yaa khalifa*, when you accuse me of ambition."

"Do you deny that you seek the *khalifa*, then?"

In truth, I desired nothing less at that moment. Abu Bakr had already committed errors that threatened to destroy everything Muhammad had built, such as sending an inexperienced youth, Osama ibn Zayd, to lead a military campaign into Syria. I was denied the privilege of joining the force, despite my stellar achievements as Muhammad's most courageous and skilled fighter. Obviously, Abu Bakr lacked the judgment needed for this important position. And he could not have chosen a worse time to send our warriors on a muscle-flexing expedition. Bedouin tribes throughout Hijaz now threatened to invade Medina, for they assumed that Muhammad's death had weakened us. With most of our warriors away, those of us who remained in Medina lived in dread of an attack we could not forestall.

Not only were our numbers too paltry to wage a competent defense, but our stomachs were as empty as gourds. Abu Bakr did not feed us, claiming the treasury had been empty when he inherited it, but he could afford somehow to stage an elaborate show of might in effort to impress our neighbors to the north.

I had no wish to be holding the command when Medina sank to its knees and *islam* breathed its final breath. Nor did I have the energy that would be required to repair Abu Bakr's damage. My uncle al-Abbas and my cousin al-Zubayr had been urging me toward the *khalifa* since Muhammad's death, no doubt because they coveted the status that would ensue for them, my relations. As for me, I wanted only what was mine, and I wanted my wife to have what belonged to her.

I lifted my chin at my adversary, knowing that if I denied his accusation he would not believe me. While I stood in silence, my raised arm weakening, my demure wife stepped forward and took the sword from me, and pointed it at the thief-*khalifa's* heart.

"If it is Ali's allegiance you covet, *yaa* Abu Bakr, then you are not as intelligent as you are reputed to be. Denying my inheritance will only increase his hatred for you. By doing this thing, you injure the *umma* with a wound that may never heal."

She handed the sword to me and I placed it in its sheath. "The rest is between you and al-Lah," she said. "This is the last time I will ever enter this mosque."

She turned and walked with her head high to the mosque entry. There she flung the dust from her heels with great ceremony. I could think of no more effective action so I merely walked out behind her. I had no worries that Abu Bakr would retaliate against us for our rudeness to him. How could he harm the Prophet of al-Lah's favorite daughter and most beloved cousin beyond what he had already done? He would lose all his support if he caused injury to either of us.

We swept past a small crowd waiting to petition the *khalifa*. Fatima ignored their curious stares; I hurled daggers with my eyes. We arrived at our home to find al-Zubayr waiting for us.

"*Ahlan*, Ali, I have come with an announcement that you will not enjoy, but that I hope you will forgive," al-Zubayr said. I waited for Fatima to hasten inside and leave us, but she remained, casting a sidelong glance at him.

"I have heard enough bad news for one day, cousin," I said with a sigh.

Al-Zubayr's gaze fell from my face to the ground, and he shifted from his right foot to his left. "I wanted to tell you before you heard it from another. I pledged allegiance to Abu Bakr this morning."

"Traitor!" Fatima hissed the word so quietly, she might have been a serpent about to strike.

"I had no choice," he said. "I need to fight in the army to earn money for my family. Only those who have pledged may join."

"So you have sold your loyalty like everyone else in Medina." Fatima rasped. "And Ali and I stand alone for what is right. So be it. Now you may leave our home, never to return."

Al-Zubayr turned to me for refutation of her vow, but, by al-Lah, I could not bring myself to contradict a dying woman. I merely stood in silence, unable to meet my cousin's questioning eyes.

He cleared his throat. "I hear and obey. I will leave you. *Ma' salaama*, Ali. Fatima."

I watched as he trudged away, then turned to Fatima to discuss the matter with her. But her head was lolling and her eyes rolled back so that only the whites were showing. I caught my gentle Fatima—graceful even in sickness—in my arms before she would have fainted at my feet.

Her skin burned; an acrid smell like singed hair made me reel. Perspiration drenched her hair and clothing. Sobbing like a man who has lost everything, and feeling as empty as if my heart had been torn from my chest, I carried my dear, dying Fatima to her bed. The moment her head touched the camel's-feed bag that served as our pillow, her eyes sprang open to stare at me in horror, as if I had transformed into a fearsome *djinni*, and she gripped my arm.

"My head," she said, gasping. "Please . . . Ali . . . help me."

I hastened next door to fetch our neighbor, Jalila, who was already caring for our children that morning. Then I ran to the market, my every breath measured for Fatima, my every thought now focused on relieving her agony. I had seen a similar expression of torment on Muhammad's face the day before he died, and I had seen A'isha administer medicine to abate his pain. From her deceitful words this morning, I knew A'isha would be unwilling to assist my wife, but the apothecary at the market would be able to dispense a remedy.

I had known Abu Shams for many years, and had benefited from his potions when, on our arrival in Medina, I had become ill after eating a variety of *kema*, desert truffles. I had also consulted with him when my oldest son, Ali al-Hassan, had been colicky as an infant and, later, when his baby's teeth had broken through his gums. Abu Shams' concoctions were always distasteful but effective, and so it was with hopefulness that I turned to him.

As I approached his stall, I was surprised to detect no warmth on Abu Shams' gray-bearded face, and to hear no greeting save a grunt from his pinched lips. Preoccupied with Fatima's illness, I ignored his reticence and launched into my request.

His expression never softened, not even upon hearing my description of Fatima's symptoms. When I had finished speaking, he regarded me with eyes as narrowed and piercing as those of a cat.

"*Yaa* Abu al-Hassan," he said, addressing me by my *kunya*, my honorary father's name, "I understand your need. Yet I am obliged to do business only with those who are loyal to our new *khalifa*." He frowned. "I hear you have not yet pledged your allegiance to Abu Bakr."

I felt as if all the blood in my body had rushed to my face, making me hot in the head yet cold in my trembling hands. Speaking in a measured, respectful tone was, for the second time that day, an excruciating struggle.

"*Yaa* Abu Shams," I said. "Excuse me. I do not see a connection between this matter and my wife's need for medicine."

He shrugged. Was Fatima's impending death a matter to be cast off so lightly? I clenched my teeth together, trying to smile.

"Only those who serve the *khalifa* receive service here," he said. "*Afwan*, Abu al-Hassan, I did not make this rule. The *khalifa* sent word of it yesterday."

In that moment, the storm that had been gathering in me all morning erupted. I snatched the neck of Abu Shams' *bishr*.

"God damn the *khalifa*!" I cried, eliciting gasps from those around us. "Will you deny treatment to the beloved daughter of the Prophet of God? What will you say of this evil deed when you face Muhammad in Paradise?

Or perhaps this act will send you to burn in hellfire, instead, with Abu Bakr and his arrogant daughter."

He tried to sputter an answer. Then, from behind me, I heard the most irritating voice in all of Hijaz. "Arrogant? That's like the camel telling the cow it's ugly, isn't it?" A'isha said. I released Abu Shams and spun away from them both, wanting as much distance as possible between myself and this hated woman. She placed a hand on my sleeve, and I turned to her. To my confusion, she did not smirk, but gazed up at me with concern.

"Is it Fatima?" she said in a low voice. "If you're trying to buy medicine for her, forget it. They won't take your money until you pledge allegiance to my father."

"Your breath is wasted," I snarled. "Abu Shams has informed me of the shameful boycott."

"You're the one who should feel ashamed," she dared to respond. "Do you realize how close you've come to destroying *islam*? People are fighting in the streets over your so-called right to rule."

I bore down on her with the force of my stare, my heated breath, and my superior height, pinning her against the stall without touching her. She merely lifted her eyebrows.

"*You* are the one who will destroy *islam*, you and your incompetent father," I said. "First you send our warriors away on a useless mission, leaving the rest of us unprotected. And now you deny Muhammad's daughter her inheritance. What was my cousin, your husband, supposed to have said? 'What we leave is alms'? I never heard him utter those words."

Uncertainty crossed her face but she masked her dishonesty with a laugh. "It's no wonder *you* didn't hear it," she said. "The dog barks too loudly to hear the eagle's cry."

Overhead, the scrape of a crow's *caw* brought to mind my beloved Fatima's anguish, and I raised my fist in despair, wanting only to bring it down upon the taunting, uncaring redhead who defied me with such impertinence. "By al-Lah, where is your shame?" I whispered, but still she would not cringe.

"You wouldn't assault a Mother of the Believers." She gazed steadily into my eyes.

A'isha spoke the truth: I could not strike her, no matter how I hated her. She was a widow of Muhammad, revered as the mother of Muslims. Nor would I strike any woman, al-Lah help me, because Muhammad had taught me to exhibit, as he did, the utmost respect for all women—even this one.

"You are mother to all Believers, it seems, except my poor wife." I took a step back from her and allowed my arm to drop impotently to my side. "She lies dying of the Medina fever, and you and your father deny her care."

"Dying!" Sorrow clouded her eyes. She turned and said a few words to Abu Shams, who scowled at me, nodded, and handed her a small pouch.

She offered the packet and I snatched it from her, part of me fearing a prank such as she would have played when she was a child. "Give it to Fatima, with my prayers," she said. "It won't cure her—only al-Lah can do that—but it will make her feel better."

And then, as I struggled to form words of thanks, A'isha hurried away from me into the market crowd—not like a lioness, as she so frequently paraded herself before the public, but, for the first time in my memory, with her head down and her eyes to the ground, humbly, as befits a woman.

A'isha

The Medina fever was no way to die, as I knew from years of tending those stricken with it. Imagining Fatima's agony filled me with compassion as I stood over her grave with the thousands of mourners who'd come to her funeral. I was grateful, for once, for the requirement that the Prophet's wives veil their faces. Otherwise, those around me might take one look at my red-rimmed eyes and whisper *See how A'isha forces her tears!*

I and Fatima had not been friends. In truth, we had despised each other. We'd clashed since the day we'd met—not in the way Ali and I did, like sharpened blades, but more quietly, like rams butting heads over a fence. Today, huddled in the drizzle with my sister-wives, I watched Ali step down into Fatima's grave and I regretted that I hadn't at least tried to set things right between us during her final weeks.

It should have been so easy. Hadn't we both loved Muhammad nearly all our lives? And weren't we fairly close in age? Those two traits alone might have made us friends. But Fatima was the youngest of Muhammad's daughters, his baby, as beloved by her father as I was by mine. She'd been glad to see her sisters marry and move into their husbands' households, leaving Muhammad for her alone. Yet he never did belong completely to Fatima, because, when I became his betrothed at age six, I took possession of a tiny piece of his heart—a piece that grew with each of his daily visits to me. When I married him, at nine, his eyes welled with love. By the time I moved into his home, when I was nearly twelve, he'd lost his heart to me completely. Meanwhile, Fatima found herself shunted off to Muhammad's temperamental cousin, Ali.

It was no wonder that she'd been jealous. Yet, as I listened to al-Abbas say the prayers over her body—normally the *khalifa's* duty, but Ali had refused to let my father—I couldn't help chastising myself. Why hadn't I tried to befriend Fatima?

In fact, I'd been jealous, also. *Love is not a dish of tharid,* Muhammad had told me once—meaning I didn't need to be greedy because the human capacity for love is limitless. Muhammad had enough love for me and eleven sister-wives, as well as an entire *umma.* His affection for Fatima had never diluted his devotion to me. Yet I'd behaved as wickedly as she, cutting her with my tongue, clinging to Muhammad whenever she visited, and, worst of all, supporting my father's decision not to grant her inheritance to her.

We do not have heirs. Whatever we leave is alms. Try as I might, I couldn't recall hearing Muhammad say these words, although *abi* insisted he had. Why had I gone along with my father's tale? If I'd argued with him or urged him to compromise, *abi* might have given Fatima some portion of the Khaybar lands, at least.

I remembered how Fatima seemed to shrink in the mosque that day until she resembled a tiny, squeaking mouse. I'd felt a stab of satisfaction at the sight of her so diminished, but now my face burned at the memory, and I realized that I was the one who'd been small.

How ridiculous I felt now, sniffling over her grave. I looked around, self-conscious. I needn't have worried about being noticed, though. Next to me, Umm Salama and Zaynab sobbed and held each other as if to keep from falling into the hole. Sawdah, who had raised Fatima from girlhood and loved her as though she were her own, wailed and moaned too, ignoring Umar's baleful glances. Even my father's eyes were moist, for, as Muhammad's longtime friend, he'd known Fatima since the day of her birth.

He's the hypocrite. The thought struck me like a blow, stealing my breath But, no. My father had denied Fatima her inheritance so that the *umma* might live, as he'd told her. In truth, she couldn't have chosen a worse time to ask for the lands. And her cold demeanor toward my father in the past—in support of Ali, who had always regarded *abi* as a rival for Muhammad's affection—hadn't inclined him favorably to her. She must have known her petition might fail. But she'd also known she was dying, and she'd wanted to make sure her family would be cared for.

My heart's edges softened even more when, as Ali scattered rose petals in Fatima's hair, their son al-Hassan began to cry and call for his *ummi*. "Come to A'isha," I said, holding out my arms to the little boy.

I patted and stroked his hair the color of wheat, his father's hair, and told him his *ummi* had gone to be with her father, Muhammad, and that she was waiting for him in Paradise. His sobbing subsided as I carried him to the back of the crowd. What was Ali thinking of, bringing the boy here? Watching the gravediggers fling dirt over his mother's body would give him nightmares for the rest of his life.

"Don't worry," I murmured. "Your *abi* is here to take care of you. And you have me to cry on, see?"

Rough hands jerked him out of my grasp, and I looked up into the savage face of Ali. "What are you doing with my son?" he said. Heat spread across my cheeks as though he'd slapped me.

"Comforting him," I murmured, lowering my eyes.

Ali laughed harshly. "Comforting the child after hastening the mother's death? By al-Lah! How Fatima would have benefited from your compassion a few weeks ago."

Murmurs rustled through the crowd like blowing sand as he swept through the onlookers, his arms gripping his little boy who had begun to cry again. As I rejoined my sister-wives, his words echoed in my head. All I could see was Fatima's wan face that sad morning as she'd petitioned *abi* for her inheritance. Again, the question tormented me: Had Muhammad in truth said *We have no heirs*?

If someone else—al-Abbas, for instance, or even his son—had claimed to hear such outlandish words from Muhammad, I'd suspect him of inventing the tale. Only three months after my husband's death, incredible stories about him were moving through the *umma*. *The Prophet said my infant son would become the mightiest warrior Hijaz has ever known*! After someone died, it often surfaced that Muhammad had predicted the time, place, and circumstances of the death and promised that person a place with him in Paradise.

I knew *abi* wasn't inventing his tale. But if what he said was true, there was one question I couldn't answer: Why would Muhammad have bequeathed his property yet neglected to appoint a *khalifa*? The resulting struggle for power had almost torn our community apart—and Muhammad's strange bequest had broken Fatima's heart.

As a warrior under Muhammad, Ali had collected plenty of booty—although, like Muhammad, he'd given most of it to the poor. Now, Ali no longer had the earnings from Fatima's work as a laundress, and his disloyalty to my father had cost him his right to fight. The income from just one of Muhammad's date plantations would have gone far to help Ali and his family. If only Muhammad hadn't left that income to the needy! But he couldn't have foreseen that Ali would lose his war booty so soon. He wouldn't have wanted his own family to go hungry.

When I'd broached these questions with *abi*, he'd frowned. *There are aspects to the* khalifa *that even you cannot understand.* But I knew a lot more than he realized. I knew Muhammad had left an empty treasury. I knew the Byzantine emperor now sent his caravans on a trade route that bypassed Medina, depriving our merchants of income or goods. I knew that, since Muhammad's death, many had turned their backs on *islam* and were refusing to pay the *zakat*, the alms-tax they'd been giving Muhammad. These were desperate times for the *umma*. That was why *abi* had said "no" to Fatima.

But Ali's support was crucial, not just to my father's ability to rule, but also to the future of *islam*. As Muhammad's cousin, son-in-law, and foster son, and as father to Muhammad's heirs, Ali held sway with Believers throughout Hijaz. If he continued to oppose my father, the Muslim community would tear like a ripped cloth, its edges too frayed to ever mend. *Abi* must gain his allegiance for the sake of the *umma*.

Ali is stubborn, my father had said to me, *but his children's hunger will weaken his resolve.*

Sitting on the courtyard grass that evening, my sister-wives fed my anxieties with their talk.

"With all respect to your father, *yaa* A'isha, I don't blame Ali for being angry," Zaynab said with a toss of her head. "What Abu Bakr did was wrong."

Hafsa leapt to my defense. "Maybe we should make you the next *khalifa*, *yaa* Zaynab," she said. "Since you seem to know so much."

"As for me, I know little," Umm Salama said quietly. "Yet I do not believe Muhammad would have wanted to leave his grandchildren in destitution."

"Why not?" Raihana said. "He left *us* without anything, didn't he?"

"Some of us," Saffiya said, cocking a jealous eyebrow at Hafsa, who wore a new robe that her father, Umar, had given her for the funeral. Like Raihana, who was her cousin, the pretty, young Saffiya had come to our *harim* a princess from a Jewish tribe—a captive who had used her wiles to captivate. She hadn't fooled any of us sister-wives—although I later befriended her—but Muhammad had been so entranced that he'd broken all the rules by marrying her on the battlefield, instead of waiting until they returned to Medina. I still grinned to remember her triumphal entry into town, for I always imagined the shock that must have followed when she'd beheld her squalid hut.

"Aw, we will be all right," Sawdah said. "We know we will be taken care of."

"By whom?" Raihana lifted her eyebrows. "You've got a lucrative leather trade, Sawdah, and the rest of you have your families to depend on. But as for Saffiya, Juwairriyah, and me, Muhammad's army killed our fathers and brothers. What's going to happen to us?"

"If we could marry again, survival would be easier," Juwairriyah said timidly.

"It's going to be a lonely life," Saffiya said with a sigh.

As they spoke, I felt as though a leather strap had been tied across my chest. How could my sister-wives talk about remarrying just a few months after Muhammad's death? Yet there was truth in their words. By forbidding his wives to marry again, Muhammad had relegated us all to lives of loneliness. He'd made the pronouncement in order to stop gossip about us, but his decree had a far-reaching effect.

Hafsa snickered. "Maybe we should follow Maryam's example and hire eunuchs to keep us company."

"Maryam seems happy enough," Raihana said. "Of course, there's only so much a eunuch can do."

"You might be surprised," Umm Habiba said with a sly smile. "I've heard tales about eunuchs that would make your toes curl."

Maryam was Muhammad's concubine from Egypt, a gift from that country's Muqawqis, or religious leader. She had brought with her a servant, a tall black man named Akiiki. His devotion to Maryam had sparked many rumors until, confronted by Ali, he'd lifted the hem of his skirt to prove that he was no threat. How I would have loved to be a fly in Ali's eye at that moment! His double-bladed sword must have dropped to the floor.

Afterwards, Ali had accused me of meddling for telling Muhammad about Akiiki. "That's high praise, coming from an expert in the art," I retorted. Jealous not only of my father, but of me also, Ali had caused problems in my marriage that I could never forgive him for.

Amused though I was by my sister-wives' speculations, I knew I couldn't let this dangerous talk continue. In spite of the restrictions Muhammad had placed on his wives, he'd resisted the urgings of men like Umar to lock us up in our homes. Now that Muhammad was gone, who would guard us from losing our freedom? If scandal touched a hair on any of our heads, we'd all be prisoners forever.

"By al-Lah! Muhammad trusted Maryam, and so should we." My voice rang harsh. "Be careful, sister-wives, not to turn against one another out of boredom or fear. Look what's happening in the *umma,* with Ali's accusations turning brothers against brothers. If we don't pull together, *islam* will die—and we, the Mothers of the Believers, will be nothing."

"We'll be a house full of widows waiting for a man to claim us," Raihana said with a shrug. "I lived through it once, and ended up here."

"Yes, but you gained Muhammad as a husband," I argued. "What other man treated women with such respect?"

"Respect is wonderful, but you can't eat it," Raihana retorted. "Without a husband, who is going to feed me, *yaa* A'isha? Your father? He talks a lot about following Muhammad's example while he lets the Prophet's wives starve."

I knew Raihana spoke truly, but I also knew my sister-wives were wrong to blame my father for their hunger. Without money in the treasury or any means of getting it, *abi* could only listen day upon day to his constituents' pleas for help—men as well as women. Our only hope was Osama's expedition to Syria. Sending those warriors had left Medina in a vulnerable position, as my father's critics loved to point out, but *abi* hoped desperately that Osama would convince the Byzantine emperor to route his caravans through our city again.

Secretly, I also questioned my father's sending Osama. Muhammad had originally appointed him, trying to assuage the boy's grief over his father's death, but things were different when Muhammad was alive: We'd been collecting taxes from outlying tribes and weren't desperate for the trade. Now that our tax money had dried up like a *wadi* in the summertime, I wondered if the critics were right, if my father hadn't sent a boy to do a man's job. But *abi* had been adamant: Muhammad, not Abu Bakr, had assigned Osama the task. *How can I fold up this flag which was unfurled by the Prophet of God, yet profess to follow his example?* he'd asked his advisors. None of us could argue.

Yet when it came to following Muhammad's example, my opinions sometimes differed from my father's. For instance, I couldn't imagine Muhammad's naming the vicious Khalid ibn al-Walid as commander of his army—and I worried that my father's doing so would lead to disaster.

And so things stood until, about a week after Fatima's funeral, Osama brought his troops back to Medina amid cheers from hundreds who lined our main street, a wide swath of dirt so dry it seemed to exhale dust whenever a donkey-cart rolled down it. Watching from the mosque, I could barely make out Osama ibn Zayd leading an army bedraggled by the long journey to Syria and back. I smelled them before I could see them, their pungent, sour stench telling me they hadn't bathed in many weeks. Emaciated and pale, they looked more like skeletons than mighty warriors, and jubilant greetings turned to shocked gasps as they passed. As for me, the sight of Khalid ibn al-Walid riding beside Osama stilled my tongue and sent chills down my spine.

The murderous warrior, once our enemy, was infamous for his cruelty. His eyes were pale and cold. A scar like a long, thick worm ran across one cheek, and his nose, broken many times, jutted like a knife blade. His hair sprung wildly about his face. Arrows stuck in every direction from his loosely wound turban. His filthy Bedouin robes hung in shreds from his broad shoulders. From the saddle of his snorting war-horse, he looked down at the crowd as dispassionately as if they were a pack of yapping pups. His glance fell on me as he passed, and recognition twitched at his lips.

A short while later, when Khalid strode into the mosque by Osama's side, the taste of ashes filled my mouth. After glancing carelessly at Talha, Umar, and Uthman, all of whom sat with me behind my father, he stared at my single uncovered eye—Muhammad had required his wives to pull our wrappers about our faces so that only one eye showed—with such intensity that I had to fight the urge to cover my face completely. Did he recall that morning long ago when Muhammad led him into the cooking-tent and assigned me to watch over him? Khalid's gaze had raked my twelve-year-old body as brazenly as if I'd been performing a dance, and his lewd remarks had made my skin burn with shame.

Osama's guileless face, as open as an angel's, seemed childish in contrast to Khalid's brooding one. As Osama stepped forward to kiss my father's signet ring, I couldn't help thinking how young, in truth, he'd been to lead an army to Constantinople.

"Our expedition to Byzantium was unsuccessful, *khalifa*," Osama said. His ears, sticking out from his head like gourd handles, glowed a bright red. "The emperor has no interest in resuming the trade route past Medina. Life is too unstable here, he said."

"By al-Lah, the situation is grave for us, then." My father's voice betrayed his fear. "We must find a way to entice the Syrian caravans back to Medina. Does anyone have suggestions?"

"Trade is the least of your worries, *yaa khalifa*." Khalid ibn al-Walid broke in without asking permission to speak. Yet *abi* leaned forward in his seat and stared at Khalid as if he were the angel Gabriel bringing a message from God.

"On our journey home, we saw Bedouin travelers crossing the desert in great numbers," Khalid said. "Five or ten thousand, at least. Our scouts informed us that they were gathering at the Wadi al-Hamd oasis, preparing to invade Medina."

"We cannot possibly defend ourselves against such an army." My father's voice shook.

"That's what we thought the last time we were invaded, remember?" I pointed out. "Then we dug a trench that kept the army out. They had ten thousand, as I recall—including Khalid ibn al-Walid, the famous fierce warrior." I tossed a haughty glance at Khalid.

"Your trench was unique in the history of Arab warfare," Khalid said to my father. "Our army was thwarted by the element of surprise. But such a device would not stop the Bedouins now. Our attackers would be prepared to overcome it."

"We'll have to devise something equally surprising, then, won't we?" I retorted.

Talha smiled at me in appreciation. "As I recall, that trench was your idea, A'isha," he said. "Of course, you've always been full of surprises." His compliment made the heat rise to my face as he turned to my father. "*Yaa khalifa*, I propose that we convene a council to discuss the matter—"

"The time for discussion is past," Khalid snapped, cutting Talha off as effectively as if he'd sliced off his tongue. "We must act now."

I opened my mouth to protest Khalid's abrupt behavior toward my cousin, but a shout from outside stole my chance. The door to the mosque crashed open. In stormed Ali, his stride long and sure, his turban wound about his head like a tightly coiled serpent.

"Forgive me, *khalifa*," he said, brushing past Khalid to kneel at my father's feet. He seized *abi's* hand and kissed his ring as fervently as if Muhammad still wore it.

"I have come to offer my allegiance to you," Ali said. His voice was hoarse with emotion and his lips trembled. "Forgive me for taking so long to do so."

My father's smile was as thin as barley mush. "If you had pledged to me earlier, would your words have been sincere?" he said. "'A truth that displeases is better than a lie that pleases.'"

I wondered if Ali's pledge *was* true, but I held my tongue. What did it matter? In those days, an Arab's word was binding, no matter what lurked in his heart. With Ali's allegiance secured, my father could at last turn his full attention to governing the *umma*.

"There is much work to be done, Ali," he said. "Khalid is telling us now of a Bedouin expedition amassing to destroy us. Some desert tribes have stopped paying their tax, and now they want to increase their insult by raiding our city."

"Then we must attack first!" Ali stood and drew his sword, Zulfikar, with its twin points at the end of a double blade. "Allow me to lead an expedition for you, and I will gouge the eyes of any apostate who refuses to pledge his allegiance."

"How quickly the wolf dons the wool of a sheep," I said to Talha, who had taken a seat beside me.

Ali glared, but my father nodded. "A'isha speaks the truth," he said. "How can any man fight on my behalf when he has recently sown dissension against me?"

Ali's features froze. "I was not free to bind myself to you while my wife lived," he said. "I am certain you can understand why."

"And I suppose your uncle and cousins forced you to oppose our *khalifa* in the first place," Talha said, smirking.

My father's glance at Talha was benign, but there was no mistaking its meaning: Talha had said enough.

"*Yaa* Ali, let me ask you something," *abi* said. "Would you appoint a man to lead your army who had no legs?"

"I would not, *yaa khalifa*," Ali said, pushing out his chest. "Such a man could not help our cause, and might even harm it."

"You have spoken truly." My father stroked his beard with one hand. "A man who cannot stand on his own principles, but who allows others' desires to direct him, has no legs of his own."

Ali's face turned as white as a fish's belly. He looked like a man on the verge of sickness.

"I have tolerated your disloyalty for the sake of the Prophet, whose love made him blind to your faults," my father said. "But, by al-Lah, I will not appoint you to fight for me."

I sucked in my breath, waiting for Ali's famous temper to strike. Did my father realize what he was doing? By chastising Ali in front of Osama and, worse, Khalid, he'd humiliated him in the worst way. Now that the army was back, Ali had only to say a few words and he'd find himself in command of half those men—many of them the fiercest warriors in Medina. Overthrowing my father would be as easy for him as pulling the wings off a fly.

But Ali said nothing, to my relief. He stepped to the side and glowered at the wall, his hands behind his back as if tied. My father turned to Khalid with the eagerness of a man seeking the face of his beloved. Beside me, Umar and Uthman frowned at each other, sharing my concerns over *abi's* enthusiasm for this *majnun*.

"How do you propose that we deal with these apostates, *yaa* Khalid? You've had many successes as a general against Muhammad's army. In truth," his grin was wry, "you were the reason we lost so pitifully at the Battle of Uhud all those years ago."

"I suggest we leave tonight," Khalid declared. "I will subdue the apostates in three days." I almost snorted at this boast.

"But—our troops are exhausted," Umar protested. "We cannot send them out again so soon."

"They begged to fight three days ago, when we saw the Bedouin curs amassing," Khalid said. "Your general, however, refused to act without orders from you." He shot an accusing glance at Osama. "We must confront the apostates now. Every moment of hesitation strengthens our enemies' resolve."

Khalid's eyes shone and I winced. He spoke as if he were already in command of my father's troops. Would *abi* reward his aggressive attitude by making him general of the *umma*'s army? I stared at my father—trying to catch his attention. Yet he couldn't see anyone but Khalid. It was as if that man's battle scars held the answers to all *abi's* troubles.

"Attack, then, with my blessing," *abi* said. "But do not harm any Muslims, or shed the blood of anyone who offers to return to *islam* and pay the tax."

Khalid lifted his arms as if in joy at my father's words. The flourish of his hands, I thought, was an unnecessary gesture.

"Hearing is obeying, *khalifa*," he said. And then I noticed something that made my heart skip: Khalid's eyes were so shot with red they seemed to float in rivers of blood.

◆

Moments later, I stepped into the courtyard with Talha by my side. "Can anything good come from Khalid ibn al-Walid?" I said.

"New turban fashions," Talha quipped. "Or were those arrows sticking out from his head?"

"He's showing off," I said. "He wants everyone to know what a fierce warrior he is."

"He is fearsome. And perhaps Abu Bakr needs a show of strength. Criticism has besieged him these past months."

"By demonstrating a strength that he does not possess, our *khalifa* creates the illusion of leadership qualities that he does not possess." Ali's voice slithered into our midst.

I whirled around to face him, my hand lifted. How I would have loved to slap his face, to feel the satisfaction of his skin against my palm, to see his face recoil from the sting! He stopped with his feet wide apart, his arms folded against me, daring me to attack.

"You could be whipped for those words, especially after you've just pledged your allegiance to my father," I said. "Apparently, your pledge was just another lie."

"There is nothing false about my allegiance to Abu Bakr. Yet, as he himself would readily admit, he is human, with flaws which he has shown in abundance today."

I snorted. "Refusing to appoint a traitor to his army indicates an abundance of leadership ability, if you ask me."

"Allowing a *djinni*-possessed murderer to lead his troops indicates a complete lack of judgment," Ali countered. "As does letting his daughter interject herself into men's affairs."

Again he made my blood rise, but Talha's eyes glinted. "*Yaa* Ali, is it worse than heeding the counsel of a eunuch?"

Ali gripped his sword. "Are you calling me a eunuch?"

Talha shrugged. "What else do you call a warrior who can't do battle?"

"Ali," I said, trying to avoid a fight, "Muhammad had no qualms about letting me 'interject.' He came to me often for political advice."

Now Ali was the smirking one. "He may have come to you often, but not for your insights."

Talha drew his sword and, in a flash, had pressed the tip of the blade against Ali's throat. "How dare you dishonor the Mother of the Believers with your filthy insinuations?" he growled.

"Talha, no," I warned, not so much for Ali's sake as to shield us all from more gossip. Our fighting would only further prevent the *umma* from joining together. If we fell apart, then *islam* would be lost.

"*Afwan*, A'isha," Talha said. "But if I were *khalifa*, I would have ordered this traitor whipped to his final breath. I have no qualms about killing you now, Ali, for the disrespect you've just shown to my cousin. Apologize, if you would save your throat."

I placed a hand on Talha's lifted arm. "Talha, I don't care. Let him go, please."

"Al-Lah forgives all," Ali said, looking Talha in the eyes. "And, as I ask Him now to forgive my insult, so has He granted my request."

Slowly, Talha withdrew his sword. "A'isha saved your life today," he said.

Then Ali did something rare: He laughed. With his mouth lifted at the corners and his cheeks plumped out like dates, he looked almost handsome. But his eyes held malice, not mirth.

"You are wrong, Talha," he said. "She has only deprived me of the pleasure of fighting, and killing. In this, she resembles her father. But my loss is only temporary, even as Abu Bakr's *khalifa* is temporary. He is an old man and will soon die."

His smile disappeared as he turned to me. "Beware of me then, A'isha, for I will be ready to claim the *khalifa* that Muhammad intended for me. On that day, you will in turn claim the legacy he intended for you: a life spent at home with your sister-wives, tending to the business of housekeeping and gossiping, and forsaking the world that God created for men." This was a strange comment, since Ali was telling everyone that he didn't want to be *khalifa*. What was the truth? I wondered if he knew.

"If Muhammad had wanted me in seclusion, he could have commanded it," I said. "He never stopped me from doing anything I wanted to do."

He narrowed his eyes. "That was his indulgence, but it is not mine. When I am *khalifa*, you will not be allowed to venture outside these courtyard walls, for you refuse to behave with the modesty required of the Prophet's wives."

Ali turned and walked back into the mosque When he was gone, Talha leaned close to my ear.

"What do you think now, *yaa* A'isha? Are you still reluctant to help me? If Ali becomes *khalifa* we are all lost. *Islam* as Muhammad intended will be a vague memory, and so will you."

I shook my head as I had so often done these past weeks when Talha had urged me to help him gain the *khalifa* after my father's rule ended. I had no desire to help anyone fight for power. Yet in that moment I did feel the strongest desire to keep Ali as far from the *khalifa* as possible.

Talha spoke truly: Ali would destroy *islam* with his self-righteous zeal and his rigidity. No one, not even my father, seemed to understand the threat he posed. In *abi*'s eyes, he was a hot-headed youth, nothing more. Only I and Talha knew what havoc Ali might wreak on the life Muhammad had built for us.

"Yes, I'm convinced," I finally said. "We're the only ones who can stop Ali. But you have to promise me one thing: When you become *khalifa*, you'll rule as Muhammad would have ruled."

He reached out and pulled my wrapper away from my covered eye, then gazed deeply at me. I blushed, feeling as exposed as if he'd removed my clothes, and glanced quickly around to make sure no one was watching.

"When I'm *khalifa*, I won't need to try to emulate Muhammad." His breath smelled of honey. He spoke so softly that I had to watch his mouth to understand him.

"When I'm *khalifa*, *yaa* A'isha, *you* will rule. Who better to lead *islam* than the one who knew our Prophet best? I might hold the title, but A'isha bint Abi Bakr will be the *khalifa* in truth. And I, your faithful cousin, will carry out your every command."

Ali

Our esteemed *khalifa* had ordered me to observe only, and to file reports of the legendary Khalid's exploits. I had balked, for in truth, as that mocker Talha had said, to cut off a warrior from fighting is to deprive him of his manhood. Yet, during the year that I rode with Khalid ibn al-Walid throughout Arabia and, now, in the Persian Sawad, witnessing countless heart-sickening murders, I thanked al-Lah many times that I was not a warrior—for then I would have been required to fulfill that demon's commands.

With a churning stomach and a sickened heart I watched from my horse as Khalid and his warriors hacked the bodies of their victims and spilled their blood into the trickle of water flowing through the *wadi*. *Please, al-Lah, color this stream the brightest of reds*, I prayed, spitting to eliminate the taste of rust filling my mouth as the blood-smell permeated my nose, my hair, my skin, and my sleep.

For three days Khalid had been slaughtering men in his *djinni*-possessed effort to create a river of blood. First he had killed all the Bedouins who had fought for the Persian empire against his army. Then, when their blood merely disappeared into the dry sand, he had ordered his troops to gather all the injured and dying among our enemies—Persians as well as apostate Bedouins—and he slaughtered them, also, to no avail. Still, he had no river of blood. Finally, this morning, he had ordered his men to round up all the citizens living in the countryside and, at the suggestion of a local *shaykh*, had the gates opened at a nearby wheat mill to release the waters stored there. The innocents' blood mingled with the water from the mill created a crimson stream. Now, perhaps, the killing would cease.

Despite my revulsion, I said nothing, as Abu Bakr had commanded. Commentary was not my responsibility on this expedition. I was not an adviser; nor, to my humiliation, was I a warrior, even though I had sworn allegiance to Abu Bakr. I knew that our almighty *khalifa* and his conniving daughter had deprived me of commanding troops for fear that I might lead a rebellion. I had not desired to do so until he refused to allow me to fight. Unmanned, I became more receptive to my uncle al-Abbas's reminders of my rightful position. *Surely you remember the time when the Prophet likened himself and you to Moses and Aaron. Did not al-Lah say, speaking through His Prophet, "Moses said to his brother Aaron, 'Take my place among my people; act rightly and do not follow in the way of those who spread corruption?'"* Muhammad, in truth, intended for me to "take his place among his people" as *khalifa* after his death.

The *qur'an*, Muhammad's recitations, also say, "Will you make in the *khalifa* one who will act corruptly and shed blood?" With these words, my uncle pointed out, al-Lah had foretold the reign of Abu Bakr, for never had there been such carnage wrought in the name of God. Khalid committed his atrocities despite my warnings that Abu Bakr would be displeased. As for me, I would have killed Khalid gladly, and stopped the slaughter. At Umar's urging, Abu Bakr had sent me to ensure that Khalid was doing the *khalifa*'s bidding, such as dealing respectfully with those who returned to *islam*. But I could do nothing to stop him when he disobeyed.

After one of the first battles, in which he had defeated our invaders with hardly an arrow slung, Khalid spared the lives of all who fell to their knees and professed for *islam*. Yet when he discovered that a group of Ghatafani had slipped away from us, Khalid vowed, "We will find the traitors if we have to comb the desert sands for them." Forgotten was his promise to return to Medina as soon as he had vanquished the Bedouin rebellion.

He led his army galloping through the parched desert, our animals' hooves sinking into hot, thick dunes, the sun glaring like an angry eye until even the camels began to swoon. By the time we surprised the Ghatafani at the Wadi al-Hamd oasis, few of our men could muster the strength to do battle. Yet his warriors' faintheartedness failed to deter Khalid.

He spied Umm Siml among the Ghatafani, her hair cropped to her neck like a man's and leather plates shielding her breasts, slashing and thrusting her sword from the hump of a rearing, kicking, belching camel. His eyes bulged in their red-rimmed sockets as he watched her slice through his men. *She is mine*, he breathed before letting out a scream and racing his black steed toward her, his black-robed body folded over the horse's back so that he could barely be seen. Khalid extended his blade and slashed the backs of her camel's knees, snapping the hamstrings. Umm Siml's mount crashed to the desert floor.

The beast emitted a shriek like that of one thousand and one terrified women, but I heard no sound from Umm Siml. She leapt from the animal's back and whirled to face Khalid, still holding high her singing sword, her chest heaving and her eyes blazing.

Any other man would have followed his opponent to the ground to conduct an honorable fight. But Khalid cared nothing for honor, only for conquest. He wheeled his horse around and yanked on its reins, causing it to rear up and kick Umm Siml in the back. She sprawled forward and our men cheered as Khalid hurled himself from his horse to land on top of her. He then yanked up his robes and committed an atrocity before the eyes of all—except me, for I had the grace, thank al-Lah, to avert my gaze. A collective gasp made me look back in time to see Khalid slitting the woman's throat with his dagger while he still abused her.

Now, as then, blood glistened on Khalid's hands and smeared his robes. He approached me, and nausea twisted my guts when he lifted his blood-slick hands to cup my face.

"Be certain to include the deeds of this day in your report to your *khalifa*," Khalid said. "Let Abu Bakr know that Khalid ibn al-Walid has subdued every apostate who threatened his people."

I wondered why I would need to tell Abu Bakr anything in Khalid's stead, since he had been commanded many times to return to Medina. Apparently, he held other desires more dear than following our *khalifa's* orders. That evening, while the waters still gleamed red and death's haze hung over the land, he called a meeting.

We gathered in his tent, one fashioned from the hides of twenty lions that Khalid claimed to have wrestled before killing. Inside, we sat cross-legged in the sand, making a circle around Khalid, who crouched in the center and turned to stare into the eyes of each of us. I could barely bring myself to look at him for fear of revealing my disgust. He smelled of sweat and urine and blood creased his fingernails. I focused my gaze on his clean robes, which he had fortunately had the courtesy to don.

"The invaders we thwarted were only the first of many who have resisted our *khalifa's* authority," he said. "When Abu Bakr sent me into Hijaz, he ordered me to subdue those who oppose him. Despite our efforts to restore peace, resisters remain to Muslim rule. There are many in Persia who would subdue *us*."

He lifted his dagger and held it close to the face of the man sitting before him. The man looked at the dagger, then at Khalid, whose queer eyes shone with a brightness that shrank his pupils to needle points. He then moved the dagger over to the next man, watching his face as if to gauge his reaction to his words.

"I have heard that in Yemama, the Bani Tamim tribe follow a whore named Suhayl who has led thousands astray with her sexual charms. She has also seduced the Bani Hanifa's false prophet, Musaylima, thus joining two tribes for us to conquer. "

I said nothing, although I knew my silence could be construed as consent or even approval of Khalid's brutality. I was loath to invite speculation that I opposed Khalid, especially while Abu Bakr suspected me of disloyalty. So when Khalid moved his blade to my face, instead of meeting his taunting gaze I took the coward's way and shifted my eyes to stare at the tent wall behind his head.

"Tomorrow, we ride to Yemama," Khalid said, moving the dagger to the face of another man, who broke into a trembling sweat. "Our mission will be this: To kill the apostates. Already the Bani Tamim and the Bani Hanifa have repulsed two teams of negotiators sent by Abu Bakr. By al-Lah, they will not turn us away! We will trample them like a stampede of elephants and make necklaces of their noses and ears. Only then will al-Lah be satisfied."

"Commander," one of the Medina *ansari* said in a voice as meek as a child's, "do you have the authority from our *khalifa* to lead this charge? The tribes you have mentioned have never accepted *islam*, nor did the Prophet force them to."

Khalid flipped the dagger on its side and pressed the blade's tip into the *ansari's* throat. "Here is my authority," he said. "Is it enough for you, or do you need more?" The *ansari* remained mute and Khalid pulled the blade away, then lifted it toward me again.

I masked my hostility by indolently lowering my eyelids. "Keep alert, *yaa* Ali!" Khalid said with a coarse laugh. "You will leave for Mecca tomorrow bearing reports of our triumph over evil."

I clenched my hands. *Yaa al-Lah*, I prayed, *please provide me with a way to prevent another massacre*. I wanted to condemn Khalid's plan as a sin before God, but I said nothing. I valued my life too highly. And I had my *khalifa's* orders to consider. I was many things in those days—including a coward, I realize now—but I was not a traitor.

While it was true that I had delayed my pledge of allegiance to Abu Bakr, having done so I now desired only to serve him and the *umma*. Abu Bakr's tactics for achieving the *khalifa* had been questionable, but I shared his goal of preserving *islam* as Muhammad had envisioned it. Khalid's brutality was a violation of all Muhammad had desired. Except for those who threatened the *umma* directly, no one had ever been forced by the Prophet to convert to *islam*. So instead of protesting, I shrugged. If Khalid discerned my opposition, he might delay my departure until his scheme had been irrevocably set in motion. I needed to return to Medina as quickly as possible to inform Abu Bahr of these new, heinous plans.

The next morning, I performed an act of utter deception by embracing Khalid and promising to sing his praises to Abu Bakr. I rode away from the encampment at a leisurely pace. Once I was out of Khalid's sight I kicked my camel into motion, sending it racing across the desert, past the grassy pastures on the desert floor which had mystified me, for no date palms or other vegetation grew there, and away from the Tuwayqh Mountains, which jutted like a jagged blade severing the Earth.

I rode through the marrow-chilling nights and the heat-pulsing days with as few stops as my camel could endure, pushing the beast to its limits, compressing what should have been a five-day journey through the Nejd highlands into a two-day trip. Once inside Medina's gates, I rode directly to the mosque, praying that I would find Abu Bakr in the mosque and also that his daughter would be occupied elsewhere.

Alas, although Abu Bakr did sit on his date-palm stump, A'isha perched by his side, her wrapper pulled over her face but not far enough to hide the animosity in her exposed eye as I walked into the room. Fortunately, Umar was with them, as well as the benign, smiling Uthman in his usual resplendent attire. Both men arose and greeted me with unexpectedly warm embraces.

I knelt before Abu Bakr and kissed his ring, the signet worn for so many years by my beloved cousin. *Al-Lah, imbue the wearer of this ring with Muhammad's spirit even now,* I prayed, then stood and delivered the news of Khalid's atrocities.

As I spoke, Umar's cheeks and nose reddened as viciously as Khalid's river of blood. Abu Bakr, however, showed no reaction save for the occasional nod of his head and, when I had finished, a thoughtful tug of his beard.

"*Yaa* Ali, you say Khalid eradicated the danger of invasion, and with few fatalities on our side?"

I stammered my reply, confused by his mild response. "Th-the rebels have all pledged their allegiance to you," I said. "Except for those he brutally murdered."

A'isha's eye dimmed. "Poor Umm Himl," she breathed.

"She would have done worse to you, *yaa* A'isha, if she had been given the chance," Abu Bakr said quietly. "Umm Himl was widely renowned as a merciless killer."

"With respect, *abi*, I'd heard she was a courageous warrior," A'isha said.

"She is a dead warrior now, and dishonorably killed," Umar sputtered. "*Yaa* Abu Bakr, it is as I have told you: Khalid ibn al-Walid is like a camel with no rider. You must pull the reins on him now, before he commits more atrocities in the name of *islam*."

"By saving Medina, he has saved *islam*," Abu Bakr said. "And I do not recall hearing you protest the use of female captives in the past, Umar, or you, either, Ali. In truth," he said, giving me a piercing look, "I recall similar stories about you some years ago, Ali."

A'isha's eyebrow shot up, and I could sense disapproval rising from her like heat. My skin flushed, betraying my embarrassment. "I was young," I mumbled. "And although I took pleasure from our captives as did other men, I never humiliated a woman by dishonoring her publicly—or covered myself in her blood as Khalid did."

"Khalid ibn al-Walid is unstable, Abu Bakr," Umar said. "He cannot be trusted. See how he has ignored your mandates! Did he offer Umm Himl the opportunity to embrace *islam* before he slit her throat, as the Prophet would have done?"

"Khalid is not the Prophet," Abu Bakr said. "We do not expect perfection from him."

"But what about mercy, *yaa abi?*" I was surprised to hear A'isha speak my thoughts.

Uthman fingered his moustache. "You did command Khalid to show mercy, as I recall."

"Khalid answers to no authority except his own," I said. "Some of the men pointed out that you had not given permission for this expedition against the Bani Hanifa, yet he insists on attacking. He plans to recruit warriors from among the Bedouin tribes friendly to us."

Abu Bakr nodded. "That is a good plan. The Bedouins are not only fearless fighters, especially if booty and women are to be gained, but they will be able to advise Khalid on how to defeat the Hanifa. I have heard that they thwart attack by fleeing into a date grove so dense, even the sun does not shine within."

"But the Hanifa have done nothing to us," I said, hating the sharp edge of my voice for I did not want my temper to deflect from my message.

"They have chosen to follow Musaylima, the false prophet," Abu Bakr said. "His devotees have increased daily since Muhammad's death, until their numbers rival those of the Believers. Musaylima is popular because he does not collect an alms tax. In truth, he does not care for the poor; he cares only for his own glory. He is leading the Arabs into the depths of hellfire. Would al-Lah have us turn our faces from this evil?"

"Muhammad would have won them with his example—" I began, but Abu Bakr cut me off.

"*Yaa* Ali, Muhammad is dead." He lowered his face, but not before I saw his eyes cloud with sorrow. "Although we are obligated to try, there is no one who can take the Prophet's place."

"We can only do our best," A'isha said. Her one visible green-brown eye, as impenetrable as that of a bird, shifted from Abu Bakr to me, and back again.

"Your best is not good enough," I said, my voice rising.

The feeble excuses of father and daughter whipped about my ears like a harsh wind, fanning the same outrage that had fueled my frantic ride to Medina. I exploded in such a torrent of criticism that, were I any other man, the *khalifa* might have ordered me whipped.

"Innocent people are being murdered at this very moment, slaughtered in the name of *islam* by a demon-possessed man of your own appointing," I raged. "The blood of the guiltless flows on the plain at Aqraba in your name, Abu Bakr. It stains this mosque, smearing your name and that of your predecessor." Shaking all over, I seized my dagger from under my robe and slashed my arm with it, then let the blood pour onto the date-palm stump at Abu Bakr's feet.

Abu Bakr leapt down from his stump and stood over me, waving his arms. "Enough of your histrionics!" he bellowed. "Leave the mosque at once."

I ignored his command, having little respect for him now.

"Why did you send me on that expedition with Khalid, *yaa khalifa?*" I asked, not attempting to hide my disgust. "Were you hoping I might be killed, and the lone dissenting voice against you silenced? Or perhaps your precious daughter desired vengeance against me. After all, did I not encourage Muhammad to divorce her, as he would have done if not for his friendship with you?"

Now A'isha leapt to her feet, also. "You don't know what you're talking about."

"I know more than you will ever discern, with your foolish woman's mind," I shot back. "Your father's fortune was crucial to *islam*. Without Abu Bakr's purse, the *umma* would have disbanded many years ago, and Muhammad would have endeavored in vain to rescue the Arabs from idol-worship and hellfire."

"Ali, I command you to cease this instant!" Abu Bakr was so furious, I thought he might jump down from the stump to strike me. I took no heed of him, for my temper had changed its course like an erratic dust-devil to attack A'isha, instead.

"You were a foolish girl with an insolent sword for a tongue and your *abi's* love as your shield," I said, using the words I knew would hurt her the most. She listened to me, as her father had not, and her whitening face and pain-brimming eyes gave me great satisfaction.

"I was an idealistic youth, concerned about my cousin's honor," I continued. "When the *umma* called you an adulteress after you disappeared with Safwan ibn al-Mu'attal, I naturally advised Muhammad to divorce you. But he chose to endure an unpleasant wife—in spite of having so many other, more charming ones—in order to retain the favor of her affluent father."

"You lie!" A'isha's voice quavered. "Muhammad loved me *and* he loved my father."

"He loved your father's purse," I said. Then, remembering my duty, I untied the serpent-skin pouch weighting my belt. "*Yaa khalifa*, I have just recalled your words upon appointing me to accompany Khalid. Did you want me to report on his loyalty?"

"In truth, that was my order," Abu Bakr said, resuming his seat. With his eyes on the pouch, he gestured for A'isha to sit, also. She pulled her wrapper more tightly about her face as she did.

"At the time, I supposed you desired me to observe his faithfulness to your commands regarding *islam* and its people," I said. "But now I perceive the real motive behind your appointment. You knew that I could be trusted to deliver your rightful share of the war spoils."

I hefted the sack in my hands. Although it had been sewn shut to ensure against pilfering—an insult Khalid had delighted in pointing out to me—I could discern from its weight and the clink of the contents that it held coins, hundreds of them, seized from those who had submitted to Khalid as well as those who had fought him and died. *Tell the khalifa this is only the beginning*, he'd said.

I handed the scaly pouch to Abu Bakr. His face seemed to shed itself of years as he tore it open and watched the dinars and dirhams spill like his victims' tears across his lap.

"Well done, *yaa* Ali," Abu Bakr said, and pressed a handful of gold into my palm. I let it drop as I turned away, not letting myself think about the cries of my hungry children as I walked into the street, utterly alone.

A'isha

After leading us with a straight back into Mecca for the *hajj*, the annual pilgrimage to worship at the Ka'ba, my father left the city as helplessly as a newborn, lying on a camel-skin stretcher as if he were being borne to his bier. His face was ashen and skeletal. Four men carried him across the desert back to Medina. I stumbled beside them, my throat clogged with unshed tears and my feet blistering and bleeding.

"*Yaa* A'isha, our men are already carrying one person. Do you want to be the second?" Hafsa sidled up and tucked an arm around my waist. "Come and sit on your camel for a while. Killing yourself won't help your father, but taking a rest will benefit you."

I flung her away and forced myself to walk upright, ignoring the wobbling in my thighs and the sting in my soles. What was the soreness of my feet compared to my father's pain, or to my grief at the thought of losing him?

"The end could come at any moment," I said. "I want him to know he's not alone." As I spoke, I dried my tears in case he opened his eyes. He would need courage from me, not sniveling.

I'd known *abi* was in trouble before we'd left for Mecca. He'd tried to hide his illness by complaining that indigestion was keeping him awake at night, but I'd noticed how perspiration stained his gown although the cool of evening bathed us in a sweet breeze. His eyes were as lifeless as coal, reflecting nothing back. His spirit seemed snuffed. I'd told myself it was fatigue sagging his eyes like filled water-skins, that the trials of leading the *umma* tremored his hands. And I watched him grow weaker and more pale every day.

My father was very sick, with the same illness that had taken Muhammad and Fatima. I knew it and he did, also. Neither of us ever said "fever," as though speaking its name would give it more power—or as though ignoring it would make it go away. But we knew, as Muhammad had known, that the Medina fever lived to kill. It was rarely defeated, and never by a man as old as *abi*.

The journey home was eerily silent. In the glow of the torches that lighted our way I saw sadness on each face, for everyone loved my father, even those who disagreed with him. He could be stern—no one knew that better than I—but he was always honest, living up to his name until the very end. And he had fulfilled the role of *khalifa* with a grace that some found surprising. His tolerance for Khalid's brutality, so controversial, had strengthened the *umma's* power and its purse. Because of Khalid's conquests, *islam* had not only been restored to Hijaz, but it had spread into new territories. Unlike when *abi* had taken the *khalifa* two years ago, we of the *umma* no longer feared invasion or suffered hunger. Now, we feared only my father's death, and what might come afterward.

"I do not know how longer I will be among you," he had said to the worshippers only a few days ago, standing atop the Ka'ba's steps. His words had elicited gasps, including from me. "But I do know that, whatever happens to me, *islam* will yet live. For al-Lah has promised to reveal the name of my successor before I die."

Then he turned his face to Ali, who widened his eyes in vulgar glee.

"When the time comes, I know you will support him," my father continued, still boring his gaze into Ali. I knew he was sending Ali this message: *Do not oppose the next khalifa the way you opposed me*. And I could tell from the brightness in Ali's eyes that he thought my father meant something else altogether. He thought *abi* meant to choose him as his successor.

I marveled that Ali could be so naive. After all his years of competing with *abi*, first for Muhammad's favor and then for the *khalifa*, did he think my father esteemed him? His behavior in the mosque six months earlier, when he'd returned from his expedition with Khalid, had only proved him to be as impulsive and temperamental as ever. I'd been stung by Ali's claim that Muhammad had loved me only for my father's purse, but then I'd shrugged off his ridiculous accusations. Muhammad had loved me. It was one reason why he had forbidden me to marry again after his death. Muhammad wanted me beside him in Paradise, and had promised me a place of highest honor. Nothing Ali said or did could diminish that fact.

As for naming Ali *khalifa*, my father would never do that. He knew, as I did, that Ali resented our family. If he ever gained power over us, we'd all suffer. We'd lose status, money, freedom, perhaps even our lives.

Now, though, picking my way over lava beds, I wasn't thinking of anything else except *abi*. *Please, God, don't take him from me*. Still I refused to cry, for his sake.

When we arrived in Medina that gloomy mid-morning, my father's young wife Asma showed no such qualms about displaying her grief. She ran to his stretcher with a sharp cry and flung her henna-decorated arms around his neck before his bearers could lay him down.

"Praise al-Lah for sending you home alive," she said, sobbing. "I would die one thousand and one deaths were you to depart from me without a final kiss."

Behind her, my mother grasped Asma's arms and pulled her off my poor father. *Abi* frowned, for he'd clearly been enjoying the attention, but *ummi* pretended not to see his disappointment.

"Did I not warn you to remain at home, you stubborn ass?" she said gently as she wiped his damp face with the sleeve of her robe. "'If you cannot ride with dignity, it is best not to undertake the journey.'" She stood and turned toward their house, signaling his bearers to follow.

I followed, also, with my arms around the weeping Asma, down the street of red dirt to my father's home, a simple stone house but, compared to the mud-brick dwellings squatting beside it, as elegant as a mansion. Its modest exterior belied the lovely interior, with its tapestries, stone floor, brass oil-lamps ensconced on the walls, and the large courtyard separating the rooms where my father and brothers lived—their bedrooms and the *majlis*, or men's sitting room—from the *harim*, where their wives and children lived and worked. The *harim* comprised the wives' bedrooms, where their husbands might sleep if they desired; a large bedroom and playroom for the children; and a spacious, windowless kitchen, where the women sat and talked on hot days. Otherwise, they gathered under the shade of the trees in the courtyard or, at night, with their husbands on the rooftop terrace over the *majlis*.

I'd never seen my father's bedroom, for my family had moved in recent years to be closer to the mosque, but I took only a cursory glance around when we entered, noting its austerity: a mattress on a platform, a dressing table holding a comb and a pair of scissors, a single chair, and a water gourd sitting in a corner. I focused instead on his face as if, by staring at him hard enough, I could make him strong again. As the men settled him onto his bed, Asma disentangled herself from me, recovered from the shock of seeing him so ashen and listless, and moved to his side to stroke his brow. My mother *hmphed* at her but said nothing. I noticed the flicker of her gaze from Asma's adoring face to my father's, which had suddenly grown calm, and to his fingers clasping Asma's free hand to his chest, over his heart. I felt my own chest tighten for the sake of my mother, who had been my father's most cherished wife for so many years. *Well worn sandals are no longer good enough for the feet of a* khalifa, she'd said with a sniff when my father had married Asma—a woman not much older than I, and who worshiped *abi* as if he were the Prophet of al-Lah.

While Asma clutched my father's hand and wept, my mother poured water from the gourd into a large basin, then dampened a rag and held it to *abi's* brow. She loosened his clothing and removed his sandals, then washed his feet. Throughout her ministrations he continued to gaze into Asma's beautiful face. I gave my mother a fierce, sympathetic look, but she shook her head as if to say, *It doesn't matter now*.

Around us, my father's Companions stood in silence, waiting for his commands, or, in Ali's case, waiting for his death. I watched Ali closely, noting the careful way he hooded his eyes and the neutral set of his mouth, hiding his mistaken hopes. Beside him, the soft-hearted Uthman blinked and wiped his tears with a red silk handkerchief, and Umar grimaced and wrung his hands. Both of them stood with bowed heads, praying. But Talha gazed directly at me.

Tenderness filled his eyes. Furrows as deep as riverbeds lined his forehead and the sides of his face, and his lips parted as if he were on the verge of speaking. His sympathy invited me like open arms to rest against him.

Then a rough cough jolted me back to the room, where Ali pursed his mouth at me and Talha as though we were misbehaving children.

Blood rushed to my cheeks. "Are you comfortable, *abi?*" I stood to open curtains, and took a date-palm fan from my mother to wave over my father's sweating face. As I passed the fronds to and fro, cooling him, I fought back the tears that, after my exhausting walk through the desert, threatened to flood my eyes. I focused on the palm leaves waving like rushes in a stream, not daring to look at *abi* and not caring, now, about Talha's beckoning or Ali's accusations. Lust, jealousy, greed, judgment: These emotions, causing so much struggle and strife in our daily lives, now seemed as insignificant as the whine of a gnat.

Umar cleared his throat. "*Yaa* Abu Bakr, now that you are in your home again you appear much improved."

My father turned his face to give his friend a wan smile. "By al-Lah, I have never known a warrior so reluctant to acknowledge death."

Umar's eyes flickered a smile of his own. I knew both men were remembering how, hours after Muhammad's death, Umar had refused to accept the loss, insisting that he and the Prophet had plans to walk in the moonlight. In spite of Umar's harshness, especially toward women, my wariness softened as I watched him struggle to accept the demise of his old friend Abu Bakr. *Abi* had always been as strong as the Ka'ba's cornerstone. In times of direst distress, Muhammad had turned to my father for help. Now, in *abi's* own hour of need, we stood helplessly by, Umar dangling his ever-present whip as if it were a dead serpent and I rummaging frantically through my medicine pouch for a cure that I might have missed.

A clattering sound came from the doorway, where the curtain fell to the floor, too roughly shunted aside. Al-Abbas, Ali's uncle, swept into the room, his belly thrusting, his eyes squinting at my father as if peering through a fog. Umar and Uthman stepped aside—that's how commanding was al-Abbas' presence—but Ali moved his gaze to the floor.

Shunting Asma aside, al-Abbas clasped one of my father's hands. "Your skin is on fire, *yaa khalifa*. I will summon a physician."

How I longed to pummel his fat face, all false concern! He'd opposed my father since before Muhammad had died. But the sharp retort on my lips deflated under the weight of my terrible grief.

My father didn't rebuke him. Instead, *abi* sighed and closed his eyes.

"I have already spoken with the best of physicians—al-Lah," my father said, slipping his hand out of al-Abbas's grip. "He said to me, 'I will do with you whatever suits My purpose.'"

His words were sharp stones chipping at my heart. God had visited *abi*? For what other purpose than to prepare him for death? I couldn't stop the tears that poured over my cheeks.

"By al-Lah, the Prophet had this fever also." Umar lifted his whip as if to frighten the illness away. "After his death, I heard a physician claim that he could have saved Muhammad. Allow me to summon this man, Abu Bakr. He may have a remedy for you."

My hopes jumped, but my father pressed his lips together. A tear quivered in his lashes. He took a violent, wheezing breath. "I am not worthy to die in the same manner as Muhammad," he said when he had finished gasping. "But may God's will be done."

He turned in his bed until he faced the wall, shunning us with his hunched shoulders and broad back. "Go," my mother said, standing to shoo us with her hands and the palm frond, which she had taken from me. "My husband needs to rest." Behind her, while *ummi* protected the man she had loved for so long, Asma had already moved to my father's side and lain in his enfolding arms.

We filed out to the courtyard and separated into groups. Umar and Uthman stood under the trees, where they murmured and embraced each another in grief over their dying friend. Outside the entryway to the house, al-Abbas made adamant gestures as he spoke to a downcast Ali. I hid indoors, on the other side of the doorway, unseen by them. Talha, who had lingered in my father's room for a moment, came up from behind me with concern on his face, but I shook my head. He lifted his eyebrows, questioning, as I pressed a finger to my lips and listened to our enemies talk."Once again you have forsaken your opportunity," al-Abbas was saying in a hissing tone. "When will you stand up and claim what is yours?"

"Would you have me request the *khalifa* while Abu Bakr's family weeps over his impending death?" Ali said. "Surely not even *you* would be so heartless."

"All your sensitivity will be for naught if he dies now before naming a successor. Every man in that room—plus one woman—covets the title. Each of them schemes to snatch the *khalifa*. You and I must devise our plan."

A whisper in my ear and warm breath on my skin made me shudder. "What's *your* plan, A'isha?" Talha murmured. "You should take Abu Bakr's place."

I turned to him, grimacing. "It would be easier to place a camel on the roof than to put a woman in that position."

Talha squeezed my hand. I drew in my breath, disapproving. His touch, skin to skin, was highly improper. But when I lifted my reproachful gaze to his face, I beheld sympathy and friendship. I relaxed, returned the affectionate squeeze, and slipped my hand away from his.

"You *should* be the one to rule." Talha led me away from the doorway so we couldn't be heard. "Everyone knows it, even your father. It's ridiculous that being a woman should stop you. Even the Persians are more advanced in this respect. I've heard that their queen, Buran, leads troops on the battlefield."

I imagined a strong, armor-clad woman racing into battle on the back of a sleek horse, hefting her sword high. Hadn't that once been my fantasy? As a child, I'd yearned to ride with the Bedouins, as free as the wind, wild and fierce. Then I'd become engaged to Muhammad, and my parents had placed me in confinement for nearly six years. By the time I moved to Muhammad's home, my dreams had become like the toys on my shelf, increasingly forgotten amid the demands of married life. Yet now I felt again within my breast the beating of that distant drum. What I'd yearned for might be possible if I'd been born in another place. But in my world, men ruled—and women submitted.

"Men like Umar and al-Abbas would never bow to a woman—not even a queen like Buran," I told Talha.

"Not knowingly. But—tell me, A'isha. You're Abu Bakr's chief adviser, aren't you?"

I nodded. "We meet several times a day to discuss the affairs of *islam*."

"Do you have any influence upon him?" he pressed, although he knew the answer.

"More than *abi* realizes. I even convinced him to appoint more generals, in order to dilute Khalid ibn al-Walid's power. But I'm not as powerful as you think, cousin. I couldn't get Khalid demoted, not even after that 'river of blood' massacre."

"You would have that power and more if I were *khalifa*." Talha's eyes darkened as he gazed into mine. "A'isha, I told Abu Bakr as much when we were in Mecca. He seized my beard and kissed me." A strange light filled his eyes, so cold it made me shiver. "I believe he may appoint me, A'isha. He knows that he would be appointing you, also."

I heard the clap of sandals on the courtyard flagstones. Ali charged into the house, the picture of confusion, his face set in determination to request the *khalifa* from my father but his eyes shifting with doubt. I stepped out of the intimate circle I'd made with Talha, my face burning. Ali's sneer said all, and of course he couldn't resist making a snide remark.

"How unfortunate that Muhammad is not here with us," he said. "I am certain he would enjoy seeing his wife situated so cozily with another man."

"*Yaa* Ali, Muhammad sees everything from Paradise." I narrowed my eyes at him. "He hears everything, also. Including secret conversations about coaxing the *khalifa* from a dying man."

Ali blanched, making me want to laugh with satisfaction. A cry from my father's bedroom, however, sent me running down the hall to him.

Inside the bedroom, my father struggled against the efforts of both my mother and Asma to keep him in his bed. "Help us, A'isha!" *ummi* called when she saw me in the entryway. "A *djinni* has possessed him."

I hurried over to wrap my arms around *abi* in a fierce hug. Heat leapt from his skin as if he'd swallowed one thousand and one suns. Uttering a silent prayer—*Please ease his pain*—I pulled back to look into his face. Fear lashed in his eyes but as I continued to gaze at him, recognition crossed his face and he relaxed, slumping against our arms.

"How sick are you, *yaa abi*, if you can fight against three strong women?" I teased gently as we laid him back down.

"I must be close to death, if I cannot win," he said, panting. "*Yaa* A'isha, call the others back into the room. I want to name a successor before it is too late."

I stood—but there was no need to call anyone. Umar, Uthman, Ali, and Talha stood in the doorway, watching and listening. Umar and Uthman's faces sagged with sorrow. Ali's eyes stared straight ahead and his jaw clenched. Talha's expression held more triumph than I would have wished. As for me, I wanted only for them and their petty ambitions to disappear. Standing in death's shadow, even the fate of *islam* seemed trivial. I buried my face in my hands.

As a child, I'd had little comfort or consolation from my mother, whose life had held too many difficulties for her to sympathize with mine. And so I had clung to my father, a gentle man with a soft lap and an even softer beard that smelled of cardamom and apple. He, not my mother, had taken pity on me in my confinement and spent long hours playing with me, teaching me to read and recite all the great poems of old and also Muhammad's *qur'an*, his revelations from God. He'd bought me Scimitar, my first horse, and taught me to ride, then taken me out late at night to gallop across the desert, where we knew we wouldn't be seen. I'd lived for his approval, which he gave so readily that I rarely doubted my abilities. So much of the woman I'd become was because of my father. When he died, what would happen to that woman?

"*Yaa* A'isha," *ummi*'s voice yanked me back to the moment. "We are waiting for you."

I looked over at my mother, who perched at my father's feet while Asma sat beside him on the bed, cradling his head in her arms. The men had gathered around expectantly, gazing down on him as if he were already in the grave. In a trance I stepped to my mother's side and knelt there, submitting completely to my father, to God, to life—and, alas, to death.

"I have prayed for al-Lah's guidance in naming a successor," my father said. "I praise Him that He has allowed me enough breath, and enough presence of mind, to announce His choice. It will be better for *islam* if things are settled before I leave you."

At that moment, my mother did a strange thing: She lifted up her voice and began to wail. I turned toward her—my mother, who had rarely displayed any emotion except anger—and stared as though she were a *djinni*. Her gray-red hair, like iron that has begun to rust, frowsed about her head, and her face contorted as though invisible hands pulled her skin in different directions. I was taken aback, but then I felt the shock of recognition as I looked into that face so like my own, a face that held my own sorrow up to me as if reflected in the blade of a dagger. I would *not* be alone. I opened my arms and pulled my mother close, and let my tears mingle with hers.

Then my father began to speak. His hands lay in Asma's and his eyes seemed to gaze far away, as if he were already leaving this world. I could see the resignation on Ali's face, the downward slide of Talha's mouth, the approval in Uthman's eyes, and the blush on Umar's neck.

"He has been harsh only in response to my mildness," *abi* was saying. "And when I was harsh, he urged me to be mild. He will make an excellent *khalifa*, and will follow in the steps of Muhammad as I have tried to do. You must all pledge your allegiance to Umar ibn al-Khattab."

THE SECOND RIGHTLY GUIDED CALIPH

◆

UMAR

634–644 A.D.

Ali

Like a jackal leading a lion to its prey, my uncle al-Abbas persisted in encouraging me to pursue the *khalifa* even as, standing in A'isha's hut, we witnessed the prayer services over Abu Bakr's grave.

"Behold the charming goddess with the painted arms," he murmured, pulling me into the crowd of mourners for a better view of our dead *khalifa's* young widow. Asma bint Umas, whom I'd always found as delectable as mouthful of honey, wept graciously in the arms of A'isha, for whom I suddenly felt an appreciation. How valiantly she comforted poor Asma, in spite of her own tremors of grief. My eyes grew moist as I watched them cling to each other as though resisting the buffets of a raging *samoom*.

I and my uncle and more than one hundred other mourners had crowded into the hut to watch Abu Bakr laid into the floor according to his wishes, with his head at Muhammad's shoulders. Outside, in the courtyard, thousands of men and women and children pressed against the walls like sea waters lapping at the shore. Inside, the crush of mourners made it difficult for me to view anything except turbans and beards. As I stretched my neck for a glimpse of Asma's face, I bristled at my uncle's "goddess" comparison, for it evoked idolatry. Yet when I beheld her, I could not argue against the characterization. Even with tear-swollen eyes and a nose like a fully blown rose, Asma held my gaze with her beauty as though she were an enchantress.

"Marry her, and you will position yourself perfectly for the *khalifa,*" my uncle whispered. "But do it now, while Umar is distracted by mourning. Soon he will discern the advantages and claim her for himself."

I had no difficulty discerning the advantages of marriage to the delightful Asma, but positioning myself for the *khalifa* was not among them. Unbeknownst to my uncle, I had ceased to covet the position. As I had stood at Abu Bakr's deathbed and listened to him appoint Umar, I realized that I would never succeed Muhammad until his elder Companions had died. In their eyes, I was too young and inexperienced to lead them, and too controversial, also, for my uncle al-Abbas had created dissension among the Medina tribes by trying to convince them that I was Muhammad's rightful heir. Of course, Umar, Uthman, and their companions assumed that I supported my uncle's divisive actions. At times I had, for al-Abbas was a smooth and constant persuader. Now, however, I wanted only to forget any foolish notions of leadership, and strive for the happiness I had once known, before those crushing six months when both Muhammad and Fatima died.

Umar was not nearly as advanced in years as Abu Bakr had been. A vigorous man, he would rule for a long time. When the *khalifa* hearkened again, many of those aged Companions would have departed this life, and I might be granted the opportunity to claim my heritage at last. In the meantime, I saw no reason why I should not enjoy myself to the best of my ability, beginning with the widow Asma's plump, perfumed body in my bed.

Umar began his sermon. "*Yaa* Abu Bakr, may al-Lah bless you," he said quietly, with tears wetting his face. "You have made the task of succeeding you most difficult."

Asma's weeping increased and so did my desire to comfort her. My heart felt so full that it pushed my emotions out of my chest and into my mouth. In the next moment, although I had not planned it, I was speaking words that I would never have imagined uttering—words of praise for Abu Bakr. The crowd turned around to view me, and I stepped through their midst to utter my own lamentations over this man who, despite our differences, had richly deserved Muhammad's love.

"May al-Lah have mercy on you, Abu Bakr," I prayed. "You were an affectionate companion and friend of the Prophet of al-Lah, a source of joy to him, and one who knew his secrets."

As I spoke, all my dislike for the man seemed to melt away, replaced by memories of his goodness. Lifting my voice as though in song, I told of the time he had saved Muhammad from starvation. Mecca's merchants, rejecting Muhammad's religion of one-God, had refused to do business with him, so Abu Bakr had donated food and other provisions to the Believers. I told how he had rescued the Prophet from Quraysh's swords by hiding with him in a cave while assassins combed the sands for him. When, after three days, the killers abandoned their quest, Abu Bakr and Muhammad slipped away to Medina with a guide paid by Abu Bakr. Their safe arrival was due in part, at least, to Abu Bakr's intelligence, courage, and willingness to use his wealth to aid his friend. I spoke of his devotion to Muhammad and to *islam*, for although he had made mistakes—of course, I did not allude to these in my speech—he had tried to his utmost to govern the *umma* as Muhammad would have done. He had failed, but I withheld this opinion.

My homage completed, I stepped back into the crowd so that others could pay their tributes. Across the grave, A'isha stared as if I had grown a new head while Asma gazed at me with gratitude—not for the last time, I hoped.

I longed to say to her: *Yaa Asma, I adored you from afar years ago, even while you were married to my brother, Ja'far. Now a yawning grave separates our bodies, but our hearts, I pray, will soon be as one.*

But in the following instant A'isha wrapped herself around Asma as if to protect her from dishonor. Hiding her from me, that she-dog led Asma out of the hut, hurling me looks that would have struck me dead had they been daggers.

I restrained myself from leaping over our dead *khalifa* and yanking my prize out of that red-haired vixen's arms. A'isha had hated me since the day, seven years ago, when I had urged Muhammad to divorce her. Even now I remained convinced of the rightness of my position. She had never repented of setting Muslim against Muslim with her irresponsible, illicit night in the desert with the young warrior Safwan ibn al-Mu'attal. Unable to admit any wrongdoing, she still blamed me for her troubles. Now I tried not to imagine the lies she would tell Asma to poison her against me.

As the crowd dispersed, my uncle and cousin approached with smiles.

"A wonderful speech, very poetic and spontaneous," my cousin Ibn al-Abbas was saying, embracing me, while my uncle nodded and leered as though I had committed a lascivious act.

"Very shrewd," he said, clasping an arm about my shoulders as we left the hut. "Now all of Medina will marvel at Ali ibn Abi Talib's generous spirit as well as his eloquence of speech. None will even remember that you opposed Abu Bakr, only that you praised him at his burial. You have positioned yourself most excellently for the *khalifa*, nephew."

My face and neck burning, I protested, telling my uncle that my words had been sincere. He laughed and winked. "Of course," he said. "Ali is the epitome of sincerity, second only to his paternal cousin, the Prophet of al-Lah."

It had been Abu Bakr's request that, on the same day that he was buried, the people of Medina should pledge allegiance to Umar. *The umma must not be without leadership for even one day,* he had said. To ensure that the people would support his choice, he had called Asma to help lift him from his bed to the window, where, supported by her remarkable arms, he summoned his remaining strength to ask the crowd outside for their approval. *Have I made the right decision in choosing Umar?* he had croaked, and they replied with a roar so enthusiastic it seemed to tremble the walls.

Now those same supporters poured like a flash flood into the mosque courtyard to profess their support for Umar as their new *khalifa*. I made certain I was the first to make the pledge, so that there would be no more speculation about my wanting the title.

Later that afternoon, with a flavor in my mouth like grape seeds, I approached Umar. I hesitated to do so while the pain of Abu Bakr's passing lay upon him like a fresh wound, yet my uncle was right that, once Umar's sorrow diminished, he would covet the exquisite Asma for his own. So as not to appear overly eager for her, I first requested the favor I had the least hope of obtaining: permission to ride into battle with my brethren. The famous general Mothanna, who had already won so many victories in Syria, had arrived in Medina last evening to recruit warriors for our Persia campaign. If Umar allowed it, I would be the first to volunteer.

But my desire to fight was not to be fulfilled at that time.

"I remember well the skills you exhibited at Badr and Uhud," Umar said, referring to two of the *umma's* greatest battles under Muhammad's green standard. We were seated in the *majlis*, which, despite the *umma*'s new prosperity, was decorated as austerely as it had been during Muhammad's time, with only a single curtain of coarse linen on the high, small window, and a plain rug, worn but clean, on the floor. In one corner of the room, near the courtyard entry, lay a pile of cushions that had supplied me and Umar with our seats. Between us on a cloth sat a yellow gourd filled with water and two bowls from which we drank.

"Allowing me to fight would ensure the *umma* many victories," I said. "Awarding me a position of command would gain you even more."

"You speak truly." Umar peered at me from beneath brows that shaded his eyes like hedges. "Yet we have already lost too many of the Prophet's Companions in our battles. You are father to the Prophet's heirs. How can I risk your life?"

I was prepared for this argument. "I fought alongside Muhammad in all his battles. You would be following his example if you allowed me a command in the Muslim army."

Umar lifted the gourd, poured water into his bowl, drank it down, poured more water, and drank again. I watched his face for clues to his thoughts, but could discern nothing.

"The situation is different now," he finally said as he wiped his mustache. "Muhammad's detractors attacked from *outside* his ranks, while you have attacked the *khalifa* from within."

I dipped my head to prevent his seeing the angry tic of my jaw. "I protected Muhammad from his enemies. I would do the same for you, *yaa khalifa*."

"Would you protect me from yourself, then, Ali?"

"By al-Lah, I have pledged allegiance to you. I will not endure these slanders!" My shout erupted like the blast from an oven, shooting me to my feet. He scowled, and I knew he was but an utterance away from denying me all I wanted. Yet the idea of again remaining in Medina while others fought was unbearable. Holding my voice steady, I looked Umar in the eyes and dared him with my thrust chin and set jaw to prove his insinuations. "I am no traitor," I said.

He arose, also, to stand over me, his height much greater than mine. "Nor are you a loyal follower," he said. "Except, perhaps, of your uncle al-Abbas."

"I want to fight. If you will not appoint me to a position of command, then at least allow me to serve as a foot soldier."

He lifted his right arm and snapped it downward, cracking the whip he infamously carried everywhere now. The sound reverberated like a slap against my ears, causing me to flinch.

"Do not command Umar ibn al-Affan," he cried. "I will not degrade you by sending you into the field as a foot soldier, nor compromise myself by making you a general. You will remain in Medina to advise me as you did Abu Bakr. Now, if that is all . . ."

His face drooped, revealing his exhaustion. I knew he needed rest, yet as he walked me toward the *majlis* door with shoulders slumped I realized my chance at happiness lay between him and that entryway.

"*Yaa khalifa*, that is not all."

He exhaled sharply. "I have made my decision, Ali."

"I hear and obey," I said. "Yet if I must remain at home, I would like to request marriage to Abu Bakr's widow."

Umar's scowl remained fixed, but a slight smile seemed to unravel its edges. "Umm Ruman? She seems advanced in years for you, well past the age for bearing children. Yet if you insist—"

"I do not refer to her!" I winced hearing the irritation in my voice, and when Umar's eyes lit up with his jest, I wished for a whip of my own to brandish. I took a calming breath. "I speak of Asma bint Omas."

"Asma? Hmm." Umar tugged at his beard. "That is a prize I had desired for myself."

My hopes, so lofty when I had approached Umar, now faltered like a bird whose wing has been hurt. I pressed my sweating palms into my robe.

"*Afwan, khalifa*, I did not intend to feast on a meal you had prepared for your own enjoyment." I struggled to keep my voice steady. "I erroneously assumed that you would be occupied—"

"Yes, yes, you speak the truth, Ali. The demands of the *khalifa* will prevent me from meeting the demands of a new wife." His curt nod sent my spirits soaring again. "If Asma consents, then you have my permission to take her."

And so with light steps I moved across the courtyard to ask the incomparable Umm Salama to act as my emissary in requesting Asma's hand in marriage. As required of all Muhammad's wives, she hid behind a screen as we spoke, shielding her expression from my view. Although she greeted me most warmly, the great lady grew quiet when I presented the reason for my visit.

"I want to marry Asma bint Omas," I said, smiling, for the act of forming her name seemed to fill my mouth with joy. "Will you honor me by approaching her with my offer? I wish to seal an agreement today."

The silence between us stretched as long and tight as the leading rope on a stubborn ass. I yearned to jump up and topple the screen to determine if she had fainted.

"*Yaa* Umm Salama," I said. "Did you hear my request?"

"I did," she said at last. "And I will do as you ask—as soon as Asma has had time to recover from her husband's death."

"No." My mouth grew dry at the idea of waiting, for who knew what might happen to thwart my desires? Another man might make an offer and be accepted. Or A'isha, who had moved temporarily to her father's home, might influence Asma against me. "Please go today," I said. "Umar has commanded it."

She was silent again. "Hearing is obeying," she said at last. "But I warn you, Ali, I think this is unwise."

"Why?" I pressed. "What is unwise about it?"

"I cannot reveal more without betraying a confidence," she said. "But I do not believe this endeavor will go well for you. Al-Lah willing, I am mistaken. At any rate, we shall know very soon."

◆

I do not mean to suggest that I had been all alone since the death, two years earlier, of my first love, Fatima, may peace be upon her. Following the Prophet's example, not long after Fatima's departure I had sought, and obtained, a wife to care for my children.

Umm al-Bunin was stolid and dependable, a loving mother to my boys al-Hassan and al-Hussein and to my girl Zaynab, and dutiful in the bedroom. However, she was also like a field that yields fruit as soon as it is touched by the seed, becoming pregnant on her first night with me and then, after she bore my son Abbas and her waiting period was completed, sprouting another son.

Being a virile man who needs his desires fulfilled, and having obtained

attack again. If they win, we will lose everything we have gained in Persia. We need fighters now. Mothanna is here to lead you. All who would join him, step forward and grasp the standard of *islam*."

Smiling as if he had not just delivered the most tepid of speeches, Umar surveyed the crowd with his chest thrust confidently forward, and waited—but no one approached.

He cleared his throat. "Great honor awaits those who volunteer, both in this world and the next," he said. "The Prophet watches, and will reward you well in Paradise."

Still no one came.

I longed to be the first to seize that standard. I envisioned myself defying Umar and volunteering here, before all of Medina, to join our troops on the Persian front. Yet I also knew these men needed more to inspire them than Umar's lukewarm invitation. They needed a fiery, impassioned speech, which Umar should be able to deliver, being one of the most eloquent orators in all of Hijaz. But he did nothing, only stood there with a drooping mouth.

Unable to restrain myself any longer, I leaned toward him and murmured into his ear. "*Yaa khalifa,* your formidable skills as a speaker were never needed more than now," I said. "You can arouse their passions by displaying some of your own."

He sighed deeply. "My heart is heavy with the loss of Abu Bakr," he whispered. "How can I inspire my men to action when I want only to retreat from the world?"

Here was an opportunity for me to gain Umar's trust and, perhaps, a position in his army! Yet I made my offer with trepidation, lest he suspect me of attempting to overshadow him. "Allow me to address your subjects, *yaa khalifa,*" I said. "Perhaps I can win recruits with tales of what awaits them in that fertile land."

And so, with Umar's permission and al-Lah's assistance, I summoned my imagination and my skills, lifted my voice, and beckoned warriors to Umar's army with poetry and promises. Riches such as they had never seen before awaited in Persia, I said. There, even the outhouses were jewel-encrusted, and the women were as ripe fruits dangling from every bough. "Join the fight against the fire-worshippers, and partake of this glorious plunder," I urged. In the next moment, Abu Ubayd, a man of about eighteen whose beard was as fine as the hair on a baby's head, stepped forward and grasped the standard. Not to be outdone by a youngster from Ta'if, scores of Medina men followed, as well as many Meccans.

Yet when the recruits had clustered around Mothanna, visions of booty swirling in their heads, and seized one another's beards in excitement, did Umar reward me with an appointment of my own? By al-Lah, he did not. Instead, he embraced Mothanna as though *he* had been the one to give the speech, then stepped over to Abu Ubayd, who had been pushed to the edge of the group. Umar grasped Abu Ubayd's right hand and held it up.

"The first to volunteer will be the first to lead," he announced. "I hereby appoint Abu Ubayd as your commander under Mothanna."

The silence that followed was more pronounced than the jubilation that had preceded it. "By al-Lah, would he appoint a boy from Ta'if to command men of Aws, Khazraj, and Quraysh?" one of the Medinans muttered to me. "Do those who served the Prophet hold supremacy no longer?"

As I struggled for a diplomatic answer I felt a tugging at my sleeve. Umm Salama stood behind me and, although I could see only one of her eyes, it was clear to me that she was agitated.

"*Yaa* Ali, we need to speak," she murmured.

"I cannot leave now," I said. "Please tell me what has happened."

"I will await you behind my screen," she said. "When we can talk privately." She turned to leave.

"No!" I cried. Praise al-Lah, the uproar that now filled the courtyard prevented my outburst from being heard. Umm Salama turned to me with her gaze lowered. "Tell me now," I said. "We must settle this matter before A'isha . . . before it is too late."

She lifted her eye to give me a tender look. "It is already too late," she said. "After hearing A'isha's tales about you and Abu Bakr, Asma's heart teems with bitterness. She refuses to marry you. I am sorry, Ali. Nothing I could say would change her mind."

A'isha

Three years after he'd sighed his final sigh Muhammad lived on, not only in the beautiful verses he'd left behind, but also, for me, in the memory of his warm copper eyes and how they'd shone when we were together. His eyes were like bronze mirrors that reflected only my loveliness and none of my flaws. With him on this earth, I'd reveled in my strengths, knowing that he relished my bold spirit like the savory taste of *tharid*, his favorite dish, on his tongue.

Now as I stood amid the festive, early-morning bustle of caravaners on the street, I had to bear Ali's glares without my husband's smile to sustain me. Yet I wasn't completely alone. Talha, packing my camel for the pilgrimage to Mecca, gave me adoring looks—which I tried not to notice. Instead, I closed my eyes and savored the excitement of the *hajj*: the bellows and grunts of the camels, the aromas of sandalwood and cardamom, the spontaneous verses shouted by men showing off their oratorical skills. When I opened my eyes again, Talha had turned away, to my relief. Despite already being married to one wife, Talha, being a man, had little to lose by flirting. But for me, everything was at stake. One rumor could rob me of all my freedom—especially now, with Umar in power.

Umar presided in the mosque wielding a whip in one fist and suspicion in the other. He watched me, in particular, waiting for me to behave immodestly—in truth, expecting it. I was one woman he'd never been able to control. Many suffered under his rolling eye. He strode through the market every day with that whip, terrifying women by cracking it about their heads. One old dear, Umm Alia, had hands that shook so badly she couldn't hold her wrapper about her head. When it fell to her shoulders, out lashed Umar's whip, which fell too hard and struck her across one eye.

Abi had predicted that Umar's nature would soften when he became *khalifa*, but I wasn't so sure. By al-Lah, a serpent that sheds its skin is still a serpent! In Umar's eyes, all women were temptresses, and that included me. Muhammad and my father had protected me from his harsh ways, but they couldn't help me now. If Umar knew that Talha visited my hut and that we spoke without a *hijab*, or curtain, between us, he'd confine me to the *harim* for the rest of my days, despite the fact that I and Talha had been lifelong friends. In truth, my laughing cousin had become my closest companion, the person whose company I treasured most, in spite of his boldness. Or maybe because of it.

Now, while loading my camel with provisions for the long excursion to Mecca, Talha noticed Ali's squint-eyed scowl and mimicked him, bunching his face exaggeratedly and causing Ali to redden.

"*Afwan*, Ali, but you don't look like a just-married man," Talha said. "I hope you're not already having troubles with the lovely Asma."

Ali grunted and hurried away. If Asma was the reason for his ill humor, I'd gladly endure one thousand and one of his frowns. An unhappy home was just what Ali deserved, given how he'd coerced Asma into marrying him.

After Ali had gone, Talha gave me a wink. Then with a grunt he hefted a sack of dates onto my camel's back.

"By al-Lah, who would believe little A'isha could eat so much?" he teased. "You're bringing enough food for the entire caravan."

"These dates will feed the poor," I said, and stepped forward to help him tie the sack onto the saddle. In a lowered voice, I added, "If Ali can resist stuffing his expanding belly with them."

"His paunch has grown nearly as large as his head," Talha agreed.

"He has a reason for his fat stomach, having four women to cook for him," I said. "But from what I can see, there's nothing but air between his ears."

Talha laughed. "*Yaa* A'isha, what would Muhammad say if he heard you?"

"He would say, 'A'isha hasn't changed at all.'"

But he would be wrong. Since Muhammad had died, Ali had denied him the funeral befitting a Prophet; he'd tried to start a rebellion against my father; and, with Umar's help, he'd forced my father's widow, Asma, to marry him. As far as my feelings for Ali were concerned, I had changed a lot in the past few years. I hated him now more than ever.

I'd known why Ali had praised the "great Abu Bakr" so lavishly during *abi*'s funeral. I'd seen him drooling over Asma as if he were a starving man and she were his next meal—while my father's spirit yet lingered among us. The earth had barely covered *abi*'s nostrils when Ali sent Umm Salama with his outrageous marriage proposal. Poor Asma was sobbing so wretchedly over *abi* that she'd barely heard a word—but she was, at last, able to choke out her refusal. Of course, Ali had found a way to win her hand: He'd encouraged Umar to propose—for himself. Faced with such a choice—the hypocrite or the wife-beater—Asma accepted Ali's offer, telling Umar that Ali had misunderstood, that she had accepted his offer but wished to delay the marriage until her grieving was ended. Yet Asma had cried for months afterward and all the way through her wedding. I hadn't seen her since, but I hoped to visit with her during the *hajj*.

Yet who could dwell on gloomy thoughts during this festive time? Around us, men and women swirled past like leaves in a breeze, laughing and chattering in anticipation of our eleven-day ride. This was the yearly *hajj*, in which we Believers braved desert heat, wicked storms, and Bedouin raids to visit Mecca, where, only a few years ago, Muhammad had rid the Ka'ba of all gods but al-Lah. Our triumphal entry into our homeland still thrilled me whenever I remembered it: how Bilal had climbed to the Ka'ba's rooftop to sound the call to prayer; how the people of Quraysh had streamed out from their homes to greet us; how Muhammad's eyes had filled with tears as, one by one, his kinsmen and neighbors had knelt before him on the Ka'ba's steps and kissed his ring. I'd sat next to him with my heart so full that love coursed through my body like a river overflowing its banks. I felt that same fullness of love every time I made the *hajj*.

I'll see you in Mecca very soon, habib. Never did I feel so close to Muhammad as during the pilgrimage, when I walked in his footsteps and prayed the prayers he had taught us. Bereft of his company and of my father's presence—had it already been a year since *abi* had died?—I needed this journey more than ever to soothe my lonely heart. Anticipation tickled the bottoms of my feet, making me smile at my camel and at Talha, making me want to kiss them both. Judging from the look in Talha's eyes, he was feeling the same impulse.

I dropped my gaze and, seeing Umar approaching with his whip, made sure my wrapper covered my face and ducked into the mosque. I slipped across the floor and into the courtyard, where my sister-wives packed their belongings. Zaynab stood among them, waving her white gown and complaining loudly.

"Outrageous for a wife of the Prophet!" she was saying. "Behold, this gown has been mended three times. In truth, mended holes are all that holds this rag together!"

I couldn't help staring at her—not because of the noise she was making, but out of shock at the paleness of her face and its tautness. Her lips were tinged a faint blue, making her beautiful teeth look yellow.

"By al-Lah, I wonder what holds *her* together," whispered Hafsa, who had sidled up next to me. I couldn't reply; my breath blocked my throat, snagged by emotion. Zaynab, I could clearly see, was very ill.

Umm Salama could see it, too. Like a wind she rustled across the drought-parched grass and enfolded her friend in her arms. "*Yaa* Zaynab, are you planning to travel tonight? I think you will need to rest beforehand."

"Rest? How can I rest when I have no clothes to wear and no money with which to buy even the coarsest cloth?" Zaynab's glance veered about the courtyard, seeming not to see any of us who watched her. Then Saffiya stepped out of her hut in a gown of pink silk edged with gold thread.

Oblivious as always, Saffiya returned our gape-mouthed stares with a smile, and twirled before us in new gold-colored sandals. "Isn't it beautiful?" she said. "I haven't worn such a gorgeous gown since I was a princess in my father's house."

"*Yaa* Princess, I wouldn't step too close to Zaynab right now," Raihana said with a grin. "Unless you want to get crowned."

"Now girls, there is no need to start any trouble." Sawdah's voice was stern, but her hands fluttered like anxious birds. "Saffiya has not been on the *hajj* before, and she does not know how to dress for it."

"I want to look my best," Saffiya said, and twirled more slowly this time. "See how the gold thread shines throughout the fabric? And it is so weightless, I feel cool even in this heat."

"But—where did you get it?" Hafsa asked.

Saffiya blinked at her, as if the answer were too obvious to state. "From Uthman," she said.

I sucked in my breath. Uthman! He was wealthy, yes—probably the wealthiest man in the *umma*. But, unlike Umar, he was infamous for his love of women. Before *islam*, the handsome, pleasure-seeking Uthman had enjoyed the company of widows, dancing girls, concubines, and virgins, all eager, it seemed, to lavish their attentions on a man so generous with his gold.

"*Yaa* Saffiya, you must return those gifts," I said.

She jerked away from me as if afraid I'd yank the clothes from her body. "Why?" she said. "Because *you* don't have them?"

"If you are seen wearing such an extravagant gown, you may bring scandal on yourself," Umm Salama said.

Saffiya frowned. "Scandal? For what? Wearing new clothes?"

"It doesn't take much to start a scandal about *us*," Raihana said with a smirk. "Looking at a man with both eyes will get you the whip these days."

"People will wonder where you got the gown," I said.

Zaynab flashed her eyes at Saffiya, although her voice was feeble. "And what you did to earn it."

Saffiya's gasp was as short and sharp as a slap "Uthman is my friend," she said, bristling. "He comforted me when Muhammad died, which is more than any of you cared to do."

"We had our own grief," Umm Salama began, but Saffiya cut her off.

"You had your own interests." She swept an arm around to indicate each of us. "All you cared about was the *khalifa* while I wept in the courtyard alone, dying of a broken heart. Uthman gave me his scarf to dry my tears, then sat and cried with me. We're friends, and nothing more."

"That's very touching," Raihana said dryly. "So when the *umma* starts whispering, are you going to give them this tale? Because I'm telling you, no one is going to believe it."

"At least, not the 'friends' part," I said. "*Yaa* Saffiya, Uthman used to have a reputation. You probably didn't know."

She turned to me. "And I don't care," she said. "I won't listen to you slander him just because you're jealous, A'isha. Although, why you should be, I don't know—not when you have your father's money!" She whirled around and stomped to her hut, kicking up a puff of dust before she disappeared inside with a slam of the door.

For a few moments, all was silent. Then Juwairriyah's quiet voice rose. hesitant.

"*Yaa* A'isha, you speak truly about the scandal," she said. "But there is truth in Saffiya's words, also. While you have enjoyed Abu Bakr's assistance, some of us have no one to provide for us. I, Raihana, and Saffiya came to Medina from other lands, and our families are far away."

"Or dead," Raihana grumbled.

"Nobody helps me." Sawdah drew herself up and spoke in a voice tinged with pride. "I have provided for myself for years."

Zaynab sighed. Her shoulders drooped, and she looked as though she might crumple to the ground. "My father used to give me money until he died. But my uncle won't give me a *dirham*. He thinks the *umma* should support Muhammad's wives."

"I receive a small allowance from my father, but his fortunes have changed since we invaded Mecca," Umm Salama said. Her tribe, the Banu Makhzum, had been one of the Quraysh clan's most prestigious families before *islam*.

"My father provides for me, of course," Ramlah said. She raised her nose into the air, its usual position. "But as the daughter of Abu Sufyan, governor of Mecca, I *should* have more money than Jewish slaves."

"Because of my father, I do not starve, either," Maymunah said. She smoothed her palm over her linen gown. "Like your father, *yaa* Umm Habiba, al-Abbas has much pride in our family's status and would never allow me to wear mended clothes. Yet he complains nonetheless. He says, 'Muhammad should have left an inheritance for his wives or allowed you to remarry.'"

"Remarry? Then we would lose our place in Paradise with him," Sawdah said. "I want to be right there by Muhammad's side, living in his palace. We'll have plenty of nice clothes then, girls."

Hafsa lowered her eyes. "My father provides for me, also. I never even wondered how everyone else gets along."

I patted her arm in commiseration, then looked up to see the gazes of my sister-wives on me. They were waiting for me to speak, but what could I say? My father had given me a generous share of his property when Muhammad had died, but I'd used it to help feed people in the tent city while *abi* tried to collect taxes from the apostate tribes. Only lately, as our men made more and more conquests, had the *umma's* treasury begun to fill. But then *abi* had asked me, on his deathbed, to share my income with my two brothers, my older sister, and my little sister, Umm Kulthum.

"I'd share what I have with all of you, but it's not mine to give any more," I said. "Soon I'll be wearing mended holes, also."

"Ah, but you have the power to do something about it," Raihana said. "You have the *khalifa*'s ear."

I laughed. "Umar? What woman has power with him? He whips his wives if they talk back."

"He listens to me," Hafsa said in a small voice. "Sometimes."

"Of course he does," Sawdah said. "What father could turn his little girl away?"

Umar could, and we all knew it, but no one spoke as we gave Hafsa nervous glances. If she petitioned her father, he might view it as a sign of disrespect—and he'd punish her severely. Yet I wasn't sure I'd fare any better if I went to see him. He wouldn't strike me, for he knew Muhammad was watching from Paradise, but he might punish me in some other way for daring to approach him. Still, loot from our conquests had been pouring into the *umma*'s treasury since he became *khalifa*. Umar might make things hard for me, but would he refuse my request?

"I'll go," I said, "when we return from the *hajj*."

Hafsa took a deep breath. "We'd better go now, A'isha. Our army killed that Persian queen, did you hear? I saw my father this morning, and he's in a very good mood. Our messengers brought back a trunkful of treasures. By the time we get back from Mecca, it might all be spent."

Together we went inside my hut to prepare for our visit. Hafsa combed my hair and pulled it back away from my face so it wouldn't show beneath my wrapper, and I removed the kohl from her eyes. "Our humble personalities won't be enough to impress my father," she said with a giggle. "If we want his help, we must embody modesty and meekness."

We hunched our shoulders, covered our faces, and shuffled into the mosque like a pair of cringing slaves. The room was dim and cool, having no windows, with trickles of light filtering through the date-palm ceiling and mottling our white robes. Umar knelt on a crimson carpet that, I could see as we neared, displayed a glorious garden of jewels: emerald grasses, trees dripping with ruby fruits, flowers of amethyst and garnet and jade, and rivers of pearl springing from a golden earth paved with silver paths.

"Exquisite," Umar murmured as his hands caressed the glinting jewels.

"It is beautiful, *yaa abi*," Hafsa said in her most childlike voice. His head jerked up at the sound of her, and he leapt to his feet.

"Yes, b-but—too extravagant," he said, his voice suddenly gruff. "The decadence of the Persian court was never more apparent. It is one reason why our disciplined warriors were able to defeat the Persian troops—that, and the fact that a woman led them."

I thought of asking Umar about the Muslim army's other victories, in which we had defeated troops led by men. Did he also think men were unfit for war? But I held my tongue, not wanting to rankle him now.

"Did our messengers bring the carpet to you, *abi?* By al-Lah, that is a rare acquisition!" Hafsa gave Umar her most winning smile. "What do you intend to do with it?"

"We will display it in the Ka'ba as a testament to the power of *islam*," Umar said, beaming at her. My spirits lifted to see him in such a benign mood. Hafsa had spoken truly: Now was the best moment to make our request. I bowed low and asked permission to speak.

"*Yaa khalifa*, we have come to ask for your help. Muhammad's widows, having no husbands to provide for us, need the *umma's* support."

"The *umma* has always shown the utmost respect for you all, has it not?" Umar said.

"I do not think Muhammad would approve of such an ostentatious display of that carpet, *yaa khalifa*."

The voice came from the shadows behind me. Irritation crossed Umar's face at the sight of Ali, but he quickly arranged his features into a smile and walked across the floor to grasp his elbows.

"Yes, of course you speak truly, Ali. I did not mean I would display this extravagant item indefinitely. It would be on view for a short time, to allow the Believers to witness the luxury of the Persian court."

"A luxury in which they lived while their subjects begged for food in the streets," Ali snapped. "These are the conditions Muhammad sought to correct with *islam*."

Although I agreed with Ali, I felt as agitated as if acacia thorns were pricking my skin. If we didn't speak up soon, our petition would be forgotten or even dismissed, as Ali's interference soured Umar's mood.

"*Yaa* Umar, as Muhammad's widow and Abu Bakr's daughter, may I make a suggestion?" I said in my meekest tone.

Umar scowled at me, but he nodded.

"*Yaa* Ali, what would you have Umar do with the Persian carpet?" I asked.

Ali folded his arms and widened his stance. "He should cut it into pieces and distribute them to the men of the *umma*. That would be the way of *islam*, to share equally with all."

"Why couldn't you display the carpet first for all to see, and then divide it?" I asked. "Then everyone could see the fruits of our conquests and give praise to al-Lah before reaping the benefits."

Umar's smile returned. "Your idea had occurred to me, also, A'isha. Now I am convinced that it is the best way." He clapped Ali on the shoulder. "You are not the only one who bears the Prophet's intentions in mind, Ali."

Then Umar turned toward the *majlis* and began to walk away. "It has been a long day for me. I need to rest."

"But *abi*!" Hafsa blurted. Umar stopped, lifted his whip slightly, and looked around at her with lifted eyebrows.

"What is it?" he asked. Then he shifted his gaze to me, and back to Hafsa. "Yes. Your petition."

I stepped forward, my head ducked in submission. "Will the widows of Muhammad receive a portion of this wonderful carpet? Selling it would do much to relieve our suffering and also to enhance your status, for the people of the *umma* would not like to see us threadbare and starving."

"I do not recommend that, *khalifa*," Ali said. Umar looked annoyed by the interruption.

"Would Muhammad object to this, also, Ali?"

"Not Muhammad. But *you* might not desire it."

"Muhammad would want us to be provided for," Hafsa said. She walked over to Umar and grasped his hand. "*Abi*, please," she said.

"If you distribute that carpet to Muhammad's widows, every woman in the *umma* will want a share," Ali said. "Shouldn't their husbands decide how the household income is allocated?"

Umar released Hafsa's hand and pulled at his beard. "Ali's argument is compelling."

Hafsa's shoulders drooped as low as my spirits. "However," Umar added, "I do not wish to leave the widows of the Prophet in destitution. You speak truly, daughter, when you say that Muhammad would not have wanted you to suffer."

He smiled at her then, his eyes as soft as kisses. When he turned his gaze to me, the warmth remained.

"I will distribute the Persian carpet to the men of the *umma* only," Umar said. "As for your sister-wives, *yaa* A'isha, I will give them each a yearly pension of ten thousand silver dirhams." Hafsa cried out and threw her arms around her father's neck, while I stood in stunned silence. What about me? Were my sister-wives to be awarded such a generous amount while I received nothing? My portion of the date harvest from my father's lands was barely enough to keep me alive.

Umar patted Hafsa's back self-consciously, being unused to showing affection. As he pulled her hands away from his neck, he smiled down at her and then at me. "Do not look so forlorn, A'isha," he said. "Would I forget my friend Muhammad's favorite wife? Because of his esteem for you and your status in his *harim*, I will award you more than they receive: twelve thousand dirhams."

"*Yaa khalifa*, do you think that is wise?"

As rude as always, Ali strode forward to stand in front of me. "We have all heard how A'isha antagonized the other women of the Prophet's *harim*. Her jealousy over Muhammad's affections inspired much resentment among her sister-wives. Awarding her a larger pension might rekindle those old animosities."

"*Afwan, khalifa*," I said. "Ali seems to be an expert on everything today. What will he say next? That he should be the *khalifa* instead of you?"

Umar heard the truth in my words. Ali had overstepped his bounds more than once. He glared at Ali. "A'isha speaks truly. I do not recall asking for your advice today on any matter, yet you have thrust your opinions upon me several times. Utter one more word, and you will feel the sting of my whip!"

He lifted his whip and jerked his wrist. Its tail snapped so closely to Ali's head that I saw his hair lift and fall. "Ten thousand dirhams for the others, twelve thousand for A'isha," he said. "Umar has spoken. I am going to leave you now—unless, Ali, you have something else you want to contribute?" Ali shrugged.

As soon as Umar had left the room, Ali whirled around and lunged toward me, forcing me back against the mosque wall. "Leave her alone, or I'll call my father!" Hafsa cried, but I knew I could handle him. Staring into his narrowed eyes, I sent Hafsa to the *harim* to tell the sister-wives our good news.

"How dare you belittle me before Umar?" he rasped when she had gone. "By al-Lah, if you had not deceived Muhammad into loving you so ardently, I would find a way to diminish you. Instead, I have forbidden any of my wives to speak to you, lest your unbecoming conduct influence theirs."

I struggled to keep my dismay from showing. Not speak to Asma! She and I had grown close after my father's death. Her grief had been so heartfelt that even my mother had ended up consoling her—and, in the end, loving her.

But I knew Ali would have a hard time enforcing his new rule during the *hajj*. Amid so many pilgrims, he'd never be able to watch all four of his wives, especially since he would ride up front with Umar while we women would be in the back.

"Hearing is obeying," I said, never breaking my stare. "Now if you'll step aside, I need to finish packing."

A slow grin spread like a shadow across his face. "You have not heard the news," he said. "And so it is my great pleasure to inform you. After hearing my warnings about dangerous rebels lurking in the desert, Umar has declared that the widows of Muhammad will remain in Medina. You will not make the *hajj* this year, A'isha. Al-Lah willing, you will never see Mecca again."

Al-Lah didn't seem to be the one making the rules these days. But before I could make the retort Hafsa ran into the mosque, her wrapper forgotten, her hair lashing the air about her head.

"A'isha, you've got to come quickly," she cried. She jostled Ali aside as if she hadn't seen him, then grabbed my hands and pulled me toward the courtyard. "Zaynab needs you. She's vomiting blood."

All was a blur as I ran to get my medicine pouch. Ali was forgotten, the *hajj* of no consequence to me now. None of us would travel while our sister-wife Zaynab lay at the feet of death. Inside her hut, I pushed my way through the sister-wives crowding her bedside. She smiled weakly, parting her parched lips just enough for me to see flecks of blood on her gums. I rummaged through my bag, silently worried, having no experience with this illness. My hands trembled as I pulled out a piece of dried ginger. "We'll make a tea from this," I said. "It will soothe your stomach."

"A'isha." Her once-husky voice sounded feeble, a mere rustle like grasses in the wind. "I spoke with Muhammad."

I heard a cry, and looked into the panicked eyes of Umm Salama, whose pale face reflected my own terror. Was Zaynab so close to death that she communicated with those in Paradise? I reached out to smooth her hair from her damp brow. Touching her skin was like putting my hand into a fire.

"*Yaa* A'isha, why do you cry?" Zaynab reached out to squeeze my hand. "Not for me. I'm going to join Muhammad!"

"No," I lied, blinking back my tears. "Not for you. For myself! I hoped I'd be with him soon."

"But of course I would be the one to go," she said. "He was my whole life, you know. But you, A'isha—Muhammad told me—you have to stay. You won't go to Paradise for many years."

"But why?" I said, sobbing now, forgetting that Zaynab was speaking out of delirium. "Doesn't he want me?"

"Of course he does." She squeezed my hand again, but more feebly. She closed her eyes and sighed. I cried out, thinking she was gone—but then she spoke again.

"You need to be here, A'isha," she murmured. "Muhammad told me. You have work to do."

"Work? What kind of work?"

"Al-Ma'thur," she murmured. "The Legacy." She closed her eyes.

"Muhammad's sword? Does he want me to use it? Against whom? *Yaa* Zaynab!" My voice rose with my fear of losing her, and my urgent need to hear more.

"Shhh, A'isha," Umm Salama whispered, and laid a gentle hand on my shoulder. "Zaynab is resting, can't you see?"

I sighed in defeat. When Zaynab awoke, she might not even remember this conversation.

Please, al-Lah, help her to remember, I prayed. *I need Muhammad's direction more than ever.*

As Umm Salama ushered my sister-wives out of the hut, I stuffed the herbs and medicines back into my pouch, wiping tears from my eyes. Zaynab was dying, and there was nothing I could do. All the ginger tea in the world wouldn't cure her, and I didn't know what would. I'd have to go to the market apothecary for help.

I stood and turned away from her—and then I heard a murmur. I looked down to see Zaynab's lips moving. "A'isha," she whispered.

I fell to my knees. "Zaynab," I said. "I'm here."

Her lips moved again, and I lowered my head so close that I could feel her breath on my ear.

"Dogs . . ." she said. "Beware the dogs."

"What did you say, Zaynab?" I whispered back. "What dogs?"

"At Hawab," she said. "Muhammad said . . . beware the dogs at Hawab."

And she fell back into her deep slumber, leaving me more confused than before.

Ali

Such pleasure it gave me to reveal to A'isha her exclusion from the *hajj*, and to see her smug expression flee like a slumbering dog startled by a hungry lion. In truth, I felt much like a lion at that moment. But the swelling of my chest, like the fullness in my belly, did not last for long. Only months after the pilgrimage to Mecca had ended, despair had become a sharp stone in my stomach as I scoured the city for barley to feed myself and my growing household. In the market, I moved from vendor to vendor with a coin-heavy purse, thanks to the pension Umar had given to me and my sons. Yet all the dinars in Hijaz would not have benefited me, for the drought we had been experiencing for more than a year had diminished our food supply. Barley and dates, the foundation of our diet, had become scarce.

Perspiring with anxiety, I snatched the sack of gold into my right hand ready to throw it in exasperation into the next sorrowful face telling me there was no barley available. Apparently seeing my frustration, or perhaps glimpsing the coins in my sheepskin pouch, the old jeweler Umm Ramzi beckoned for me. In a hushed voice he told of a caravan that had arrived that morning bearing wheat from Egypt. The owner of that caravan was none other than Hassan ibn Thabit, our city's esteemed poet. For this useful news, I gave Umm Ramzi a dinar. His expression brightened: It was an outrageous amount. But I would have paid twice the price to ensure that my family would be fed while I was in Syria.

These were desperate times for Hijaz. From Khaybar to Ta'if, the ruthless sun beat strong men down to dust, shrinking spirits as well as bodies. Springs had vanished, sucked dry by the earth's thirst, shriveling the date crop before flowers could form on the trees. Prayers for rain filled the mosque like birds too exhausted to fly, flapping their tired wings against the dirt floor. One afternoon, dark clouds choked the sky with eerie promise—but the few drops of rain they spat dried up before reaching the ground.

And so with a gladdened heart I entered the mosque that evening, a sack of wheat hoisted upon my shoulder and news for Umar of more grain available from Hassan ibn Thabit. Relief from starvation, at least, was near at hand. Now we could turn our energies to other problems.

"You must put an end to the decadence of your warriors if you wish to end the drought," a wizened *shaykh* said to Umar as I walked into the mosque. "We hear tales of excess from the conquered lands in Syria and Persia. Al-Lah is punishing us for straying from the Prophet's ideals."

I could not argue with this reasoning. My cousin had modeled an ascetic life, for he believed material possessions distracted men from spiritual pursuits. In truth, the pleasures in my life provided by a pension and four wives had lulled me into a malaise like the sleep into which a man lapses after a large meal. Yet we had heard rumors of a greater decadence in Syria, where our warriors had abandoned their fight for the love of dice, dancing girls, and exotic foods.

"By al-Lah, I know these tales, and I will determine their truth," Umar said to the *shaykh*. "We have finished our preparations and leave for Damascus tomorrow. If we find our men engaged in sinful pursuits, I shall order all to return to Medina immediately. If we find the governor condoning this behavior, I shall replace him. By al-Lah! I will put an end either to the wagging tongues or to the causes for God's displeasure."

And so we departed the next evening, one hundred men but no women, for Umar had forbidden wives to join us. "*We must not risk exposing our women to corruption*," he'd said, causing many to grumble. I held my tongue, but with difficulty. Without Asma to accompany me, the excursion would be only a duty to be endured.

Yet Umar had selected a propitious time for this expedition. As we were mounting our camels, the young warrior Said ibn Utba rode up on horseback. Said was dressed in a most amusing fashion, more befitting a eunuch than a man, in a Damascene silk tunic of pale indigo patterned with the figures of horses. "*Yaa khalifa,* I bring news from Khalid ibn al-Walid," he said, panting. Umar invited him into the *majlis*, delaying our departure until Said had eaten from our meager stores, drunk the last of the *umma's* goat's milk, and rested an hour from his long journey.

"We have taken Jerusalem, the holy city," Said announced that evening, as he sat in the *majlis* with me, Umar, Uthman, and Talha. "That prize was not easily won. We besieged the city for weeks until its patriarch, Sophronius, offered to surrender. But he says he will only submit to the *khalifa* Umar."

And so Jerusalem was added to our expedition, and with a sinking heart I contemplated additional months away from Asma's bed.

In his winter robe, mended countless times, Umar set out that night with his advisors and supporters. My cheeks still wet with my darling Asma's tears—for my kindnesses had at last, after two years, won her heart—we made the arduous trek to witness our warriors' behavior in Damascus and to claim Jerusalem, the city Muhammad had once deemed most holy in the world.

Besides Asma's absence, the journey held another disappointment: Umar had invited Talha, whose provocations would certainly irritate me like a blister that refused to heal. I endeavored to remain as far from that mocker as possible.

Avoiding contact while we traveled was not difficult, since the majority of our journey occurred after dark. Nighttime in the desert is frigid, requiring a man to swaddle himself in blankets as though he were a newborn. And so with little effort I was able to avoid his dancing eyes.

Undistracted by Talha's unpleasant jokes, I focused on the pleasures of travel: the contours of the sand dunes, like the curves of a woman; the glassy moon; the sweet, sharp exhilaration brought about by the richness of the desert air in my lungs; the pungent earthen aromas arising from the camels; the acrid smell of burning oil on the torches our men carried to light our way; the *yip* of jackals and the song of men's voices reciting verses invented in the moment. The latter was a skill at which I excelled, having been reared in the household of Muhammad, the Greatest Poet of all.

Only occasionally during our weeks-long march did I happen upon Talha. My uncle al-Abbas was another matter. He had ingratiated himself so thoroughly with Umar as to become one of his chief advisors along with Mughira, a leader of the Quraysh tribe. Mughira was a big, ugly, one-eyed man on whose breath I had smelled both women and wine, but who professed the utmost piety. He prescribed the severest of punishments for those accused of those same transgressions. My uncle cared little for Mughira, knowing him to be the most odious of hypocrites. Yet he visited the man's tent, and urged me to do the same, for power's sake. *Mughira holds the* khalifa *in his palm. He could be a valuable ally for you.*

I said nothing, fearing that I might burst into laughter and reveal the disrespect for my uncle that had planted itself in my heart. The time was not right for these ambitions. I burned in shame at the memory of the deeds I had committed in the interest of my advancement. In truth, I had never approved of al-Abbas' tactics for pursuing the *khalifa*—not Muhammad's secret burial; not the defiance I was encouraged to display once Abu Bakr had been chosen; and not my uncle's recruitment of spies and rebels from the *umma*'s army, men who pledged they would support me as *khalifa* although I was not a contender.

I tried demurring, but my uncle refused to listen.

"In the eyes of Quraysh, I am too young to lead," I insisted.

He frowned. "You are less young than you were before, and you will be older tomorrow than you are today."

"But the Bedouins will not support a relative of Muhammad's."

My uncle *tsked*. "Ali, these are not your obstacles. They exist only in others' minds."

Perhaps, but they were no less real to me. I might never be the *khalifa*. I had accepted this. I felt no urgency to press for the position while Umar held it. Severe though he might be at times, Umar strove to uphold Muhammad's vision for *islam*. Nothing else mattered, in my view.

And when Umar needed guidance in administering *islam* according to Muhammad's ideals, to whom did he turn? I possessed the most intimate knowledge of the Prophet's heart, and I most advised the *khalifa* on these matters. I only regretted that he did not seek my opinions regarding his treatment of women. I would have made life easier for those gentle creatures. This, I knew, would have been my cousin's desire.

As Umar's Companion, I was able to make nearly as great an impact on the future of *islam* and the *umma* as if I had held the *khalifa*. And after giving my advice, I returned home to my delightful wives and growing brood of children. Would I be more content if I held Umar's position? I could not imagine it.

When we reached Damascus, we found that beautiful city in disarray. Women dressed in dark blue huddled at the ornate arched gate and screeched like crows as we entered. In the city, men and women scurried about like ants when they beheld our approach, as though we had come to invade their city a second time. As we entered the heart of the city I could only wonder whether we Muslims controlled anything within its sand-colored walls. True to rumor, we spied men wearing warriors' clothing hunched in the narrow streets and casting dice of carved stone. Pieces of gold lay scattered at their feet. The rattling of tambourines greeted our ears along with the lilt of women's voices, and as we rounded the corner we beheld the form of a fleshy dancer in a dress the color of the sea, whose bare arms and throat dripped with jewels and who gyrated her body more sinuously than any serpent's for the pleasure of a growing crowd of men. Heat spread across my lap as if my robes had caught fire, and I averted my eyes for the dancer's sake, for al-Lah's, and for that of my own soul. *Yaa al-Lah, allow us to reach this poor woman with Your message.*

Instinctively I sought Umar, who rode at the front of the caravan and whom I followed at a distance so that I might avoid Talha's distasteful company. Yet as I spurred my camel forward along the line, I saw that mocker gazing at the woman's body with every swing of her hips. Talha's mouth twitched at the corners, as it seemed always to do. He inclined his head toward that of his young friend Abdallah—my cousin al-Zubayr's son, A'isha's nephew—and said, "By al-Lah! Behold the woman's spasmodic twitching! Has she swallowed a honeybee, or an entire hive?"

With skin the translucent hue of milk and the graceful upward sweep of her hair—red hair, reminding me unpleasantly of A'isha, whom I had sought to escape on this journey—the dancer's feminine delicacy was apparent, even if her morality was not. With equal measures of approval and worry I watched Umar stomp up to the unsuspecting woman, his whip in his right hand. How imposing was his figure! Certainly she would cease her flagrancy as soon as he commanded her to cover herself.

He lifted the whip and brought it down with a crack upon her tender, exposed bosom. The dancer screamed and crouched, covering herself with her arms, but his next strike fell on her back, leaving a welt so angry it oozed droplets of blood. No one rushed forth to protect her, and when her admirers realized her admonisher's identity, they scurried away like startled rats.

My pulse pounded like a fist against my throat as I watched Umar strike the woman, his pocked face as livid as a bruise; as I heard her shrieks of pain, which rose and echoed off the stone buildings; and as I saw the blood rise upon her pale skin. How could I end this punishment? Muhammad would not have condoned this.

The poor, sobbing dancer fell to the street while I watched. Indecision paralyzed me. Should I interfere? Muhammad would certainly have done so, but he was the Prophet of God. Yet as Umar raised his whip again I was commanding my camel to drop to its knees, and then running toward the fallen woman as if pushed by some hand other than my own. When I reached her I yanked off my woolen robe and flung it over her shuddering body, protecting her from Umar's sting and hiding her from his unforgiving eyes.

I half expected to feel the lash of Umar's fury on my shoulders and head, but my interruption had halted his assault. He stood with his hand suspended, the whip dangling against his wrist, his eyes narrowed.

"I have ended her offense, *yaa khalifa,*" I said. "She is now covered. Al-Lah willing, she will remain so, now that you have pointed out her error."

He did not reply. Instead, he turned and stomped back to where his camel awaited. My face burned: Surely he suspected more than ever that I would usurp his authority. An act of retribution would be necessary, I knew, to place me again into my proper position.

As I turned to the woman at my feet, I could not regret my actions. I reached down to help her with my sleeve over my hand, showing my respect for her by placing a barrier between my skin and hers. From the moment Umar's whip had welted her, she had ceased to be a sinner in my eyes and had become, instead, a human being deserving of compassion. When I touched her, however, the robe slipped away from her hair and I noticed again its color, the orange-red of a cactus flower. The memory of A'isha cast its long shadow across my mind.

But I helped this fire-haired woman more gently than I had ever even thought to touch A'isha. As a young girl, A'isha had aroused my ire many times with her pranks and her tart mouth; as a young woman, she had inspired my dislike with her petty jealousies over Muhammad, her disrespectful treatment of my beloved Fatima, and her relentless ambition to become queen of the *harim*. I had fantasized many times about seeing her punished, but now, beholding this woman who reminded me of her, I recognized A'isha as woman who could be hurt and humiliated, just as this dancer had been.

"I owe you my life," she murmured in a voice like the breeze. Her egg-blue eyes gazed through a veil of tears as she offered up my robe, but I waved it away.

"Please keep it so that you may hide yourself from the eyes of men," I said to her. "The Prophet admonished us to clothe ourselves in modesty so as not to incite sinful desires."

Her tears disappeared. "Am I to be ashamed of that which God has given me?" she said, tossing her head and spilling red hair across her bared arms. "No, and not ashamed of the stripes your leader has marked me with, either. I will display them so that my fellow Syrians can see the pain this new *islam* inflicts. Our Christian God—" she lifted her chin "—is a God of love."

As she handed my robe to me, I thought again of the arrogant A'isha. I hastened to my camel, donning my robe and glaring at all I passed, daring any man to comment while hoping someone might. I hungered for a fight.

I noted the eyes of Talha in the crowd, eyes that danced with laughter under his ridiculous yellow turban. Young Abdallah, A'isha's nephew, had disappeared and had been replaced by the warrior 'Amr, who was seated beside Talha on his horse. As I passed the pair, Talha bowed to me as if in deference, although I knew he meant to mock.

"The red hair of a woman is to Ali as a flickering flame to a moth," Talha said. "Attracting and scorching at once. Do I speak truly, *yaa* Ali?"

The lilting tone he used was like a bellows to my smoldering rage. In the flash of a blade I held Zulfikar, my double-pointed sword, mere inches from Talha's face. He laughed no more.

A single thrust and I could have pierced both his eyes at once. I imagined Talha's howl, his smirk lost in rivers of blood. 'Amr's sword clashed against mine, calling me back to the moment.

"*Yaa* Ali, is that dancer so important that you would fight over her?" 'Amr asked. "If you attack Umar's Companion Talha, our *khalifa* will deprive you of every advantage you now enjoy. And, despite your closeness to the Prophet, he would certainly have you whipped."

'Amr's warning deflated my passion, leaving me cold. He spoke truly: Umar enjoyed Talha's wit. I sheathed my sword without deigning to respond and walked away to my camel.

As we neared the former Byzantine church—now a mosque—I felt my spirits lift in anticipation of a good meal and a soft bed. The journey had been long, comprising several weeks of straddling camels and chewing on dried barley. Even the sturdy Umar must be in need of rest and a proper meal.

But my spirits sank when I beheld a retinue of men in gold-embroidered robes and bejeweled turbans stepping forth to greet us. Their long beards were sleek and trimmed, delicately curling about the edges and oiled with perfumes that made them glisten as if dipped in starlight. Their hands, which carried colorful pillows laden with plump figs and purple grapes, were smooth and free of calluses, and their fingers flashed with gold rings. Umar's camel knelt at their approach. I could not see Umar's face, but I knew he would not appreciate such finery.

The tapping of tambourine bells, pleasing to all ears except Umar's, kept time with the rhythmic stepping of the servants. Behind them walked an elaborately manicured and extravagantly clothed man at whom I had to stare for many moments before recognizing the savage warrior Khalid ibn al-Walid. Gone was his crude turban stuck with arrows; in its place, a snow white hat perched like a dove atop his head. In his right hand he held a scepter wafting incense, which he waved before his flaring nostrils. His robe, in contrast to those worn by his servants, was a deep, lustrous indigo, embroidered in a rainbow of colors to depict the feathers of a peacock in full plumage.

"By al-Lah! How dare you parade before me in this way." Umar dismounted his camel in a spry leap to tower over the men who greeted him. He was so tall that he appeared to be on a horse even as he stood with his feet on the ground. His height rarely failed to intimidate.

The servants halted at his shout and folded their bodies around their goods as if to guard them from being scattered to the ground. But Umar was a frugal man. He grabbed an empty sack from his camel, pulled it open, and scooped the pillowed fruits into the bag. He did the same with all the food, and then, while we in his caravan watched with watering mouths, he motioned for me to descend and come forward.

"Take this bag and distribute its contents among the poor," he said. "Take nothing for yourself." He raised his voice so all our men could hear. "Because Ali has challenged my authority today, you will all feel the effects. I alone will sleep in the room prepared for me tonight, while the rest of you will spend the night in your tents." No one dared complain, but several of our men glared at me as if they might slit my throat while I slept. I dropped my gaze to the bag in my hand, contemplating with dread another night on the hard ground, with no bath to refresh me.

But Umar had more punishments in store. "I also command you all to partake only of the rations provided you at the beginning of our journey," he thundered. "I alone will dine with the governor of Syria tonight."

I continued staring at the ground, trying to swallow my disappointment with a closed throat. By disciplining all for my sin—the sin of compassion, by al-Lah!—Umar had meted to me a most undesirable punishment: the resentment of my fellow travelers and, with my humiliation, the loss of their respect.

"*Yaa khalifa*, how long must we endure these painful conditions?" Abdallah ibn al-Zubayr, my cousin's son, dared to ask. The whip was Umar's answer, lashing at the youth's cheek and leaving a welt there.

"There is your pain!" Umar roared. He placed his hands on his hips. "Does anyone else have a complaint?" No one responded. He narrowed his eyes at me. "*Yaa* Ali, are you waiting for Ramadan to distribute those goods?" As I did so, he continued to rant. "By al-Lah, I am astounded at the frowns I see on the faces of my men, Muslim men. Should we enjoy these rich fruits while so many hunger? Barley and dates satisfied the Prophet. They will satisfy us, also."

How could I argue? I agreed with Umar in principle, for I knew Muhammad would not have allowed a single fig or a grape to pass his lips while the streets of Damascus held even one malnourished child. I distributed the delicacies among the eager Damascenes: a girl with a face like a skull and hair that fell in clumps about her shoulders; a *shaykh* with a back bent in two and hands that shook as he accepted my gifts; a woman, clutching an infant to her breast, whose large, expressive eyes spilled tears as she chewed a fig and placed the paste into her baby's mouth.

When I had finished, my stomach continued to feel empty but my heart, by al-Lah, brimmed like that mother's eyes. Others in the caravan grumbled about giving away what was rightfully ours—and as I passed Talha on his horse, I heard him tell 'Amr that *the khalifa has repaid us well today for Ali's interference*.

I knew that he had wished for me to hear it. I stopped and turned toward the grinning men with an exaggerated bow.

"No, Talha, he has done the opposite," I said. "By assigning to me the task of feeding the poor, Umar made me the Prophet's surrogate. With this honor, Umar demonstrates that, although he is the political *khalifa*, I am my cousin's spiritual successor."

I groaned to myself as soon as I had spoken these words, knowing that they would reach Umar's ears and increase his suspicions of me. Yet they served my purpose. Talha narrowed his eyes—allowing me, for once, to be the grinning one.

"Do not worry, Talha," 'Amr called as I stepped away. "Someday, while Ali is distributing alms to the poor, you will sit in the *khalifa*'s seat, commanding the world."

I laughed at this remark, for it revealed the true nature of Talha's ambitions. As I glanced at the men around us, however, I did not see anyone else who appeared discomfited. In truth, I could see no indication that anyone had even heard 'Amr's comment, for the entire caravan was slumping to the ground as the camels knelt to allow their riders to dismount. We would not sleep or eat here, but we would all enter the mosque to greet Syria's governor, Yazid ibn Abi Sufyan.

As I directed my servant to feed and water my camel, I heard Umar's sharp cry from the front of the caravan. I raced to his side. He was shouting and waving Khalid's scepter as though he might strike Khalid with it.

"How dare you appear before me dressed in such finery!" Umar yelled. "By al-Lah, I do not know what has happened here. The rumors of decadence in Syria appear to be true, and I appear to be a fool! In truth, I see no warriors, but only soft, vain women in perfume and jewels."

Khalid lifted his hands to his embroidered garment and ripped it open to reveal his trousers, leather jerkin, and fitted shirt—his battle uniform.

"We attired ourselves to honor you, *yaa khalifa*," he said in a low, even tone that sent chills rippling along my arms and neck. "As you can see, I remain a warrior."

Umar narrowed his eyes. "And beneath the battle gear? Only al-Lah can view your heart." He brought the scepter down on a large rock, breaking it in two, and handed the pieces to Khalid. "When I have prayed, perhaps He will reveal your heart to me, also."

As Umar swept past Khalid, leaving us all in his wake, I could only stare at the man who had once been the *umma*'s fiercest general. With his beautiful robe rent open and hanging like mourner's rags and the pieces of his scepter in his hands, Khalid appeared broken also, a pitiful contrast to the haughty figure he had once presented. The scar on his cheek writhed like a worm as he tensed his jaw against these humiliations. As I passed him, I glanced down at his feet and saw a pair of golden sandals glittering with jewels. I could have sworn that I detected the aroma of wine rising from his body.

In contrast to the chaos outside the mosque, I expected to find order within. Yazid was heralded not only as a shrewd commander on the battlefield but also as an effective governor, popular with his Syrian subjects. Despite my reservations when Umar had appointed him—he was, after all, the son of Abu Sufyan, who had once been Muhammad's mortal enemy—I had to admit that the choice had been a wise one. The congenial Yazid had charmed the Damascenes into forgetting that they had been conquered.

Yet it was not he who greeted us but his brother Mu'awiyya, a tall man with fair hair, like mine, and piercing eyes the color of sand. Unlike the fat, red-bearded Yazid, Mu'awiyya had inherited his features from his mother, Hind. And, unlike Khalid and his courtiers, Mu'awiyya wore a simple gown and turban of the deepest blue—the color of mourning.

His eyes gazed warmly into Umar's, as if they were long-time friends, and he clasped Umar's elbow as boldly as if he were the governor instead of his brother. Mu'awiyya was but a mere warrior under Umar's command. Like his father, who had tried many times to kill Muhammad, Mu'awiyya appeared to hold an inflated opinion of himself. But Umar, preoccupied with other matters, apparently did not notice the insult.

"I am pleased to see you, Mu'awiyya, but where is Yazid?" Umar said. "I am anxious to speak with him."

Mu'awiyya's eyes filled with tears—conjured tears, I was certain, for he had never shown any love for his brother, and had once threatened to kill him in the market at Mecca until their father intervened. "Yazid died yesterday," he said. "We have suffered a terrible plague in our city—"

"By al-Lah, you are infested with a plague and we are only learning this now?" I cried. "Why did you not send messengers to alert us? By allowing the *khalifa* to enter the city, you have endangered his life."

Umar placed his hand on my arm. Mu'awiyya turned his disturbing eyes upon me. I had seen that cold expression before, when he was but a youth, as I had pressed my sword against his father's neck and demanded he convert to *islam*. Mu'awiyya watched Abu Sufyan grovel before me and heard him beg, and he had hated me ever since.

"Excuse me for being preoccupied with my brother's demise as well as that of his two sons," Mu'awiyya spat. "Family is extremely close to the hearts of Abu Sufyan's sons and daughters."

"But surely you knew we were approaching," I said—but again, Umar silenced me with a touch.

"My deepest condolences, Mu'awiyya," Umar said. "Your brother was a superior general and a great statesman. He will be difficult to replace. Who has assumed the leadership here?"

Mu'awiyya's expression became as stone. How clever he was, such an expert at concealing his true emotions. "Your general Khalid ibn al-Walid has graciously taken on this difficult task," he said.

Umar's frown deepened. "And you?" he said. "Why did you not take your brother's place?"

Mu'awiyya wiped a false tear from the corner of one eye. "I did not wish to presume," he said. "Such an honor is only the *khalifa*'s to confer."

"Khalid had no such qualms," Umar muttered to me and my uncle a few moments later, as Mu'awiyya led us down a long, dim hallway to the *khalifa*'s sleeping quarters. I could have spoken for hours about Khalid ibn al-Walid's arrogance, his cruelty—so antithetical to *islam*—and his ruthlessly ambitious nature, but I said nothing, loath to reveal my inner thoughts before the cunning Mu'awiyya. When Umar entered his rooms, beckoning me and al-Abbas to join him, I knew he would be seeking our advice. "Send Mughira to me, also," he said as he dismissed Mu'awiyya.

Inside, I gazed around the spacious rooms, my mouth hanging open like a child's. These quarters were more luxurious than any I had seen, with ceilings so high even ten men standing on one another's shoulders would not be able to reach them, large arched windows, plush carpets and tapestries, and a bed whose plump stuffed mattress could accommodate four men. I tried not to think about my own sleeping quarters that night, a thin pallet on the hard-packed earth in a tent that smelled like camel sweat, torch smoke, and body odor.

Umar walked to a window and beheld the view, but it did not calm him. He drummed the fingers of one hand on the sill and, with the other, picked a thread hanging from his robe.

"Khalid is guided by his impulses," al-Abbas said. "Behold his behavior today."

"He is obsessed with power and wealth," Umar said. "I am certain that he has been stealing from me. How else could he afford such extravagances as embroidered silk robes and golden incense burners?"

"And jewel-encrusted gold sandals," I added. "The price of his shoes alone could feed Medina for a month."

"Damn him." Umar slammed his fist on the windowsill, scattering the birds that had gathered outside. "I have heard that the men in his command were not paid last month, although I sent Khalid a sack full of silver for them. By al-Lah, where is Mughira?"

"You must punish Khalid for this treachery." I began to pace the smooth stone floor. "If you do not have him whipped, you will appear weak."

"Khalid is popular with his men," al-Abbas said. "*Yaa* Ali, do you wish to cause a mutiny?"

"If he has that much power, Umar must strip him of it," I said.

"Your advice is sound," Umar said. "I need to question him about these newly acquired riches. If he does not answer satisfactorily, I will deprive him of everything he owns."

Umar sent me back to the mosque in search of Khalid, whom he desired to interrogate immediately. Before I entered, a familiar, annoying laugh stung my ears, stopping me in place.

"Did you behold the anger on Umar's face when he heard that Khalid had taken the governorship?" Mughira said. "Soon you will be in a better position."

"It was a move that I knew Umar would dislike," Mu'awiyya said. "That is why I encouraged Khalid to make it."

I remembered the task for which I had been sent, and turned away to seek Khalid. But then the men began to talk again.

"*Yaa* Talha, like the Bedouins, I try always to support the winning side," Mu'awiyya said. "Who has pledged support for you as *khalifa*? Someone powerful, I hope."

"He has the love of A'isha bint Abi Bakr," Mughira said. "As the Mother of the Believers, she holds more influence than any man."

"She thinks she will rule if I am appointed," Talha said.

I heard footsteps behind me, and saw Khalid ibn al-Walid walking down the hall, clutching his rent garment. I hurried to him, not daring to call his name lest I be discovered by Mu'awiyya and his cohorts.

"*Afwan*, Khalid. Umar sent me to look for you. He desires to speak with you now, in his quarters."

Khalid regarded me as though I were a piece of dung on his shoe. "Tell Umar that I will be there," he said, "as soon as I have changed my clothes."

By al-Lah! Was the whole world so filled with disregard for the *khalifa*? These men would never have treated Muhammad so lightly.

I said nothing as he disappeared down the hall, for I was eager to return to my eavesdropping. When I peeked into the mosque again Talha was gone. Mu'awiyya had taken a seat on the governor's throne as though he had been born in it, and Mughira was kneeling before him and kissing his ring. Both men were laughing.

"With a single stroke, I have conquered all of Syria today," Mu'awiyya said. "Next, with the help of the ambitious Talha and his naive whore A'isha, I will hold the *khalifa* in my hand."

"You must be the most clever man in the world," Mughira said. "And the most under-appreciated." Now I was the one wanting to laugh. The evening before, the fawning Mughira had spoken the same words to me.

"Do not fear," Mu'awiyya said. "Soon all the world will praise the name of Mu'awiyya ibn Abi Sufyan—even as they kneel before me."

A'isha

During the months when Umar and his Companions were in Syria, I and Maryam began taking morning walks together. In spite of our tempestuous start years ago, when I'd been jealous of Maryam's exotic blond curls and eyes the color of sky, I now loved her as though she were my own sister instead of merely a sister-wife—or, to be exact, a sister-concubine. She had declined to marry Muhammad so she could remain a Christian, and so she wouldn't have to veil herself.

Our first morning walk came about when, the morning after Umar, Ali, Talha, and the rest had departed, I went to her house in tears. If only I were a man so I could go along on the expedition. I knew Maryam, who cherished her freedom, would be sympathetic. And so we started spending time together. When the group returned with tales of a plague killing thousands in the north, I felt better about staying in Medina.

"Thank the Lord our men did not bring the plague home to us," she said a week after Umar's triumphant return, as we climbed to the crest of the hill behind her house. "I lived through a plague in Egypt. I saw my mother's body swell and ooze and her skin turn black. I could not imagine the extent of her suffering! God willing, we will not be stricken here."

We unfurled our prayer mats on the cracked ground and called our greetings to al-Lah, I in the Muslim fashion and she in the Christian way.

Our spirits alive and our toes tingling with the chill, we sat and watched the sheep nibble at the weeds poking up from the parched earth and reminisced about life with Muhammad, commiserating over the loneliness that haunted us both.

"I know people whisper about me and Akiiki," she said, whispering also. Unlike me, Maryam cared what people thought of her. The rumors that she was sleeping with her skinny black eunuch—a notion I found completely laughable—niggled at her like a sore tooth that she continuously tested with her tongue.

"How could people say such things?" she fumed. "I was Muhammad's concubine, not his wife. I could marry again if I desired. My decision to remain faithful to him should inspire praise, not gossip."

Our being forbidden to remarry had caused tongues to wag about all of us. We'd discussed this in the *harim* many times, but since Maryam lived in her own house—we'd once treated her so badly that Muhammad had separated her from us—she didn't know that we suffered from gossip, also. "The women who tell lies about us are jealous of our status," I told Maryam, "and the men want us for themselves."

She gazed across the fields. As the sun touched our hair, she lifted her face, cascading her curls down her back and revealing her throat. Then I saw the swelling in her neck, as if she'd swallowed a stone.

"By al-Lah!" I drew back from Maryam. Did she have the plague? "Stay right there."

I had heard stories about this dreaded illness. "It begins with lumps in the neck and quickly becomes a fever that kills," Talha had told me. And, he'd said, few of its victims survived.

Please, al-Lah, let Maryam live, I prayed as I ran to my hut to get my medicine pouch, across the rolling meadow that separated her house from the city.

On the road, I dodged bedraggled Bedouin caravans, their riders looking for water and the handful of dates that Umar provided to all who asked—a poor ration, but it had saved many from starving. I fled through the market, praying for Maryam, past the sad-eyed vendors whose numbers had dwindled because of the drought to almost nothing. Without rain there was no milk to sell, no fruit, no wheat, no meat.

I raced into the mosque, where I stopped to tell Umar about Maryam's illness. As I gave him the news, his face drooped even farther than it had already sunken these past months. Gone was the fat he'd once stored like acorns in his cheeks. I'd heard that he'd given all his precious butter and honey away, saying he couldn't indulge in those luxuries while his people starved.

"*Yaa* A'isha, you must not return to Maryam's house," Umar said. "She is in al-Lah's hands now."

"Not go back?" I frowned. "And let Maryam die in agony, alone?"

"She will not be alone." A faint smile tugged at the corners of Umar's mouth. "Her eunuch can care for her."

I lowered my eyes, remembering to show submission. "But I may have remedies, *khalifa*," I said in a soft voice.

"There are no remedies for the plague." Umar's tone was curt. "You will not return to her."

"You don't care if Maryam dies!" I cried.

"If she has the plague, she is going to die."

"And she'll die in agony if I obey you." I glared at him. "But who cares about Maryam's pain? She's only a woman. If she's not giving pleasure or sons to a man, she's less valuable than your cattle."

Umar raised his whip and cracked it down hard against the mosque floor. "She was the mother of Muhammad's son," he shouted. "And she is a model of womanhood, while you are the opposite."

"Praise al-Lah for that!" My laugh mocked him. I had no respect for Umar's order to keep away from Maryam. I turned around to address our audience: Ali, Uthman, and Talha had come into the mosque and stood behind me.

"Behold Maryam's reward for her exemplary behavior. The 'model of womanhood' is now being left to die alone like a dog. In that case, I'll happily be her opposite."

Ali folded his arms and smirked at me. "We are aware, A'isha, of your desire to be a man. Unfortunately, al-Lah has not blessed you with the attributes you need."

"And what's *your* excuse, Ali?" I fired back. Talha laughed out loud at my retort, and even the tactful Uthman smiled. Umar stomped over and cracked his whip over my head.

"Enough!" he said. "A'isha, you have gone too far."

"I haven't gone far enough," I said. "Not until I've gone back to Maryam's house."

I ran past him and into my hut, intending to grab my medicine bag and return to her, but in my haste I spilled the contents all over the floor. By the time I'd stuffed everything back inside and opened the door, Talha stood outside. His stricken expression was such a rare sight that I dropped my bag again.

"What are you doing here?" I said. "You know if Umar sees you—"

"I'm enforcing your confinement." He bent down and picked up my pouch. "Umar sent me."

"Confinement?" My body tensed. My childhood imprisonment in my parents' home pressed like walls against my memory. Did Umar think I was contagious? I *had* hugged Maryam and kissed her cheek this morning.

I lowered my voice. "Thank al-Lah that you're the one he sent! Is anyone watching? I'll slip out to Maryam's house and return in an hour. You stay here and pretend I'm still inside." I started to move around him, but he held up his sword.

"No, A'isha." I grunted in exasperation and he averted his face—avoiding the plague. "It is as Umar said: You cannot return. This pestilence has already killed twenty-five thousand. We can't risk spreading it in Medina. You must remain in your hut until we know if you've been infected."

"No—" Emotion filled my throat, making my voice sound choked and far away. I lowered my head and tried again to step past him, but he flung out his arm to block my way. I retreated into my hut, glowering. "What about Maryam?"

His gaze was tender. I peered over his shoulder, yearning for escape, not wanting to see love on his face that I couldn't return.

"Maryam is in the hands of al-Lah," he said. "As are you, A'isha. And I, for one, am praying for your good health."

◆

Several weeks later, I'd been pronounced plague-free but Maryam was dead—not from plague, after all, but from a tumor. At her funeral, more tears watered the ground than had fallen all year. Thousands came from all over Hijaz to pay homage to the mother of the Prophet's son, Ibrahim, who had died when he was two. Maryam's service was simple, not befitting her status, but since she hadn't been a Muslim, Umar had refused to say the prayer over her grave. Her sister, Sirin, who had come with her from Egypt, led the service—while Umar, who disapproved because she was a woman, stood frowning beside her.

We sister-wives sobbed as we looked down at Maryam lying in the ground, her body shrouded. Over the years, she had become like a sister to us all, soothing our worries with her encouraging words. Even the hard-hearted Ramlah loved her, and no wonder. Maryam always honored Ramlah by calling her by her *kunya,* Umm Habiba. And when we'd heard of the death of Yazid, the Syrian governor and Ramlah's brother, Maryam had given her a bag of dried dates—such a sacrifice during this famine—in consolation. How unjust that death should claim Maryam so soon! But al-Lah knows best, as Muhammad used to say.

Our cries could barely be heard over the ecstatic weeping and moaning of Akiiki, Maryam's eunuch servant. As he tore his clothes and tried to hurl himself into the grave, members of the *umma* watched from the corners of their eyes, not wanting to encourage such wanton behavior yet curious about the blackamoor and his relationship with Maryam.

How eagerly Akiiki had followed Maryam about, always at hand to do her bidding, ever anticipating her needs. He was, in truth, like a smitten lover, gazing at her with limpid eyes as though she made a vision too bright to behold, yet too enchanting to look away from.

She, in turn, had seemed to rely on Akiiki for much more than a master usually asked from a servant. The eunuch dressed her, styled her hair, massaged her feet: Imagine my shock to see his hands move up her legs to caress and knead her calves, and to hear Maryam's moans of pleasure as he did so! He danced and sang with her, and held her head in his lap and stroked her hair. He cooked her meals, murmured in her ear, and called her *habibati,* meaning "my beloved." In short, he did everything a husband might do—and more, for who ever heard of a man cooking a meal for his wife?

I'd seen them laugh together, seen how their eyes locked in the secret knowing that lovers share. Was there more to their relationship than Maryam would admit?

This was the question on people's lips after Muhammad had died. Gossips like Umm Ayman had found Maryam's situation too exciting to resist. Yet they'd also paired most of us in the *harim* with a man. Some had paired us with each other. I'd heard rumors about me and Hafsa, to my bewilderment and Hafsa's amusement.

Often, people talked in order to forget their hunger. Drought and famine had made skeletons of us all, killing babies in their mothers' wombs, drying up mothers' milk, cracking and swelling lips, leaving too little energy to brush away flies. Each day was consumed with thoughts of food and water. Because of our status, we sister-wives were among the first to receive rations, but most others were less fortunate. Hundreds died miserable deaths of slow agony. Plague and its quick delirium might have been preferable.

Umar had tried to alleviate the suffering—in ways that I, sometimes, didn't approve. Now that we'd conquered Persia's queen and taken all her country's wealth, he'd awarded every man in Medina a stipend from the *umma*'s treasury. He'd built houses for the inhabitants of the tent city and enlarged the mosque, replacing its date-palm pillars with ones of stone, tearing out its tree-stump platform and building a *minbar* of marble in its place. I knew the expansion was needed, for we had many more converts coming for prayer services now, but I'd hated to see Muhammad's examples of humility cast aside. Much had changed about *islam* these past ten years. Not all of the changes, I knew, would have pleased my husband.

Yet neither silver, gold, nor renovations could compete with the distracting power of gossip.

"Behold how the blackamoor embarrasses himself," old Umm Ayman said to Sawdah at the funeral.

"He embarrasses us all," Hafsa murmured to me. "From the way he's acting, people will decide the rumors about him and Maryam are true."

I didn't answer: In truth, I admired Akiiki's passion. If not for Umar's anger over my outburst when he'd forbidden me to return to Maryam's bedside, I might have risked his displeasure and descended into her grave to kiss her forehead and sprinkle her body with rose petals. But these gestures were permitted for men only. If not for Umar's dislike of public mourning, I might have torn my clothing, spread ashes on my face, and cried out to al-Lah the question that seemed to haunt me so frequently these days: *Why?*

Why did you take Maryam, and not me?

"Al-Ma'thur," Zaynab had gasped on her deathbed when I'd asked a similar question. "The Legacy." I'd been puzzling over the answer ever since. Muhammad had given me his sword named al-Ma'thur before he had died, and admonished me to use it in the "*jihad* to come." The struggle. There had been plenty of struggles since Muhammad's death, but nothing calling for my sword. Our only battles had been fought far afield, and I wasn't allowed to leave Medina anymore.

Umar placed new restrictions on women every day. Now, for instance, every woman had to wear a veil. He boasted about upholding Muhammad's vision for *islam*, but my husband had given women more rights, while Umar took them away. The battle for my freedom and the freedoms of my sisters was what I needed to fight now, and for respect for women such as Maryam, whose funeral was nearly as paltry as if she'd been a slave—and as full of scandal as if she'd been a prostitute.

Then, as if summoned by my grief, a poem burst on my lips and poured like scented oil over poor Maryam's body:

"*Let us weep at the remembrance of our beloved, at the sight of the station where her tent was raised . . .*

A profusion of tears is my sole relief; but what avails me to shed them over the remains of a deserted mansion?"

When I had finished reciting the verses, I stepped forward and removed my gold arm band, a gift from Maryam, and dropped it into her grave. "*Yaa* Maryam, blessed mother of us all," I said, ignoring Umar's scowl and Ali's stern glare.

"The generosity you have shown to me I now return to you, Maryam," I said. "May your spirit float on the sea of our tears all the way to Paradise, and may al-Lah bless you and welcome you there."

Having given her the eulogy she deserved, I stepped back among my sister-wives and welcomed their embraces. "Thank you," Umm Salama whispered, "for doing what I should have done." Yet I noticed that Ramlah, like Ali, was shooting me disapproving looks. I didn't need to ask what either of them was thinking, for I had heard it from them both before: *Once again, A'isha has to make herself the center of attention.* Of course, if I had been a man—an Arab man, I should say, considering the baleful looks Akiiki was getting—no one would have disapproved. In truth, everyone would have murmured agreement with my sentiments.

As the crowd began to drift away, leaving the gravediggers to cover

Maryam's body with dirt, I felt a tug at my sleeve. I turned to face Talha, who gazed at me as though I were the full moon. I had to bite back a response: *Save those adoring glances for your wife, or, if you're looking for another wife, save them for someone available to you.*

"*Yaa* A'isha, your verse was quite appropriate," he said. "Such a beautiful homage you gave to the honorable Maryam. Muhammad would be very proud."

And what would he think of you, blatantly displaying your desire for his widow?

Before I could say anything, though, we heard a splintering scream. We turned in the direction of the cries to see Akiiki's long body fold and tumble into Maryam's grave, a dagger in his stomach and his blood gushing.

"By al-Lah, the eunuch has taken his own life," Uthman cried, holding out his arms toward Akiiki as if to catch him.

"He has gone to join his beloved," old Umm Ayman said with a knowing nod to Sawdah.

"He loved her, everybody knew that," Sawdah said. "But Maryam was faithful to Muhammad."

"That is not what people are saying about her," Umm Ayman said. "Or about your sister-wives, either. Behold A'isha and Talha, for instance. How closely they stand to each other. Does he not visit her hut from time to time?" I took a step backward, and pulled my wrapper closer to hide the flush of heat spreading across my face and neck.

"Get that blackamoor out of Maryam's grave," Umar gruffed, then walked away shaking his head. As he passed me, he added, "*Yaa* A'isha, I want to talk with you in the mosque. Immediately."

My stomach pulled tight. I turned to follow Umar, feeling Talha's gaze as I walked away. What did Umar want? Would he chastise me for speaking at Maryam's grave? Or had he, also, heard rumors about me and Talha? That would hurt Talha's chance of being named the next *khalifa*. Umar would never name a successor who had been tainted by scandal.

As I followed Umar, Mughira, and Ali to the mosque, a small, dark man stepped into Umar's path. "*Afwan, yaa khalifa*, forgive me for intruding," he said. "I am Abu Lulu'a, a former slave. I earned my freedom two years ago but your Companion Mughira still enslaves me. He takes two pieces of silver per day from my earnings as a carpenter. I beg you to lift this unfair tax."

Umar turned Mughira beside him, who shrugged. "He learned his craft under my sponsorship," he said. "It is only fair that I should benefit."

"You have so much wealth, while I have nothing," Abu Lulu'a screeched. "This is not fair."

Umar drew back as if Abu Lulu'a had spit at him, and gave the little man a stern frown. "Would you have me insult Mughira, one of my most valuable advisors, for the sake of a slave such as you?"

Abu Lulu'a bowed again. "According to the Prophet, we are all one in the eyes of al-Lah."

Umar nodded. "You speak truly. But Mughira is important not only to me, but to *islam*. When you have demonstrated that you are equally important, than I will admonish him." He started to walk away, but the little man stepped backwards and blocked his path again.

"What can I do to prove my worthiness to you?"

"Hmm." Umar tugged at his beard. "That is a very good question, *yaa* Abu Lulu'a. What can you do? Hmm." He tugged at his beard as if deep in thought, but his wink at Mughira told us he was far from serious.

"By al-Lah, my answer has revealed itself," Umar said with a snap of his fingers. "Abu Lulu'a, as you know, our wells in Medina are so depleted that we cannot retrieve their water. Can you build a windmill for pumping the water? If you can do that, then I will speak to Mughira on your behalf." He grinned at his advisor, who grinned back.

"A windmill!" A whine edged Abu Lulu'a's voice. "I am skilled, but I am not a *djinni*."

Umar shrugged. "That is unfortunate for you. But at least I gave you a chance."

He began to walk again, motioning for us all to follow, leaving Abu Lulu'a standing with his arms akimbo.

"You will be sorry for this," he cried. "Al-Lah will punish you!"

Umar inclined his head toward Mughira. "*Yaa* Mughira, I think a tax of two *dirhams* is not enough in this case," he said. "I suggest you charge him three." Mughira grinned, showing his ugly yellow teeth.

At the mosque entrance, Umar ordered his Companions to take their leave, then beckoned me to follow him inside. At his behest, I sat across from him. He poured us each a bowl of water and we drank, but my gaze never left his face as I tried to figure out why he'd brought me into his *majlis*, Umar's male sanctum.

Finally, he put down his bowl, wiped his beard with his sleeve, and looked at me.

"A'isha, I am sure you have heard the rumors," he said. My intuition had been correct. Angry over the lies swirling through the *umma*, Umar was going to banish me from Talha. I cast about for arguments. *Yaa al-Lah, give me the words to change his mind.*

But, as it turned out, Umar hadn't brought me here to discuss Talha.

"As you know, I can offer her an excellent home," he was saying. "And my other wives will treat her kindly. If you will give your consent, of course."

I shook my head. "What about Talha?" I said frowning.

He shook his head. "It seems grief over Maryam has settled like a fog on your ability to reason," he said. "No one has mentioned Talha." His eyes narrowed. "Unless there is something you wish to reveal."

"No." I took a sip of water. "You speak truly about my mind being confused. Did you say something about a marriage?"

He let out a short, impatient sigh. "Yes. I want to marry Abu Bakr's youngest daughter," he said. "Your sister Umm Kulthum. If you will give your consent, of course."

Suddenly I felt as if I had plunged headlong into the Sea of Hijaz. My thoughts flailed. Umar's eyes watched me steadily, waiting—and again I felt grateful for my *hijab*. With it, Umar couldn't see the turmoil I felt. Send my little sister to live with a man who beat his wives for speaking above a whisper?

"Umm Kulthum?" He nodded. "But she is only four years old. Why would you choose her?"

"Betrothal to a daughter of our esteemed *khalifa* Abu Bakr would enhance my status," he said. He gave me a thin smile. "And Muhammad has forbidden you to remarry."

Praise al-Lah for that. I cleared my throat. "I—I don't know what to say."

"Why not say 'yes'? The match would be advantageous for your family, also."

"Yes, but —" Needing more time, I forced a cough. Umar poured the last drops of precious water for me and I sipped them slowly.

Umar folded his arms over his shrunken belly and smiled, his eyes gleaming as he anticipated my assent. His eagerness sweetened the taste of my lie.

"She—she is spoken for," I said. "Talha asked my father before he died." I shook my head. "By al-Lah, I can't believe *abi* never told you. You two were so close."

I don't know which delighted me most—Umar's disappointed frown or his obvious embarrassment. "I and your father did not often discuss family matters," he said. "But it makes no difference. What is done is done."

"I hope your heart won't suffer from losing my sister's hand," I said sweetly, goading him.

He reddened even more. "Of course not. What kind of man would I be, to lust after a four-year-old? I told you, the marriage would have been political, and nothing more."

I bowed to him. "It will be the same for Talha. He hopes to be *khalifa* some day. If al-Lah wills it."

"Yes, yes." Umar stood, and I followed. "I am sure he would be an excellent candidate." He stepped toward the *majlis* entryway and, with my head meekly lowered, I followed him. Then he stopped and turned around to peer at me, his eyes glinting.

"In truth, marrying your sister will enhance Talha's chances at the title," he said. "Much more so than the *other* route he has been pursuing."

The accusatory lift of his eyebrows told all, and I thought I should defend myself against his insinuations.

"What route is that, *khalifa*?" I said.

"A route that leads directly to Hell," he said. "Dangerous to all concerned, especially you."

I lowered my head to hide my guilt. "I didn't know you cared," I said wryly.

"I do not," he said. "Not in the way you are thinking. I do, however, care about the reputation of the Prophet's widows, and the deleterious effects of gossip. If Talha's engagement to Umm Kulthum will restore some peace among the tongue-waggers, then I will give the couple my full support."

I lifted my head to offer him a smile and say something truthful, at last. "I couldn't agree more. This marriage will be good for everyone concerned." Now, all I had to do was convince Talha—and hope that being married to my sister would, someday, turn his thoughts away from me.

Ali

When Umar insulted Abu Lulu'a with his offer of freedom in exchange for a windmill, I thought little of the incident. Slaves approached the *khalifa* daily with complaints, and Abu Lulu'a should have known that Umar would display little sympathy. Although Muhammad had encouraged Muslims to free their slaves, Umar lacked my cousin's tenderness of heart.

So when my cousin Abd Allah ibn al-Abbas came to my home to announce that Umar had been stabbed, the news struck me like a fist to my chest. Abd Allah's face shone as brightly and excitedly as if he were announcing a birth instead of an impending death.

"Praise al-Lah, the path for you is cleared at last!" my cousin said. I led him into my *majlis*, where he seized my beard with such vehemence that my eyes began to water.

"Umar lies dying in the mosque, may al-Lah be with him. His Companions are gathering to hear his instructions. *Yaa* Ali, you must come and let him know that you are a contender for the *khalifa*. The future of *islam* depends on your appointment."

I wanted to tell him that *islam* had survived very well without me as its leader, but in truth I did not believe that it had. Grandiose mosque expansions, a pension system that pitted Qurayshi against Bedouins and early converts against new ones, the appointment of that deceiver Mu'awiyya to govern Syria—so many of Umar's initiatives had, in my view, served to corrupt the *islam* revealed by Muhammad. I wanted to return the faith to its origin—to restore equality among men, respect for women, and honesty and humility in government. Could my time be at hand?

We stepped outside into mayhem. Everyone in Medina, it appeared, had surged into the street: men with bared teeth and fire in their eyes, veiled women crying their children's names, and children re-enacting with sticks the terrible attack that had befallen Umar as he had walked from his home to the mosque that morning.

We wove our way through the swirl and crash of children, men, *shaykhs*, women, dogs, horses, camels, goats, and ubiquitous flies to hurry into the mosque, where Umar lay on a mattress, holding his side to stem the flow of blood that the reddening bandage wrapped around his waist could not. His face had turned an unpleasant ashen color. Beside him sat his first-wife, Zaynab bint Maz'un, patting the hand of her weeping daughter Hafsa, who had remained inexplicably attached to Umar despite his harsh treatment. A'isha knelt beside Umar's bed and mixed a poultice to apply to a clean bandage, which she laid across the terrible gushing wound.

Umar paid little attention to the ministrations of the women but clung, instead, to the robe of his friend Abd al-Rahman. In spite of the drought and famine, the wealthy Qurayshi merchant had somehow managed to cultivate three chins under his dyed black beard.

"There is no better man," Umar was saying between gasps. "Please accept, so that I can die in peace."

I murmured a greeting, hiding the alarm that I knew must be flashing across my face. Umar was attempting to appoint Abd al-Rahman to the *khalifa*. Such an action would only increase the corruption of *islam*, for Abd al-Rahman loved only one thing more than money, and that was status. I had heard him speak disparagingly about Bedouins, Persians, Yemeni, and Egyptians, whose members now made up most of the Muslim populace. I knew he had donated generously to Umar's mosque expansion in exchange for coveted positions for his sons, brothers, and cousins. As *khalifa*, he would place a relative into every governorship throughout our territory, which would heighten complaints that *islam* had become a religion of, and for, Quraysh.

Abd al-Rahman's reply alleviated my concerns. "I am honored, *yaa*

Umar, but I cannot accept this appointment. Have you not said many times that the *khalifa* should be chosen by the people? I beseech you to convene a *shura*. If its members elect me, I would gladly, and humbly, serve."

Although I knew there was nothing humble about Abd al-Rahman, I could not dispute the wisdom of his words. After Abu Bakr had appointed Umar, many had muttered, wondering why I, the father of the Prophet's heirs, had not been considered. My supporters among the *ansari* and the Bedouins stemmed partly from my blood relationship to Muhammad and partly from my respect for them. Under Umar's harsh reign, the complaints about my being overlooked for the *khalifa* had lately increased. For Umar to appoint his successor would surely cause a rift in the *umma*. That in turn could leave our vast empire vulnerable to conquest by that power-monger Mu'awiyya.

But my hopes plummeted as Umar named the men who would serve on the electing council: Abd al-Rahman; the esteemed general Sa'd, who had served under my command as a foot soldier at Badr and Uhud; Umar's oldest son, Abdallah; Uthman, and al-Zubayr, my cousin, who had supported me in the beginning, refusing to pledge allegiance to Abu Bakr, but had then turned against me. My name was not mentioned.

"And what about Talha?" A'isha said, although she had not been asked to offer her opinion. "You've relied on him often enough for advice."

"You speak truly," Umar wheezed.

"*Yaa khalifa*, I request your permission to speak." My cousin Abd Allah stepped forward and bowed. He suggested that I be included, also.

"There are rumors of Talha's ambition for the *khalifa*," Abd Allah said. "Also, many Believers support Ali for the position. To avoid dissent, why not appoint them both to your council? Then no one could say that Umar had unfairly cheated Ali of his birthright."

"People are going to talk no matter what you do," A'isha began, but Abd al-Rahman cut her off, earning from me a measure of respect that would, alas, be short-lived.

"I agree with the son of al-Abbas," he said. "Our highest hope for the continuation of the *umma* and of *islam* depends on having an impartial, balanced council choose your successor."

And so with spirits lifted, I stepped forth from the mosque a member of the prestigious *shura* that would decide the future of the Islamic community. We were to meet almost immediately, but first, the members needed to be summoned, and Umar needed to rest. "Do not worry," he said, gasping, "I will not take my final breath until a successor is named." Yet the way he struggled to focus his gaze and the parchment-like pallor of his skin told us that his time, and ours in which to choose a *khalifa*, was very short.

For his comfort we closed the mosque to all except his family and the *shura* members. A'isha had advised against moving Umar to his home, saying the pain would be great for him and that doing so might shorten his life.

I hurried to the home of al-Abbas with the news of my appointment to the *shura*. For all my doubts about my uncle, I could not dispute his shrewdness in political affairs, and I desired his advice before entering into the deliberations that could shape my destiny.

"Praise al-Lah for Abd al-Rahman!" he cried when I had related the tale of the *shura*'s formation. I cringed to think of praising that smug sack of goat-grease, but then my uncle added, "His lack of intelligence is our gain. What he has unwisely refused, we will seize for ourselves."

I did not like the greed in his eyes, for I neither intended to "seize" anything nor to claim the *khalifa* for my uncle's sake. His ambitions, I had learned, could prompt me to perform deeds against my conscience. As I walked to my home to tell Asma the news, a scream more deafening than a howling *samoom* bounced against the building next to me. I ran in one direction, then another before finding Umar's assassin, Abu Lulu'a, lying in the street, his face smeared with mucous and blood, his throat slit open. Beside him stood Umar's youngest son, Ubayd Allah, a blood-dripping knife in his right hand and a grimace on his lips.

"Now begins my vengeance!" he cried. His eyes were bulging and unfocused, staring into the crowd gathering around the slain man. "Let his collaborators beware, for they will be the next to taste death's dust."

"*Yaa* Ubayd Allah," I said, eyeing his knife warily. "Of whom do you speak? Umar angered Abu Lulu'a, and Abu Lulu'a attacked him in return. Now you have avenged your father, and the blood-price is paid. Any more killings would make you a murderer."

"Murderer!" he snarled. He took a step toward me, his eyes gleaming. The aroma of blood pierced my nose. I gripped my sword handle. "The dogs of Persia are the ones who have murdered today," he said. "By al-Lah, before night falls the streets of Medina will be steeped in Persian blood!"

He turned and, shouting his father's name, fled into the crowd. I hurried back toward the mosque, forgoing the embraces of my lovely Asma in order to alert Umar to the dangers his son posed. Ubayd Allah was like a stampeding bull, and I had no doubt that he would hunt down additional Persians to kill. But once I reached Umar's bedside, I knew he was not the one to tell. He lay on his back with his hands folded on his chest, his face flushed and shining as though it had been rubbed with oil, his breathing like water bubbling through gravel, his bandages soaked and dripping onto his mattress.

I spat onto the dirt floor. Damn A'isha! Her task was to tend to Umar, yet she had left him alone without man or woman to greet him should he awaken. Once again she had proved herself as irresponsible as a child.

And she was as gullible, also. She would try to help Talha take the *khalifa*, I had no doubt, although how much influence she would wield was unclear. Talha was in Khaybar, inspecting his date plantation and enjoying the cool date-palm breezes created by his crowd of servant girls. Without being here to advocate for himself, he had almost no chance of being chosen today.

I knocked on the door of A'isha's hut, but heard no response. I looked for her in the cooking tent, but it was empty. At last I stepped into the treasury, intending to inquire of Abd al-Rahman. I found him there, but I also discovered the other men of the *shura*—plus, to my astonishment, A'isha, who was pleading her favorite's case.

"Talha can't possibly ride all the way back from Khaybar in such a short time," she was saying.

"Umar was clear," Abd al-Rahman said. He folded his hands and studied us all with the gravity of a man who has assumed a weighty role against his inclinations. "He has directed me to choose his successor within three days. To leave the position unfilled for too long will cause strife in the *umma* and give others an opportunity to put forth their own candidates. We must avoid the confusion that would result."

"But Talha was appointed by Umar," she said.

"So were we all," I interjected. Heads turned at the sound of my voice. "But the rest of us are here in Medina, not lounging in the cool Khaybar oasis."

A'isha's face reddened. "Talha is working, and you know it. He has date plantations to manage and workers to pay."

In truth, I did not relish the presence of Talha in these *shura* meetings for I knew he would campaign aggressively against me. Judging from what I had overheard in Damascus between him and Mu'awiyya, his election would bring a complete corruption of *islam*. Talha thought only of his own ambitions and very little of the desires of al-Lah. Preventing his ascension to the *khalifa* was more important to me, therefore, than my own appointment. Yet, as I pondered the alternatives, I felt certain that I was right for the task.

"You speak the truth, A'isha," Abd al-Rahman said, nodding like a sage old *shaykh*. "Umar did appoint Talha—at your suggestion, and possibly without recalling that he had departed for Khaybar. I have sent a messenger to request his return. He will certainly arrive as soon as possible. In the meantime, I agree with Umar that we should begin our deliberations."

He glanced around the room, but I barely met his gaze. I stared angrily at A'isha. I knew she had summoned the other *shura* members, and purposely neglected to include me. She would do anything to undermine my candidacy—as she proved with her next words.

"*Yaa* Abd al-Rahman, why not allow me to speak in Talha's stead?" she said. "As you know, I and he agree on every matter."

"An excellent idea!" my traitorous cousin al-Zubayr exulted. By al-Lah, what had brought those two so closely together? My mouth felt dry. I said nothing, knowing that I must appear nonchalant if I desired success.

"*Afwan*, *yaa* Abd al-Rahman, but I do not think my father would approve of a woman's involvement in these talks," Abdallah ibn Umar said. I suppressed a smile. A'isha glared at him. "Forgive me, Mother of the Believers," he murmured.

Uthman cleared his throat. "I agree with Abdallah, although I wish it were not so," he said, inclining his head toward A'isha. "You have much wisdom to contribute, A'isha, and you can speak for our Prophet, also. But Umar did not appoint you, and I think it would be wrong to violate our dying *khalifa*'s wishes."

"Holding the *shura* without Talha will violate his wishes, also," she pressed. She turned her eye on each of us, but no one replied. "Don't fool yourselves," she said with a snort. "It's not the *khalifa's* desires you're protecting, but your own." She stomped from the room with her head high.

The relief I felt at her exit must have been experienced by others, also, for immediately we began to talk as we lifted cushions from the corner of the room and placed them around the long, low table Umar used for counting and disbursing money. Abd al-Rahman placed himself in the center position, assuming the leadership.

"Before we begin the deliberations, we must know who desires the *khalifa*," he said, gazing at each of us with the shrewd, piercing eyes of a bird. "Anyone who wishes to compete, place your right hand on the table."

Silence fell about our heads like dust settling after a storm. As wary as if we were predators stalking the same prey, the six of us watched one another and waited for the first hand to appear. Finally, Abd al-Rahman placed his hand, palm down, on the table and said, "I will begin by announcing my own interest. Who joins me?"

I looked down at my trembling hands, unable to lift either, wondering if my desire to lead the *umma* sprang from the will of al-Lah or from myself. *Please, God, guide me in this momentous decision*. If I vied for the *khalifa* now and lost, I might never again have the opportunity to try again. But if I did not make the attempt, would I be failing al-Lah, *islam*, and all those who had supported me? I knew I could rely on Sa'd. I had saved his life at Uhud, and encouraged Muhammad to promote him after the Battle of the Trench. But who else here would vote for me? Umar's son, Abdallah? We had fought together, also, but he was indolent and I had been harsh with him. Al-Zubayr, that traitor? Perhaps. And certainly Uthman, one of Muhammad's closest Companions, would support me. He knew how often Muhammad had relied on my aid and advice

But, no. Across the table, Uthman coughed, covering his mouth with his hand, said "*Afwan*," and set his hand down on the table. A sense of urgency flared in me, urging me to declare myself. I could not bear to see either of these men governing the faithful and guiding the Believers in the ways of *islam*.

"Excellent." Abd al-Rahman beamed at Uthman, his brother-in-law and close companion. "It looks as though we two are the only contenders for this *khalifa*. And since I am advanced in years and lack the energy that the position requires, I will happily—"

Hurry hurry hurry hurry you are losing it all—stop him now!

The slap of my palm on the table made Abd al-Rahman's eyes fly open as though a bucket of cold water had been slung in his face. Uthman twisted his mustache and frowned.

"Ah. Ali." Abd al-Rahman's smile was a thin attempt at pleasantness. "Of course you still desire to fill the Prophet's place." He cleared his throat and glanced brightly around the table again. "Any others? No? Then please note the candidates: Me, Uthman, and Ali. Those in favor of me, place your hand on the table."

He left his hand there, and Umar's son Abdallah added his own. "Because it is my father's desire," he said.

Next came the vote for Uthman. Al-Zubayr, that deceptive dog, planted his hand beside Uthman's. "I had thought of vying, also," he said, "but to compete against a man so generous would feel dishonorable. You have treated my wife well." I felt a smirk creep across my mouth. Was al-Zubayr unaware of Uthman's reputation with women?

And at last Abd al-Rahman spoke my name, and the only remaining hand—that belonging to the estimable young general Sa'd—came down for me. "I have not forgotten your years as my commander," he said. "Never did a man wield a sword so expertly or so bravely. Your courage and skill would translate well to the *khalifa*."

And so, without Talha to cast a seventh vote—thank al-Lah!—we found ourselves with no winner. "Does anyone wish to nominate a man outside this room?" Abd al-Rahman said.

"What about Talha?" al-Zubayr said.

"Are you nominating him?" Abd al-Rahman said. "Then you must withdraw your support from Uthman."

"Would Talha offer himself as a candidate against such formidable opponents?" Abdallah said. "Which of the candidates might he support, instead? Since we have no way of knowing, I think we have to omit him."

Abd al-Rahman called a second vote, but the results were identical. For a long while we sat in confusion—until at last Abd al-Rahman said, "It is important to have a clear consensus regarding the *khalifa*. If we cannot decide who will lead us, how can we expect the *umma* to support our final choice?"

He called again for a vote, but the results did not vary.

"Praise al-Lah, He has handed us a challenge," Abd al-Rahman said, but his voice sounded weary rather than excited. "And now I will attempt to meet that challenge with this offer: I will remove my name—if you all will allow me to choose the next *khalifa,* with al-Lah's direction."

That sly son of Satan! He and Uthman were the closest of friends. It was no mystery whom he would select.

"An excellent idea, Abd al-Rahman," Uthman said, smiling. "As a flawlessly pious man and Companion to the Prophet, you will rely on al-Lah for assistance in this important decision, I know."

"I will fast and pray until He reveals His will to me," Abd al-Rahman said.

I hesitated to protest, fearing that I might seem overly contentious. Seeing that Sa'd was not going to question this dubious offer, however, I allowed myself to speak. "And what if He does not reveal His will, Abd al-Rahman?" I said. "On what basis will you choose between me, whom you have never supported before, and your relative, who also happens to be your bosom companion?"

"*Afwan*, Ali, but you are speaking without thinking," al-Zubayr said. "Abd al-Rahman is well respected in our *umma* as the most faithful of Believers. Did not the Prophet say, 'Truly, You hear all prayers?' Surely al-Lah would listen to the man our *khalifa* would have chosen as his replacement."

The treachery of al-Zubayr, my long-beloved cousin, made me gnash out the words I had repressed for so long.

"And you, cousin?" I snarled. "You supported me in the past, but you have turned with the prevailing winds like an inconstant flag. How many dinars did Uthman pay for your vote today?"

Al-Zubayr leapt to his feet, his hand on his sword. "Insulting Uthman, the Prophet's beloved Companion! If not for Muhammad's love for you, I would cut out your tongue this very moment."

I stood, also, and touched my sword hilt. "The only man I wished to insult, cousin, was you."

"*Yaa* Ali," my lone supporter, Sa'd, said quietly, "this is not the way to gain the *khalifa*."

I glanced down at him and then at the other faces, all like locked doors. Why should they disagree with Abd al-Rahman's offer when he would gladly perform this difficult task in their stead? Once again I would be denied the *khalifa*. I turned and I stormed out of the room—and, on the other side of the doorway, collided so violently with someone that I nearly fell.

When I had steadied myself I looked down into the flushed face of A'isha, who lay in an awkward sprawl at my feet. Her wrapper had slipped down, allowing her hair to float like a fine red mist about her face. She looked so vulnerable that I might have offered my hand to help her from the floor—until she reached out a sandaled foot and kicked me in the shin.

"Watch where you're going, in the name of al-Lah!" she growled as she pushed herself upward.

"*Afwan*," I said, hiding with a scowl my unbidden—and unwelcome—feelings of compassion. "I should have expected to catch you spying, the same as when you were a child. How foolish of me to think you might have grown out of it."

"I have an interest in those proceedings, the same as you," she said. "Unlike you, though, I was forced to leave."

"Why would I remain? To witness yet another act of treachery by your bosom friend al-Zubayr?"

She laughed. "Al-Zubayr is no friend of mine. He supports Talha and the return of *islam* to its original state, the way Muhammad envisioned it."

I wanted the same thing, I could have said—but she already knew that. I was the one she hated, not my beliefs. "Supporting that weakling Uthman will do nothing to help *islam*, as you and al-Zubayr should know," I said.

She pulled her wrapper aside for one instant, to taunt me with her wicked smile. "He's keeping you out of the *khalifa*, isn't he? Talha will be here soon. Then, we'll see—"

A shout from outside the mosque interrupted us. I frowned to see Abu Hurayra with his ever-present cat cradled in one arm and the other arm flailing as if he were trying to fly.

"Murder!" he was crying. "Murder in the streets of Medina! *Yaa* Ali, heir to the Prophet, I beg you, protect us, hide us from the killer of Persians!"

His words were a hand squeezing my throat. Ubayd Allah! In my surprise at seeing the *shura* convened, I had forgotten my concerns about the son of Umar's vengeful rampage.

I ran to Abu Hurayra and grasped his beard, sending his cat scrambling to the floor. "Tell me of whom you speak and I will have him arrested."

"Ubayd Allah, son of Umar," he said in a quaking voice, confirming my worst fears. "He has killed two Persian men, and now he wants my Persian cat."

Just then Ubayd Allah burst into the mosque gripping his bloody dagger. His eyes blazed as he lunged toward Abu Hurayra.

I possessed little affection for the pest Abu Hurayra, Muhammad's self-appointed servant, who had annoyed me immensely by following Muhammad everywhere—into the *majlis*, into his wives' bedrooms, into my home—and, after my cousin died, inventing sayings by Muhammad to suit his every convenience. Yet I did not wish to witness more bloodshed, and I certainly could not condone killing in the mosque. I yanked Zulfikar from its sheath and sliced my trusty blade against the right arm of Ubayd Allah. He dropped his dagger and slumped to his knees.

"*Afwan, yaa* Ubayd Allah," I said. "I cannot permit any more killings."

Abdallah and Sa'd rushed into the room—but stopped at the sight of Ubayd Allah bleeding on the floor. "*Yaa* brother, what has happened?" Abdallah said, glaring at me.

"The Persians have murdered our father," Ubayd Allah groaned, holding his arm. "I have taken revenge."

"One Persian did the deed, not all of them," I corrected him. "And your father yet clings to life. Who knows whether he will defeat this wound and return to rule us all?"

"You are mistaken, Ali," Abdallah Ibn Umar said in a thick voice. Tears spilled over his face. "Our father breathed his final breath today in my mother's arms—while we of the *shura* fought over the *khalifa* like scavengers over scraps of meat."

A'isha

Where is Talha? In spite of the anticipation and excitement filling the mosque on the day the next *khalifa* was to be chosen, I felt only anxiety as I waited for Talha to magically appear. In the eight years since Muhammad's death, *islam* had taken some disturbing turns away from its original path. Conquest and booty drove the *umma* now, rather than love for God. Orphans, slaves, and women, the people Muhammad had helped, were forgotten as men strove for wealth and military honors. Talha hated these changes as much as I, and, as *khalifa,* would work with me to restore compassion and generosity to *islam*. But we had to begin now—before it was too late.

Umar had doubled the size of Muhammad's mosque, but I could see from my hut's doorway that it wasn't nearly big enough on this day. The spacious room filled quickly with men and their chatter, hundreds of voices rising in a confused swarm that stung my ears with the name of *Ali* and soothed them with the murmur of *Uthman*. If only it had been Talha's name soaring to the sky! We could have accomplished so much for *islam*. But alas, he wasn't here and the *khalifa* was about to be given to someone else—and all I could do was pray that it would be someone other than Ali.

Standing with my sister-wives pressing around me, I watched as Ali and al-Abbas entered to a smattering of cheers. Even from this distance, I could smell al-Abbas's perfume, an unctuous musk scent that made me gag. He had been busy, I'd heard, recruiting supporters for Ali, but he widened his eyes at the chanting men as though he'd never seen such an astonishing sight. Ali climbed the steps to the marble platform and faced the crowd, his jaw tight and his hands clenched. He had dressed plainly for the occasion, in a simple white gown and robe the color of sand—clean but a bit tattered, despite his generous pension. Of course, he had a family and a stomach to feed, both of which seemed to be growing all the time.

On the other side of the platform stood Uthman, his mustache slick and curling over his copper-dyed beard and his mouth smiling as though he'd just filled his belly with warm milk, which he probably had done. His rich red robe and saffron gown told me he expected to be appointed today, and why not? Abd al-Rahman, his closest companion, was making the choice.

Uthman's eyes met mine and his smile widened. I nodded and smiled back to him. Although I had desperately wanted Talha for the *khalifa*, in truth I would have supported a donkey over Ali. If Ali were named, not only would I lose my pension and my freedom—for he'd be certain to tighten the restrictions Umar had imposed, and banish me to my hut—but *islam* would lose its soul to the greed of Ali's uncle.

"Listen to those men chanting Ali's name," Sawdah said from her cushion on my floor, where she busily sewed leather leggings for our warriors. "The Prophet would not have liked this, believe me."

"You speak truly," Juwairriyah said from behind me, shaking her head and filling the room with the scent of lavender from her hair. "Muhammad always admonished us to treat one another kindly."

"There's nothing kind about that chanting!" Saffiya's eyes shone and a red dot glowed on each of her cheeks. "Think how poor Uthman must feel."

"I'm sure he feels anything but poor." Raihana rolled her eyes.

"He has to expect opposition if he's going to try for the *khalifa*," Hafsa pointed out. "A'isha's father had competition, and Umar had detractors, also."

"But they had already become the *khalifa*," I said. "I agree with Saffiya—advocating for Ali like this is rude. Those men should be made to leave the mosque."

"Who will send them out, A'isha? You?" Ramlah's laugh was harsh. "Unsheathe your sword and demonstrate, by al-Lah! I, for one, would like to see that feat."

"We all know whom *you* would like to see named *khalifa, yaa* Ramlah," Maymunah said. "But your brother Mu'awiyya is not a contender."

"Not yet," she said. "He would be a much stronger ruler than either that soft-handed Uthman or that hard-headed Ali."

"Mu'awiyya's head is every bit as hard as Ali's," Umm Salama said.

"Not to mention his heart," I chimed in. I'd heard how Mu'awiyya had tricked Khalid ibn al-Walid into declaring himself governor of Syria, then spread rumors that Khalid had stolen from the treasury. Too proud to speak in his own defense, Khalid—who'd conquered Syria—had been stripped of his rank and Mu'awiyya had become Syria's governor. As much as I disliked Khalid—and feared him, for his steely eyes never looked at me without violence—I couldn't condone Mu'awiyya's deceit. I wouldn't have been surprised to learn that the unctuous Mu'awiyya had murdered his brother Yazid to gain his seat.

Yet I didn't want to think of Mu'awiyya that day as we waited for Abd al-Rahman to arrive. Visions of Talha racing across the desert, urging his camel onward, filled my thoughts even as the impossibility of his getting back in time made me dig my fingernails into my palms. *Why, al-Lah, did You let him leave Medina?*

I must have whispered the prayer, for Hafsa squeezed my arm and gazed at me with eyes as large and sad as a doe's. "Why did al-Lah let my father die? Why did He allow my brother to become possessed? *Yaa* A'isha, let me know if God answers your questions, because He has ignored mine."

I realized how selfish I was being. What was I worried about except power, while Hafsa mourned the loss of her father and the possible execution of her brother Ubayd Allah, whom she loved most in all the world? Yet what was more important than the *khalifa*? Our next leader would have the power to do tremendous good, to instill the values of equality and mercy throughout our empire. Or he would increase the divisions, resentments, and greed taking hold of our people as our wealth grew.

"Here comes Abd al-Rahman now," Saffiya breathed. "Please, al-Lah, let him name Uthman."

The softness of her eyes and mouth as she spoke Uthman's name told me she was in love with him—but, contrary to several years ago when I'd first suspected it, I felt no disapproval now. Loneliness was my companion, and that of my sister-wives. How could I blame Saffiya for wanting to escape our fate?

The room fell silent as Abd al-Rahman made his way slowly from the mosque's entryway, across the room, to the platform. His step was sluggish and his white robe seemed to droop from his bent frame, which stooped as though he carried the Ka'ba on his shoulders. He ascended the platform on Uthman's side and walked to the center, to stand between the candidates. His skin, normally as pink and fresh as a newborn lamb's, sagged in folds the color of ash below his sunken eyes.

"Poor thing, he has not slept since Umar died," Sawdah said. "Umm Ayman took him some food but he wouldn't let her in the door. He said he was praying night and day until al-Lah told him who to pick."

"He was probably hoping he'd die before he had to make this decision," Raihana said. "Can you imagine the burden?"

"He offered to do it," I told her. Of course, he'd seemed certain at the time that God would guide him. Judging from the way he looked today, his prayers hadn't been answered.

He lifted trembling arms. "Men of *islam*," he began. His voice sounded like he'd eaten sand for his morning meal. "Today marks a momentous occasion."

And then, despite his exhaustion, Abd al-Rahman spoke for a full hour. Spellbound at first, his listeners soon became restless, murmuring to one another, shifting from foot to foot, tugging at their beards, and rolling their eyes at one another. My legs grew tired and I was tempted to sit down with Sawdah, but I didn't want to lose my vantage in the front of the group. So I let my mind wander to thoughts of Talha, envisioning his race across the desert, kicking up sands, picturing his laughing eyes and brilliant smile. If he were here now, I'd be grinning at his quips instead of fretting and chewing my fingernails. Unless, of course, he spent the time caressing me with his eyes and murmuring tender words.

My pulse quickened at the memory of our last moments together, how his eyes had shone as he praised my eulogy for Maryam. How, I'd wondered, could he display his desire so wantonly when I was still married to the Prophet of al-Lah? I'd been as irked by his attentions as if he were a stray dog trotting at my heels. Yet, ever since he'd left for Khaybar, I'd found myself beset by thoughts of Talha. During the day, I tucked away amusing stories to tell him, imagining how he'd laugh. At night he filled my dreams, caressing my hair with his hands. I awoke feeling guilty—could Muhammad discern dreams?—and more determined than ever to turn desire, his and mine, into a love as innocent as that of a sister and brother.

Yet—was I an alchemist, able to transform these forbidden feelings into gold? Loneliness and its salt tears had never been my favorite flavors. Having betrothed Talha to my sister Umm Kulthum, I had no choice but to try.

How I rued, now, my impulsive request! Talha had been reluctant, to say the least. His eyes had dulled when I'd asked him to marry my sister. Since he already had one wife, I'd assumed he would readily agree, to save Umm Kulthum from Umar and his whip. I'd also hoped the engagement would change his feelings for me. Now, though, I despised the thought of his holding my sister close, of the intimacy they would someday share.

If only I had known that Umar would die before my sister came of age. But al-Lah knows best—and, in truth, Talha's marriage to my sister might be best for us all. My dreams told me that I was in danger of succumbing to temptation. I hadn't been intimate with a man in eleven years, and Muhammad and the threat of hellfire seemed so far away. But now, Umm Kulthum's honor was at stake. I'd have to take care not to let my newly discovered feelings for Talha show.

Dwelling on these thoughts, I missed most of Abd al-Rahman's speech. But then he said "Ali," and my thoughts jerked back to the mosque. I listened and prayed he would not appoint the wrong man.

"We of the *umma* are privileged to have as a candidate the beloved cousin and son-in-law of the Prophet," he said. "Many believe that, as father to Muhammad's heirs, Ali ibn Abi Talib is best qualified to follow in the Prophet's footsteps." The roar of the Bedouins and *ansari* in the crowd—neither group being known for its manners—made Abd al-Rahman pause. "And in truth, Ali has proved himself impeccable in all aspects: in piety, in intelligence, in his knowledge of the *qur'an*, and on the battlefield as the Prophet's most distinguished swordsman."

Each word he spoke made the wings of my heart flap harder. Abd al-Rahman was about to name Ali to the *khalifa*.

"For these reasons," Abd al-Rahman went on, "it might be my desire to name Ali our next *khalifa*." A great roar like a burst of thunder shook the walls as men shouted Ali's name and waved their swords. Ali's eyes grew bigger as Abd al-Rahman spoke—but Uthman didn't move a hair. His smile stayed on his face as if he'd painted it there, and he nodded his head and twisted his mustache as though he'd written Abd al-Rahman's speech and it were now being delivered just the way he'd intended.

Abd al-Rahman held up his hands to quell the noise. "Unfortunately, it is not that simple," he said when Ali's supporters had settled again. "I promised al-Lah that I would allow Him to choose the next *khalifa*. And although I know that both candidates are excellent, He has not indicated which man, Ali or Uthman, I should appoint."

"Uthman belongs to the prestigious clan of Abd Shams," a hook-nosed man in a silk robe called out. "His credentials are *adab*. Gold! Ali, on the other hand, is only a Hashimite."

"As was the Prophet," al-Abbas cried out. "And Muhammad raised Ali as a son. There are no better credentials."

"Ali is young. Inexperienced!" the first man cried. "Uthman is a respected *shaykh*."

At this last remark, Abd al-Rahman gave a slow nod of his head. He pressed his lips together. His eyes, whose gaze had been bouncing about the room, fixed themselves on Uthman. My pulse pounded like frantic fists on a locked door.

"*Yaa* aunt, are you well?" The words pulled my attention from the floor. My nephew Abdallah stood in front of me.

"I'm well, by al-Lah, but far from calm!" I said. "Umar has banished women from the mosque, and I need to participate in these proceedings."

"Let me help," he said. "I'll be your messenger."

"Yes. Go tell Abd al-Rahman that I have thought of this test for the candidates." I leaned down and murmured into his ear.

A smile leapt onto his face. "By al-Lah, aunt, you're the most intelligent person in this room!"

"And *you* need to be the speediest," I said. "Hurry, Abdallah, and whisper my suggestion to Abd al-Rahman. Tell him the Mother of the Believers wants to know the candidates' answers."

I prayed as Abdallah pressed through the crowd, calling Abd al-Rahman's name. Al-Zubayr, standing on the platform with the others in the *shura*, tapped Abd al-Rahman's shoulder and pointed to him. While everyone else in the mosque squabbled over the *khalifa*, I breathed a great sigh of relief. *Thank you, God, for giving me a voice in these proceedings*.

Hafsa nudged me with her elbow. "By al-Lah, I should have known you'd find a way to get involved!"

I shrugged, pretending none of it mattered. "Umar knew Ali's weaknesses. He wouldn't have wanted him to be the *khalifa*."

Hafsa slanted her eyes at me. "He wouldn't have wanted *you* to help with that choice, either."

"I only made a suggestion." She spoke truly: Umar would decry any woman involved in choosing a *khalifa*. But I knew Umar's distrust of women was misguided, and Hafsa knew it, also. His distrust of Ali, on the other hand, was both accurate and wise.

I held my breath as I watched Abdallah climb the steps to the platform and huddle with Abd al-Rahman. When had my nephew become a young man, and so handsome? The *shaykh* nodded, to my relief, and a smile washed like cool rain over his face. He straightened his stooped back. He squeezed Abdallah's shoulder and sent him down the steps, then turned to address the crowd.

"Al-Lah has answered my prayers at last," he announced. "He has sent me a question for the contenders, the answer of which will guide me to His will." The shouts and murmurs among the onlookers faded to the hush of one thousand and one breaths.

Abd al-Rahman turned to Ali. "*Yaa* Ali ibn Abi Talib, I will pose the question first to you," he said. I felt a cry in my throat. Let Ali answer first? Would his response overshadow anything Uthman might say?

Abd al-Rahman gestured toward Ali, who stepped forward. "If you are appointed to the *khalifa*, will you rule according to the precedent set by Abu Bakr and Umar?" he asked.

My heart beat wildly. *Say no say no say no*—for, although I considered "no" to be the proper answer, since Muhammad, not my father or Umar, was the man to emulate, I knew Abd al-Rahman had revered both and that he would appoint the man who promised yes, to follow in their paths. Ali knew this, also, as I could see in the emotions roiling across his face.

For twelve years now, ever since Muhammad's death, Ali had been grumbling over the decisions that my father, then Umar, had made for the *umma*. My father's support for the cruel Khalid ibn al-Walid as general had made Ali argue and fume. When Umar had assumed the *khalifa* with his whip in hand, Ali complained of his harshness. They were strange objections from a man who drew his double-bladed sword whenever he was provoked.

I, also, had disagreed with these stern measures because I knew Muhammad would never have condoned them. But Ali's hatred of me took him far from Muhammad's path. He had complained about my father's consulting me for advice—which Muhammad had also done—and about Umar's paying me a larger pension than my sister-wives received, an act which my husband would have encouraged. Ali, follow in their footsteps? The idea made me want to laugh.

For a long time, Ali didn't answer Abd al-Rahman's question. He stood and gazed at the eager faces of his supporters, men nodding and, no doubt, mouthing to him to *say yes*. He searched the eyes of Abd al-Rahman, certainly hoping to see the correct response there. He looked down at his clasped hands and closed his eyes, probably praying for the right words.

At last he lifted his face to Abd al-Rahman's, and his look of calm filled me with dread. Whether with al-Lah's guidance or with Satan's, he had arrived at an answer. If Abd al-Rahman chose him, *islam* would be lost to the dishonesty and greed of Ali and his relatives, and I'd have to watch from the confines of my hut the ruin of everything that Muhammad had worked for.

"Thank you for the opportunity to address this very important matter." Ali bowed first to Abd al-Rahman and then to the crowd. "Of course I am aware of the many virtues possessed by Abu Bakr and Umar, not the least of which was their love for my cousin Muhammad, the Prophet of al-Lah."

Cheers rose from the crowd again. "If I were appointed *khalifa*, I would try very hard to follow the example of my predecessors. I would certainly do so to the best of my ability. I might decide on a different direction than these men might have chosen, but only after consulting al-Lah. And if I should fail in any matter, I would be forgiven and my errors rectified by God. For I have no doubt that He would prefer the man closest to His Prophet's heart to lead His people."

Ali's supporters burst into cheers and Abd al-Rahman's face took on creases and folds like shifting dunes. As for me, I had to lean against the wall to keep from slumping to the floor. How wily was Ali! He had managed to answer my question without commitment or denial—in truth, without saying anything except to remind us of his ties to Muhammad.

Ali returned to his place and Uthman stepped forward. His smile was bigger than ever, so that it seemed to surround his face instead of just covering it. Abd al-Rahman turned sad eyes to his friend as though he already knew his answer would be inadequate, as though he were apologizing for having to appoint Ali.

"Uthman ibn 'Affan, I ask you the same question," he said. "If appointed, do you vow to rule according to the example set by first Abu Bakr and then Umar?"

Uthman began to nod. He looked out at the expectant crowd as though he had already rehearsed this moment with them. Yet, like Ali, he said nothing at first. Ali's answer had impressed this group, and Uthman, who had never been known for his skills as a speaker, now had to outperform him. Even as I knew he couldn't do it, and as his smile started to look foolish and his mustache, ridiculous, I prayed that God would give him the words, just this once.

"What is your answer?" Abd al-Rahman asked. "If appointed, do you promise to follow the example of your predecessors?

Uthman was still nodding. "Yes, I do," he said. And he folded his arms over his belly and stood like a ben-tree in a storm, proud and strong.

"Oh, no!" My cry was lost in the clamor of men shouting Uthman's name. A simple "yes" was his answer? Around me, the sister-wives who supported Ali hugged and kissed one another, while those who wanted Uthman slumped in place, our eyes blank as we contemplated life under Ali. I gazed around my hut, at the colored glass hung by threads from the ceiling, at the paintings on my mud-brick walls, at the colorful cushions I had sewn, at Muhammad's grave and that of my father, and I sighed. It was a good thing I loved my home, because, with Ali as *khalifa*, I wouldn't be leaving it.

Maymunah was beaming. "*Yaa* A'isha, a most excellent question you asked. Now we Hashimites will have the respect we deserve."

"Yes, thank you, A'isha," Ramlah said dryly. "Your meddling has destroyed *islam*. I'm sure my brother Mu'awiyya will be very grateful."

To think of Mu'awiyya's suffering made Ali's appointment almost bearable. I was about to say so when Hafsa shushed us all. "By al-Lah, the contest isn't over."

Abd al-Rahman lifted his hands raised toward the ceiling and shouted like a man struck by lightning, "*Yaa* al-Lah, which is the answer You sought?" Buffeted by indecision, Abd al-Rahman leaned first toward Ali and then toward Uthman.

Then he began to nod, his eyes closed, as if listening to a voice no one else could hear. "Yes, yes," he said. "Yes. No equivocating, no faltering, no excuses. Only a simple 'yes.' God is pleased with you, *yaa* Uthman. You have given the best answer."

He opened his eyes and beamed at the crowd. "It is my pleasure to announce that Uthman will be the new *khalifa*," he said. "*Yaa* Uthman, please stretch forth your hand so that I may pledge my allegiance to you."

Now I was the one cheering, and Hafsa, while Saffiya wiped the tears from her cheeks and gave a hug to Ramlah, who pulled back with a wince. Uthman held out his hand, and as Abd al-Rahman kissed him, his supporters chanted and cheered while Ali's supporters yanked off their sandals and used them to smack the heads of the others. Abdallah took a blow to his face as he made his way back toward me. I broke free of my sister-wives to go to him.

And then three miraculous and unexpected things happened. The crowd of men parted when they saw me approach, and many of them bowed to me. "Make way for the Mother of the Believers!" someone cried. I blushed to realize that, in my haste, I had forgotten my wrapper, but the eyes of these men were not gazing upon me with desire or disrespect. I saw reverence, as though I were the angel Gabriel appearing in their midst. And I saw something else in these men's eyes: love. Not the love of a man for his bride, but, rather, of a man for his mother.

"Please," I said, feeling a new power, a mother's power, "respect our new *khalifa* with your good wishes and your allegiance. Think how Muhammad must feel, watching Muslims fighting Muslims."

Then the second miracle occurred. On the platform, Ali dropped to his knees and kissed Uthman's hand, which now wore Muhammad's signet ring. Standing beside my nephew Abdallah—who was unharmed, he assured me—I watched, stunned, as Ali professed his allegiance to Uthman with a graciousness that he'd never shown either to my father or to Umar. When he'd risen, he asked everyone in the room to profess his allegiance, also. All around me, men lifted their hands and spoke Uthman's name, and I lifted my hands also, at one with these men, the only sons I would ever know. I bowed my head for a brief prayer of thanks. When I looked at the platform again, I felt Ali's eyes on me and I returned his gaze. And I wondered: Had Ali pledged his allegiance with a sincere desire to unify the *umma*, or had he done it to draw the crowd's attention away from me and back to himself?

Then came the third miracle. While the room full of men shouted and slapped one another's backs, and as Ali and I stared at each other, a mighty crash assaulted our ears. And we heard a hissing like that of a giant serpent. Abu Hurayra, the cat-lover, rushed out into the courtyard and ran back into the mosque—dripping wet.

"Praise al-Lah, the drought is ended!" he cried. "God has sent us rain to signify His pleasure with the day's events."

From my hut I heard my sister-wives squeal before they disappeared from my doorway. I found them all in the courtyard, barefoot and bareheaded, and dancing like children in the blessed downpour. For five years we had waited for rain, had prayed for it, had licked our cracked lips in memory of the feeling of water on our skin. So many springs had dried up that the public baths had closed and we had to chew dry barley for want of water to cook it in. Many had died of dehydration, including my mother and Abu Sufyan, Ramlah's father. Today, as the rain fell in cool, misted sheets about our bodies, we forgot the dust that our skin had become and the thickness of our parched tongues in mouths that felt lined with linen. Today we danced. We tossed aside our robes made heavy by the rain and squished our toes in mud and threw it at one another. What man would dare to enter the courtyard, knowing we were here? Our gowns clung to our bodies and our mouths opened like baby birds' to the wonderful, drenching, cleansing rain and we didn't care at all about the outlines of our bodies or the glisten of water like diamonds on our skin. We danced until our gowns dragged at our feet. We cared only about soaking it in, all of it, filling ourselves from the outside in with this elixir as precious as life.

Through the curtain of rain I thought I saw a man's shadow appear by my hut, then disappear inside it. Who would dare to enter my home? Ali, wanting a confrontation? No one else would be so audacious. I snatched up my robe and my sword and tramped through the muck, across the courtyard and into my hut.

"By al-Lah, what are you—" I began, but when I saw the intruder, I dropped my sword and threw my arms, instead, around his neck.

I closed my eyes and breathed him in, dust from his long journey, and sandalwood perfume. "Talha," I said. "If only you'd arrived an hour ago."

"Al-Lah knows best," he said, and smiled down at me. "I'm glad to be here now."

I hadn't realized how much I'd missed him until that moment, when I saw him there in my room with those dancing eyes and those smiling lips that beckoned me, always, like a sweet honey that I had never dared taste. Until now.

Our lips touched and seemed to melt together and my breath stopped and then, on the verge of fainting, I heard Muhammad's voice. *Beware this sin*, I heard him say. *Beware this man*.

Fear ripped through my body as I pushed Talha away so violently he staggered backward, his face a jumble of emotions. I stared at him, my hand pressed to my chest, wondering if he'd heard Muhammad also, but he only laughed.

"By al-Lah, I did not realize you were so frightened of thunder!" he said.

Chills wracked me. Shivering, I crossed my arms over my chest to warm myself and to hide my body from his view.

"Thunder is the least of my fears," I said. And I ducked behind my screen to put on some dry clothes and the facade, at least, of dignity. Mother of the Believers? At that moment, I felt more like a reckless, foolish child.

THE THIRD RIGHTLY GUIDED CALIPH

Uthman
654–656 A.D.

A'isha

It was the day I had dreaded, yet I had to appear as happy as if the wedding were my own. I knew I could do it, al-Lah willing. I'd become good at pretending after that day in my hut, ten years ago, when I'd been swept into Talha's arms. *I was delirious from the rain, and thrilled that Ali wasn't named* khalifa, I'd explained to him later. *I felt I had to kiss someone, or burst.*

He gave me his usual grin, so I didn't know whether he believed me. In any case, he became an expert at pretending, also, for Talha never touched me again—although his eyes spoke blatantly of desire whenever he looked at me, while my longing for him tugged at my heart, my fingertips, my eyelashes.

Today, for instance, as he greeted his wedding guests in the mosque courtyard, my gaze returned to him again and again as if his face were the changing moon and my blood the tide-driven sea. Sorrow weighted my body to see him laughing into my sister's eyes. He looked as handsome as a peacock in his magnificent garments of green and gold silk, while I stood in the shadows, my future as bleak as the grave.

I had known for a decade that this day would come, that Talha would marry Umm Kulthum when she turned fourteen. I'd seen him grow more and more fond of her as she matured into a young woman with as quick a tongue as mine, yet with a grace and composure I could only marvel at. Recently, when curves had molded her young body, Talha had begun standing closer to her, his hands hovering near as if to touch her. I'd seen it all, had cried into my pillow at night, mourning the loss of Talha's love, asking Muhammad *Why did you do this to me? Why would you deprive me of loving again?*

I'd tried teasing Talha about his burgeoning desire for Umm Kulthum. But the words stuck in my throat like barley mush. Now, watching him feed my sister a bite of bread and hummus with glances that suggested greater pleasures to come, I had to turn away. My dignity was a threadbare garment, threatening to fall about my feet and expose my naked desires. *Al-Lah, help me to hold myself together.*

My brother Mohammad, Asma's son, a strong and handsome youth of sixteen, approached with a cup of galangal water. Seeing him reminded me of another struggle I faced today. With talk of rebellion against Uthman swarming like bees through the *umma*—talk instigated by my brother, who'd grown up in Ali's home and loved him as a father—I had to keep politics out of this event. As much as I envied Umm Kulthum, I loved her more, and I'd do anything to make sure her wedding day was peaceful.

"*Yaa* sister, who died?" Mohammad was grinning as he handed me the cup. "Take this, by al-Lah, before you faint!"

"Yes, this heat is really affecting me." I unclasped my veil to gulp the delicious water and handed the cup back to him, wanting to be alone with my thoughts. "Go fetch me some more, brother."

He regarded me soberly, looking every bit like our father. "Only if you stop lying and tell me what's really bothering you," he said.

"Lying!" I frowned and shook my head, pretending to be stern. "That's the problem with the younger generation. No respect for elders."

"Elders?" My brother's friend Ibn Hudhaifa, Uthman's foster son, stepped up before I could cover my face, bearing another cup of galangal water—which he handed to me with a flourish. "*Yaa* Mother of the Believers, of whom are you speaking? I was so dazzled by your youthful beauty that I forgot to listen."

I rolled my eyes and laughed. "You are Uthman's son, to be sure."

His happy expression disappeared like the sun in eclipse. "Please, Mother of the Believers, do not call me this. Uthman would not deal with a son as he has dealt with me."

Behind him, I saw Uthman walking toward us. I raised my eyebrows, trying to alert Hud, but he was frowning and looking at the ground. "Uthman refused to make Hud a governor," my brother said. "He said he lacks experience on the battlefield."

"And in truth he does," Uthman said. His clothing was even more ostentatious than the groom's: indigo silk laced with fine gold thread over a pure white gown studded with jewels.

"Being the leader of a country is a great responsibility." He turned to Hud. "How can you send troops into battle, or lead them there yourself, unless you have first become a respected warrior?"

Hud's face turned a deep red. "I have been trying to join the new navy ever since I became of age one year ago. But your governor Mu'awiyya will not appoint me."

Uthman shrugged. "He desires sea-warriors who are familiar with the ways of water. You do not even know how to swim."

"You told him not to appoint me," Hud yelled. With a nervous glance at the bride and groom, I shushed him. Hud lowered his head and kicked at the ground with the toe of one foot. "You don't want me to fight; you've told me so many times."

"I admit it," Uthman said. "I do not want to lose you, Hud. Before your father died I promised him I would take good care of you."

"I feel the same way about my brother," I said to Hud. "There's no real need to do battle anymore. We're not being invaded, or trying to get rid of idolatry, or conquering new territories. We're just squelching rebellions in Persia. Anyone can do that."

"*Yaa* sister, as long as there are men there will be battles," Mohammad said. "We will always need to prove ourselves."

"Especially those of us who want to be governors." Hud glared at Uthman again, who cleared his throat and excused himself.

I shook my head at the boys. I had my own opinions about Uthman's rule—or, rather, the rule of Marwan, Uthman's scheming cousin who had his ear so completely he now sat in a chair beside the *khalifa* and gave him advice on every petition. Tales about Marwan's love for women and gambling, and his stealing from the treasury, circled the *umma*. Yet, in spite of my own concerns, I was determined to keep the peace today.

"That was rude," I said. "Not only is Uthman your foster-father, *yaa* Hud, but he is also our *khalifa*. He deserves respect."

Hud snorted. "*Afwan*, Mother of the Believers, but you may be the only one who still feels that way."

I frowned. "Who told you that?"

"Everyone," my brother said. "People are complaining. Uthman only appoints his relatives to the good positions, he pretends not to notice as the *umma*'s money is misused, he ignores scandalous tales of his appointees drinking, womanizing, gambling, and worse . . ."

I rolled my eyes, hiding my unease. "These are the same rumors that plagued Umar."

"And they were true!" my brother said. "I've heard Ali's tales of traveling to Syria—"

"Uthman isn't interested in the truth, not if it will reflect poorly on his relatives," Hud said. "People come to him from Egypt, from Kufa, from Basra, complaining of corruption and what does he do? He promises to investigate but then does nothing."

"He's losing his support," Mohammad said. "Even here in Medina, people are speaking against him. Behold the finery he adorns himself with." He spat on the ground. "He vowed to follow the example of Umar, Abu Bakr, and the Prophet. But that was a lie in order to defeat Ali."

Listening to him, it was clear whose home Mohammad had grown up in. My brother might have *abi's* eyes, nose, and mouth, but his demeanor—the twist of his lips, his bitter accusations—was pure Ali.

"Even God has withdrawn His support," Mohammad said. "Didn't al-Lah snatch the Prophet's signet ring from Uthman's hand?"

I shook my head. "That ring fell off Uthman's hand and into a well. Al-Lah didn't 'snatch' it."

Hud narrowed his eyes. "Then where did it go? Every man in Medina tried to find it. They dug up the well, dug up all the dirt around the well, and nothing. It disappeared."

Mohammad leaned closer to me and lowered his voice. "Some say it's a sign from God."

I crossed my arms. This conversation was getting more and more ridiculous—and disturbing. "A sign of what, by al-Lah? Of a *shaykh*'s weight loss?"

"Do not be upset, Mother of the Believers." Hud resumed his formal diction, showing his respect. "Your brother and I are not inventing these opinions, nor are we exaggerating them. Our *khalifa* ruled well for his first six years, but lately he has turned away from the people, while raining down favors upon his kin. Even your brother-in-law Talha shares our view."

My brother leaned in close to me. "It is time to prune the diseased branch from the tree."

The words *brother-in-law* hit me like a slap. "I don't agree," I said. "And I think you're mistaken about Talha. But al-Lah knows best." Shaking my head, I stepped away from those troublemaking youths, lest they notice my distress. Was Talha encouraging mutiny?

Muhammad's voice in the thunder ten years ago came back to me now: *Beware this man.* The warning had haunted my nights, tossing me in my bed as I'd tried to discern its meaning. Except for his desire for me, what was there to "beware" about Talha? Like me, he'd rued the turning of *islam* away from Muhammad's vision of charity and equality, and the scrambles for money and power that had gripped our ever-expanding *umma*. Like me, he opposed Ali. Beware Talha? Must I also beware myself?

Unable to find an answer, I'd put the warning out of my mind. But lately I'd seen disturbing changes in Talha. With Uthman's blessing, Talha had traded his date plantation in Khaybar for fertile land in the Persian Sawad, the so-called "Gardens of Quraysh," and he was now one of the wealthiest men in all of *islam*. Being engaged to the daughter of Abu Bakr had increased his status even more, which didn't bother me at first—I had, after all, asked him to marry Umm Kulthum. Recently, though, during one of Uthman's lavish parties, I'd heard Talha boast about his engagement while talking to 'Amr, the famous conqueror of Egypt. *It is but another example of Abu Bakr's high regard for me.* The lie had taken me aback, and made me wonder if I knew my cousin anymore.

"It's a game, *yaa* A'isha," he'd said with a laugh when I'd confronted him later. "Every man eyes the same treasure, but I, and you, have the wits to win."

"Leave me out of any game that involves lying," I'd snapped then. Now at the wedding, I'd say the same thing to him about mutiny. Despite my dismay over the direction *islam* was taking, I also felt bound to support the *khalifa.* If al-Lah wanted Uthman to step down, He would make it so—without Talha's help, and without mine.

My worries were forgotten in the next moment, as I beheld my long-lost friend Asma stepping into the courtyard.

A pale linen cloth covered her nose and mouth, and her matching gown clasped high at the neck and hid her feet, but I couldn't mistake those large, round eyes or that graceful walk that made her look as though she floated above the ground. Love warmed me as I approached her for the first time in twelve years. My arms were open, my lips smiling with the pleasure of speaking her name—when Ali stepped into the courtyard and gave me a look that would have felled a camel.

"I commanded you to refrain from approaching my wives," he said, stepping in front of Asma.

I had to laugh. "By al-Lah, that edict is so old your breath smells of ashes when you speak of it!"

His face looked as hard as stone. His eyes held no expression. Arguing with him would be as fruitful as debating with a statue. Yet my heart longed for just one word with Asma, who had known and loved my father, and whose tenderness after he'd died had helped me endure the most painful days without him.

"*Yaa* Ali, I respect your desire to rule your household," I said as he turned away from me, still sheltering Asma from view. "But I'm also surprised at the way you're treating Asma. Does she lack a mind? It's hard for me to believe you were brought up by Muhammad. He gave his wives choices in most matters."

"Yes, I noticed," Ali said. "And I also saw how he suffered for it. You, especially, caused him a lot of trouble with your 'choices.'" He stepped away from Asma, clearing the space between her and me. "But you do speak truly, A'isha. My cousin allowed his wives much freedom, and it is my desire to follow his example in all respects."

Then he turned to Asma and gestured toward me "Asma, I leave the choice to you. Speak with A'isha if you desire, although it means contradicting my wishes. You may decide for yourself whose love you value more, hers or mine." He walked stiffly across the grass to join Mohammad and Hud under the date-palm tree.

Face to face with Asma at last, I greeted her with a smile that I hoped showed my love for her.

"I've missed you so much all these years." I stepped toward her for an embrace. To my shock, she backed away from me. Her gaze darted about.

"We were friends once, but that was long ago," she said, shifting from one foot to the other. "Now my allegiance is to my husband. *Afwan*, A'isha." And she scurried off like a frightened rabbit to huddle under the palm tree in the protection of Ali's arms.

I stared after her with a hollow feeling in my stomach. How completely Asma had changed! She was devoted to Ali, it was clear. *It is my desire to follow his example in all respects*, Ali had said without blinking. Ali, following Muhammad's example? How easily lying came to him. Once again I said a prayer of thanks that Ali had not been given the *khalifa*.

As I made my way through the crowd, talking to one opulently dressed person after another, I noticed more keenly than ever how the basic principles of *islam* had been cast aside. Muhammad had taught equality, but the Muslim people had created a hierarchy. At the top were members of the tribe of Quraysh, Meccans who bragged about their blood ties to Muhammad even though they'd tried to assassinate him. Next came the Medinan *ansari*, or Helpers, who'd allowed Muhammad and his followers to flee persecution and live in their city.

Lower down on the ladder were the apostates, Bedouin tribes who had turned away from *islam* after Muhammad's death, then later returned to the fold. My father had contributed to prejudice against them by forbidding them to fight in his army. Umar had relaxed that prohibition, in part because he'd needed more warriors; but he'd also increased the jealousies and divisions by giving more pay to longer-time Muslims and less to new converts. Umar rewarded men for their faithfulness, but he'd also created a lot of resentment.

Uthman, to his credit, had done away with Umar's "merit" system and equalized pensions among all, depending on rank, not longevity. Yet he'd awarded the best, highest-paying positions in the government and the army to members of his family. I'd advised against it, warning him that the Bedouins, especially, would grumble. *Does not a wise leader appoint men whom he knows and trusts?* Uthman had said with a smile.

I liked Uthman. He was a generous man who had given large sums of money to Muhammad, saving him from starvation more than once. Yet, like my brother, I wasn't sure he was the best man to lead the *umma*. He wasn't strong enough to refuse favors to his family members, and he never denied himself anything. His knowledge of the *qur'an* seemed thin, and his health always seemed to be failing. During his first year as *khalifa*, he hadn't been able to lead the pilgrimage to Mecca because of a nosebleed that wouldn't stop. Now that he was eighty, everyone seemed to be waiting for him to die—and jostling for position in the contest for the *khalifa*.

Ali, I could see, still thought the job should be his. But instead of increasing his status with money, he'd focused on building a huge household of wives, concubines, and thirty children.

"By al-Lah, is he trying to rival Solomon?" Hafsa said to me now as, plucking grapes from a bowl outside the cooking tent, we watched Ali place his hand on Asma's swelling stomach.

"Yes, and not just in wives and children," I said. "He wants to be a king like Solomon, also." I told her about my conversation with Mohammad and Hud, and her eyebrows lifted.

"Do your brother's opinions come from Ali?" she said. "I've heard similar talk elsewhere."

"I'd wager my next month's pension that these rumors of unrest are coming from Ali," I said. "Of course, he's too feeble-hearted to start a rebellion by himself. But his uncle al-Abbas is perfectly capable of doing the job."

Servants marched past bearing platters of food: loaves of wheat bread as light as air; rice scented with saffron; lamb stewed with figs; tender asparagus braised with leeks and ghee; cheeses of various textures and colors made from the milk of goats, sheep, and cows; and sesame cakes drizzled with *rummaniya*, a syrup made from pomegranate juice. They wafted behind them a scent trail to make our mouths water—cumin, cinnamon, cloves, and lemon—yet I couldn't help remembering a time, while Muhammad lived, when a feast like this would have made our stomachs flip in delight. Back then, our household subsisted on barley, dates, and water. Most of the rest of the *umma* had fared only slightly better. But Persia was closed to us then, and caravans from Egypt and Syria were rare. Now we owned those lands and imported their foods, and money to buy them was ever at hand. Only the poorest among us ate barley bread these days, or relied on dates to survive.

Behind the servants lumbered Sawdah, nearly seventy now and barely able to walk ten steps without resting. "I see you two hungering after the meal. It is good, the best feast I have ever been in charge of," she said proudly, mopping sweat from her face with a handkerchief. "But you know you can't eat, A'isha, until you congratulate the bride and groom." She narrowed her eyes, giving me a look so pointed it prodded me across the courtyard to Talha and Umm Kulthum, the disturbingly happy couple.

"A'isha!" My sister glowed as if she'd been dipped in starlight as she kissed me. What a difference between her wedding day and mine! She certainly wasn't the frightened bride I'd been. Of course, I'd been nine, and terrified that Muhammad would want to consummate our marriage that night. If I'd known that my new husband was willing to wait until I was ready—and beyond, as it turned out—would I have collapsed on the floor during the ceremony, crying, while our families and friends looked on? Or would I have smiled as radiantly as my sister was doing now? She loved Talha. She would have married him the day they became engaged, when she was just four, if I'd let her. He, on the other hand, was supposed to love *me*. So why did his eyes sparkle deliriously as he invited me now to the Sawad?

"I've built a huge house, big enough to get lost in, with lots of rooms, patios, fountains, and servants," he said. "Why don't you join us? Plan to stay a few weeks so you can view every room."

"Yes, come with us, A'isha." Umm Kulthum grabbed my hand and squeezed it as she snuggled into Talha's embrace. "It'll be a nice change for you, and very restful."

I shook my head. Watching Talha fondle my sister didn't sound restful to me. "I don't feel comfortable in big houses," I said. "Like Muhammad, I prefer simplicity."

Umm Kulthum frowned. "I've noticed. That gown you're wearing is older than I am. A'isha, there's no need to live so austerely anymore. We're not fighting for survival the way you did in the olden days. The *umma* has money now."

Talha nodded. "Your sister speaks truly, A'isha," he said. "People are once again measuring a man by his wealth. With my great house in the Sawad, I'm more respected, and my chances of becoming *khalifa* are increasing. Things are changing—and Umm Kulthum, my fresh young bride, can help prepare us for the future."

They turned together as one and, arm-in-arm, floated like lovers into the mosque. Beside me, Hafsa tugged at my sleeve.

"*Yaa* A'isha, you're crying!" she whispered. In truth, I was. I dropped my gaze, hoping no one could see the tears spilling onto my cheeks as my sister-wife led me into the mosque for the wedding feast.

I plopped without grace onto a cushion, as I struggled to control my emotions. How often Talha used to gaze at me the way he now gazed at Umm Kulthum! A dish of lamb was placed before us but I barely noticed it. Umm Kulthum, of course, was a beautiful girl, with skin like dew and a mouth as plump as ripe figs. I, on the other hand, was an old woman of forty. It was obvious why any man would prefer her to me. *My fresh young bride*, Talha had called her. He'd never see me the same way again.

Praise al-Lah for that, a voice inside me admonished. *Doesn't Umm Kulthum deserve happiness?* I shook off my self-pity and reached for a piece of bread and a bite of lamb so tender it fell apart on my tongue. My little sister was the closest thing to a child of my own that I would ever know. Her happiness was everything to me—as I'd proven by giving up the man I loved for her sake. Tears filled my mouth, choking out the taste of my food. I was a married woman, promised to Muhammad for eternity. I shouldn't be having thoughts about men and love that didn't involve my husband.

Things are changing. In truth, they were, and not all for the best. What had Talha said—that people were again measuring men by their wealth? He hadn't seemed to disapprove of that attitude, while Muhammad had adamantly rejected it. *A man's money means nothing to al-Lah, unless he uses it for the good of others*, he'd said many times. Now, just twenty-one years after his death, people were forgetting the true meaning of *islam* and honoring men for their possessions instead of their hearts. Uthman, who flaunted wealth, was partly to blame. But so, in my opinion, was Ali.

I looked at him now, escorting Asma to a group of women far away from me before joining the men's side of the banquet. He was wearing his old military uniform, the most modest apparel at this event except, perhaps, for my old gown. But his swagger bespoke arrogance, and his choice of seating—with 'Amr, the Egyptian governor-conqueror, and the despicable Marwan—told me that power was still on his mind.

When we'd finished our meal, and the dishes and cloths had been gathered up and carried away, Uthman creaked up the steps to the platform, preparing to lead a prayer for the bride and groom. But when he turned to face the crowd, the heavy doors to the mosque creaked open. In walked the skinny, gray-bearded *shaykh* Ibn Masud, one of Muhammad's most respected Companions. Until my seclusion at age six, he had dandled me on his knee during many visits to my parents' home.

Murmurs flurried through the mosque as he stepped up to the platform, as spry as a man half his age, and shook his cane at Uthman. "*Yaa* Uthman, I am told that you have refused my petition for a hearing today," he shouted. "A man of my status and age should not be refused, especially when he has come all the way from Kufa."

Uthman frowned. "As you see, Ibn Masud, we are in the midst of a wedding ceremony. I am afraid your complaint will have to wait."

"There is no waiting when you are as old as I am," Ibn Masud said. "As you should know."

Uthman reddened, being a vain man who preferred not to talk about his age. "*Yaa* Ibn Masud, were you invited to this wedding? If not, I must ask that you leave the mosque and come back tomorrow."

"I may be dead tomorrow," he said, waving his cane. "Here is what I came to say. Listen to me now. Your brother Walid is the mortification of Kufa. I left that lovely village on the day he led the prayer services drunk on wine. He vomited on the mosque steps." Gasps punctuated the room.

"Enough!" Uthman cried. "*Yaa* Ibn Masud, I told you I would see you in the morning."

The old man stomped his foot. "You must correct this now," he said. "It is blasphemy against al-Lah and an embarrassment for you, *khalifa*. And as keeper of the treasury of Kufa, I have come to tell you in person what my messengers have told you many times: Walid has been stealing dinars and dirhams for his own enrichment. For example, he uses the money to pay dancing girls for private performances. When I complained he suggested I take some gold for myself, which of course I did not do. Uthman, with your brother setting the example, corruption pervades your administration!"

"I said that is enough," Uthman cried. "If you do not take yourself out of the mosque this instant, I will—I will—"

"He will have you forcibly removed," Marwan called from his seat on the floor.

Uthman nodded. "Marwan speaks the truth. I will have you forcibly removed."

"But *khalifa,* there is more. Your attempts to compile the *qur'an* into a single version are tainted."

"That is enough!"

"I am an old man, but my mind is as sharp as a dagger. I can recite every word of the Prophet's recitations exactly as they fell from his lips. Your compilers are making changes."

"I do not want to hear this!" Uthman cried. "I warn you for the last time, Ibn Masud."

"Changes in God's word, Uthman! This is the greatest sin of all, and if you do not correct it, you are in danger of hellfire."

"Where are my men?" Uthman was screaming now, his face wizened with rage. Two of his guards ran up to the platform, wiping pomegranate syrup from their mustaches. Uthman pointed a quavering finger at the *shaykh.* "Throw him out! Now! And I mean *throw* him, as far as he will go!"

I leapt to my feet as the men picked up Muhammad's old friend. "No! Stop!" I yelled as they ran with him toward the open door. I raced toward them, stepping on platters, kicking over cups, calling out to the guards to be careful, that he was the Prophet's Companion—but I was too late. Just before I reached them, the guards tossed the poor old man high into the air, his arms and legs flailing, to land hard on his stomach, wheezing and bleeding from his nose and mouth.

How I yearned to run my sword through the gut of the rat-faced guard who stood chuckling at Ibn Masud! The poor old man lay in a heap. "That should teach you to obey our *khalifa,*" the other guard said with a sneer. I ran to Ibn Masud and knelt by his side.

"I am unharmed, Mother of the Believers," he said. I blushed with pleasure at the honor of hearing him use my *kunya.* He tried to stand and found that he could not. "My ribs," he said, sitting on the ground, doubled over in pain. I ran my hands along his ribcage and found two jagged breaks trying to tear through his skin. By al-Lah! He would need treatment, and soon.

The guards had gone back inside the mosque, slapping each other's backs in congratulation. No one had followed me. Did no one care about this important *shaykh,* a reciter of the *qur'an* and one of the last honest men in the Muslim empire?

As if in answer to my question, the two Mohammads—my brother and his friend Mohammad ibn Hudheifa—burst forth from the mosque. "We would have come sooner," my brother murmured, "but Uthman insisted on leading the prayer."

"While the most pious one lay in the dust, mistreated at his behest?" Heat rose from my belly. Leaving the Mohammads to help Ibn Masud, I snatched up my sword and stomped back into the mosque—just in time to confront Uthman before he began his descent from the *minbar*.

"What has happened to you, *yaa* Uthman?" I snapped, forgoing the praise and ring-kissing he enjoyed before being addressed. "Have you forgotten your promise to follow Muhammad's path? Or have you decided the Prophet's vision for *islam* is now out of date?"

"A'isha, please seat yourself," Uthman said—gently, for he knew that having *me* thrown out would start a mutiny. "Honor your sister Umm Kulthum and your cousin Talha with your silence. I and you can speak of this later."

"I am not the one who has dishonored this ceremony, and I will not be silent." I raised my sword—Muhammad's sword—high into the air. "I'm disgusted by what I saw here today. What kind of man beats up a wizened old *shaykh*? Not much of a man at all!"

Cheers arose from the men's side of the mosque, emboldening me even more.

"For years I've defended you against every criticism, against every accusation, but I'm finished with that now. In my opinion, you deserve every damning word that comes your way."

With that, I turned and walked to the front door of the mosque, ceremoniously shook the dust from my sandals, and, with my head high and my heart broken, stepped out the door.

Ali

I should not have gone to Kufa. My stepson Mohammad ibn Abi Bakr, reclining in my new, spacious home after a delicious meal, invited me to accompany him to that city on the Euphrates. He planned to enlist in the battle against the rebellious Persians resisting our rule. As he told me about it, a foreboding fell upon me like the cold of a desert night.

"You must come, *yaa abi*," he'd said. "Every important man in Medina is moving his home to Kufa. It's said that Paradise is the only place more beautiful."

After much coaxing, I set aside my reservations and agreed to the journey, for I longed to escape the increasing unrest in Medina over Uthman's rule.

But I also desired to see Kufa, the new garrison city Umar had built that, I had heard, outshone the sun in splendor. My son told me of a river engorged with water year-round, of trees bejeweled with the sweetest of fruits, and of a mosque so dazzling that to pray under its shining dome seemed to lift the soul to the lap of al-Lah. To view delights such as these would certainly divert my thoughts from the irksome urgings of my uncle to join the agitation against Uthman and position myself for the *khalifa*.

"The *ansari* have already pledged their support to you," al-Abbas had said the day before as we walked home after the Friday services. I held my tongue, not pointing out that the *ansari* had always supported me. "The Bedouins are more receptive to you, also," he'd added, as if hearing my thoughts. "They had feared a monarchy if you succeeded Muhammad, but many are saying now that Uthman's nepotism is more deplorable."

I found this talk of mutiny thoroughly disgusting. I wanted only to distance myself from it as quickly as possible. So, despite my apprehensions, I told my son that I would accompany him to Kufa—and regretted my decision before we even set out. For, at the front of the caravan, next to Mohammad, rode his bosom companion Hud, Uthman's foster son and relentless detractor. I would not escape complaints about Uthman, after all.

"It is an honor to have our *khalifa* accompany us," Hud said, his face alight with pleasure.

"Your eyesight must be deteriorating, *yaa* Hud, and at such a young age," I said to him. "It is not the *khalifa* who sits before you, but only Ali."

His eyes shone. "I am too eager for this change. In my view, you already are the *khalifa*."

"But without a whip, or evil advisors," my son added, coming up behind me on the camel I had given him.

At that point, I should have changed my mind and stayed at home. But before I could retreat, the *muezzin* sounded the call to prayer. Then, after we had rolled up our mats, Mohammad gave me his first embrace in years. What father would turn back after that happy event?

We rode during the night, as was our custom, with blazing torches lighting our way across a land bereft of oases or water. In the so-called sand desert, we had to place blankets as stepping stones under our camels' hooves so they could walk without sinking. The dunes were impossibly soft and deep, blown into great, sea-like billows by the most violent of *samoom* winds. We labored for six nights to cross that treacherous land, fearing a storm might swoop down like the hand of a *djinni* and smother us with its whirling, devilish *zauba'ah*, pillars of stinging sand.

By the grace of al-Lah we were able to avoid that gruesome fate and cross the sand desert in safety. Yet by the time we reached the other side, I had begun to fear a different foe—one equally out of my control. Each time we camped, the bitterness of Mohammad ibn Hudheifa toward his foster father poured forth from his mouth to taint our food, disgruntle our camels, and disturb my sleep with visions of our blessed *qur'an* impaled on the tip of a sword and spurting blood.

"People think Uthman is generous, but he only gives when he knows he'll get something back," Hud would say. "That's why the numbers of poor are growing while our treasuries overflow with gold. Uthman's relatives benefit, because they help keep him in power." He poked our cookfire with a stick, causing sparks to fly. "Let me correct myself. *Some* of his relatives benefit."

On and on he went, complaining about how Uthman would not appoint him to a governorship until he had proven himself a worthy warrior on the battlefield, snarling over his difficulty obtaining a position in the Egyptian navy, and vowing to wreak revenge on Uthman for treating him poorly.

I had held my tongue many times through this diatribe until, one night, my agitation overcame my sensible nature and I answered Hud with sparks of my own.

"By al-Lah, if you knew how you sounded with these complaints you would never speak another word against Uthman," I said to him. "You only prove your lack of maturity by focusing on yourself."

I did not point out to him that I, who had been denied the *khalifa* three times, had never complained about my lack of status. Of course, Hud had been a young child, no more than seven or eight years old, when Abd al-Rahman had granted the *khalifa* to his friend Uthman on the strength of a single, disingenuous "yes." In contrast to his promise, Uthman had not followed the examples of his predecessors, not even in the smallest of ways.

Hud raised his stick and pointed it at me across the fire—disrespectful behavior, but better cannot be expected of a man who, as a child, enjoyed the fulfillment of every whim. "Focusing on myself?" he said with a scowl. "I spoke of the poor, didn't I? That's more than I've heard from *you* tonight."

"*Yaa* Hud," my estimable son Mohammad said. "Ali is like a father to me, remember?"

"Father?" His laugh clattered about our heads. "You speak the word as if it were hallowed, as if I should prostrate myself with respect. I do respect you, Ali," he said, lowering his stick, "but not because you are a father."

"Raising another man's child is no simple task," I said, able to defend

Uthman on this point, at least. "It requires time, attention, and money. From what I have seen, Uthman has met his obligations to you exceedingly well."

"He had to," Hud said. "He owed money to my *abi*. That's the one obligation Uthman ibn 'Affan can understand."

I said nothing more, for it was clear that Hud was not interested in truth, but only in revenge. The more he spoke, the more I understood Uthman's refusal to grant this hot-headed young man a leadership position. At the same time, I sympathized with Hud's frustration. Had I not been denied the *khalifa* because of my impulsivity, quick temper, and youth?

Of course, I had also faced A'isha's opposition. She seemed to follow me like a shadow, appearing in the mosque, in the market, everywhere but in my house, from which I had wisely banished her. Her challenges to me seemed relentless and without reason. Did she nurture a grudge for my words and deeds of more than twenty years ago? We had been scarcely more than children. Yet now, as then, she could not admit to wrongdoing of any kind.

When she railed at Uthman about harming the old *shaykh* Ibn Masud, I had wondered if she regretted supporting that weakling Uthman's appointment—but her refusal to tend to Ibn Masud at my home, where my son had brought him to convalesce, told me she still clung to her erroneous choice. Impressed by her speech on the *shaykh's* behalf—a speech I should have made, instead of merely sitting and watching Ibn Masud's mistreatment—I had decided to lift my ban and allow A'isha into my house. But A'isha had sent a surgeon to set Ibn Masud's broken bones and her servant girl to check on his progress. As always, she held herself above me and made certain that I was aware of it. And so my grudge against her returned.

The farther away from Medina I traveled, the smaller my concerns over the *khalifa*, A'isha, and Uthman seemed to become, as if they diminished on the horizon. Even Hud grew tired of grumbling. Instead, he played the *tanbur* around the fire while we drank coffee.

After one month, we arrived in Kufa, and soon I felt as much at home as if I had never lived anywhere else. Kufa was a remarkable city, with its houses laid out around the central mosque in a most orderly fashion. The mosque was an imposing building of stone, each side the length of two spear throws, with a row of marble columns across the front. A deep, wide trench—similar to the one that had protected Medina from invasion in the Battle of the Ditch—surrounded the city, whose eastern border was traversed by the green-shaded Euphrates River.

As soon as I had entered the splendid city, my chest expanded with affection and with the fresh, scented air. The weather was cooler than in Medina, and the gentle breeze blowing from the Euphrates reduced the number of flies. Although the climate was dry, grasses of every texture and hue blanketed the ground, and fragrances of thyme, sage, and fennel enveloped us like a perfumed cloud.

Within an hour of entering, I was transformed. Gone was the listlessness into which I had sunk in recent years. Losing the *khalifa* to Uthman had weighted my spirit as if a wet woolen cloak had been thrown across my shoulders. But now, as the citizens rushed into the street with faces of joy and shouts of *yaa Ali!* on their lips, I perched myself on my camel with a straight back and a light heart.

Even meeting the besotted governor, al-Walid ibn 'Uqba, did not quell my enthusiasm for the city. Standing in the spacious, sunlit mosque, I hid my shock at the sight of Uthman's scandal-ridden brother. His skin was as red as if gossip had placed him in perpetual embarrassment, and his nose had spread and softened into a fleshy blob. He seized my beard in an show of friendship as he greeted me in a blurred voice. I smelled wine and spiced mutton on his breath.

"I trust you have not come to spy on me," he said, wearing a large grin that revealed lips stained a red darker than blood. "You would find the employment very dull."

"My visit to Kufa is for pleasure only."

"Ah." He winked and slapped my back. "So I have heard. Like me, you have embraced pleasure for its own sake, eh?" He lowered his voice. "I have recently obtained from Syria a lovely singing girl with hair as red as A'isha bint Abi Bakr's. I know she would entertain you."

I felt the hair prickle on the back of my neck. Could this woman be the same performer I had rescued from Umar's whip in Damascus? How tenderly I had regarded her huddled on the ground, her hair spilling like rusty tears over her damp cheeks, and how churlishly she had responded to my admonition for modesty. In spite of A'isha's many faults, I could not accuse her of immodesty, not since the day twenty-five years ago when she'd ridden into Medina with her arms around Safwan ibn al-Mu'attal and her neighbors' shouts punching her like fists.

A beardless man wearing a tall, narrow cap appeared before al-Walid. "I bring an urgent message for you, *yaa* governor," he said. "That group to whom we have been referring is scheduled to meet tonight."

Al-Walid lifted his eyebrows at me as if apologizing for the interruption. "Why are you telling me this?" he barked. "Of course you will have them all arrested."

"Some of them are prominent men," the messenger said. "Others are sons of prominent men."

"Arrest them all and bring them to me." Al-Walid excused himself and escorted his visitor from the room. The two Mohammads pulled me out the mosque door, saying hot food and soft beds awaited us. After a month of chewing on dried meat and dates I was eager for a meal. I was not disappointed at the repast laid out for us in the *majlis* of al-Ashtar, the legendary Bedouin warrior.

"I approached 'Amr for a position in his navy, but before he could appoint me, Uthman had deposed him," Hud said over olives, lemony hummus, skewers of lamb, golden wheat bread, saffron-scented rice, and plump figs. "He did it only in order to appoint his foster brother, whom everyone hates. Uthman doesn't listen to anyone except his relatives, and all they want is power, status, and money."

I barely heard a word, so occupied was I filling my stomach—until al-Ashtar entered the room in an undyed linen gown and a matching head-covering with a red band.

"Praise al-Lah, He has sent you at last," he said. "*Yaa* Ali, we have been praying that you would come."

Five or six other men followed him into the *majlis*, all regarding me with faces as bright as those of children beholding a long-lost father.

"I told you we would succeed in meeting Ali, with the help of al-Lah," al-Ashtar said to his men. They settled themselves on cushions, and servants carried in fresh platters of food. He nodded at the Mohammads. "And with the help of these two, also. Now, we can begin the task to which al-Lah has called us."

I turned to Mohammad with lifted eyebrows. His face pinkened, but his eyes shone at al-Ashtar's praise.

"Yes, *abi*, I brought you here for a purpose," my son said. "Your time has arrived, and with it a new era for *islam*."

I stared at him, dumbfounded. The boy sounded full of zeal, like myself at his age.

"My time for what?" I asked, although I had already discerned the answer. I held my expression still lest my feelings—apprehension, excitement, disbelief, fear—shift across my face, exposing my ambivalence. Indecision was a weakness that I would not want anyone to see except my cherished wife, Asma, who had held me in her arms during long nights and assured me that no one truly knows himself.

"For the *khalifa*!" Hud leaned forward so that his knees touched the floor, threatening to topple him into the bowl of hummus. He jabbed the air with a crust of bread. "It should have been yours all along. You're next in line to the Prophet."

"Lower your voice," I rasped. If anyone heard this mutinous talk, we might all be executed.

"I am aware of my lineage," I said, and then, noticing the shadow of petulance crossing his face, I reached for a piece of bread to stab playfully back at him. "But the *khalifa* belongs to Uthman."

"Uthman is no leader," al-Ashtar said. "His cousin, Marwan, that fox, is making the decisions."

I shrugged. Behind every ruler is a wily advisor.

"Marwan is also stealing from the treasury," al-Ashtar said. "He has taken thousands of dinars. I learned this when 'Amr was governor of Egypt. Marwan rode into Alexandria, demanded the keys to the treasury, and stuffed his purse with gold and jewels. He left with heavy pouches and a light step. 'Tell anyone, and I will have you deposed,' he threatened. 'Amr told Uthman, and one week later he had lost his position."

I frowned. I had never cared for Marwan—he smiled all the time and talked excessively—but I had regarded him as harmless. I had never believed the characterizations of Uthman as corrupt. Muhammad had respected him, and who besides my cousin was a more able judge of men? Yet al-Ashtar's accusations made sense.

"*Yaa* Ali, we have decided to rid *islam* of this scourge," al-Ashtar said.

"Scourge?" *Run*, a voice in my head urged. *Get out now, before it is too late*. Yet I knew al-Ashtar would be a dangerous enemy, and the wildness in his eyes warned me not to incur his displeasure. I glanced downward and busied my hands with dipping bread into hummus. "Do you seek to eliminate Marwan, then? You have said that he is the corrupt one."

"I speak of Uthman ibn 'Affan." He lunged forward and grasped my robe. Holding me with both hands, he pushed his face so close to mine that I could feel the spray of his words on my skin.

"Uthman must go," he said. "His weakness is destroying *islam*. He has allowed his relatives to plunder our treasuries. He has ignored our pleas for mercy while his cousins and brothers inflict cruelties on the innocent. He condones drunkenness, greed, and lasciviousness. He changed the *qur'an* and altered the rituals of the *hajj*."

"All you say is true, al-Ashtar," I said, trying to maintain an even voice. "Yet I do not know what you would have me do. Uthman does not consult with me. He listens to Marwan only, as you stated."

Al-Ashtar released my robe and sat back on his cushion. "What would we have you do? Is that not obvious?"

My son cleared his throat. "*Yaa abi*, we want you for the *khalifa*." His eyes seemed to be sending me an urgent message but I could not hear his thoughts.

"When Uthman dies—" I began, but al-Ashtar cut me off.

"We want you for the *khalifa*," he said. "Now."

As I stared at him, unable to believe the suggestion behind his words—mutiny! perhaps even murder—we heard the slamming of a door, then shouts. My son leapt to his feet and gripped the hilt of his sword. His face was pale. I stood beside him with my blade in hand. "Do not be the first to attack," I murmured. "It will only give them a reason to kill you."

"Let them try," Mohammad said. Yet when the men burst into the *majlis*, his hands fell away from his weapons. The ten of us could not hope to subdue these thirty big warriors, all in armor, with their swords drawn. Their leader was the man who had interrupted my talk with al-Walid earlier that day with news of a secret meeting.

"You are under arrest by order of the mayor al-Walid ibn 'Uqba," the man said.

"Arrest? We are merely sharing a meal," al-Ashtar said, struggling against his captor's effort to constrain him. "When did that become a crime?"

"When the purpose of the meeting is to plot the overthrow of our *khalifa*," al-Walid's man said. "By al-Lah, I hope you filled your bellies, because it is the last meal any of you will enjoy for a long time—perhaps forever."

A'isha

While the governor of Kufa was riding into Medina with Ali in his custody, I sat in the cooking tent hiding from the afternoon sun and arguing with my sister-wives about Uthman. Like everyone else in the *umma*, each of us had an opinion that all the arguments in Hijaz wouldn't change.

"He has the heart of a lamb," Saffiya said, eyeing the new bracelet Uthman had given to her.

"And the cunning of a fox," Raihana scoffed. "*Habibati*, no man gives jewelry like that unless he wants something in return."

"Or unless he has already procured what he desires," Maymunah said with a sly, sidewise glance. Saffiya opened her mouth to protest, but Umm Salama cut her off.

"It is not necessary to be unkind," she said calmly. "Uthman is a man of honor."

"Honor?" Hafsa snorted as she drew henna designs on my hands. "What's so honorable about letting your friends and relatives plunder the people's treasuries?"

"I see no honor in his harsh treatment of those who disagree with him," Juwairriyah said. "My father used to say that new points of view enriched the tapestry of government. As leader of our tribe, he listened to every man."

"Uthman listens to women," Saffiya said with a little smile. "He likes women."

"So we've noticed," Raihana quipped. Maymunah laughed, as eager as ever to discredit Uthman.

Ramlah, on the other hand, staunchly supported him. "My cousin Uthman is the best of men, and was beloved by our own Muhammad, do not forget," she said, never looking up from the sewing in her lap.

Hearing her call Muhammad "our own"—as if her father, Abu Sufyan, hadn't tried to kill him many times—made me grit my teeth. "*Yaa* Ramlah, Muhammad died twenty-four years ago," I said. "Would he approve of Uthman's actions today?"

"Now, A'isha, none of us can answer that question," Sawdah said, trying to keep the peace.

"But we can guess!" Hafsa cried. She lifted her brush and jabbed it in the air. "Uthman promised to follow Muhammad's example, and my father's, also. Yet I've seen him do nothing good."

"His first years as *khalifa* were not controversial," Ramlah pointed out.

"Beginning with his appointment by his brother-in-law?" Maymunah huffed. Beads of sweat popped onto her brow, which she dabbed with her scarf. "That display of favoritism set the tone."

"A'isha knew Muhammad best." Saffiya grasped my hands, hoping I'd redeem her beloved patron. "*Yaa* A'isha, what do you think about Uthman? What would Muhammad think?"

All heads turned toward me, the first-wife of the *harim*, Mother of the Believers, and now, apparently, the authority on the Prophet Muhammad. I stared back at them, not sure what to say.

What *would* Muhammad think about Uthman? How could I know when I wasn't sure what *I* thought? I'd been relieved when he was appointed, because it meant Ali wouldn't be our next *khalifa*. I'd never considered him a strong leader, but I didn't dislike him. He'd always treated me with respect. And, in truth, during his first half-dozen years as *khalifa*, I'd had few complaints about his rule.

Ever since Talha's wedding, though—a sad event that I kept trying to forget—I'd begun to see Uthman in a new light. His harsh treatment of Ibn Masud had shown me an arrogance I'd never even suspected. Then he'd cut my pension. *I have heard complaints that you hold yourself above your sister-wives, yaa A'isha. I do not believe these rumors, but I have no wish to fuel hostility in the Prophet's household by giving you more than they receive.* I was glad for the veil that covered my smirking lips. It was clear to me why he was reducing my income, and my sister-wives had nothing to do with it. He was punishing me for publicly chastising him.

Muhammad might have approved of Uthman's decision, since he'd been careful to treat all of us wives the same. But he would have cried to see poor Ibn Masud writhing on the ground. He also would have deposed al-Walid and ordered him flogged for his drunkenness. Uthman, however, had refused to admit there was a problem, and had lost respect from members of the *umma.*

Now Ali stood accused of conspiring to overthrow Uthman, a charge that, if true, would have angered Muhammad. I, also, frowned on talk of mutiny, but I understood the frustration behind it. Every day I had more difficulty defending our *khalifa,* even to myself. Instead, my criticisms became more vocal, until I hated the sound of my own strident tone. To quell my dissenting voice, Uthman had banned me from the meetings in the *majlis*. For the first time since girlhood, I had to lurk in the shadows and spy in order to stay informed.

Listening outside the doorway one morning, I'd heard the news about Ali's arrest. Uthman's slippery advisor, Marwan, told the tale with a quaver of glee, but Uthman had shaken his head and said he didn't believe Ali would plot to overthrow him.

"I and he served Muhammad together as Companions," he said. "Ali is a man of integrity. His accusers are mistaken."

But Marwan had spoken forcefully and persuasively against Ali. "*Yaa* cousin, who has more to gain from your abdication than Ali ibn Abi Talib?" he said. "Abu Bakr and Umar both watched him with a wary eye. Follow their example. Do not underestimate Ali's power, or you may lose yours."

As much as I distrusted Marwan, I couldn't help agreeing with him. As a youth, Ali had been quick to brandish his sword and call for attacks against the enemy. I could easily imagine him doing the same in Kufa during his meeting with al-Ashtar. He'd claimed that they'd only been planning a demonstration against Uthman, but the Ali I knew would have urged the others to rebel. He'd never been good at compromise, and I guessed that, with the *khalifa* at his fingertips, he'd be more excitable now than ever.

As I pondered Saffiya's question—what would Muhammad have wanted?—my sister-wives watched me, waiting for my answer. "I—I think Uthman has made some mistakes," I said. "But he is the *khalifa*, and he deserves our support."

A shout from outside the tent interrupted our talk—a man's shout, familiar to my leaping heart, calling for Umm Salama. My body quivered like a plucked *tanbur* string when Talha thrust his face into the cooking tent.

"*Afwan*," he said "I am sorry to intrude, but Umm Salama must come now. Your brother is hurt, *yaa* Umm Salama. A'isha, we also need you and your medicine bag."

Our group rushed outdoors, with me in the rear. To my surprise, Talha stood at the tent as though waiting for me to appear. I averted my eyes to the ground, avoiding his insistent gaze, and hurried past him to my hut, where I grabbed my medicine pouch and some bandages. When I stepped outside, a sob cracked the air.

Across the courtyard, next to the mosque entrance, Umm Salama knelt beside her brother, her long, loose hair like a waterfall of tears covering him from sight. I ran over to them and gasped at the sight of Ammar, whose face and hair glistened with blood.

"By al-Lah, what has happened to my brother?" Umm Salama glared at the men who'd carried him in: the narrow-faced Marwan with his skeletal sunken cheeks and snapping eyes; Talha, who'd made his way through the crowd of exclaiming sister-wives to return to Ammar's side; and al-Zubayr, who cradled the poor man's head in his lap.

"*Yaa* Umm Salama—" Talha began, but Marwan cut him off with a tone as sharp as his nose.

"Your brother is a traitor." He spat on the ground. "He accused our *khalifa* of deception and thievery, after we so graciously made him a governor. Perhaps after today he will think one thousand and one times before displaying such ingratitude to the beneficent Uthman."

Having finished his speech, Marwan turned and walked into the mosque. When he had gone, Talha told us what had happened.

"Ammar came into the mosque and confronted Uthman about jewels missing from the Medina treasury." He glanced at Saffiya's braceleted arm, then away. "They belonged to a woman whose husband had offered them as security in lieu of taxes, while he awaited a payment on his date crop. Uthman's new wife, Naila, was seen wearing a necklace of lapis lazuli recently. One of the missing pieces fits that description."

"And a ruby bracelet, I'll bet," Raihana drawled. Talha reddened, but not as vividly as Saffiya. She yanked back her arm, hiding her bracelet under her sleeve.

As for me, I cared only about poor Ammar. His every breath was a labored gasp as Talha and al-Zubayr carried him into Umm Salama's hut. As I smeared a soothing sandalwood paste on his skin and then applied bandages, my pulse increased from a slow thud to a rapid drumbeat, calling me to action.

"By al-Lah, this can't continue!" I forced my trembling hands to fasten Ammar's bandages gently. Red bled at the edges of my vision until, finished at last, I fled to my hut.

I paced my floor for long minutes, Ammar's whimpers haunting me, Marwan's contempt setting my teeth on edge. When had honesty become a crime? My father had been called *al-Siddiq*, "the Truthful." Muhammad's nickname had been *al-Amin*, "the Trusty." What would they say now to the terrible punishment of men who followed their example? What would they do to correct it? *Help me, al-Lah. Show me Your way.*

I stopped my frantic pacing and began to breathe more slowly and deeply. My confused thoughts dissipated like dust clouds and I focused on Muhammad's bejeweled sword, lying on a shelf, waiting for its moment of glory. *Use it well in the* jihad *to come.* My beloved's words rang in my ears as if he were speaking them now. I reached for the sword but my hands fell instead on Muhammad's relics, lying beside the sword: his long, dark curls, snipped from his head before his burial and bound at the ends with string; his linen shirt, unwashed since the last time he'd worn it; and one of his sandals, made of twine and goatskin, poorly mended many times by Muhammad.

After insisting these past two years that the *khalifa* should be respected, and after criticizing those who talked of a revolt, how could I, the Mother of the Believers, approach Uthman with a sword in hand? My goal was to show the *khalifa* how far he had strayed from Muhammad's example, and from the Prophet's vision for *islam*. What could be more effective than presenting him with these items, which still contained Muhammad's essence?

I wrapped them carefully in a piece of cloth and carried them to the mosque—but Marwan, sitting in the cushioned, gold-trimmed chair that Uthman had placed on the *minbar* for himself, informed me that the *khalifa* had retired for the day. "He has left me in charge of the *umma*'s affairs," he said, looking down his nose at me. "Which, naturally, refers to the concerns of men."

I stomped out the front door of the mosque and into the street, heading for Uthman's palatial home on the edge of town—another change that Muhammad wouldn't have liked. As Medina had doubled in size with converts from our conquered lands, the squalid tent city, once on the far edge of Medina, became the center of town. Convinced by Marwan that the *khalifa* belongs in the center of the city—and wanting to claim the now-valuable land—Uthman had sent the tent city's residents again to the far edge of Medina and put his three-storey white palace in their place. Then he'd sold the rest of the land to other wealthy men, where they'd built their own fabulous houses with terraces, fountains, shaded patios, and rooftop gardens. It was there that I expected to find him, resting under the canopy in his leafy courtyard and sipping galangal water while his new wife fanned him with date-palm leaves.

I was surprised to see him strolling through the market in his saffron robe, nibbling meat from a skewer and plucking roses from the arms of Abu Hurayra, who walked beside him, to present to the young women he encountered. His smile widened when he saw me, and he pulled a yellow rose from Abu Hurarya's gourd.

"*Marhaba*, A'isha," he said, holding the flower out to me. "You look as if you might desire some brightness in your day."

The roses' cloying fragrance made me want to retch. I snatched the flower from his hand and flung it to the ground, then stomped on it with my bare foot, heedless of the thorns. "This is truly a dark day," I said. "I have just come from the bedside of Ammar, who lies near death by your command, punished for telling the truth."

I heard gasps and murmurs. I looked around me at the faces of my neighbors, *shaykhs* like Ibn Masud and young men like Ammar, beautiful women like Saffiya smiling coyly and sniffing the roses bestowed upon them by their charming *khalifa*—women who had no idea what Uthman ibn 'Affan had become. Did I want to humiliate him before these people, his admirers? Did I want to incite them against him?

Just behind Uthman I spotted Umm 'Umara, the warrior woman I had envied long ago at the Battle of Uhud, one of our early fights against the Meccan Quraysh. She was an old woman now with skin as tough as untanned leather, and she had been given no flower while the lovely young woman beside her held a rose of brilliant red. Uthman had overlooked the old *hajja*, who'd saved Muhammad's life in that battle, because she had nothing to offer him in return. Raihana had spoken the truth: Uthman gave generously to those who could benefit him with money, status, or, in a woman's case, a pretty smile. Those who had nothing to offer received nothing, and if they dared question him, they were whipped, imprisoned, or killed. They were the people I was speaking for—those to whom Muhammad had given a voice, which Uthman had taken away. As the Mother of the Believers, I was well suited to defend them, because not even Marwan would harm a single hair on my head. Muhammad watched, as did Believers everywhere.

I pulled out the shirt, the sandal, and the hair, and held them high overhead.

"How soon you have forgotten the ways of the Prophet, even though these parts of him have not perished!" I cried. Uthman's eyes bulged at the sight of the relics, and his face turned as pale as if he beheld a *djinni*. The crowd drew closer.

"The Prophet gave to the poor, while you take their lands away," I said. "The Prophet respected the truth, while you abuse it. The Prophet despised corruption, greed, and drunkenness, while you tolerate these sins."

"By al-Lah, she speaks truly!" Abu Ramzi, the jeweler, selling necklaces at a stall, called out. "The Prophet gave everything away and kept nothing for himself, while Uthman gives nothing away and keeps all for himself."

"Unless you are a member of his family," Umm 'Umara cried. "Or a young woman at the height of her beauty." She snatched the rose from the woman next to her and flung it to the ground, then stomped it with her foot the way I had done.

"Hail, Mother of the Believers!" she cried, lifting her hands toward me. "Uthman imprisoned my grandson for refusing to sell his date-palm plantation to Marwan. That was land the Prophet gave to me for my bravery."

Other shouts arose from the crowd, and fists began to wave. "His governor Sa'id in Basra forced my daughter to dance for him," I heard someone cry. "She was a woman of virtue, yet Uthman did nothing to punish Sa'id."

From the corner of my eye, I saw a tall, dark-skinned man pull out his sword. Alarmed, I leapt atop a date-palm stump and spread my arms, showing that I carried no blade.

"Please, put away your weapons," I said. Inciting a *fitna*, or battle between Muslims, had not been my intention. "Our *khalifa* was chosen by al-Lah, and deserves our respect," I said. "Do not forget: *Islam* means 'submission.'"

"But did not the Prophet say, 'If people see *munkar* and they do not try to remedy it, they incur divine punishment'?"

The voice behind me felt like fingertips on my skin. I turned to see Talha, his sword in hand, his hazel eyes muddled with darkness. He must have heard that I was in the market confronting Uthman, and come to protect me.

I nodded to him. "Muhammad did admonish us to remedy injustice. That is why I've come today, to ask Uthman to correct these errors. But, as you see, I've left my sword at home. Would our Prophet want us to use our weapons against his dear Companion?"

"Make way! Let me through. I have urgent news for the *khalifa*."

Marwan elbowed his way into the melee, glaring at me as he swept past. He murmured something in Uthman's ear, then whipped out his sword and waved it around, sending men and women stumbling backward to avoid its sting.

"Go home, all of you," he snarled. "Or you'll find yourselves in the desert before nightfall, looking for new homes."

"Death to Uthman!" someone cried as the crowd dispersed. Marwan whirled around to discern who had made the threat, but it was impossible to pick out the angriest face—other than Uthman's.

I leapt to the ground and stood before him, my relics still in hand. "*Yaa* Uthman, the people are becoming more agitated with each abuse," I said. "You know this is not what Muhammad would have wanted."

"God damn you, A'isha," Uthman said in a low growl. "What are you doing? I was enjoying a pleasant afternoon until you appeared. If the people are agitated, it is because of you, not me. And if you continue with these confrontations, I will assign a guard to keep you in your hut."

Marwan's eyes glinted. "An excellent idea, *yaa khalifa*." How I wished for my sword then, so that I might silence him once and for all. He placed a hand on Uthman's plump waist and steered him toward the mosque. "*Yaa khalifa*, you are needed in the mosque," he murmured. "Your brother al-Walid is here with Ali."

Uthman stopped and exchanged whispers with Marwan. Then he turned to face me again. "*Yaa* A'isha, good news," he said, smiling. "I am permitting you to make the pilgrimage to Mecca this season. Matters here will detain me this year, but I have appointed the son of al-Abbas to lead the caravan. It departs tonight. I trust you will join it, for I may revoke the privilege again next year."

"That snake," Talha said as the pair walked away. "You know he wants to get rid of you, A'isha. This is a dangerous time for Uthman, and he doesn't want the Mother of the Believers here to make things more difficult."

"By al-Lah, he doesn't need my help for that," I said. "He's destroying everything Muhammad built, and the people won't endure it much longer. However, I will go on the *hajj*. Then, when he's turned the entire *umma* against him, he'll have no one to blame but himself."

"I could use your support here in Medina," he said softly.

I felt my blood rise. "You have Umm Kulthum for that, remember?" I snapped. I couldn't help wondering: Why had Talha come today? To protect me, as I'd first assumed? Or to place himself in line for the *khalifa* with me at his side?

"A'isha," he said, "I married Umm Kulthum for your sake. You asked me to, remember? Since our wedding, you've avoided me. Two years, A'isha! If you looked into my eyes, you would see the same love I have always felt for you. We were once so close. We shared the same vision for *islam*. We still do. Unless you've changed."

I looked up into Talha's eyes, and, yes, something *was* different. Gone was the breathless, trusting love that had once swept over me whenever he was near. It had vanished when I'd seen the sultry gaze he'd given my sister at their wedding—a look I'd thought he reserved for me alone. The pain I'd felt had reminded me of the tears I'd shed whenever Muhammad had married a new bride. He'd take a wife supposedly for political reasons, but then, during the ceremony, gaze at her as adoringly as if she were his only wife. I'd thought Talha was marrying Umm Kulthum out of love for me, but his face had shone at their wedding. Now I wondered: What did he *really* want? My love, or my influence?

"*Marhaba,* Talha, my old friend." I turned to see 'Amr ibn al-As, Egypt's conqueror, a broad-shouldered man with pure black eyes and a trim beard sprinkled with gray. He seized Talha's beard and then smiled at me. "*Yaa* Mother of the Believers, your speech was eloquent and full of truth, as usual."

"*Marhabtein.*" Talha grinned at his old battle companion. "What brings you to Medina, *sahib*?"

'Amr glanced to the left and to the right, then lowered his voice. "Come with me to al-Zubayr's home, and you will find out."

They started to walk slowly away, leaving me there in the street with Muhammad's shirt, sandal, and hair. Whether or not Talha loved me, it was clear that he still wanted the *khalifa*. Did his meeting with 'Amr have anything to do with that? Could anything good come of colluding with this conqueror, who bore a grudge against Uthman for deposing him? I tried to call out, to warn Talha, but I only made a strangled sound. Yet it was enough to turn the heads of Talha and 'Amr.

'Amr smiled at me again. "*Yaa* Mother of the Believers, will you join us there? Please wait five minutes and then come in without knocking. It is best if you are not seen with me."

My body tensed, as if I were riding a horse headed for the edge of a cliff. I knew I should refuse, but I was curious.

"Are you sure you want me?" I said. "I'm just a woman."

Talha grinned. "*Yaa* A'isha, you are more than just a woman. You are *the* woman. The Mother of the Believers. Of course we want you."

He stepped back over to me and looked deeply into my eyes.

"Please join us, A'isha," he said softly. "You have much to offer. Look at what you did today!"

And then he said the words I'd yearned to hear from him for so long.

"Of course we want you, A'isha," he said. "*I* want you. More now than ever before."

Ali

During my years as a warrior, I saw men's faces writhe in anguish as they beheld my uplifted sword. Their eyes held a terror that anticipated the agony and annihilation of death. I had not encountered fear's disfigurement since the days of Muhammad, when I had last wielded my sword in battle. But I saw it on Uthman's face when his brother al-Walid led me into the mosque with chains binding my hands. Behind us, a rabble of shouting malcontents from Kufa, Basra, and Egypt streamed in, making a noise as mighty and alarming as if the earth had split asunder.

Uthman beheld me in those chains and his mouth trembled. For all his foolish mistakes in recent years, he saw clearly the error his brother had committed in humiliating me, the father of the Prophet's heirs. It would have been better for al-Walid to behead me in Kufa and declare me a traitor than to lead me, shackled and weak, into Medina before the eyes of my relatives and supporters.

Even worse for Uthman was this: My son Mohammad and his friends, exiled to Egypt, had learned of al-Walid's journey and hastily convened a group to support my cause. They'd escaped from prison and fled to Kufa to occupy al-Walid's palace and rally men in that city, as well. In Basra, Kufa's sister city, malcontents had also gathered. They all rode forth, then converged at Mecca and marched as one to Medina. Meanwhile, that tippler al-Walid dragged me through the desert, my wrists bound so tightly that I lost feeling in my hands, my mouth parched from the paltry amount of water he allowed me, and my feet blistering from the heat of the sand he made me stumble through while he rode, jerking my tether. Only when I fainted would he allow me to slump over a camel's back, and then only until I recovered from my swoon. Each loss of consciousness was a blessing, not only because it afforded me a ride, but also because it silenced my fears. What form of torture would Marwan inflict for this charge of treason? How could I convince Uthman of my innocence? Why would he believe me, when neither Abu Bakr nor Umar had trusted me? *Help me, al-Lah, to survive.*

God answered my prayers as we neared Medina. The rebels joined us on the outskirts of town, provoking glares from al-Walid and his warriors but nothing more, for these protesters numbered in the thousands. At the gates, one hundred of these men continued into the city with us. I and al-Walid entered the mosque as in an angry swarm. Uthman, sitting on his elaborate throne of ivory and gold, stood as quickly as his aged legs would allow and ordered his wine-stinking brother to release me without delay.

Al-Walid shrugged, too relaxed by his breakfast imbibing to generate enthusiasm for any effort except another drink, and gestured to his men to free me. No sooner had the chains clanked to the floor than did our escorts begin to cheer and chant my name. I rubbed the soreness from my wrists and ankles and willed myself to remain standing. Uthman descended the steps to stand before me, his eyes glaring but his mouth as soft as a lover's. He was waiting for me to thank him, but I was too dizzy and sick to think. In the next moment he slapped me so hard that I fell to my knees, my ears ringing.

"Were you plotting my overthrow?" he shouted over the protests of the rebels. "My heart sickens to hear this charge."

"It is but a rumor, *yaa khalifa*, and a false one," I said, spitting blood and struggling to my feet.

Al-Walid burst into laughter. Uthman turned to him.

"He was dining with al-Ashtar, who has escaped from prison with the help of his friends and now occupies the governor's palace in my absence," al-Walid said.

The mercurial al-Ashtar, leader of these dissidents, pushed his way through the Kufan guards.

"As you can see, *yaa khalifa*, I occupy no palace," al-Ashtar said. "I have come with an urgent petition to correct the injustices that your governors in Kufa, Basra, and Fustat have imposed."

Uthman drew his mouth into a tight frown as he turned to his brother. Al-Walid's bald head had turned a fiery red and he was glaring at al-Ashtar with bulging, blood-shot eyes.

"Is it as this man says, *yaa* brother?"

The drunken man emitted a guttural sound not unlike Mount Layla's belching before she had rained brimstone upon our city a few years before.

"How dare you insult me with this ridiculous question?" he screamed at Uthman, who drew back from him. "You would take the word of this camel's teat over that of your beloved brother?"

Uthman hastened to ascend his platform in time to avoid the spray of outrage spluttering forth from al-Walid's mouth.

"Do you not know me after all these years?" the governor continued to shout, turning now to rail at the empty mosque. "Brother, instead of challenging me you should be flogging these traitors with barbed whips! You should remove their heads with dull blades! By God, I should have done that deed for you. By God, I will do it now!"

He clumsily pulled his sword from the sheath under his arm and stumbled toward al-Ashtar, who sidestepped him with a flourish. The raging drunkard fell to his knees on the floor, the position I had occupied only moments earlier. Al-Walid's guards assisted him to his feet. After brushing himself off with great care, he thrust out his chin and reeled toward the mosque entrance, anticipating, no doubt, his next draught from the flagon on his horse's saddle.

"By al-Lah, *yaa* brother, you have filled me full of shame," al-Walid said over his shoulder. "I will retire to my quarters and await your apology."

I heard laughter and looked to the courtyard entrance where Talha was winking at al-Zubayr and nudging the arm of the broad-shouldered general 'Amr. Beside Talha stood A'isha, properly covered, for a change, yet affecting a stance—feet wide apart, arms folded across her chest—that indicated her attitude was far from demure. Unlike in the past, however, I did not resent her presence in the mosque. She, at least, was willing to confront Uthman over his unjust behavior.

Uthman glared at them as the Egyptians shouted and embraced their beloved 'Amr.

"Here, *khalifa,* is our choice for Fustat." Al-Ashtar gestured toward 'Amr. "Reappoint 'Amr as governor of Egypt and we will be appeased."

Uthman sighed and sat heavily on his throne. "I do not know," he said. He closed his eyes and leaned his head against the back of his chair. "Can I unseat Abdullah? He is my foster brother. And he was an early Companion to Muhammad."

"Yes, and the worst kind of Companion!" A'isha called out. "First Abdullah pretended to be a Believer; then he went to Mecca and told lies about Muhammad."

Uthman sat up quickly and pointed at A'isha. "I banished you from these meetings!" he cried. "Go to your hut, and do not come out until I summon you."

Shouts of outrage filled the mosque from the rebels who stood behind me. Encouraged by their support, A'isha walked into the mosque to stand before the *minbar,* her chin lifted even higher than before. Uthman slumped in his seat again like a sail that has lost its wind.

"Yes, A'isha, Abdullah offended the Prophet, but the Prophet forgave him." Marwan entered the mosque. His narrow eyes jerked about, taking in the gathering: I and the rebels; Talha and his cohorts; A'isha, openly returning his gaze and inspiring me to do the same; and Uthman, slumping in his king's throne and appearing anything but royal.

Marwan's sandals slapped across the tile floor and against the marble steps as he ascended the platform. He settled himself on a second throne, newly installed for him, of polished wood.

Uthman continued to sprawl in his chair like a drooling old *shaykh.* Marwan tapped a forefinger against his chin and perused us like a slave buyer eyeing shoddy merchandise. "*Yaa* Mother of the Believers, why have you not embarked on the *hajj,* as the *khalifa* so generously permitted?" he said.

"Al-Abbas's son has delayed the caravan's departure, at my request," she said, turning her focus to Uthman and ignoring the impertinent Marwan, who behaved increasingly as if he were the *khalifa.* Gossips said that Marwan had put himself forth as Uthman's successor. Uthman had been wise not to assent, for the day he agreed would be his final day on earth. He would die either by Marwan's hand or that of al-Ashtar, who would do anything to prevent Marwan from becoming *khalifa.* Over supper in Kufa the night we were arrested, al-Ashtar told me how he had risked his life long ago to carry the injured Marwan off the battlefield—and then been insulted in return.

"Instead of thanking me, he called me a 'filthy Bedouin,'" al-Ashtar had said. "He complained that, because I had touched him, he would have to be purified." For this humiliation, al-Ashtar nurtured a vicious grudge.

A'isha, on the other hand, advocated negotiation, not killing. "*Yaa khalifa,* I strongly advise you to listen to these men," she said.

"I do not recall your being asked—" Marwan began, but A'isha interrupted him, gaining another measure of esteem from me.

"Uthman, they came all this way to talk to you," she said. "And they're only asking you to appoint a new governor in Egypt. It seems like a fair request."

Cheers arose from the rebels, which brought Marwan to his feet. "Enough!" he cried. "You have overstepped your boundaries. Abdullah and al-Walid will remain in office at the command of the *khalifa*. Now, depart before I call our guards, who will show you Bedouin scum how *real* men behave."

His insult fanned the flames of the rebels, who would have rushed onto the platform and attacked him with their swords if al-Ashtar had not urged me to the front alongside A'isha.

"*Yaa khalifa,* Abdullah has been a cruel governor," I said. Marwan began to speak but Uthman, sitting up, shook his head at him.

"If you knew the tales I have heard, you would be aghast," I said. "Muhammad would not want any Muslim to be abused as these men have. As for al-Walid, his weaknesses outnumber his strengths. It would be better to keep him in Medina as your advisor than to leave him to his own counsel in Kufa."

"We want 'Amr!" al-Ashtar shouted. " 'Amr in Egypt and Mohammad ibn Abi Bakr in Kufa."

Marwan's eyes glinted. "Mohammad ibn Abi Bakr is your stepson, is he not, Ali? It is no wonder that you have allied yourself with these men. His appointment would certainly enhance your status."

I flushed. "I was not aware of any movement to have my son appointed governor," I said. "Although, in truth, he would perform excellently."

"'Amr and Mohammad! 'Amr and Mohammad!" the men cried, rushing to the platform and crowding so closely around me and A'isha that we were pushed against each other. Her wrapper fell from her face and her eyes widened in alarm as we were jostled about. She appeared so tiny and fragile that I feared she might be crushed against the marble, but when I reached out an arm to protect her, she whirled around, narrowed her eyes at seeing me so close, then leapt onto the platform.

"*Yaa* Uthman, do something!" she cried, holding her sword high in defiance of the mob. She refused to meet my eyes, although I could not remove my gaze from the sight of her. She was so courageous and strong, not like any woman I had ever seen and certainly not the rude, brash girl I had once despised.

Marwan said something into the ear of Uthman, who nodded and then stood. He walked to the edge of the platform with his hands out to quell the crowd.

"I will do as you ask," he said. " 'Amr will be governor of Egypt and Mohammad ibn Abi Bakr may rule Kufa. Forgive me for ignoring your complaints for so long. My territory is vast, and there is always much to be done. Now, please, in the name of al-Lah, go home, and allow the Mother of the Believers safe passage to her hut."

He inclined his head toward me. "As for you, Ali, it is evident that you sympathize with the rebels' complaints but not their tactics. I am dismissing the charges against you. You are free—but, in the future, choose your dining companions more wisely."

The room fell silent as we men regarded one another in stunned shock. Had Uthman capitulated so easily? Relief washed over me and I uttered a prayer of thanks to al-Lah.

"I thought we would have to negotiate for weeks or even months," Mohammad said as we filed out the front door.

"Did you see that scoundrel Marwan whispering in Uthman's ear?" Al-Ashtar's laugh was coarse. "By al-Lah, he is plotting something evil or I am not a filthy Bedouin."

"*Yaa* Mohammad, that sister of yours is quite persuasive," Hud said. "I'll bet 'Amr is glad to have her on his side."

I bade farewell to al-Ashtar and my son at the city's main gate, declining their request that I join them for the evening meal. I had already endured weeks of imprisonment because of associating with al-Ashtar and his group, who were, in truth, too radical for my liking. *Thank you, al-Lah, for Uthman's acquiescence.* If he had not accommodated them in some measure, they would take his head, or Marwan's.

Uthman had spoken truly: Although I agreed with the rebels' complaints, I did not wish harm upon the *khalifa*. If any life was sacred, it was that of Muhammad's successor. Al-Lah had rid the *umma* of that usurper Abu Bakr only two years after he had deceived his way into the position. Would God allow Uthman to rule for twelve if He had not wanted him for the *khalifa*?

But I also denied the men's dining invitation for another reason: I wanted to be alone to ponder all that had happened today, from the unexpected appearance of the rebels outside the city gates to Uthman's refusal to acknowledge his brother's drunken behavior, to my shocking response to A'isha—admiration!—on the mosque floor. I walked slowly down the street to my home—but then, at the door, turned away. I needed to delay the cacophony of wives, concubines, and children for just a few minutes more. As I walked to the *hammam*, the public baths, I pondered the day's occurrences, as well as the question that Hud had posed: What *did* A'isha gain from helping 'Amr?

I recalled the scene in the entryway, when the laughing Talha had winked at al-Zubayr, then 'Amr, and I knew. Placing 'Amr back in Egypt would be the first step toward procuring the *khalifa* for Talha—and, in A'isha's view, power for herself. For I knew that, being a woman and therefore unable to claim the position, she would instead sit by Talha's side and issue commands for him to carry out. Or so she mistakenly imagined. Judging from what I had heard between Talha and Mu'awiyya that day, Talha's ambitions extended to no one but himself.

◆

As we soon discovered, we were *all* mistaken, every one of us: me, A'isha, Talha, al-Zubayr, 'Amr, al-Ashtar, Mohammad, Hud, and one thousand dissidents. Even Uthman was mistaken, for he apparently thought his decisions would be honored. But as the rebels crossed the desert on their way home, one of their scouts overtook and captured an Abyssinian messenger whose black skin had attracted their notice but whose errand, they discovered, was even darker.

He had in his possession a letter addressed to the Egyptian governor Abdullah and sealed by Uthman's ring. *'Amr is coming with a letter proclaiming that the khalifa has appointed him the new governor. Pay no attention to it. This is a ruse designed to place him in your hands. Dispose of him as you wish.* The treacherous order bore Uthman's signature.

This time, the men did not pitch tents outside Medina's gates. This time, one thousand men crashed into the city like a raging, tumultuous, flooding river, trampling Abu Hurayra's cherished cat, scattering screaming children from the streets and running roughshod over their toys, and summoning me from my home, where I had dandled my delightful baby girl on my knee and amused her with a song. (In truth, this child was the only member of my family able to endure my pitiful, discordant voice.) The clamor of their invasion was so sudden and so heart stopping that I thought Mount Layla had erupted. I jumped to my feet, heedless of the baby's startled cries, placed her in her mother's arms, and ran to the door. A blur of horses' hooves and flowing gowns and snarling men went scudding and tumbling toward the mosque. I turned and ran out the back door of my home to take a more expedient path to the mosque. Inside, I found a white-lipped al-Ashtar, backed by dozens of his followers, screaming at poor Abu Hurayra, who cowered and sniveled and insisted he had only come in search of his cat, Queen of Sheba.

"Why do your eyes dart about as we question you?" Al-Ashtar pointed his dagger at the little man's throat. "You know where the *khalifa* is hidden. Tell us!"

"*Yaa* Ashtar, Uthman has probably retired to his home to escape the afternoon heat, as he does every day," I said. "He will not return until the evening."

"By al-Lah, he will never return!" al-Ashtar cried, and in the next instant he had sprung to his horse's saddle and was leading his men to the palace, where the unsuspecting Uthman lay in the shade beside his fountain enjoying the cool drinks, moist cloths, and breezes from the date-palm fan waved by his lovely young wife Naila.

Sweat poured into my eyes as I hurried to the stable for my horse then rode at full speed to Uthman's palace. As always, I rankled at the ostentatious display of wealth this grand edifice presented. Fashioned not of mud-and-straw bricks as were most homes in Medina, Uthman's palace was built of stones carried in from the cliffs outside the city, large rocks of gray and rose, held in place by thick stripes of white mortar. Instead of the single story or, at most, two, that characterized the ordinary Medina home, Uthman's palace had three floors. Outside, around the ornate fence of stone and its gleaming copper gate, carefully tended roses and pomegranate trees stunned the senses with beauty and fragrance. A whitewashed balcony jutted out over enormous first-floor double doors of polished teak that had been transported on elephants from India. A garden spanned the entire flat roof, its foliage spilling green and flowers over the outside walls. Muhammad would not have liked this house. My cousin had not frowned on wealth that was used for others' good, but he disapproved of any man's flaunting his riches, just as he frowned on women's publicly displaying their beauty. Nevertheless, when I arrived I stopped a group of men from battering down Uthman's gate. As much as I would have enjoyed destroying the shameful structure, so contrary to the teachings of *islam*, I could not condone such violence against our *khalifa*.

Gaining entry to the palace was difficult, for Uthman's servants were allowing no one indoors. Having prepared for this possibility, I attached my ring to an arrow and shot it onto the roof. In moments, Uthman's wife Naila stepped out to the gate and beckoned me inside. The throng of attackers moved aside as I stepped through their midst and into Uthman's home.

To my disgust, the palace's interior was even more opulent than the exterior. The entryway, whose ceiling seemed to reach the heavens, could have held several rooms of my new house. Red and blue carpets from Persia lined the white marble floor, and bejeweled tapestries sparkled from the walls like stars on a clear night. Lamps of ornately worked gold lined the marble stairway, and the mahogany rail gleamed so pristinely that I hesitated to touch it.

Naila climbed the stairs. I followed her into a spacious bedroom containing more rugs, tapestries, and furniture including a bed nearly as large as the mosque's *minbar*. Closets filled with gowns and robes lined the room, their doors gaping like stuffed mouths, their contents spilling onto the floor. Uthman stood before a mirror, donning a rich blue robe embroidered with flowers of gold thread. His fingers were trembling. His wife retrieved the indigo turban she had been winding and placed it on his head.

"I see you are preparing to greet your visitors," I said. "Take care, Uthman, for they aim to seek revenge."

"Revenge?" His voice sounded high and reedy, like the whine of a gnat. "For what, by al-Lah? I gave them everything they asked for."

I showed him the intercepted letter, and his florid skin drained of color. He seized my beard and stared into my eyes. For the second time that day I beheld that desperate, horrified look I had seen on the battlefield so many times.

"B-by al-Lah!" he gasped. "This is not my d-doing."

His shocked response told me he spoke the truth. "You will have to convince al-Ashtar," I said. He started for the door, but I seized his arm. "Not out there," I said, "unless you have ceased to value your life. Uthman, these men want to kill you. Do not place yourself within reach of their sword points. Greet them from your balcony overhead—and wear your chain mail in case someone shoots an arrow at you."

Bewilderment crossed his face, and I realized that he probably did not possess a chain-mail suit or any other battle accoutrements. Uthman had never fought in a battle: not at Badr, for he had remained at the bedside of his dying wife Ruqayya, Muhammad's daughter; nor at Uhud, for he had been among those who fled back to Medina at the first glimpse of the enemy streaming like a silver tide over the sand. Muhammad forgave him for that defection, for he admired the gentleness of his friend's heart despite its timid beat.

I stepped outdoors to inform al-Ashtar that the *khalifa* was preparing to greet them, but then Uthman appeared on the balcony, the letter in his hand. "I did not write this, al-Ashtar," he said in a stronger, more resonant voice than I had ever heard him use. "I demand to know why you forged it. Do you hate me so much that you would invent reasons to kill me?"

"Was that a forgery?" Mohammad yelled. He pushed the Abyssinian captive to the front of the crowd for Uthman to see. "Here is your messenger. If you don't recognize him, say so, and I'll behead him where he stands."

"Rahman," Uthman said. "Of course I know him. He is from my household. You may release him, for he was only obeying a command. Not *my* command, however."

"He lies!" Hud cried.

"Ask the messenger, then," I suggested. I turned to the poor, shivering man and asked who'd given him the letter, but he only shrugged.

"He is mute," Uthman said. "His tongue was cut off when he was younger, as punishment for telling a false tale."

"*Yaa* Uthman," I called, "who can verify that the handwriting in that letter is not yours?"

He frowned. "A'isha has helped me with spelling on some documents. She knows my writing very well. Unfortunately, she may have left on the *hajj* by now."

I had seen her caravan, packed and waiting for the cool of evening, as I had raced my horse down the street to the palace. I turned to Mohammad. "Go and fetch your sister," I said. "She is likely in her hut, resting for tonight's ride."

An excruciating hour passed. Al-Ashtar delegated a group to collect water for the horses, and others opened barley sacks to feed them. Another contingent went out to establish camps before nightfall. Hud complained about the delay, but al-Ashtar gave him a sensible reply. "We must be certain of the *khalifa*'s guilt before we take further action," he said.

To my irritation, he then walked over to stand beside me under the shade of a ghaza'a tree, as though we were colluders in this siege. Yet I did desire to know what the rebels would choose to do. If they decided on violence, I would stop them.

Before I could decide my next course of action, Mohammad appeared with A'isha beside him, attired in a fine linen gown of pink and a robe of dark red, her hair hidden by a white wrapper, her face veiled. She was attired as I had long believed she should be, with the modest demeanor befitting the widow of the Prophet Muhammad. As I looked upon her, I felt a surprising impatience for her to look up into my eyes as she passed.

"Mother of the Believers!" Al-Ashtar bowed before her; she barely inclined her head toward him, I noticed. He noticed it too, and scowled as she swept past him to enter Uthman's house. After many excruciating moments, Uthman, who had disappeared from his perch on the balcony, re-emerged with A'isha at his side.

"*Yaa* Mother of the Believers!" someone shouted. "May al-Lah heap blessings upon you." Soon the air resonated with cries of her name and praise for the Mother of the Believers. Looking up at her, I felt a rush of emotion. How erect was her bearing, how proud and honorable. She cleared her throat. She held up the letter. She glanced down at al-Ashtar—and then at me. Yet in a flicker of her lashes—dismissive? indifferent?—she was lost to me. She turned her gaze upon the shouting, leaping crowd.

"Uthman did not write this letter," she said.

Grumbles rolled across the crowd. "Then who did write it?" Hud shouted. "A *djinni*?"

"I don't know," she said, retaining her calm in spite of the shouts and hisses spluttering through the men. "It was sealed with Uthman's ring, which he has been missing. Perhaps a servant in his household wrote it, or maybe one of his advisors. Whoever it is wanted nothing good for any of you—or for Uthman."

Marwan was the thought that blossomed in my mind at the same time al-Ashtar shouted it. "For the answer, you need look no farther," he said. "Let us confront Marwan. Where is he now, *yaa* Uthman?"

Uthman's scowl seemed directed inward. "I do not know Marwan's whereabouts," he said. "I have not seen him since yesterday, when you all left Medina."

"*Yaa abi*, do not try to protect him," Hud said. "For your own sake, hand him over to us."

A'isha gave the young upstart a pointed look. "*Yaa* Mohammad ibn al-Hudheifa, the *khalifa* said he doesn't know Marwan's whereabouts. Aren't your ears working? Or are you shouting too much to hear what's going on?"

"Uthman is a liar!" someone yelled. I winced at this accusation, knowing it could lead to no good.

"Ignorant old *shaykh*!" another man cried. "His mind is so feeble he doesn't know what is happening in his own household."

Al-Ashtar raised his sword. I hurried away from him, then, not wanting to be associated with this treacherous behavior

"You hear your constituents, Uthman," al-Ashtar said. "They have lost faith in you. It makes no difference who wrote that letter or who used your seal. Either you did it yourself, which makes you a liar and not worthy to rule, or you lack control over your own household, which also renders you unworthy. It is time you stepped down from your position and gave it to another, someone who is ruled by *islam* and not by corrupt family members."

He nodded his head toward the place where I'd stood. Then, when he realized I had moved from my spot under the tree, he glanced around, searching for me. I uttered a prayer of thanks to al-Lah for prompting me to move when I did.

But then the swarm of men beside me parted to a cry of, "Make way for the Companions of Muhammad!" Talha and al-Zubayr hastened with drawn swords and puffed chests to Uthman's front door.

"We have come to offer our protection, *yaa khalifa*," Talha announced. A wave of revulsion crested in the pit of my stomach. For as he stood beneath the balcony flexing his heroic muscles, A'isha gazed upon him with tender admiration. Given our conflicted past, our mistaken present, and our irredeemable future, she would never look at me that way.

A'isha

Uthman begged me not to go.

I would be haunted by the memory for the rest of my life.

He pleaded with me, his eyes red and rheumy, his face drooping, his voice shivering.

"Do not leave me, A'isha. You are a powerful orator. You can change their minds with one speech."

I stared at him. Hadn't he practically pushed me out the city gates, urging me to make this *hajj*? He didn't want me waving around Muhammad's relics again and stirring up trouble. He'd wanted me gone.

Now, after I'd rushed around to find camels, buy food, pack, bathe, and help my sister-wives get ready for the trip, Uthman looked at me with the eyes of a whipped puppy and begged me not to make the *hajj*.

Standing on his balcony after Talha and al-Zubayr had gone and after that traitor Ali had disappeared with his *djinni*-possessed friend al-Ashtar, Uthman pleaded with me to change my plans and stay in Medina.

"You can change their minds, *yaa A'isha*," he said. "Your words would be as charms placed upon their ears."

"Their hearts are what need changing," I said. "Only you can do that."

I turned toward the door, intending to leave, for I had planned to meet in secret with Talha, al-Zubayr, and 'Amr. I felt a tug at my sleeve, and looked down to see Uthman's hand. I yanked my robe out of his grasp and

he grabbed my wrist. I was so astonished that he would touch me that I didn't even try to pull away.

"A'isha, you must forgo this pilgrimage," he said. "You alone can save me. Do you not recall how those men cheered for you? 'Mother of the Believers,' they were chanting. They revere you as if you were their mother! You only have to warn them against harming me, and they will desist. You only have to tell them to return to their homes, and they will obey."

I recalled the glow on the faces of the men today who'd shouted my name and my *kunya,* the honorary name given to women who'd borne a child. Since, to my sorrow, I had never given birth, the title *Umm al-Mommaniin*, "Mother of the Believers"—shared by all my sister-wives—struck an especially poignant note in my heart. Uthman spoke truly: I was like a mother to the people of the *umma.* Perhaps I could persuade his persecutors to leave the city, and the *khalifa*, in peace. But did I want to?

I'd come to Uthman's aid reluctantly today. I'd already heard about the mysterious letter, and I'd guessed that it had been forged, and by whom. Marwan, who would never be able to gain the *khalifa* honestly—for he had neither the credentials nor the integrity to lead us—held too much influence over Uthman. The only way to get rid of Marwan was to remove Uthman from office. Before, I'd stood against ousting the *khalifa*, but now I realized it would be the best thing for the *umma.*

Ai! How wrong I turned out to be! If only I'd listened to my instincts, which told me to leave the *khalifa* in the hands of al-Lah—

Marwan was an evil man. Uthman was merely old and hapless, his mind grown feeble, his judgment compromised by devotion to his family. It wasn't difficult to see what would happen if things went on as they were. Something had to change. In truth, change had come in the form of one thousand men on thundering horses. I had no desire to stop it.

Uthman fell to his knees. Blood rushed to my face and neck. I glanced around to make sure no one watched us. In the doorway his wife Naila stood with a straight back, her black eyes flashing, as if to make up for her husband's lack of pride. I looked down at the weeping Uthman, his gray curls quivering, his hands clasped as if in prayer, his eyes lifted to me, his savior, he said.

"A'isha, have mercy," he said. "Only you can save me."

I had no idea what to do. Not about going to Mecca—I was determined

to make the journey, for I needed guidance from Muhammad about the future of the *umma* and my role in the struggle he'd foretold that seemed, at last, to be at hand. I knew that the rebels wouldn't harm Uthman during this sacred month, for bloodshed was forbidden during the time of the *hajj*. But I didn't know how to get Uthman to his feet, to make him behave with dignity befitting the *khalifa*. I looked over at Naila again. She must have guessed the questions on my furrowed brow, for in the next instant she was gliding across the room, pulling Uthman up off the floor and into her arms and leading him away, cooing to him that he needed rest.

Left alone, I looked over the balcony at our oasis city, green and lush with palm trees and flowers and springs bursting from the earth. The heady fragrance of lavender, which grew in profusion over the hillsides, filled my nose, soothing and uplifting me all at once. It was hard to imagine violence here in this peaceful haven, a refuge for the Believers in our time of persecution and, now, a destination for so many. From Alexandria to Oman to Azerbaijan they came, converts to *islam* desiring to meet the Companions of the Prophet, to see where Muhammad was buried, and to pay homage to his widows, grandsons, and other relatives.

Our latest visitors, it seemed, had come to see Ali. I'd heard them cry out to him, hailing him as "*khalifa*." I'd seen the zeal on their faces. I'd heard the excitement in their voices. And I'd seen him standing with them, not against them, as I'd done—standing beside al-Ashtar, that inciter, more impulsive than Ali had ever been and more dangerous, I feared, than even Marwan.

These men cried out for Uthman to resign, and they wanted Ali in his place. Somehow, they'd decided Ali was next to Muhammad in al-Lah's eyes, that because he'd fathered Muhammad's only surviving male heirs, he carried something special in his blood. To them, Ali was sacred, more so than the *khalifa*. More so than their own lives, which they'd come to risk for his sake.

I couldn't stop them. No matter how well they regarded me, those rebels adored Ali more. If he wanted Uthman dead, they'd kill him.

I went inside. My heart swelled with pity for Uthman, who was not, after all, a bad man. *What should I do, yaa Muhammad?* No answer came to me, but I hadn't really expected one. In Mecca, the city my husband had loved like a mother, I would know his desires.

I climbed the stairs to the rooftop garden, where Uthman lay in the shade under the breeze of Naila's date-palm frond. His eyes were closed; his face, uncreased. He looked so peaceful that I hesitated to disturb him. But the caravan for Medina would be leaving at any moment. Now was the time to make him see the truth.

"*Yaa* Uthman," I said. When he opened his eyes they were bright, hopeful. I swallowed, feeling sorrow like a fist in my throat.

"I am sorry, but I cannot do as you request. I have been unable to make the *hajj* for many years, as you well know, and I cannot miss the opportunity now that it has been granted to me."

"Tarry, A'isha, and I will personally escort you next year," he said, sitting up a little.

I shook my head. "I need to be near Muhammad, to rest my eyes again on the places he loved, to remember being there with him in his last years. I need his counsel, Uthman, more than ever."

He lay back and closed his eyes.

"While I am in Mecca, I will pray for you and your safety," I said. "Although I know al-Lah will protect you from harm. Nothing will happen before I return. This is the sacred month, and those men are Muslims. They won't attack you now."

He lay as still as if he were sleeping, but his deep, resigned sigh told me he was very much awake. I pressed on, speaking more rapidly, imagining I heard the tinkle of the camels' bells as they began the long march to Mecca without me.

"Uthman, please heed my advice and abdicate the *khalifa*," I said. "Al-Ashtar's men have vowed on the black stone of the Ka'ba that they will not leave Medina with you in power. You must remove yourself—or they will remove you."

He sat up quickly, his eyes blazing, and began tying his robe with sure fingers.

"Am I to remove the mantle laid upon me by al-Lah?" he said, and gave me an eerie smile. "No, I do not think so."

My hopes fell like a stone dropped in a deep well. "Talha and al-Zubayr are both good men," I said. "Either of them would gladly serve in your place—"

Uthman's smile became a sardonic laugh. "As would Ali, and Marwan, and every other man in this *umma*," he said. "As would A'isha, if not for her womanhood." He stood up on his own, despite Naila's rushing over from the corner to help, and gave me a fatherly shake of his head. His face, I noticed, was no longer drooping and his voice no longer quavered.

"By insisting on making this *hajj*, you are ensuring my death," he said. "Sacred month or not. But it will be as al-Lah desires. At least, if I am assassinated, *I* will go to my grave with a clear conscience. You, on the other hand, will not be able to do the same."

Ali

Al-Ashtar and his rebels besieged Uthman's palace for weeks. Heedless of the sacred status of the month of the *hajj*, they bragged among themselves about the merciless death they would inflict if the *khalifa* were to leave his home. Their violence confined me also to my house, where I could safely ignore the pleas of both al-Ashtar and Uthman for aid and support. For, while I hated the corruption of Uthman's reign, I abhorred violence against him. Rather than be compelled to join either side, I stayed indoors, away from their eyes and, I hoped, their thoughts.

Sequestered, I remained ignorant of the events at the palace, except what I gleaned from rumors or from my son Mohammad, who beseeched me daily to join al-Ashtar's cause. At times he nearly succeeded, for the information he passed on filled me with anger—not against Uthman, but against Talha.

"*Abi,* we're fighting on your behalf and you're not even there," my son said with a pout. "My friends are saying you've become soft and fearful in your old age."

I said nothing in response to this ridiculous remark, an obvious tactic designed to inspire me to take up arms. Instead, I repeated the phrase I had uttered many times since that first meeting in al-Ashtar's home. "I do not advocate killing anyone, and that includes Uthman."

"Uthman is ignoring our demands!" Mohammad paced the floor, sword in hand, as I had done many times at his age, in the *majlis* with Muhammad and the other Companions. "We asked him to hand over Marwan, but he refused. We demanded that he step down as *khalifa*, but he said 'no.' We've asked him to negotiate, but he won't let us inside his house, nor will he come out to us." That was a wise choice, I could have told my son, for I knew al-Ashtar would strike Uthman dead. He was determined to remove him from the *khalifa* at any cost.

Mohammad's news about the proceedings *inside* Uthman's home incited my rage even more. "Talha and al-Zubayr have sent their sons to protect the palace, but they've told us secretly that they support our cause," he said.

I snorted. "They are like the Bedouins, helping whichever side they deem most likely to benefit them."

Mohammad frowned. "Why do you say that, *abi*? They have given us many dinars for weapons and food."

I sucked in my breath at this news. "I cannot imagine why they would expend their wealth only to hand the *khalifa* to me. I and Talha have long shared enmity between us, and Al-Zubayr has turned against me for reasons I do not understand."

Mohammad grinned. "I know why they're helping us. Each hopes to be *khalifa*. Al-Ashtar promised they'd be considered, but of course he only wants you. We all want you."

"They want to be *khalifa*!" I spat on the dirt floor. "Talha, that adulterer?" Mohammad's eyes widened. Not wanting to start rumors about A'isha, whom I felt certain was spotless, I hastened to add, "Or at least he desires to commit adultery. I detect it in his face and his body whenever I see him with A'isha."

Mohammad's face reddened. "By al-Lah, if he ever touches her, I will kill him myself."

"It is enough that he has risked her reputation with his inappropriate behavior," I said.

Mohammad watched me with a hopeful grin as I growled and kicked a cushion across the floor. That deceiver Talha was only encouraging the rebels for his own gain, taking advantage of A'isha's absence. She certainly would not approve of his conspiring with them. Then another, very disturbing notion filled my head. Had A'isha made the *hajj* to distance herself from Talha and al-Zubayr's activities?

Perhaps A'isha knew of Talha's plan, and had gone away in order to disassociate herself from this *fitna*. Being far away in Mecca would enable her to claim ignorance of the situation. That would serve her well later, if her lying cousin succeeded in gaining the *khalifa*.

But would Talha commit murder to achieve his ends? Fearful for Uthman's safety, I sneaked like a thief one night among houses, behind shrubs and trees, in order to view the proceedings at the *khalifa*'s home. The overcast sky shrouded the moon, but torches provided me with a view of the happenings there. What I saw astonished me: Not only had al-Ashtar and his men encircled the palace, at which they shouted insults, but they also had inflicted great damage to the building and its grounds. They had uprooted the flowers in front of Uthman's gate, and had chopped down the pomegranate and ghaza'a trees. As I watched, a group of men tore stones from the fence surrounding the palace and hacked at the gate with axes, while others dragged the limbs of the butchered trees to the base of the fence and tried to set them on fire.

A camel in green silk lined with tassels approached, stopped, and knelt in front of the palace. Out of the green-and-saffron *hawdaj* emerged a woman covered from the top of her head all the way to the ground in a flowing rose-and-gold gown and robe. She spoke to the men guarding what remained of the gate. They replied, and soon she was waving her hands and shouting. I slipped closer to hear their exchange, and discovered the woman to be Saffiya bint Huyayy, one of Muhammad's widows, bringing water for Uthman.

"He's dying of thirst in there," she said. "You know how hot these days have been."

"I am sorry, Mother of the Believers, but our commander has ordered us not to let anyone in or out of this house."

"Take the water in to him yourselves, then," she said, sounding as shrill as a peacock. Witnessing her agitation, I wondered if the rumors about her and Uthman were true. But how could they be? Al-Lah sees all, and would surely have struck her dead if she had betrayed Muhammad.

The chastised warrior shook his head. "The *khalifa* will not admit us for any reason. We tried offering him water, but he refused."

"That's because he knew you were trying to trick him. How foolish of you to think such a weak strategy would deceive Uthman ibn 'Affan!" She laughed, which made the warrior lower his head. "He'll let *me* in, I assure you. Step aside."

She turned to take the reins of the ass she had brought with her, a beast that stumbled under the weight of the filled goatskins it carried, and began leading it down the stone path to Uthman's door. The warrior drew his sword and stepped in front of her.

"How vile of you to treat a widow of the Prophet this way!" she huffed. "May al-Lah curse you for it."

"I would rather face the wrath of God than the displeasure of al-Ashtar," he said, lifting his sword,. "Take even one more step and I will have to arrest you."

Realizing the futility of arguing, Saffiya mounted her camel and rode away, leading her ass beside her. But as I continued to watch, I saw Talha knock on the door of a neighbor's home, confer with him, then disappear inside. Moments later, the two men were placing wooden planks across the space between the neighbor's house and Uthman's. Meanwhile, Saffiya walked her beast around to the neighbor's door and began handing the water skins to a servant. Talha emerged from the front door to greet Saffiya, who beamed at him with clasped hands.

When Saffiya had ridden away, several men in dark clothing and Bedouins' headdresses slipped up to Talha, who ushered them inside and closed the door. Dread filled me as I watched the men emerge on the roof with water skins in each hand. Then the clouds moved away from the moon, and light illuminated the water-bearers' faces. I clapped my hand over my mouth to muffle my cry. Among the men creeping over the boards to Uthman's palace was my own stepson, Mohammad.

His grim expression bespoke murderous intentions. *Why, al-Lah, did You allow this to happen?* The pulsing of my blood filled my ears as I hurried back to my home and bolted the door behind me. After some deep, calming breaths, I forced myself to walk slowly into my *harim*. Masking my agitation with a broad smile, I took my baby girl into my arms in full sight of my wives and concubines. They would remember, if asked, that I was at home during Uthman's assassination. If necessary, I would testify that Mohammad had been with me, also. I would rather be punished by God for lying than to have my son stricken down before he could pray for forgiveness. I fought back tears as I imagined his assassinating al-Lah's chosen *khalifa,* a deed that might consign him to hellfire for eternity.

I lay that night with Asma in my troubled arms, feigning sleep as I tried to make sense of the night's events. I had no doubt about why Mohammad had entered the palace, or about why Talha had assisted him in gaining access. Damn that self-serving mocker! He would never be *khalifa,* not as long as Ali ibn Abi Talib remained on this Earth. I would muster an entire army to challenge him if he tried, and I would die defeating him, if necessary.

I was not surprised by the screams that pierced the early morning twilight, or by the clamor of running feet and shouts filling the street outside my window. I did not arise to join the curious in their rush to the palace, for al-Lah had sent me a dream which told what had taken place: Uthman had been stabbed in the forehead by my son and impaled through the neck by another. His blood poured over the floor and soaked the clothing and hair of his wife Naila, who had flung herself across her husband's body to protect it from further desecration—and lost two of her fingers.

Poor Uthman, whose only crime had been weakness, who had died for it even though, at the end of his life, he had demonstrated uncommon courage by ordering his servants and wives to leave his house. Only a couple of loyal servants had insisted on remaining, and they lost their lives defending Uthman, may peace be upon them all.

As I lay in my bed, trembling with fear for my son, I saw Asma's eyes questioning me. Whispering, I told her what I had beheld that evening, and what I feared had occurred. Our son, I told her, might now be dead. She sat up with a cry.

"By al-Lah, husband, what are you doing in bed with these terrible thoughts? Get up, *yaa* Ali, and go find Mohammad. We must protect him, no matter what he has done!"

And so, with a heart that seemed to crumble like the house of Uthman, I dressed myself and donned my turban, strapped on my sword and dagger, and opened my door. The sight that greeted me there would have made me slam it shut again, save for al-Ashtar's hands seizing my beard while the crowd gathered in front of my house chanted my name.

"*Yaa* Ali, I bring you the best of news! The evil *khalifa* Uthman is dead, and two thousand men stand ready here to pledge their allegiance to you."

He lifted his hand in a beckoning motion. Mohammad, in fresh clothes, and Hud emerged with their daggers pressed to the throats of Talha and al-Zubayr, who glared at me as if I had ordered their humiliation. In truth, it did not displease me to see them treated roughly.

Al-Ashtar raised his sword and ordered both men to their knees. "Make your choice," he said to them, "Be the first to pledge allegiance to our *khalifa*, Ali ibn Abi Bakr, or prepare to meet your friends in Hell."

A'isha

The *hajj* had been a success. I packed up my camel, my heart filled with love and longing for Muhammad and hopes for a speedy return to Medina. *Show me what to do about Uthman,* I'd prayed in the spare, windowless Ka'ba, prostrating myself among thousands of Believers in the very place where Muhammad had destroyed idols and dedicated all of Mecca to al-Lah, the One God. Not only had I received my answer, but I would carry home precious memories of Muhammad, so vivid that he almost seemed alive.

I'd been with him on the day he'd reclaimed Mecca for his own. I'd sat beside him on the stone steps while he'd accepted the allegiance of every citizen including Abu Sufyan. Although we hadn't been touching, I'd felt Muhammad's joy radiating from his skin. In the city where he'd been born, raised, married, widowed, persecuted, and forced into exile, Muhammad had found acceptance at last.

Returning to Mecca had been his dream for nearly a decade before he'd ridden triumphantly into the city. Now, making the *hajj* for the first time since Umar had forbidden the Prophet's wives to travel, I'd felt his presence here as keenly as if he sat next to me again. As I'd prayed for guidance about the *khalifa*, I'd suddenly sensed Muhammad's wishes as clearly as if the *muezzin* had shouted them from the rooftop. Today my goal was to return home as quickly as possible, before the sacred month ended, and to shame those Bedouin friends of Ali's into showing some respect for Muhammad's old Companion. I'd block his door with my body, if I needed to. *In protecting Uthman, you protect the* khalifa, *and* islam, I'd heard Muhammad say.

Lost in my thoughts, I didn't notice the camels thundering up the street until they were practically on top of me. I cried out in delight when I saw that their riders were Talha and al-Zubayr, their eyes red with dust and sleeplessness, their faces creased by sun, wind, and fatigue. My spirit quickened at the sight of my cousin, come to pray, I assumed, or to visit me on the way to his gardens in the Sawad. I handed my bedroll to a helper and stepped into the street to greet Talha with a smile.

But the grim set of the men's faces told me they hadn't raced through the desert for prayer or pleasure. Before Talha's camel had fully knelt, he flung himself from its back, then marched up to me and laid his hands on my shoulders. His man's touch, so rare, so forbidden, made my pulse jump, and I drew away from him, not wanting to risk my sister's honor.

"Uthman is dead," he said. "Assassinated."

As I stared at Talha in disbelief, a slow chill crept down my spine.

Uthman assassinated! I found my breath and began to wail. "I killed him. *Yaa* al-Lah, why? Why did I leave Medina?" I lifted my hands to claw at my face but Talha grabbed my wrists and pulled them gently toward his chest. "He begged me to stay, but I wouldn't listen. *Ai!* Talha, I killed him."

"A'isha." My wrists still bound in his hands, Talha gazed into my face. "You couldn't have stopped them. Do you hear me? They were determined to see him dead."

"Who did this terrible deed?" Al-Zubayr walked over to us and, in a sorrowful tone, told how al-Ashtar's gang had crept in and attacked Uthman, how Naila had thrown herself over him and lost fingers from her right hand, saving his body from mutilation. His story made me wish the earth would quake apart and swallow me. Naila had sacrificed her fingers while I, whom he'd begged to stay in Medina for his sake, had refused to sacrifice my plans.

I wrenched my hands from Talha's grasp and placed them over my face, for not even my veil was enough to hide my loathsomeness from my friends' eyes—or to stem the torrent of tears now gushing from mine.

"I could have saved him," I sobbed. "By al-Lah, I could have stopped those murderers. But I was selfish. May God strike me down today! *Yaa* Muhammad, I failed your *sahib* Uthman." I felt my heart empty of the love I had known these past weeks, a glow and a comfort that had come, I knew, from Muhammad. His presence had swirled through me like perfume, as if Mecca were a garden filled with flowers instead of a harsh, rock-strewn desert. But now, my feelings of communion with him fell away.

"Help me move her indoors," I heard Talha murmur to al-Zubayr, and with a tug of my sleeve they led me to the house my father had bequeathed to me, past Umm Salama and Hafsa who were busy packing their camels. Hafsa rushed over and pressed her hand against my shoulder. I crumpled against her, grateful for her woman's arms offering me the comfort and support that Talha and al-Zubayr, as men, weren't allowed to provide.

Once we were inside my home, I collapsed on a cushion with Hafsa and returned her embrace, burying my face in her clothing. "It's my fault," I kept saying. "Uthman asked me to stay, but I refused. I killed him."

"*Yaa* A'isha." Talha knelt beside me and would have touched me, but Hafsa hissed, "What are you doing?" and pulled me backward, out of his reach.

"A'isha, listen to me," Talha said. "You did not kill Uthman. Al-Ashtar killed him. Do you think he would have listened to you? Do you think Ali would have? They had a plan, and no one could have stopped them. That became clear very quickly. As soon as our *khalifa* breathed his last breath, al-Ashtar and his friends grabbed me and al-Zubayr and dragged us to Ali's house. They proclaimed Ali the new *khalifa* before Uthman's body was cold. And they forced me and al-Zubayr to our knees, held swords over our heads, and forced us to pledge our allegiance to him."

His words pelted me like stones. I leapt to my feet and ran outside. I felt as if a raging torrent of flame had erupted inside me. Grit filled my open mouth. I smelled horse sweat, then roasting meat as I flew from my house and past the market. I didn't know where I was going, nor did I care. Ali, *khalifa*! My only desire was to flee from this awful news, from my guilt over Uthman's death, from the heartache of watching men like al-Walid and al-Ashtar and, soon, Ali, destroy what Muhammad had given his life to create, and from the nightmare that my life would become now that my nemesis had become the *khalifa*.

Ali, *khalifa*! How many times had he promised to confine me to my home as soon as he had the power? I'd thought his threats were empty; I'd been sure he'd never be chosen. What had he done to deserve it? Yes, he'd been a great warrior in the days of Muhammad, but since then he'd done nothing but marry, breed, and get fat. Talha, on the other hand, had increased his wealth by running a successful date plantation and investing in land, and he'd made friends with many prominent men. He also practiced his sword fighting regularly to keep his body and reflexes fit for the battlefield. He was ready for the *khalifa* in every way. I'd be surprised if Ali could even lift his sword anymore.

I had been too complacent. I could see that now. But how could I have known that Ali would seize the *khalifa* while I was away? To think this had all occurred during the holy month of Dhu al-Hijjah, during the *hajj*!

If I'd been in Medina, I'd have stood on Uthman's balcony and given speech after rousing speech condemning those men who'd dared to threaten the life of a man chosen by al-Lah. With me in Uthman's home, the assassins wouldn't have dared to enter. No one would approach the Mother of the Believers with an unsheathed blade. Even if Uthman had been killed, I'd have stopped Ali from claiming the *khalifa*. I would have exposed him for what he truly was: a man interested in helping his family gain prestige, not in following Muhammad's example, as I and Talha were. In that regard, he was no better than Uthman. In truth, he was worse, for Uthman had never pretended to care about the poor, or about punishing corruption. If only I'd stayed in Medina. If only . . .

Breathless, I slowed my pace to a walk, wiping my tears with my sleeve, when I heard the call of the *muezzin* to prayer. The Ka'ba was just ahead. I didn't have my prayer rug with me, so I went inside and fell to the stone floor. In truth, I relished the sharpness of the pain and the dull ache that spread across my knees afterward. My discomfort prodded me, reminded me to stay alert, for which I was thankful. I'd been asleep, it seemed, for too long.

Al-Lah, please show me what to do. I bent and knelt and pressed my forehead to the floor. Yaa *Muhammad, use me as your tool*. And I prayed for my husband to come back to me, to let me feel his love again, but nothing happened. Was it possible that Muhammad wanted Ali to be the *khalifa* now? But how could that be, if Ali had been complicit in Uthman's murder?

No more complicit than you, A'isha. The thought brushed my mind like a crow's wing. My prayers finished, I sat in place while those around me rolled up their prayer mats and exchanged greetings. How much blame *did* I bear for Uthman's death? Had I really wanted so badly to make the *hajj*, or had I left Medina to absolve myself of responsibility in case anything happened to Uthman?

I remembered when Uthman had given me his permission to go, how the timing, which coincided with his brother al-Walid's arrival, had made me think he wanted to get rid of me. But when I'd told my sister-wives we could join the pilgrimage at last, Hafsa's cry of delight and Umm Salama's joyous smile inspired me to get excited about the journey. When I'd told myself that Uthman would be safe, I had genuinely believed it.

Ali was a traitor; there was no doubt in my mind. He and his friends had corrupted *islam* more thoroughly than Uthman would have done. But knowing all this was useless to me. I was in Mecca. Ali was in Medina. If I returned and tried to challenge him, he'd place me in confinement—a situation that, after six years of *purdah* as a child, I'd do anything to avoid. But if I stayed here who would dare to oppose him? He'd eventually order me to return to Medina, anyway—and I'd have no choice but to obey. And then my life would end.

"*Yaa* A'isha!" Talha rushed up. "I've been searching everywhere for you."

"Talha!" I turned wild eyes to him. "Why didn't you protect Uthman?"

His face reddened as he shook his head, making me sorry I'd asked. Was I so desperate to blame someone besides myself that I'd point the finger at my cousin?

"I'm only one man, A'isha," he said.

I took a deep breath, clearing my head of all questions except one. "What do we do now?"

"Here." He held out my sword and shield. "I brought this for you from Medina. I knew you wouldn't carry it with you on the *hajj*, but I thought you'd want to have it now."

I frowned. "Why, Talha? Are we going to fight?"

His eyes narrowed. His nostrils flared. I drew back from him even as I took my sword. This new, angry Talha was so unlike the joking, laughing rascal I'd always known and loved.

"We didn't ride all this way simply to convey news to you, A'isha," he said. "We need your help. Ali has refused to bring Uthman's murderers to justice. This cannot be. If they escape punishment, then *islam* becomes as lawless as life during the *jahiliyya*."

"Ali won't punish them because he owes his power to them," I said as I strapped on my scabbard. "But what can we do? All of Medina has pledged allegiance to him now."

"Perhaps." Talha looked over the crowded Ka'ba, at the men who talked of the weather and the date crop, for they hadn't yet heard of the *khalifa*'s terrible death. "Medina might be lost to us. But Mecca is not."

"You speak truly." By bringing Talha here with my sword, I realized, Muhammad had answered my question about what he wanted from me. I might have missed the opportunity to stop Ali in Medina, but that was only one small part of the Islamic territory now. I had Mecca before me, and Basra after that, and, perhaps, Damascus.

Use it well in the jihad *to come*. I heard Muhammad's dying words, spoken as he'd handed me this sword. I pulled al-Ma'thur out of its sheath, lifted it in the air, and walked toward the *minbar* at the front of the room.

"*Yaa* A'isha, where are you going?" Talha called.

"To recruit an army," I shouted over my shoulder.

Now was the moment I had been moving toward all my life. This was the *jihad*, no longer to come, but happening. Now.

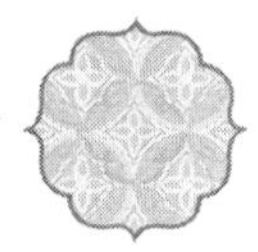

Ali

When I heard that A'isha had recruited an army against me I realized that, despite my hopes, she had not ceased in her hatred of me. In truth, her animosity seemed to have increased, while my memories of her addressing the crowds in the mosque, and from the balcony at Uthman's palace, filled me anew with admiration: her tone as clear as the *muezzin's* call; her proud stance more regal than the Queen of Sheba's.

From my seat on the *minbar*, where I awaited the ceremony that would inaugurate me as *khalifa,* I imagined the figure she had cut in the Ka'ba, hoisting Muhammad's bejeweled sword and enticing warriors to her cause. It was a brilliant speech, I had heard, made more so by its impromptu nature, "nearly as impressive as your own spontaneous verses," Abu Hurayra had fawned. I did not doubt this rumor, for I had heard excerpts that rivaled the rhetoric of our city's most esteemed poet, Hassan ibn Thabit. *We reproached Uthman. . . . He recanted and asked al-Lah for forgiveness. But Ali was not satisfied! He increased the strife that led to the murder of our khalifa, a single finger of whom was better than the whole of Ali.*

Her insults stung me, and I rankled also at her outrageous assertion, for it was she, with her dramatic monologues and her hair, shirt, and sandal, who had roused the public ire against Uthman. Yet I could not help admiring the efficacy of her speech. Her well-chosen words had mustered an army, a feat that many men had struggled, and failed, to accomplish.

But she had rallied her army to fight against me. And kill me. The corners of my mouth dragged at my face like desperate hands. In her forty-three years, had A'isha never discovered one quality that made me worthy of life? Had she not come to recognize any of my good qualities, as I had come to recognize hers?

I lowered my head to my hands. *Not even the stars, or the shining moon, could illuminate the vision I have seen / Of brother killing brother over the spoils of God / And their Mother at the fore, inciting them with words / Her lust for my smitten blood courting hellfire for us both.*

I groaned aloud at the feebleness of my verse. By al-Lah, was my talent for poetry now "smitten," also? Before I could try again, my uncle's booming voice intruded on my thoughts. "On the verge of the *khalifa,* our Ali sleeps in his chair. *Yaa* Mughira, I hope this is not an omen."

I stepped to the floor to greet my uncle al-Abbas, my cousin Abd Allah, and al-Mughira, that one-eyed, lecherous opportunist who had flattered his way into Umar's circle of advisers.

"Apparently you have heard the news about A'isha," my uncle said, leaning on his cane. "It is, of course, no surprise. She was born a fighter, and where there is no conflict, she creates it." He shook his head. "By al-Lah, she is not like any woman I have ever seen."

"Woman?" Al-Mughira snorted. "She seems more like a hermaphrodite." His laugh was coarse, laced with dirt.

"Be mindful when you speak of her, Mughira," I warned. "A'isha was the Prophet's most beloved wife. When you insult her, you insult Muhammad."

"By al-Lah!" my uncle's eyebrows flew together. "Ali, defending A'isha? *I* must be the one who has fallen asleep."

"Ali speaks truly, *yaa abi,*" Abd Allah said gently. He lifted his hand to his father's elbow to keep al-Abbas from toppling off his cane. "We must be mindful of our speech concerning A'isha. People will not tolerate disrespect toward the Mother of the Believers."

"That is exactly the point I was trying to make," I said, nodding. *Be calm, Ali, or they will guess your change of heart.* "I do not want to offend my followers."

My uncle frowned. "Hmm," he said. "Well, whatever you think of A'isha, one thing is clear: She would rather challenge you on the battlefield than support you as *khalifa*. That makes her an insurgent, and she should be arrested immediately. Whipped, also, in my opinion."

"She has been deceived by Talha and al-Zubayr." I walked about the room so my uncle could not see my face. "They pledged their allegiance to me, then raced off to Mecca to form an army against me."

"So you must form an army, also," my uncle said. "And you must do so immediately."

I stopped at the courtyard entrance, gazing out at the widows' huts, remembering all the times I had seen A'isha sitting under the date-palm tree and feeding milk to her runt lambs with her pinky finger, or heard her exuberant laughter from inside the cooking tent. Were we now to face each other in battle, one of us to be slain, the other to live in guilt and remorse?

As great a fighter as I knew A'isha to be, she was no match for me and Zulfikar, my double-bladed sword. I would best her in any contest. But after I had struck her down, would I then desire to turn my blade upon myself? For I knew Muhammad would not forgive me for causing A'isha injury or death—and I knew, also, that I would never forgive myself.

"What is this? Hesitancy?" My uncle rapped his cane on the tile floor. "After all your bitterness over not being allowed to do battle?" His laugh was incredulous. "And now, when faced with a challenge from your most formidable enemies, you gaze through the doorway as though you wanted to flee."

I whirled around to face the old prodder. "I wonder, Uncle, who is my enemy and who is my friend? Is my friend the one who compels me to take actions against my nature, simply to gain power and prestige for himself and his heirs?"

My uncle's eyes widened. "You must fight. Or else you will lose the *khalifa*—everything we have striven for since before Muhammad's death."

I sighed, and my bravado whooshed out from me like the air from a goat's-bladder ball. "You speak truly," I said, and gave him a thin smile to compensate for my earlier, disrespectful words. "Yet I do not relish the waging of any war that pits Muslim against Muslim. I do not desire another battle between Medinans and Meccans, between Quraysh and Quraysh. Did not Muhammad say, 'Never should a Believer kill another Believer'?"

"Yes, and he also said, 'Did you think you would enter the Garden without first proving which of you would struggle for His cause?'" My uncle bore his gaze into me. "This is the struggle for al-Lah's cause, Ali, and also for Muhammad's. *They* have declared war on *you*, not the other way around. Would you fight, or hand the *khalifa* to Talha?"

I cringed thinking of it. I knew well that Talha was greedy and foolish. I had heard him curry Mu'awiyya's favor. I had not heard the end of their discussion, but I guessed that Talha had pledged his support for that serpent in Syria in exchange for Mu'awiyya's assistance in the contest for the *khalifa*. My uncle spoke truly: Muhammad would have preferred me to rule *islam* over any man alive, and especially over Talha. As for al-Lah, if He had not desired me for the position, I would not now hold it, for I had done nothing to promote myself. And, contrary to A'isha's assertions, I did nothing to bring harm to Uthman.

"The first thing you must do, *khalifa,* is to gain the support of your governors," al-Mughira said with a dip of his head, as if he possessed a date-seed's worth of humility. "Al-Walid will certainly assist you—"

"Al-Walid is governor of Kufa no more," I said. "And Abdullah no longer rules Egypt. I sent messengers out today. Every man Uthman appointed is deposed. I will appoint righteous men in their places."

Al-Mughira gasped. "Deposed, all? But who will muster your army?"

"I will recruit an army myself. Beginning today, during the ceremony."

"But—" From his glance at al-Abbas I deduced that they had already spoken of these matters, and reached an agreement among themselves. Resolve was a metal plate on my breast. *I* was the *khalifa,* not my uncle, and certainly not al-Mughira. "You would be making a grave error if you deposed Mu'awiyya," he said. "He is a man of *hilm,* a true leader, very popular in Syria, and his army is loyal to him. I suggest you retain him, at least."

"Mu'awiyya!" I spat his name out. "That double-tongued politician is worse than his father Abu Sufyan. No, by God, he will not remain in office under my rule."

Al-Mughira smiled without showing his teeth, as though he held a secret behind his lips. That was the last time I ever saw him, thank al-Lah, for he left for Damascus that night to offer his services to Mu'awiyya.

As for me, the mention of Uthman's corrupt relatives motivated me, so that by the time the Believers had gathered in the mosque, I was not only ready but eager to establish myself.

"At last Ali, the Prophet's kin, is welcomed as your leader, after you spurned me for so long," I said, glaring at the men who turned up their faces to me as though I were the angel Gabriel. "Now, God has laid down two cures for you: the sword and the whip. Should I be merciful to you, when you have had no mercy toward me?" I turned away from them and began to pace, as though pondering their fate, as though I held the power to crush them all or let them live.

"*Yaa khalifa*, forgive us!" someone cried. I stopped and looked over these men, hundreds filling the mosque and beyond, my heart bursting with gratitude for their allegiance yet not wanting them to see that I was grateful. After twelve years of Uthman, the *umma* needed a strong leader. *Let me be up to that task.*

"Do not call me *khalifa!*" I shouted. "That title has been sullied by the one who came before me. He was like a raven whose only care is its belly. It would have been better for him, and for us all, if his wings had been clipped years ago.

"Do not call me *khalifa*. I am your *imam*, your leader. And forgiveness—" I turned a stern eye upon the crowd "—is the gift of al-Lah. I will ask Him for it on your behalf. But it may be too late for you. You are like sheep that escaped from your pen long ago and have grown accustomed to life in the wild. Can you now return to the fold of austerity, of righteousness, of the values espoused by our Prophet?"

Some of the men in the room began to grumble. Judging from the finery in which they clothed themselves, a return to austerity was not their desire. I held my breath as I watched them turn and walk, two or three at a time and then twenty and thirty all at once, out of the mosque. I retained my mask of outrage, determined that none should see worry or doubt on my face, hoping none could hear the slamming of my heart.

I waited while one-third of the men left the mosque, and those remaining, six hundred or so, crowded eagerly to the platform to shout, wave, and cheer. A glow like the dawn spread through me, casting out my dread that they would all depart and leave me standing alone with my outmoded principles. "Praise be to Muhammad and to his heir Ali!" a man cried. The familiar voice pulled my gaze to the center of the crowd, where al-Ashtar, my son Mohammad, Hud, and others who had assisted with Uthman's assassination stood waving their swords and pledging their allegiance to me.

I had my army, or its beginnings. My spirits soared, but falteringly. If my leadership stood on the shoulders of assassins, how stable would it be? If I displeased al-Ashtar in some way, might he kill me next?

"Death to A'isha, Talha, and al-Zubayr!" al-Ashtar called, and the men's roar like crashing sea waves filled the room. My eyes stung at the thought of that brave woman slain, and of the death of my childhood friend al-Zubayr, whom I had loved. I stood above these frenzied men, waving my sword, mindful of the hands grasping at my feet. If I lost my vigilance, even for one moment, they would pull me down.

A'isha

◆

The night was as still as a stopped heart. Outside the city of Basra, I, Talha, and al-Zubayr waited in dread for Ali's army to arrive.

"Seven thousand men," Talha's voice trembled as he paced the dirt floor of the same spacious tent of red camel's hair that Muhammad had used during battles. "How, by al-Lah, did Ali conjure such a force?"

"Not Ali, but his son al-Hassan." Al-Zubayr smirked, looking every bit the general in his gleaming chain mail. "It seems that someone in the family, at least, possesses charm."

Both men turned to me, awaiting my response. I was shocked to hear of such a mighty army under Ali's command. Seven thousand men could stamp out our small gathering, just a few thousand strong, like a sandal over an anthill. A shiver swept over my bones as I remembered again the strange barking and howling we'd heard a few nights earlier when we'd stopped to water our camels. The cacophony had made the hair on my neck stand up and my palms perspire as I remembered Zaynab's cryptic warning before she died: *Beware the dogs at Hawab*.

"What is this place?" I'd asked, but my driver didn't know. The noise continued as I asked first one man, then another, for the name of the well from which we drank. Then Talha came over and stared at me—and what a sight I must have made, frenzy-eyed, my voice rising with each query.

"*Yaa* A'isha, this is Hawab."

"We have to turn back," I'd told Talha. "Muhammad sent a warning."

I'd been adamant, despite Talha's coaxing and, finally, his teasing. "You don't believe in deathbed predictions, do you, A'isha?" I retreated to my tent and remained there for the rest of the night and the next day, praying for guidance. I waited and listened, but no guidance came—only a deep calm, as I realized that, barking dogs or not, I had come too far to turn back now. Three thousand men had heeded my call to arms. Then Al-Zubayr warned that Ali was on the verge of overtaking us, and I agreed to move on to Basra.

Now I felt that sense of calm return. This battle had been foretold. It was destined to happen. I straightened my shoulders, ignoring the tiny voice of fear tugging at my ear. What we were doing was just and honorable—and, I was convinced, it was the will of al-Lah.

"Ali couldn't talk a flea into jumping on a hound," I said. "But his sons resemble Muhammad, and they're both as gentle as lambs. It was brilliant of Ali to send al-Hassan to recruit the warriors of Kufa. Unfortunately for him, though, his honey-tongued son won't be helping him on the battlefield. Al-Hassan is not a fighter."

"You speak truly, A'isha." The twinkle returned to Talha's eyes. "Ali has the charisma of a stick."

I imagined Ali on the battlefield, waving his double-bladed sword, his belly swelling like a shifting dune. Instead of the hatred that usually knotted my stomach at the thought of him, though, I felt something else. I closed my eyes against the idea of spilling his blood. I reached out a hand, longing for a wall to support me, for Muhammad's shoulder to lean against. How had this happened? Was this what my husband would have wanted?

"Let Hassan's admirers come to the battlefield," al-Zubayr was saying. "What concern is it of ours? We have the Mother of the Believers. With one glimpse of A'isha, Ali's army will abandon him and rush to our side."

I pictured myself on the hillside behind us, waving al-Ma'thur, challenging Ali as I'd dreamt of doing since I was fourteen. I was still haunted by that awful day when I'd ridden into Medina with another man and endured the jeers of my neighbors. *Al-zaniya!* they had called me—adulteress. And *fahisha,* whore. Worst of all, though, was hearing Ali urge Muhammad to divorce me.

You will easily find another child bride, he'd said. As if that were all I meant to Muhammad. As if my young girl's body had drawn him to me in the first place. As if he had not loved me above all others. As if the allegations against me were true.

From that moment, my hatred of Ali had been bound up with my love for Muhammad. Yet I had never envisioned myself killing Ali or declaring war against him. He was my husband's kin, as beloved to him as a son. How could I fight him in battle?

Yet how could I *not* fight against him? First, Ali had let Uthman's assassination occur. Now he refused to prosecute the men who had broken into our *khalifa's* bedroom and pierced his head and throat with their knives. I'd sent him letters, as had Talha and even Mu'awiyya, but he'd ignored us. Of course, we all knew his reasons: The Bedouin al-Ashtar, who had planned the assassination, was Ali's biggest supporter. He was the reason so many Bedouins marched against us today. If Ali punished him, he would lose more than half his army—and also the *khalifa*. But by not bringing al-Ashtar and the rest of the assassins to justice, Ali was committing a grave sin against *islam*. How could the religion of Muhammad survive under a blood-stained *khalifa*?

It was for this, the future of *islam*, that I was willing to fight. Yet I dreaded such a battle, for, as in the old days, we'd pit brother against brother, father against son. On our side we had the Quraysh of Mecca and the men of Basra, plus their Bedouin allies. Most had relatives in the approaching army. And so did I—my youngest brother, Mohammad ibn Abi Bakr.

I shuddered to think of his death at our hands—but the alternative, the death of *islam*, was much worse. I moved my fingers to the hilt of my sword—Muhammad's sword. *Use it well in the* jihad *to come*. With his bequest, Muhammad had established my destiny—and now I was about to fulfill it.

So why did I feel so empty?

A boy of about fifteen—the minimum age on the battlefield—stepped into the tent, his long hair spilling over his shoulders. I caught my breath: He reminded me of Safwan, the youth I'd loved, or thought I loved, and for whom I'd almost risked Muhammad's honor all those years ago. Ali's hiss filled my mind again: *Divorce her*. Looking at this boy, with his high cheekbones and almond eyes, made me remember how, at fourteen, I'd dreamt of Safwan while the Prophet of God lay next to me. What a foolish girl I'd been, planning to run away with that boy! Willing to risk *islam* for him. Muhammad would have been wise to divorce me—if al-Lah hadn't given him another way out. And, with this realization, my hatred for Ali flew out the window.

I gasped, drawing the stares of Talha, al-Zubayr, and the messenger. I kept my gaze on the boy, not wanting my friends to misread the alarm in my eyes. My heart pounding, I listened to him deliver his message. "*Imam* Ali approaches and requests a meeting," he said.

"A meeting," Talha sneered. "As I suspected, the brave Ali possesses more courage on the *minbar* than he does on the battlefield."

I was stung by Talha's swaggering manner. Was this my lifelong friend, the man who shared my opinions? Apparently, his feelings differedfrom mine in, at least this regard: I wanted to avoid killing our kin, while he seemed eager to fight.

"If Ali wants to talk, why not indulge him?" I said. "It may be a sign of weakness on his part, but if he gives us what we want, you'll have the *khalifa* in your hands."

Al-Zubayr cleared his throat. "*Afwan*, A'isha, but please consider: I, also, would make an excellent choice."

I frowned at him. "Choice? For what?"

He cleared his throat again. "For the *khalifa*."

By al-Lah, I could have toppled over! I'd had no idea al-Zubayr was interested in the position. And, although he spoke truly—a famous general, a loyal Muslim, and a wise man, he would make an excellent *khalifa*—I felt my stomach sink at his words. Of all the times to make this announcement, now was the very worst. On the cusp of battle, we needed to pull together for one common cause, not split into factions.

But the damage had been done. Talha's face looked as though a thundercloud had settled on it, and his pressed-together lips told me he was biting back a response. Not wanting Ali's messenger to report that we were fighting amongst ourselves, I sent him to his *imam* with an invitation to join us. When the boy had gone, I turned to my fuming cousin and my defiant brother-in-law, wanting to smooth over the tension between them.

"By al-Lah, what a perfect team we make!" I said with a laugh. "We all want the same things: a return of *islam* to its origins, justice for the killers of Uthman, and, now, the *khalifa*."

My remark served its purpose, bringing a smile to the lips of both men. The idea of my being *khalifa* was ludicrous. How could I, a woman, be a leader of men, my superiors in every way?

"But this isn't the time to argue over the *khalifa*," I said. "We've got to focus on defeating Ali. We can't do that if we're bickering."

"You speak truly, A'isha, as usual," al-Zubayr said. "It is a pity that you cannot rule." He swept out of the tent to his own next door, to rest and wash up.

As soon as he'd left us, Talha exploded. "By al-Lah, we should have known better than to trust that backstabber." He paced the floor of my tent. "Do you remember how he urged Ali to rebel against your father when he was appointed? Then he turned against Ali and pledged to your father. He's like a Bedouin, shifting his allegiance to whomever he thinks will help him the most." He spat into the sand. "In this case, his allegiance is to himself."

Given Talha's eagerness to fight Ali, I was tempted to argue that he, also, served his own interests. Why would he balk at a meeting unless he worried that Ali would agree to our demands? If that happened, Talha might lose his chance at the *khalifa*, but more good than bad would come of it. Muslim lives would be spared, and if Uthman's murder were avenged, the blood that now stained *islam* would be washed away.

"The last thing we need is a weak, vacillating *khalifa*," Talha was saying. "After Uthman, we need a man of strength. Not al-Zubayr, who acts on impulse and changes his mind every day, and not Ali, who forces allegiance with his sword. We must prevail, or the spirit of *islam* will die."

I agreed with Talha—to a point. I, also, wanted Ali to resign from the *khalifa*. Yet, judging from the size of his army, he had something that we didn't: power. He had the support of seven thousand men, while our army numbered less than half that. His blood ties to Muhammad made him, to many, nearly as sacred as the Prophet. And his being the father of al-Hassan and al-Hussein, Muhammad's sole male heirs, increased his status. I could only marvel at the contradiction: Bedouins hated the idea of dynasty, yet they supported Ali, whose sons would certainly inherit the *khalifa*.

"Those Bedouins will race one another to join our ranks once we have defeated their *imam* in battle," Talha said. "But to hold their allegiance, we'll have to kill Ali." He walked to the tent entrance, gazed across the grass and scrub, then turned and looked as deeply as a lover into my eyes. But the look I saw was urgent, not romantic.

"Think about it, A'isha," he said. "With Ali gone, so many of our problems would be resolved. But if he lives, we'll always have to worry about his trying to retake the *khalifa*. He would never accept my rule and I couldn't force him to." He turned and faced outside again, then smacked his fist into his hand. "As for his keeping the position, I would rather die than allow that to happen."

Only a few hours earlier, I might have agreed with Talha. Now, though, I wondered: Was the *khalifa* worth killing for? Or were there more important considerations—such as justice?

Listening to Talha rant, I realized we should accept Ali as our ruler if he agreed to our other terms. If Ali gave us al-Ashtar's head, I would have to pledge my support to him. Without it, as he knew, he'd never have the people's loyalty, which he needed if he was going to hold onto his position. Ambitious men—predators—such as Mu'awiyya were already sensing his weakness and preparing to pounce.

"*Yaa* A'isha, do you have nothing to say?" Talha turned toward me again. "Or have you, like al-Zubayr, shifted your allegiance away from me?"

I tried to meet his gaze, but my own slid away. "My allegiance is yours, of course." I cleared my throat. "But—"

"But! But what?" My cousin's face bunched up like a fist he might use to hit me. "But you don't want to fight?"

"I don't want to fight our own kinsmen," I said. "I don't want to kill Muhammad's foster-son. Muhammad loved Ali! It doesn't feel . . . right."

"I don't believe what I'm hearing." Talha's laugh was sharp. "Is that A'isha I hear sniveling like Abu Hurayra?"

Heat flooded my face. "Is it Talha I hear hurling insults at me?" I drew myself up and looked him directly in the eyes. "By al-Lah, you won't get far with that kind of attitude toward A'isha bint Abi Bakr. If you don't respect the Mother of the Believers—"

"Now who is insulting whom? You pretend to oppose Ali for the sake of all your 'children,' and for the sake of *islam*. Perhaps you've convinced yourself. But I know better."

He placed his hands on my shoulders, but I slapped them away. "I don't know what you're talking about," I snapped. "And you know it's not proper to touch Muhammad's wives."

He cocked an eyebrow. "Is A'isha so proper now, after years of meeting me in private? You know exactly what I'm talking about."

"I'm afraid I don't." I turned away from him, not wanting him to see the truth on my face. In the next instant I felt his arms around me, holding me tight against him, and his hot breath on my ear, making me shiver.

"You hate Ali, but not for the sake of *islam*, or the Believers, or the memory of Muhammad," Talha murmured, his voice like silk. "You're still nursing a young girl's grudge. That's why you're here now, with your sword and your self-righteousness and your demands for justice. You came for revenge, A'isha. Revenge, and nothing more."

Ali

This much was apparent to me: My foes were divided.

I entered A'isha's tent with a quivering in my chest like a plucked *tanbur* string—a plaintive note. I knew this tent well, having conferred with Muhammad many times inside its walls. But with my first glimpse of Talha and al-Zubayr's faces, I had to restrain my mouth from smiling.

Talha, whose rust-colored beard had sprung filaments of gray, stood with his arms folded and his eyes shooting arrows at al-Zubayr. Al-Zubayr puffed out his chest in a comic fashion and held his body as stiff as if a date-palm trunk had been inserted along his spine. He focused his sights on some distant prize, most likely that of the *khalifa*, which, I knew, he had been told he might soon possess. I gave silent thanks to al-Lah for preparing my path to victory by creating dissension among my enemies.

Yet my task was neither complete nor my victory assured, for between these petulant men stood A'isha with the bearing of a queen. Her level gaze, which never left me as I greeted her companions, told me she regarded the quarrel between Talha and al-Zubayr as inconsequential, a rift easily mended. I had come amply supplied to change that situation.

A'isha's intensity made me feel as if we were alone in the tent, and that our conflict, mine and hers, was what truly mattered. In truth, if we had been alone, events would have transpired differently. For her demeanor, always before as closed and tight as a date seed, had opened today like a rose in the first stages of bloom.

For the first time in all the years we had known each other, I felt possibility in her presence. I felt hope. Perhaps we could, after all, avoid spilling our brethren's blood onto this foreign land. We might be able to reach an agreement that would satisfy us both. Perhaps—my pulse leapt at the thought—perhaps we could find a way to work together, side by side, I as *khalifa* and she as my adviser. For I had begun to suspect even then, before our initial talks, that we both held close to our hearts the same dream for the future of *islam*.

"*Assalaamu aleikum*," I said, wishing her peace. Muhammad had instructed us to do in greeting fellow Muslims, but in that moment I sincerely meant the words.

"*Wa aleikum assalaam*," she responded, and the lift in her voice and the brightness in her dark green eyes told me she, too, desired peace. She dipped her head in deference, but Talha and al-Zubayr made no show of respect.

A'isha turned to the cushions arranged around a pale linen cloth on which platters of food had been placed. My stomach rumbled loudly at the sight—dates, figs, rice, dried meat, honey—for I had barely eaten since leaving Kufa a few days earlier. My stomach had been twisting and turning, filled with apprehension over the coming fight. Now, with hope in the air, I felt relaxed enough for water to flood my mouth.

We sat before the repast, which I was somehow able to restrain myself from falling upon too eagerly. Long moments of silence followed as I and A'isha partook of the meal, while her companions only nibbled as they glared at each other. Then, when we had satisfied our bodies' needs and were able to focus on the confrontation at hand, A'isha spoke—but not, to my relief, to demand al-Ashtar's head.

"*Yaa* Ali, your seizing of the *khalifa* inspired this uprising against you," she said in a quiet voice. "Muhammad would not have wanted it, as I'm sure you know. He always told me that leadership must be earned."

"Mother of the Believers, *you* must know that the Prophet would not have wanted me to be denied the *khalifa* again and again. He and I were like two seeds in the same pod. Only you were closer to him than I. As for my seizing the position, you did not witness the events in Medina after Uthman's death. You must rely on the reports of witnesses—which may not be as accurate as you believe." I shifted my glance to Talha, who glowered at me, and al-Zubayr, who cleaned his fingernails and avoided my gaze.

"You forced us to pledge our allegiance by holding swords to our throats," Talha gruffed.

"*Yaa* Talha, I forced nothing." I looked at A'isha, which was a pleasure that seemed only to increase with each glance. "Others called for my appointment until the streets of Medina filled with a river of supporters. They swept me into their current with affection and clamoring joy. Those who tried to swim against them were turned about by the sword. I witnessed this sad distortion of *islam*, but my protests were lost in the city's cries."

"You stood helpless, flapping your arms and squawking like a hen, in the presence of tyranny," al-Zubayr said quietly, looking up at me. "That was excellent leadership."

I frowned. Given what I knew about al-Zubayr—thanks to the sleuthing of al-Ashtar—he would be wise to hold his tongue against me. But I kept my secrets for a while longer, wanting more time with A'isha, still hoping an agreement could be forged. To reveal my discoveries now would be like crashing a frightened horse into the tent, distracting us all from the business of avoiding war.

Given the number of men supporting me and the obvious rift in my opponents' unity, I knew that I would prevail in a battle between us. Yet the cost of that war—Muslim lives lost, *islam* further steeped in blood, my own chances destroyed of gaining A'isha's support and that of her followers—was prohibitively high. Also, I knew the Bedouin mind. A single erroneous rumor could send half my army scurrying to my opponents' side. The defection of al-Ashtar would certainly have that effect.

Now, as I had expected, A'isha uttered her dreaded ultimatum: al-Ashtar's head and those of Uthman's assassins—or war. "We can never support you until the blood-price is paid," she said. "And without my allegiance, you hold no power in Mecca and little in Medina."

She spoke the truth, but her implication was not as dire as she imagined. Clearly, she did not know that I had moved the *khalifa* to Kufa, a city more centrally located in our expanded territory, where support for my rule was nearly unanimous. Yet I desired A'isha's endorsement, for I coveted her advice and her companionship in my new position. Working together, we could not fail to restore *islam* to its original purpose: that of glorifying al-Lah, not men, and of caring for all God's children, not just a privileged few.

Yet how could I meet her demands? If she knew what she asked of me, she would not make such a request. To execute or even punish al-Ashtar would mean the loss of half my supporters, but that was only one reason I could not offer him to the vengeance-seekers. Mohammad, my beloved stepson and A'isha's brother, was another. As the one who had thrust the dagger into Uthman's forehead, Mohammad would certainly have to die. My eyes burned at the thought. He was Abu Bakr's son, but he belonged to me in a way that al-Hassan and al-Hussein never had. They possessed the Prophet's sweetness and his gentleness of manner, while my foster son Mohammad had somehow acquired my uncompromising idealism and the bold spirit that I had once possessed, but that had seemed to slip away during my years of banishment from the battlefield.

In my stepson I saw myself as I had once been, and as I longed to be again. How could I sentence him to death for taking action according to his principles? Uthman had been weak; his appointees, corrupt. Mohammad had suffered the results of that failed *khalifa* first-hand, in the Egyptian prison where he, Hud, al-Ashtar, and their companions had been sent for conspiring against Uthman. Had they not escaped, both would be dead now, or tortured so severely that they would be praying to die.

I had taken great pains to hide my son's role in the assassination, sending Naila with my wife Asma, to Ta'if for recovery from her wounds and, I had told her, for protection from further harm. Except for al-Ashtar—who would tell all if I persecuted him—and the men who had accompanied Mohammad into Uthman's home, no one else knew the truth. As for A'isha, I wanted to tell her—but how, with those two in the tent with us?

I lowered my head. "I am sorry. I cannot do as you wish. Al-Ashtar swears he is not the man you seek, and I will not punish him or anyone without proof of guilt." It was a defense that limped on a broken leg—and, when I glanced up at A'isha's disappointed face, I knew she was making the same assessment.

"Then we have nothing to discuss." She stood, then walked to the tent flap and held it open for me. I stood slowly, ignoring the murderous glares of Talha and al-Zubayr. A'isha did not realize what she was asking for—the execution of her brother. And she did not know how tenuous was her position. Behold her lifted chin, her calm demeanor! She fancied that her side was strong. Now was the time to disabuse her of that notion.

I ducked as if to leave the tent, then turned toward al-Zubayr and Talha, who now stood together as if bound by their common dislike for me.

"*Yaa* cousin, I almost forgot." I drew out a piece of parchment, whose seal I had broken, and handed it to al-Zubayr. "We intercepted a messenger from Mu'awiyya and took this note from him. It is addressed to you."

Al-Zubayr took the packet from me. Talha eyed the exchange with lifted eyebrows.

"You will find it interesting," I continued. I turned to A'isha. "*Yaa* A'isha, I advise you to read it, also, for it contains a promise from Mu'awiyya."

I left after stating my desire for another meeting—but my words were lost in the confusion and curiosity now whirling like a *zauba'ah* through the tent. Once outside, I let myself smile—and my cousin Ibn Abbas, who had listened from the flap, seized my beard in congratulation.

"By al-Lah, there will be no unity in their ranks from this day forward," he said as we began walking back to our camp, across the scrubby field where the battle, if there were one, would take place.

"Yes, by offering his support to al-Zubayr as *khalifa*, Mu'awiyya has secured our victory," I said. But my words sounded flat, saddened as I was by the thought of fighting A'isha.

Ibn Abbas shook his head. "I am confused. Mu'awiyya is known for his shrewdness—yet by dividing our enemy, he has assisted you, whom he professes to hate."

I nodded. "I, also, wondered at Mu'awiyya's sudden incompetence—at first. But now, I realize that he wants us to win."

"He delivers speeches against you every day, but he desires you as *khalifa*?"

As we neared our camp, I stopped so that we would not be overheard. "Mu'awiyya is known for his shrewdness, as you say," I said. "But he is also known for his ambition. If I remain *khalifa*, then he can continue his campaign against me. Eventually, if I cannot depose Mu'awiyya as governor, he might cause me to be overthrown and win the *khalifa* for himself. But if Talha wins the *khalifa*, with A'isha by his side—"

"Then Mu'awiyya remains governor of Syria." Abd Allah's frown deepened. "But isn't that what he desires?"

"So he says." I pulled my cousin close and murmured low, so that only he could hear my words. "By al-Lah, cousin, it has become clear to me whom Mu'awiyya really supports. As you have guessed, it is not me. Nor is it al-Zubayr, and it is certainly not Talha. Mu'awiyya's choice for the *khalifa* is none other than Mu'awiyya. And, as he has shown, he will resort to the most devious tactics to obtain it."

A'isha

For the first time in many weeks, I slept the deep sleep of the satisfied. I'd fallen into slumber with a prayer of thanks on my lips for the compromise we'd finally been able to strike—an agreement that would save countless lives and rescue *islam* from a future steeped in blood. In my dream, reliving the events of the night before, I clasped Ali's elbow and he mine, sealing the agreement that would avoid war between us. Then mayhem jolted me awake, and the day began that would change my life forever.

But before that happened, what an alliance—A'isha and Ali! It had been an exasperating four weeks of negotiations, partly because of Talha and al-Zubayr. Each seemed intent on doing battle with Ali, and on establishing himself as the man to take his place. Talha offered little more than smirking comments—*A man with thirty children should have no difficulty punishing a few unruly Bedouins*—while al-Zubayr challenged Ali directly, thrusting his face close enough to spray him with spittle as he accused Ali of being *a weak-livered embarrassment to the Hashim clan*. The remark made Ali's skin pale but he turned his attention back to me, where it remained for the rest of our talks.

As for me, I continued pressing Ali to bring the assassins to justice, but he continued to refuse. In return, he offered the weakest of proposals, including a promise to make the three of us top advisors in his *khalifa*.

I'd wanted to laugh out loud. Would Ali listen to us later, when he ignored our advice now? Punishing Uthman's killers might cost him some Bedouin supporters, but it would gain him my allegiance and that of Quraysh, and it would take away that jackal Mu'awiyya's excuse for seizing the *khalifa*. Why, then, did Ali stand so firmly against us? Try as I might, I couldn't understand, and, try as he might, he couldn't make me see.

Until, at last, we spoke in private.

Here's how it happened: Our "negotiations" were proceeding as usual, meaning they weren't proceeding at all. At one point, Talha took the last piece of bread just as al-Zubayr was reaching for it; al-Zubayr muttered that Talha's selfishness knew no boundaries, and Talha leapt to his feet with his sword unsheathed. "Arise and fight, you hypocrite, or I will cut the insult from your tongue!" Al-Zubayr jumped up, but I stood between them and demanded they settle their argument elsewhere.

"Come back when avoiding bloodshed, not shedding blood, is your intent," I said.

As the tent flap closed behind them, I took a deep breath—and, all of a sudden, felt as if the air in the room had become lighter. I turned to Ali, whose lips curved in the faintest of smiles.

"*Yaa* A'isha, I would never have believed that I would say this, but I am pleased to meet with you alone."

"If you think things will be easier for you now, you're mistaken. Being a woman doesn't mean I'm weak."

He laughed. "I would be the weak one if I held that opinion after knowing you for so many years." Then he stood and went to the tent flap, which he pulled aside to gaze at the night sky the way Muhammad had done, as if looking for answers in the shifting of the stars or on the face of the moon.

"Yet I must confess, A'isha. I have been disappointed that you would not confer privately with me."

I shrugged. "Negotiate in private, without Talha and al-Zubayr? I can't think of a way to insult them more."

"I am glad, then, that their discord has caused them to leave us." He turned to look directly into my eyes. "I have a matter to confess, A'isha, one that will explain my refusal to punish Uthman's assassins."

I shook my head. "I'm not sure I want to hear this without Talha and al-Zubayr present. They're the ones in charge, not me."

"They are the reason I have stilled my tongue," he said. "My information must remain confidential."

"But you can tell me?" I arched an eyebrow. "Because we're such close friends?"

"No, A'isha." He stepped back over to stand before me, and for a moment I thought he'd place his hands on my shoulders the way Talha liked to do. I took a step back, just out of his reach, and noticed his eyes flicker.

"I can tell you this secret because it concerns someone you love," he said. "Someone we both love." He cleared his throat. My heart began a deep, slow pounding.

"Mohammad, my stepson and your brother, is the man who killed Uthman," he said. I gasped, but his words only came out more quickly, like river waters bursting through a dam. "He and another man gained entry to Uthman's house. They surprised him and his wife, Naila, in his bedroom. Mohammad was the first to strike, piercing Uthman in the forehead with his dagger. The other man plunged his blade into Uthman's throat."

My own throat felt as though it had been pierced. "Mohammad." I slumped to a cushion and pressed my face into my lap, hiding my head with my arms as though I were under attack. My funny, impassioned little brother, the very likeness of *abi*, with a fire in his breast that reminded me of myself—Mohammad, a murderer! My beloved brother was the man I'd been urging Ali to behead.

What he'd done was wrong. A small voice reminded me of that fact as I pressed my face into my knees. If others discovered his deed, he'd die—justly. Yet I could not be the one to send my brother to his grave.

"I would have never forgiven myself," I said. "By al-Lah, if I'd caused Mohammad's death, I would have killed myself."

"There is no need to blame yourself." I felt his hand on my back and I jerked as if burned. Who was he now, this new Ali, who would break the rules of propriety by comforting a woman, who would risk his own position to save my brother's life, who would take me, his nemesis for more than thirty years, into his confidence? When my father had named Umar to the *khalifa*, he had predicted that the responsibility would make that fearsome man more gentle. It hadn't worked—but maybe *abi* had seen into the future, because it seemed to be happening now, to Ali.

"Ali," I said. "thank you for protecting Mohammad. He made a terrible mistake. He's so young and idealistic—"

"Thanking me is not necessary." His eyes grew moist. "I did not do this for you, A'isha. I love Mohammad as my own son. I would do anything to shield him from dishonor."

"And I, also," I said. I straightened my back and, my dignity regained, patted the cushion beside me. As he settled himself on it, I picked up the gourd on the cloth before us and poured a glass of water for him, then one for myself.

"Since beheading the assassins is now impossible, there is only one way to clean *islam* of this blood-taint," I said. "You must resign as *khalifa* and allow a *shura* to choose Uthman's successor. You may yet be chosen."

There was a long pause as he drank his water and pondered my words. "And whom would you support for the position, A'isha?"

I lifted my own bowl of water, glad for an excuse to shift my gaze away. I was about to betray Talha—my cousin, friend, and confidant for most of my life. But I'd witnessed his childish behavior toward al-Zubayr. I'd seen how greed and ambition had corrupted him. How could I support him as *khalifa*? Ali's first deed as *imam* had been to empty the treasury and give the money to the poor, the very thing Muhammad would have done. Ali had patiently negotiated with me for a month in an effort to avoid war, even though his army far outshone ours in numbers and strength. And he had risked his honor, had risked everything, in order to protect my brother.

I stood and he rose, also. I looked him full in the face, my heart open to him for the first time, this man whom my husband had loved. We were bound to each other in that way, also, by the love of Muhammad. How could anything tear us apart now?

"Don't worry about me," I said. "If you call an election, I won't oppose you. The opposite will happen. My allegiance will be yours, Ali."

Tears filled my eyes as we cast off taboos and dared to touch, not skin-to-skin but my hand on his sleeved elbow and his on mine, clasping each other to affirm our pact. There would be no battle, no brothers killing brothers, praise al-Lah!

In my dream that night, the pact ended with *a clamor of shouts and cheers, and spoons pounding against cooking pots, and camels bellowing as their bells were shaken.*

And in the next instant I was awake, sitting straight up in my bedroll, my thumping pulse adding to the shouting and bellowing and clanging and crashing that pelted my tent like hailstones. The noise bespoke a calamity as dire as if the moon and stars had plummeted from the sky. Then my tent flap flew open and in careened a man with the long headdress and rotting teeth of a Bedouin. He growled at me with eyes aglow until I snatched up my dagger and ran toward him, sending him howling out again.

Standing at the entrance, I peered out into the camp: Bedouins everywhere, their daggers waving, ripping open barley sacks and spilling the grain on the sand, smashing gourds against rocks and laughing maniacally as the precious water they contained disappeared into the dry earth, pulling down tent poles and breaking them, grabbing our sleeping troops and slicing holes in their beards. I stood paralyzed and confused, not comprehending until, in the roil, I spied the narrow face of al-Ashtar and I knew this had to be the work of Ali.

Ali! I sucked in my breath. How typical of him to say one thing and do another! How naive of me to believe him! For all his talk about returning *islam* to its pure state, he cared more about holding on to the *khalifa*.

I heard a guttural cry and looked around to see al-Ashtar slitting the throat of one of my warriors. I strapped on my dagger and grasped my sword. "Get ready to fight!" I cried, running through the camp, waving my blade. "Form your ranks, men! Arm yourselves for battle—Ali has declared war!"

When al-Ashtar saw me running through the camp in my gown, my hair uncovered, his eyes bulged and he quickly stuck his dagger into its sheath. "M-Mother of the Believers," he said. "I did not know you were camped among the men. Forgive me—"

"Get your men out of here now," I said, cursing the flush of heat across my neck and face, for why should I be embarrassed? "And tell your cowardly *imam* that, as gullible as I might be, at least *I* still have my honor." To my surprise, he ordered his men back to camp—making me wonder what Ali's real motive had been in sending them here.

Al-Zubayr and Talha came running up—al-Zubayr scowling, Talha waving his sword as though we had already fought the battle and won. "How dare you order the troops into formation!" al-Zubayr grumbled at me. "Next you will appoint yourself general in my place."

"If you're sleeping and I'm awake, and the need for a general arises, I'll gladly do the job," I snapped.

"Of course you would," Talha said, looking as though he wanted to embrace me. I stared at him. How enlivened he appeared by the idea of slaughter! "Quickly, let us go inside and plot our victory. *Yaa* 'Alqama! *Yaa* Jawn! Into the tent!"

As Talha and his men stepped inside the tent where I had negotiated peace the night before—alone, for neither Talha nor al-Zubayr had returned before I'd gone to bed—al-Zubayr's countenance darkened.

"I do not share Talha's enthusiasm for this fight," he said. "I would gladly lead as *khalifa*, but not with Muslim blood on my hands." He turned and walked away, into the swirl of men gearing up for battle. I called his name, but he continued as though I were merely a squeaking mouse.

Talha thrust his head through the tent flap. "Do not worry, A'isha. He will return," he said. "Al-Zubayr covets the *khalifa* too much to forgo the fight for it." My nephew Abdallah, al-Zubayr's son, rushed up in search of his father. Talha waved him in, suggesting he take al-Zubayr's place for the time being.

Soon the men had drawn their battle plans on a date-palm leaf and were marching forth from the tent. Talha bowed to me before following them. "We will prevail, A'isha. I feel victory in my bones. Al-Lah is on the side of the just, and you know that we are just."

I did know that, especially after Ali's betrayal today. My hands trembling with indignation, I dressed for battle, and possibly for death, in the white gown I'd worn for the *hajj* to Mecca. And, as women did during that holy pilgrimage, I declined the veil. Here, as there, my face and heart would be exposed to al-Lah. Nothing would be hidden from Him.

When I'd finished dressing, I went out to review the troops. They stood in long, straight lines, spears and swords in hand, chain-mail suits covering their bodies and leather helmets strapped onto their heads—but, to my alarm, their faces drooped and their shoulders sagged. Only Talha stepped like a jaunty bird among them, oblivious, it seemed, to their listlessness.

I approached him. Appreciation glinted his green eyes. "You look like an angel in Paradise," he said.

I raised my eyebrows. "Paradise is where we'll be in a few hours if we don't do something about these men. Our troops look like they'd rather go back to bed than fight the enemy."

"We'd heard there was a treaty with Ali." Abdallah came up from behind us. "Our hearts were gladdened by the news, because we've seen the members of the other camp. Our men don't want to kill Muslim brothers."

"I don't blame them," I said. "But unfortunately, it's either kill or be killed." I strode over to a large tree stump, careful to make each step long and purposeful. As the men's eyes turned to me, I leapt nimbly to the top of the stump.

"*Yaa* men of al-Lah," I called out. "*Yaa* defenders of justice!"

"*Yaa* Mother of the Believers!" my nephew Abdallah shouted back, al-Lah bless him. "*Yaa* most courageous of women!" Soon others were shouting my praises, also.

"I know you have heard that we reached a settlement with Ali. In truth, I sealed a pact with him only hours ago, in which he promised to resign as *khalifa* and let the people choose a leader. But, as you saw this morning, Ali is not a man who honors his agreements. He betrayed me, and all of you, by ordering this invasion of our camp."

"He betrays the Prophet of al-Lah!" Talha yelled. "Death to Ali!"

I felt a pang at his cry, recalling how I and Ali had grasped elbows the night before. I'd felt as one with him in our love for Muhammad and our shared mission of restoring *islam*. My heart had swelled with affection for him. Kill Ali?

But this was no time for sentiment. Ali had lied to me—not for the first time, but certainly for the last.

"Some of you are reluctant to fight against our Prophet's beloved cousin," I continued. "I, also, have resisted. For a month I have been seeking a compromise with Ali. But now, he has allowed his greed for the *khalifa* to overcome his sense of right and wrong. I know, and he knows, that Muhammad would not have wanted him to seize the position, with only the support of a few—"

"Filthy Bedouins!" someone shouted.

"Camel's milk drinkers!" another cried.

I lapsed into an uncomfortable silence, for we had several Bedouin tribes in our camp. Yet as the men yelled insults and lifted their daggers, I didn't admonish them, not wanting to dampen their enthusiasm for war. Their lives, and the future of *islam*, depended on it.

Al-Ahnaf ibn Qays, leader of the largest Bedouin tribe among us, stepped up to the date-palm stump. His mouth twisted as if he had chewed a bitter herb, and he kept his gaze on my knees.

"*Yaa* Mother of the Believers, I have come to a decision. I will not fight against the Prophet's beloved cousin. Neither will I fight against his beloved wife. May al-Lah forgive me for ever thinking otherwise." He turned and walked through the maze of men and out again, toward the grove of date-palms where our camels were tethered, cutting a swath through the formation as one hundred men in flowing robes followed him.

As I watched the defection of these Bedouins from our outnumbered force, I had to stop myself from crying out in dismay. We couldn't afford to lose even one man. But I knew there was nothing I could do. After the shameful insults our Qurayshi warriors had hurled—*Ai*! If only those old men had defected, instead of the young, fierce fighters who followed al-Ahnaf now—. But this wasn't the time for regrets. We had a battle to fight—and win, with al-Lah's help.

"*Yaa* men of al-Lah, listen to me," I cried, yanking al-Ma'thur from its sheath and hoisting it into the air. "Our enemy has more men, but we have God on our side. Remember the battle at Badr! We Believers were sorely outnumbered, yet with God's help, we prevailed." Never mind that many of those here, Meccans, had fought against Muhammad's army in that battle. "Al-Lah willing, we will prevail today. Now, let us go and fight for what is right—for the future of *islam*!"

"For *islam*!" Talha rode up on his horse, stirring the troops with his impressive entrance. "For *islam* and al-Lah!"

"For *islam* and al-Lah!" someone else cried, and a few others followed suit. But as our men turned to follow their leaders onto the battlefield, I noticed that many of them shuffled in the dust, their footsteps reluctant. I pressed my hands to my breast. *Help us, al-Lah,* I prayed, and stepped down from the date-palm stump with legs that trembled so violently, I could barely walk.

My nephew Abdallah stood nearby, ready to escort me to my vantage on the knoll in front of our camp. His eyes were as dark as eclipsed moons, and he chewed his lower lip. We walked without speaking to the top of the ridge. Wanting to give him some comfort—for this son of my sister's was like a son to me—I kissed his cheek and smiled into his eyes.

"Farewell, nephew, and don't lose heart," I said, somehow managing to keep my voice calm. "We'll see each other again in victory, or in Paradise. Either way, the reunion will be joyful."

As he turned and walked away, his bent head revealing the soft down at the back of his neck, I realized what I'd just said. Within hours—or minutes, by al-Lah!—Abdallah, who'd curled in my lap so many times as a boy, who'd been my faithful companion as a young man, might lie broken and dead on the battlefield. Tears ran in long, hot fingers down my face. Abdallah, dead! Talha, gone! Everyone I loved would fight for me today, would risk, and possibly lose, his life in part because of the grudge I'd harbored all these years against Ali.

As I walked to and fro along the ridge, willing myself to be brave, gripping the hilt of my sword and refusing to let any more tears fall, I remembered Talha's hissing words like the bite of a serpent stinging my ear. *You came for revenge, A'isha. Revenge and nothing more.*

I'd shrugged him away, not bothering to honor his accusations with a denial. Now, in the glare of impending death, I could deny nothing. Talha had spoken truly. I'd hated Ali ever since he'd urged Muhammad to divorce me. Yet he had been correct to urge divorce. I'd deliberately gotten stranded in the desert with Safwan, thinking I might run away with him and join the Bedouins. My disloyal act could have destroyed Muhammad's credibility in the eyes of the *umma.* Only God, by sending him a revelation of my innocence, had saved me, and *islam.* Without that miracle, divorcing me would have been the only way my husband could retain his honor and his position.

Perhaps that was why Ali had changed his mind about giving up the *khalifa*. He'd probably gone back to his tent and remembered the past, how I'd stood in his way at every turn ever since Muhammad's death. Why should he trust me? I'd been pretending all these years to be righteous, when actually my reasons for keeping Ali from the *khalifa* were more shameful than his reasons for pursuing it.

And now, my lust for revenge and my craving for power would send men on both sides to their deaths. I covered my face with my hands, hiding from the piercing gaze of Muhammad on high. What would he think as their souls entered Paradise and they told him what I'd done? What was he thinking now?

Ali

The wild eyes of al-Ashtar, so enlarged that they seemed to engulf his lean face, hovered above me as I surfaced from the first restful slumber I had experienced in many nights.

"You must awaken, *yaa imam*. The world is at an end!" His shout jolted me out of the last peace I would ever know in this world. He threw open the tent flap, revealing a sky bleeding and raw. I struggled to my feet and stumbled over to stand beside him.

When I looked across the field where I and A'isha had agreed *not* to do battle, I beheld lines of men in chain mail crossing the ground like an iron barrier, battle formations of men facing our camp, poised to attack—men from the camp of A'isha, with whom I had sealed a peace agreement only hours ago.

"By al-Lah, what has occurred while I slept?" I cried. I hastened to remove my gown and don my trousers and shirt, my chain mail suit, my leather jerkin and helmet, and scabbards for my sword and dagger. "I told you last night, al-Ashtar, there was to be no war. How has everything changed so completely?"

"I do not know, *imam*," he said. "I only beheld this treachery moments ago. I sounded the call to battle to alert our men, then came to find you."

"You—what?" I hated the whine in my voice, but in truth dismay wrapped its hands around my throat. Even as I had watched A'isha's troops lining up against us, I had calmed myself with a promise to correct any misunderstanding, to avoid the fight that seemed, suddenly, imminent. But once the call to battle was sounded, the fighting must commence. To stop now would cast us all into dishonor. Al-Ashtar's hasty response had sealed our fates, and that of *islam*.

I rushed out into our bustling camp with al-Ashtar following, my eyes taking note of the cheerful dispositions of the men who had grumbled these past days about inaction while I negotiated peace: *Did we abandon our women in order to sit on our bottoms and sharpen our swords?* Even al-Ashtar was restless; his eyes had lost their light the night before when I had told him that there would be no battle.

"We have reached an agreement," I had said. The droop of his mustache caused me to lay a comforting hand on his shoulder. "Al-Ashtar, this is for the best. All will be lost if Muslim brothers fight one another. We must put our own interests aside for the sake of *islam*."

There were no shadows on his face now, by al-Lah, only bright enthusiasm as we walked through the camp and greeted our warriors and chiefs. Sa'id ibn Ubayd al-Ta'i, chief of the Bedouin clan Banu Tayyi, with his gray-flecked beard extending to his navel like a batt of carded wool, lifted his sword and recited an extemporaneous poem declaring me as Muhammad's "legatee," prompting cheers from his fellow clansmen. 'Amr ibn Marjum, chief of the Basran clan the Banu al-Qays, who had defected from A'isha's side to join mine, bowed so low I thought he might embrace my ankles. Ammar ibn Yasir, the white-haired *shaykh* who had fought alongside me in Muhammad's army, seized my beard and admonished me to lift my head and add swagger to my step.

"By al-Lah, are you walking to your funeral?" he said, his dark blue eyes snapping so fiercely that I thought he might strike me. "I have never seen a military leader appear so forlorn. *Yaa* Ali, where is the spirit I witnessed in you at Badr, at Uhud, at the Battle of the Trench?"

Where, in truth? I heeded Ammar's advice and changed my shuffle to a strut, feigning excitement over this fight while inventing verses of my own—one of my talents of which I was most proud—to chastise the Mother of the Believers for ignoring the will of al-Lah. As I shouted my exhortations, I began to sense the truth in my words: By calling this battle, A'isha had committed a host of sins, beginning with the breaking of her contract with me. As deceptive as a black widow spider, she had ensnared me with her promises of cooperation and support, luring me into a sense of security and then, while I slept complacently, organizing her forces to attack me. My face burned as I remembered her tears during our talk, shed with seeming sincerity, and my naive willingness to believe that her heart had changed so dramatically, so suddenly, and so completely to favor me after all these years of hatred.

I had been a fool. And vain, also: Why else had I bargained with A'isha, and agreed to gamble my birthright, the *khalifa*, which I had hoped for since Muhammad's death? Although I had told myself I wished only to avoid spilling the blood of my fellow Muslims, my motives for the agreement had been, in truth, far less noble. The expression of gratitude and admiration in the eyes of A'isha, whom I had come to esteem above all other women, had puffed my chest full of satisfaction and, yes, pride. Once I had experienced her good will, I wanted only to increase it—and so I agreed to step down as *khalifa* and allow a *shura* to select Uthman's successor.

Yet now I saw her tactics clearly: a ruse to weaken me so that she, with her meager force, might gain the advantage of a surprise attack. Why else would she rally her troops without even notifying me? Although, only moments before, the presence of al-Ashtar by my side had prickled like a burr, I slapped his back in camaraderie as we walked back to my tent. How valuable his vigilance had been! Had he not spotted the movements in the enemy camp, we might all be slain in our beds now, victims of A'isha's treachery.

My outrage bubbling like the molten brimstone in Mount Layla's belly, I glowered at the sight of my foolish cousin al-Zubayr walking in agitated circles before my tent entrance. Why had he come here, risking his life before the battle had even begun? When I approached, he merely inclined his head as though he suffered from a sore neck. "Thanks be to al-Lah for returning you to your tent," he said. "It is most urgent that I speak with you. God willing, we can avoid spilling Muslim blood."

I looked askance at him, wondering if this was part of A'isha's manipulative plot. "The time for avoiding war is past, *yaa* al-Zubayr," I said. "As you see, the battle lines are drawn and the men are forming. The outcome is in al-Lah's hands now."

"But you can avoid the killing of the innocent by surrendering the guilty!" He frowned at al-Ashtar, who hovered beside me. "Do so now, Ali, I urge you! Is this Bedouin hothead worth thousands of virtuous lives?"

Al-Ashtar lunged forward but I grasped his sleeve and held him back. "I had nothing to do with Uthman's death," al-Ashtar snarled. "I stood at his front door trying to prevent violence, while you and Talha sent your sons with swords to inflame the crowd."

"We sent our sons to guard the *khalifa*'s door," al-Zubayr said. "While your henchmen sneaked into his house and murdered him."

"They were not acting under my command, I swear it before God. And"—al-Ashtar yanked his sword form the sheath on his belt—"I challenge anyone who asserts otherwise!"

"Your disavowal of violence is most impressive." Al-Zubayr turned his attention to me. "*Yaa* Ali, surely you will not continue to shield this man at the expense of Muhammad's Companions, many of whom are fighting on our side. What would the Prophet say of this sacrilege? Did he not say, 'Never should a Believer kill another Believer'? Did he not say, 'You who believe, do not kill each other, for God is merciful to you'?"

I did not know whether to laugh at my cousin's audacity or run him through with my sword.

"Your invocations of God's word are most convenient, and no doubt suit your purposes well," I said. "But Muhammad also said, 'Hold fast to God's rope all together; do not split into factions.' And he said, 'Do not be like those who, after they have been given clear revelations, split into factions and fall into disputes: A terrible punishment awaits such people.' You, Talha, and A'isha have broken this commandment by forming an army against me, and you have multiplied the sin, al-Zubayr, by soliciting the aid of that traitor Mu'awiyya."

At that moment, the *shaykh* Ammar strode up as youthfully as if he were twenty, instead of ninety-three. "The boy Jabar is prepared to begin," he said. I had ordered the youth to preface the battle by holding up the *qur'an*, then calling for unity, not discord. This departure from the traditional method of beginning warfare, which entailed hand-to-hand combat among men selected from each side, would be my final effort at peace. For, despite my arguments with al-Zubayr, I was well aware of al-Lah's admonishments against *fitna*.

Calm descended upon me, and supreme clarity, as it had in days of yore when I had fought for Muhammad. "Let us begin." I turned to take my leave of al-Zubayr—and noted how his face drained of blood as he stared at Ammar.

"By al-Lah, did not the Prophet predict that Ammar would be killed while fighting on the side of the righteous?" he rasped.

"That is the legend," I told my cousin. "I recall his making a similar comment about me and you. Do you remember? We were only boys, yet I have never forgotten his words." His eyes widened.

"Muhammad's wife Khadija, may peace be upon her, remarked on the closeness of our friendship, and said, 'May it always be so,'" I told him. "Then Muhammad responded, 'Days of strife will plague these two someday, to my sorrow. I have seen it in a dream. Al-Zubayr will challenge Ali in an unjust fight.'"

Al-Zubayr's face colored so quickly, I wondered if he were choking. "By al-Lah, I do recall that incident," he said. "I had forgotten it until this moment."

He turned and began walking away from me.

"*Yaa* al-Zubayr, where are you going?" my cousin Ibn al-Abbas, who had just joined us, called out to him. "The battle is the other way."

He turned and regarded the three of us. "I will not fight against you, cousin," he said. "Muhammad spoke truly: This battle is not just."

I would have embraced my long-lost cousin, now returned to me, except that he yet belonged to the ranks of the enemy. "Then join us," I urged, for not only did I love al-Zubayr, but he was a first-rate warrior and a shrewd commander.

"I cannot, by al-Lah," he said. "My son is fighting with A'isha. He is one of many Muslim men whose blood I would dread spilling—on either side.

Then, with his head down and his hands dangling by his sides, al-Zubayr, my cousin and lifelong friend, turned and left our camp, and the battlefield, and his dreams of Muslim unity. As he walked away, into the desert, I felt a hole open in my chest as though his love, along with A'isha's, were now lost to me forever.

A'isha

◆

For a moment, I knew hope. Standing on a knoll that overlooked the battlefield, I watched a boy ride into the center of the field with a sheaf of parchment held high in his gloved hands. Fear dilated the pupils of his eyes. His chain mail clanked. His hair lifted in the breeze like an angel's wing, then lay on his head. *He should be wearing a helmet*, I remember thinking. As if armor could truly guard us from death.

"*Yaa* warriors for Ali and for the Mother of the Believers, take heed of this, the holy *qur'an*!" The boy waved the sheaf. "Our blessed *imam*, Ali ibn Abi Talib, sends me here with an admonishment: Remember al-Lah and His Prophet, may peace be upon him, and remember the prohibition against Muslims fighting Muslims. Al-Lah watches us today!"

As he spoke, hope surged in my breast. Did this appeal to the *qur'an* mean that Ali wanted to call off this battle? The *qur'an* warned Believers repeatedly about *fitna* as though al-Lah had seen this day coming. If Ali and his men followed the *qur'an*, they would stop this fight before it started.

I held my breath as I waited to hear the boy's next words. Then, to my horror, an arrow struck him in the forehead and he toppled from his horse. A huge roar arose as each army blamed the other for the attack, and then men and horses rushed in a torrent onto the field while arrows darkened the sky.

I heard my name and turned to see Talha standing beside me. His chestnut steed stood behind him, pawing the ground. "That arrow was launched by al-Ashtar," he said. "I saw him crouching behind the great rock on the field's edge."

I narrowed my eyes, searching, suspecting who really wanted this war. Al-Ashtar, the instigator behind Uthman's assassination, would have had the most to fear from mine and Ali's agreement. Everyone, including the powerful Mu'awiyya, was demanding al-Ashtar's head. If Ali had resigned the *khalifa,* would he still be able to protect his friend?

I turned to Talha, unable to speak. Had al-Ashtar been carrying out Ali's command in attacking our camp this morning? Or had Ali slept, as I had, while al-Ashtar and his Bedouin friends had broken dishes, dumped out our water skins, toppled tents, and stabbed men—without their *imam*'s blessing?

"By al-Lah!" I cried, staring at Talha while the morning's events raced through my mind. "We must stop this battle. Talha, can you call a truce?"

Talha shook his head. "Men are already killing each other. The Bedouins wouldn't stop fighting now if Gabriel himself descended onto the field." He paused, watching the swords and spears, screaming horses, and falling bodies. "I came to ask if you have seen al-Zubayr. One of our men saw him talking with Ali."

I scowled. Had Ali convinced al-Zubayr to abandon our army and join his force, as several Bedouin clans had done this morning? But—no. Al-Zubayr was no allegiance shifter. He was a seasoned general who had vowed many times to knock Ali from his horse and from the *khalifa.*

"He must be out on the field." I lifted my eyebrows. "Which is where you're supposed to be."

Talha grinned—able, somehow, to keep his sense of humor even in the face of death. "Hearing is obeying, Mother," he said. His gaze locked with mine. "I came to pay my respects to you, A'isha. We are vastly outnumbered and outspirited, I fear, and destined to lose this fight. But—"

Panic swept through me, for if al-Zubayr had deserted us in body, Talha seemed to be doing so in spirit. "Lose? Never, by al-Lah! Get out there and show us all how a real *khalifa* wages war. We can do it, Talha! I feel victory in my soul. You don't need al-Zubayr; you don't need anyone."

He stepped forward. I saw his intentions. and moved out of reach an instant before he tried to embrace me. His face reddened and, with a wry glint in his eyes, he winked. "I need you, A'isha," he said "Knowing you are watching and praying for me gives me all the confidence in the world. And there is something I want you to know: Before we left Mecca, Umm Kulthum told me she is pregnant. If the child is a girl, we will name her A'isha."

Tears pushed against my eyes but I willed them away, wanting him to see only courage on my face. Their child, named for me! My sister must have known of Talha's love for me. With this act, Talha had made our friendship a cherished gift, and Umm Kulthum had given it her blessing. If I died today, I would do so with a conscience free of guilt and a heart brimming with love.

"Thank you," I whispered. "May al-Lah be with you, cousin." He mounted his horse and rode down the hillside, galloping into battle with his spear pointed before him.

From my vantage, I watched the fighting with my heart slamming against my throat. That was my brother Mohammad clashing swords with my nephew Abdallah. Whom was I supposed to encourage in that duel? *Please, God, protect them both from harm.* What kind of prayer was that to offer during battle? How could al-Lah answer my prayers if I didn't know what I wanted?

Horses whinnied, reared, and fell to the parched ground. Men ululated the fierce Bedouin war cry as if gargling blood. Bodies fell to the dirt. Boys scurried about with water skins—for Umar had long ago banished women from the Muslim battlefield—and knelt over the fallen, bandaging the wounds of the injured. I strained to see al-Zubayr's horse with the chain-mail blanket, Talha's yellow turban, and Abdallah's tall figure, but the fighting and the dust were too thick for me to discern which side was winning.

Several hours later, my throat was hoarse from shouting, my water skin was empty, and the day's heat was stifling. I eyed the shade of a small thorn-tree and wondered dizzily whether it was acceptable to sit while my troops toiled and bled in the sun. Then I saw my nephew Abdallah running toward me, his face streaked with dirt, sweat pouring down his skin, his helmet gone, his leather shield ripped. Talha followed behind, his chain mail broken and his hands smeared with blood.

"*Yaa* Aunt," Abdallah said, gasping, "we need you on the field!"

My heart's pounding filled my ears as, with hands that shook like leaves in the wind, I grabbed the shield Muhammad had given me and clumsily pulled my sword from its sheath. Here, at last, was the *jihad* for which Muhammad had armed me. I took a ragged breath, then lifted my chin and straightened my back. Despite my heart's sickness at the pitting of brother against brother, of Muslim against Muslim, the facts behind the battle were undeniable, and the verdict was this: Righteousness was in our camp, and so was victory. Ali was in the wrong. So I told myself.

"Come on, let's go," I said, and took a single step down the hill before Talha grabbed my sleeve to stop me.

"We can't let you walk into this battle," he said. "Your death would dispirit our men and ensure our loss."

"But I thought you needed me!" I bristled with impatience.

"We do," Abdallah said. "But not on foot. Like this!" He gestured with his hand toward our camp below, where a group of five or six men ran toward us leading a camel by its reins. A green-curtained *hawdaj* covered in chain mail swayed and clanked on its back.

"You want me to fight from the back of a camel?" I laughed in disbelief. "By al-Lah, are you *djinni*-possessed?"

"It's the way they used to do it, in the olden days," Abdallah said. "My grandfather Abu Bakr told me. When an army began to lose a battle, the men would bring a woman onto the field riding a camel, to rally the troops. Everyone would fight harder to protect her."

I stuck my sword back into my belt. "I don't want to perch myself on a camel while you fight," I said. "I'd be much more valuable to you on the ground, killing the enemy, than sitting like a figurine on a shelf."

Talha frowned. "By al-Lah, our army loses more men every minute you stand here protesting," he said. "Do as I say, A'isha, for once. Trust me. With the Mother of the Believers in their midst, our men will increase their fighting. When Ali and his warriors see you, they'll falter. This is the only way we can prevail."

As much as I wanted to argue with him—I'd been practicing my sword-fighting with him, and we both knew I was not boasting when I'd said I could kill many men—I also respected this new Talha who had emerged, this serious, commanding general. I didn't dare challenge his authority, not in front of my nephew and certainly not in front of these men who now had the camel kneeling before me. So without another word I mounted the *hawdaj* and took my seat, peering out at my cousin as the animal stood and, swaying, took me into battle with Abdallah holding her reins.

"Remain inside!" Talha shouted as he walked beside me. "Don't open your curtains for any reason, do you hear me? If you are even injured, we are lost. The chain mail will keep you safe, but only if you hold your curtain tightly shut."

I let the fabric drop shut and sat back in my seat, intending to do his bidding. When the camel had stopped, I listened to the commotion and tried to figure out what was happening. "A'isha, the Mother of the Believers!" I heard Abdallah cry, and cheers flew up all around me. The clanging of swords followed, and shouts. The rich, metallic stench of blood and the reek of bowels made me gag. The air felt thick and hot inside my enclosure. I longed to pull the curtain aside but I remembered Talha's commands. He would be the *khalifa* and I only an adviser. It was what I had wanted, and so it was my duty to obey him.

Then I heard a familiar cry. Gulping, I moved the curtain a few inches to see my beloved nephew falling to the ground, an arrow in his neck. His hand dropped the reins of my camel and another man rushed forward to grab them. I must have made a sound, for the man's eyes turned upward to me and, in the next instant, he was impaled in the stomach by the spear of an enemy fighter, who then fell to the ground, stabbed by one of our warriors, who then took my camel's reins.

I dropped the curtain and sat back in my seat, my stomach wrenching. Abdallah, dead! And another man, too, beloved by someone, a man who had given his life for me, his Mother. By al-Lah, I'd never wished for anything as much as I wished for my own death in that moment! Who was I to deserve these sacrifices? A spoiled, stubborn girl who'd been forced at a young age to marry the Prophet of God, who'd almost dishonored him because of her own selfish desires, and who'd spent the rest of her life in pursuit of two goals: revenge against Ali for judging me, and power and prestige for my family members.

Yaa *al-Lah, please end my life now,* I prayed, feeling as cold as if the fingers of a skeleton were scuttling along my spine. *If you are even injured, we are lost,* Talha had said. Wouldn't my death mean an end to this battle? Suddenly, the question of the *khalifa* seemed as insignificant as the question of which robe to wear on a given day. *Take my life now, God, and give the* khalifa *to whom You will. The decision was never in my power to begin with.*

Then a strange *ping!* sounded in my *hawdaj*. Distracted from my prayers and my grief, I looked around for the source. There was only me and my wretchedness inside this curtain. Another sound like the last, but sharper, drew my gaze to an arrow sticking through the cloth.

My pulse raced as I realized that Ali's men were shooting at me. Another arrow hit the *hawdaj*, and then another, until soon it sounded as if hailstones pelted my curtain. I felt my camel lurch under me, and heard a man shouting, *Hold that beast steady, or we will lose our Mother!*

Our Mother. My heart lifted at the words. I was a Mother to them, just as Muhammad had been a Father. They had come to *islam* as meekly as lambs, like the runts I used to suckle with milk on my finger. These men had given up their homes and their families, their wives and earthly mothers, to come and fight for me—for me, the Mother of the Believers, for wasn't I the one who had given the speeches denouncing Uthman's assassination? Hadn't I called them to arms? How could I have done all that simply out of revenge? No, my cause was just: to honor the memory of their Prophet by keeping alive his vision for *islam*.

Each arrow's *ping!* made my pulse skip and skitter more wildly. What kind of Mother hides away when her children need her help? I had prayed to die, and now it looked as though I would. But by al-Lah, I might as well die in a manner befitting the favorite wife of God's Prophet.

With a trembling hand I pulled al-Ma'thur, Muhammad's legacy, from my sheath. Cowering had never been the way of A'isha bint Abi Bakr, as my husband had known. *Use it well in the* jihad *to come*. Here it was, the struggle he'd spoken of, and now it was incumbent upon me to do my duty. Then, when I met Muhammad in Paradise, I could tell him I'd done my best until the end, and that his sword had enabled me to die with honor.

I took a deep breath and pushed the curtain of my *hawdaj* aside, struggling, for the chain mail made it heavy. I thrust myself through the opening and kept my knees bent so as to move with the camel. I lifted my sword, intending to bring it down on Marwan. I was a moment too late, for he had just speared Talha in the leg, pinning his knee to his horse. Talha struck Marwan down in return, then glared at me. "Get back inside, A'isha!" he shouted. "Or you'll be killed!"

Then he grabbed his leg and lost consciousness, slumping on his horse. The man next to him fell, his arm severed by an enemy's sword, leaving the reins of my camel unguarded. Before I could take a breath, a Bedouin man had seized the reins—but when he glanced up at me, I noticed that it was one of our own warriors. He fought bravely, fending off attacker after attacker. I raised my sword, wanting to fight but my camel lurched, throwing me backwards into the *hawdaj*, where I landed hard on my tail bone. Wincing, I rubbed the sore spot—and realized that I had lost my sword. I poked my head out of the curtain again to search for it—and found it had been flung out of reach and was sticking in one of the ropes tethering my *hawdaj* to the camel. Every movement pressed the rope against the blade, fraying it more. Death seemed certain for me now. If arrows didn't pierce me, my *hawdaj* would surely topple to the ground.

Yaa Muhammad, I will be with you very soon. I closed my eyes to imagine my beloved's handsome face, his beautiful eyes like copper coins gazing with love at me. In an instant, though, my vision changed—and I saw myself standing on my camel's back and fighting, holding on to my *hawdaj* with one hand and slashing my blade with the other. I pulled the curtain aside again to meet death courageously, face-to-face, as Muhammad would have done.

I threw myself over the back of my camel and grabbed my sword, ignoring the arrow that pierced my arm and the pain shooting through my shoulder. I stood shakily, preparing to fight as I had in my vision. Arrows fell all around me, but I never heeded them. Instead, I stared into the coal-black eyes of Ali, whose mouth opened at the sight of me, then pressed shut in determination. I watched as he urged his black steed forward to race toward me like a whirling *zauba'ah*.

Ali was coming. Here was the contest I had longed for all my life, and now dreaded as if it were my brother I faced. Yet even as I watched him, I knew my time on Earth was ended. After all that had passed between us, I could not harm Ali.

Ali

The battlefield is not the place for fear. If fear makes its residence in a warrior's heart, his enemy can smell it, for it is an aroma most sweet, portending victory for the man who detects its subtle mingling of sweat, sex, and milk fresh from the udders of a goat.

For this reason, more than any other, accomplished warriors learn to banish fear on the battlefield. I, who had participated in many bloody and gruesome fights in my youth, had never allowed myself to become afraid during a fight, and so I had invariably defeated my foes. But during that terrible slaughter that would come to be known as the Battle of the Camel, when I beheld A'isha crouching atop her camel with her sword in hand while arrows flew about her head, fear seized my throat like the teeth of a hungry jackal.

I had never seen a sight as awe-inspiring—or terrifying—as A'isha bint Abi Bakr astride that lurching beast, her mouth a rictus of fury, her left hand gripping the bar of her *hawdaj* and her right hand holding high Muhammad's jewel-encrusted sword. Blood smeared her white gown and pale arms, and from her shoulder protruded an arrow that she seemed not to feel. My heart swelled as I watched her among my best and bravest men—men who would not hesitate to kill her if they could, for many of them were new converts to *islam* and therefore unhindered by the reverence for the Mother of the Believers that those who had known Muhammad still felt.

Death seemed at hand for one of the most exemplary women al-Lah had ever fashioned and the most infuriating, also. In that moment I forgot the mayhem and stood admiring this woman whom I had previously hated.

Al-Lah only knows how long I might have watched A'isha challenge me with her eyes and raised sword. But then my son Mohammad rode up and urged me to save his sister's life. "If you don't, then, by al-Lah, I will!" he shouted. "If it means giving my life for hers, then let God's will be done. I would rather die than see my sister dishonored by Bedouins."

And then I recalled another warrior-woman, one as fierce, if not as beautiful: Umm Himl, the apostate warrior whom Khalid ibn al-Walid had brutally raped and murdered in battle. Perspiration broke out on my face and hands as I realized how imminent was a similar fate for A'isha.

I knew that there would be no halting this battle, not by command, for this was the moment for which I had prepared these men with my rousing speeches condemning the actions of the Mother of the Believers. I had labeled her an "affront to *islam*" and a "flaunter of the wishes of Muhammad, who ordered his wives to remain in their homes, hidden from the lustful eyes and hearts of men." After stirring their passions, could I now rush in and forbid them the very prize with which I had lured them? No. If I tried to stop them, they would ignore me, or, worse, turn against me.

I remembered how Khalid had felled Umm Himl, and I saw the answer to my dilemma. "We must slice the hamstrings of A'isha's camel," I said. "The beast will fall to its knees, and the fight will be ended."

Mohammad frowned. "What if she falls to the ground? She'll break her neck."

"That is a possibility," I said. "But if we do nothing, she will certainly die."

A scream pulled our attention back to the fight. One of my warriors had grabbed A'isha's blade and, in spite of his bleeding hands, yanked and tugged in attempt to pull her to the ground. She wrested the sword away from him, but it was clear that she was tiring. Now was the time to save her. She looked up and our gazes locked, and, for the first time, I saw terror in her eyes. Holding my breath, I kicked my horse into action and raced toward her, not thinking about what I had to do, but relying solely on God's guidance.

Such a feat as I had to perform would be difficult, for it would require maneuvering a horse around the crowd and back in, like thread through a weaver's loom, then reaching out with a blade and slicing the backs of her camel's legs even while the animal shifted and lurched—and doing all without getting kicked, stepped on, or killed by the enemy. Then I would have to leap to the ground and into the fray, to land by A'isha's side. The task would be incredibly complicated; impossibly difficult for most. But not for Ali ibn Abi Bakr, the greatest warrior who ever fought by Muhammad's side.

I glanced at her as I approached, my sword lifted, hoping to convey my intention so that she might hold on tightly to her *hawdaj*, to prevent a deadly, headlong tumble. I beheld her luminous eyes, brimming like bowls of tears as she lowered her sword. She had determined not to fight me!

I ululated a blood-chilling trill and bore down upon the group surrounding her so that they dispersed. I pulled back on my horse's reins in an attempt to slow down, then reined him to the side to avoid the flurry of panic-stricken men. My steed skidded, nearly throwing me from his back.

In an instant, however, my horse had regained its footing and had skirted around the camel's side, then behind its back legs. I eyed my target, the backs of its knees. As I neared its far flank I leaned out as far as I could go and thrust my double-bladed sword toward its knees.

I felt my blade sink into the camel's tendon and slice through; then I cut the second hamstring even more quickly, and lowered my head to my horse's neck as we passed on its lee side. My eyes watered from the stench of the dung the poor beast had dropped in its terror. The camel's shrill scream, so human-like, brought chills to my body. I wheeled my horse around as the camel fell to its knees, its hind legs buckling first, then its forelegs—howling and rolling its eyes as its body crashed to the ground. I never heard A'isha make a sound, but I did see her topple backward, thank al-Lah, into her *hawdaj*.

No one spoke. The cacophony of battle had ceased as all, followers of both A'isha and Ali, beheld the fallen beast and listened to its agonized groans. Mohammad rode up and pierced its neck with his blade, ending its misery. I leapt from my horse and ran to the *hawdaj*, which somehow had remained upright. I wanted to hurl myself to the ground in prostrations of thanks when I saw the torn green curtain ripple and heard the chain mail clink like a woman's bracelets.

"Are you harmed, *yaa* Mother of the Believers?" I called, every muscle tensed against a "yes" answer, or, al-Lah forbid, no answer at all.

"No, I am uninjured," she said, and my relieved sigh was audible, I was certain, to all. "Only this arrow in my shoulder," she added feebly.

I leaned in to help her, and our gazes met again—but only for a moment, until she covered her face with her wrapper. In that brief encounter, however, I beheld a mingling of sadness and grief that would haunt my dreams until my dying day. Tears welled in my eyes as, working slowly and gently, I extricated the arrow's head from her flesh and blood spurted anew from the wound. I tore a strip from my bandage belt and wound it around her arm. Then I extended my hands to help her emerge from the *hawdaj*, but she refused my assistance. As soon as she emerged, the men around her began to shout her *kunya*.

"Mother of the Believers!" they cried, including those who had just fought against her. "The hearts of Muslims weep with love for you, *yaa* Mother."

Mohammad approached to lift her into his arms, but she shook her head and murmured something. Then she stood leaning against him and narrowed her eyes at me. I think she took note of my foolish smile. It was unmanly and might have appeared gloating to her, but I could not suppress it, for I was relieved. In spite of the tears making their slow roll through the grime and blood on her face, A'isha appeared to be in good condition.

"May al-Lah protect you, *yaa* Mother," one of my men called.

I almost laughed to see her famous smirk. "I can protect myself well enough from the likes of *you*," she said in a curt tone. "As you've just witnessed."

She nodded to Mohammad. He lifted her and walked, cradling her in his arms, to her camp. I stood in place to watch their retreat, whispering thanks to al-Lah for preserving her, before turning to my men.

"This battle is ended," I said, surprised at the weariness of my voice, as though it had traveled far to be here. "Congratulations, men. We are victorious."

Their cheers sounded forced to my ears as I mounted my steed and rode slowly away, guiding my horse with care around the bodies, and body parts, of men I had known and respected. I moaned to see Tarif, the lighthearted eldest son of my faithful warrior Adi "The Generous," whose wounds in this battle left him only one eye with which to cry for his loss. I shook my head at the dismembered bodies of al-Saq'ab and Abdallah ibn Sulaym, brothers of Muhammad's Companion Mikhnaf, killed along with so many members of their clan while holding the reins of A'isha's camel. I wept over the broken body of Abd al-Rahman ibn 'Attab, a friend of my cousin al-Zubayr's, a quiet man who had been like a father to al-Zubayr's son Abdallah.

My eyes swam in tears at the sight of these good men slain, and for what? For the *khalifa* to remain in my possession? The fact that I had resigned myself to giving it up, had even embraced the notion of a *shura* to choose a leader, and had gone to sleep the night before with a heart lightened by A'isha's respect, made this bloodshed even more sickening. Sitting on my horse, my heart swelling with admiration and constricting with fear as I'd watched A'isha in the midst of the battle, I'd had to struggle to keep my face impassive when an arrow stuck in Abdallah's neck. Yet when Marwan's spear had pinned Talha's knee to his horse, making him faint, I had, with equal difficulty, suppressed my glee.

As if conjured by my reminiscences, Talha appeared before me, lurching toward his camp. His hands gripped his thigh, where the blood spurted out whenever his fingers slipped, and his parchment-pale face shimmered in rivulets of sweat. A taste like hot metal filled my mouth and a voice like a lion's roar urged me to finish the job Marwan had begun. One blow of the sword, and I would be rid of him at last.

But I could see that I would not need to deal that blow. Death had locked its talons around Talha's neck and was rapidly squeezing the life from him. I dismounted and pulled another strip from my bandage belt, then bound Talha's wound in effort to stop the bleeding. It was to no avail. Marwan's spear had struck an artery.

Alas, Talha was unable to assist me as I tried to place him on my horse, intending to transport him to his tent. So I propped him against a thorn tree in the sparse, mottled shade and gave him water from the skin on my belt. He drank deeply until every drop had been relinquished.

"My son . . . " he said, gasping.

"He is fine," I lied. "His wounds were superficial." I had seen the young man's severed head on the field just moments ago.

"A'isha," he said. His eyes stared into the distance, as though the far horizon held the answers to his questions.

"She is well," I said. "She will be glad to hear that you are alive."

"Alive!" He gave to me, then, the first grin of his that I had ever appreciated. "You must learn to lie better," he rasped.

I returned his smile. "I have never been good at lying. Haven't you heard? The truth is ever inscribed on my face for all to read."

He closed his eyes. "You and A'isha," he said. "Just alike." And then he exhaled, and his head drooped, and the candle that had been Talha's life flickered, then snuffed, leaving only darkness behind.

I said a prayer over him. *Forgive him for his misdeed. He succumbed to avarice and the lust for power, as many have before him. But he loved your Prophet,* yaa *al-Lah, and he loved A'isha above all others, as Muhammad did, also.*

Riding to my tent, I thought of A'isha, her blazing eyes, her furious wielding of the sword from the back of that camel. She'd tried to defend the men who had held her animal's reins, men who had vied to give their lives for her sake. How grief-stricken she must feel now, with the blood of her loved ones staining her hands!

I bathed in the Euphrates that night, inviting the cool waters to awaken me from the horrific dream I had been living all day. The battle was finished. I was the *khalifa.* I had won the title at last, and no one, not even Mu'awiyya, could take it from me. By granting me victory, al-Lah had demonstrated His will. Yet—why did I feel so dissatisfied? The prize I had coveted for so long was mine at last. But the winning of it was tainted by the knowledge that A'isha had betrayed our pact.

I yanked on my clothes with increasing fury as I relived the events of the night before and of this morning. How could A'isha have sealed an agreement with me in which I would have given up everything in exchange for her support—which, in truth, meant more to me than the *khalifa*—and then summoned her troops to attack? I had always known her to be a manipulator, but I never would have imagined outright treachery from her. Had she lied in order to gain the advantage of surprise? Or had her cohorts Talha and al-Zubayr convinced her to break her oaths?

I determined to visit her the next day and demand answers, no matter how shattered she might be by the news of Talha's death. This tragedy was of her making. I would have upheld my part of our bargain. If not for her, these men would not have died. A'isha was as guilty of their deaths as if she had murdered them all in their beds—and as *khalifa*, I held the power to make her pay any price for their blood. Unless she convinced me otherwise, I would exact my revenge in the worst possible manner for her. I would take away her cherished freedom. By al-Lah! She would never leave the mosque again.

◆

I arose well before the sun the next morning, bristling with anxiety about the task before me. After dressing in the finest robes I had brought on this journey, I performed my morning *raka'at*, bows and prostrations before al-Lah, and then stepped out of my tent as soon as the maddeningly slow dawn had at last taken possession of the sky.

To my dismay, her servant denied me entrance to her tent. The foreign woman's knowledge of Arabic being so limited, we were reduced to hand signals until, frustrated, I cried out to A'isha and told her she must allow me entry. She did not answer. I called again, but she remained silent.

I shouted. "*Yaa* A'isha, have you forgotten your crushing defeat on this very ground only yesterday? I am your *imam*, no longer to be defied. I command you to admit me, or I will order your tent dismantled."

In the next breath her tent flap moved and I glimpsed her face—or a portion of it, as she had veiled herself.

"*Afwan*, *imam* Ali," she said quietly. "If you have entreated me before to enter my tent, I was unaware. My sobs of remorse were all that I could hear."

Her formal tone stung me. Yet I reminded myself that this manner of speaking connoted her respect for me. As I stepped inside, I drew on a mantle of authority, playing the role for which I had fought, and for which men had died.

She, also, played the part that had fallen to her. She lowered her head, hiding her face completely, showing complete submission, and took a seat on the ground. I should have been pleased, for I had envisioned this moment ever since she had married Muhammad and lifted her nose at the sight of me. Yet, with a scowl, I urged her to stand.

So much enmity, so much strife had passed between us since that early morning pact—had it been only yesterday? I could not fathom it—after the oneness of purpose, and of heart, we had achieved. In our common love for my son, her brother, we had forged a bond greater than ourselves and our ambitions. But she had destroyed that bond with her capriciousness, and now, no matter what was said in this room, we would never be able to recreate it. The realization made me want to strike her, to view pain on her face such as I was feeling.

"*Humayra of Iram!*" I cried, pointing my finger at her. *Humayra*, "Little Red," had been Muhammad's nickname for her, and I invoked it to shame her. Iram was a fabled tribe, the greatest before Arabs had inhabited Hijaz. According to legend, the tribe was destroyed because of the foolish actions of its leader—just as she, with her capriciousness, had nearly destroyed *islam*.

Her eyes flickered and she tossed her head. "*Humayra* was an endearment reserved for my husband's use," she said. "And, although you like to think so, you're not Muhammad, nor do you bear the slightest resemblance to him in character."

I glowered at her, remembering what I'd always disliked about A'isha. Only a woman of extreme arrogance would speak to a man in this fashion. And only A'isha, the most arrogant woman of all, would insult me after suffering such a devastating loss.

"Character?" I bared my teeth at her. She did not flinch. "Who are you to speak of character, you oath-breaker? I, at least, honor my pacts."

She lifted her arms toward the ceiling and laughed, as if to ask al-Lah whether He had heard my jest. "Which pacts have you honored recently, Ali?" she said, letting her hands drop and looking me full in the eyes. "I can think of at least one that you violated in a most dishonorable fashion."

I was imagining seizing her by the shoulders to shake her to her senses, when a call at the entrance to her tent interrupted me.

"*Assalaamu alei—*" A'isha began, pulling aside the tent flap, then stopped. "Oh, it's you," she said in a flat tone.

"I have come for *imam* Ali." I heard al-Ashtar's voice. "It is urgent."

"Please enter," I said, ignoring A'isha's frown. He stepped inside and bowed to me, then extended a long, blanket-wrapped item that he carried in both hands.

"This was brought to your tent this morning," he said. "It was found in the desert, on the road to Medina, beside the body of a man. He could not be identified. He had been stabbed many times, indicating an ambush. This was his sword."

My hands shook as they pulled away the cloth. The image of al-Zubayr walking away from my camp, headed toward the Medina road, flashed across my mind. Who else from my camp had seen him depart? I glanced up at al-Ashtar, who had stood beside me and watched al-Zubayr's retreating figure, and who had often bragged that he would kill him on the battlefield. His blank expression only fueled my suspicions.

I groaned when I beheld the sword al-Ashtar had presented to me. Al-Zubayr had hammered its wide, flat blade from the armor of a Byzantine warrior he'd killed; its tarnished brass handle had come from a sword that al-Zubayr's father, my uncle al-Awwam, had wielded. Tears cut against my cheeks. Behind me, A'isha's voice broke on the edge of my grief. Her sobs echoed my own slow pulse of sorrow, and we were joined again by our love for a man better than us both.

I handed the sword to al-Ashtar with instructions to carry it to al-Zubayr's son Abdallah, who lay in his tent recovering from his injuries. My arms longing for comfort, and for comforting, I turned to A'isha, who had fallen into a heap on her bed and buried her face in her arms.

Moved by her grief, I stepped over to kneel beside her. "A'isha," I said. "Al-Zubayr died with more honor than any of us."

"He colluded with Mu'awiyya," she said. "I saw the letter you gave him."

"That was Mu'awiyya's scheming," I said. "He wanted to cause dissension in order to strengthen himself."

"But then, when Talha took command of our army, al-Zubayr deserted us." Her shoulders began to shake. "He ran away."

"He did not run away," I said. "He walked away after refusing to fight. He begged me to surrender al-Ashtar to you, and when I refused he said he would rather die than turn his sword against a fellow Muslim." I covered my hand with the sleeve of my robe and ventured a tentative touch to her shoulder. She shrugged me away so vehemently, I took a step backward.

"Which is more than you could say!" A'isha said in a snarling tone.

I stood. "I do not know what you imply," I said. "I tried everything short of walking away to avoid that battle."

"Such as sending your Bedouin friends over to destroy our camp?"

I blinked at her. "What Bedouin friends do you speak of? If your camp was attacked, it was not by *my* command."

She laughed. "Am I supposed to believe that, Ali? Your bodyguard, al-Ashtar, came over with his friends in the early morning to slit our men's throats. Fortunately, I'm a light sleeper, or they might have killed me, also."

As she spoke, I realized what had happened that morning. I began to bellow like A'isha's hamstrung camel.

"Al-Ashtar," I said. "By al-Lah, I will have his head for this." I told her how I'd returned to my tent after our talks were completed, too exhausted to tell al-Ashtar anything except that we would not fight. "He must have feared that I'd succumbed to your demands, and that he would be punished for Uthman's death."

She pressed a hand to her throat. "You didn't order the attack?"

"No. I was sleeping, A'isha. Just as you were."

Her mouth quivered. "By al-Lah! It was all a mistake."

We stared at each other. Aisha's eyes were as wide as if she beheld a *djinni*, but I knew she did not see me. Like me, she was reliving the horrors of the past day.

"All those men," she whispered. "Dead, and for what?"

For *islam*, I could have told her. Every man in the battle had fought for the future of our religion and of our *umma*. Yet the words stuck in my throat. *Islam*, I feared, had been the greatest casualty of all. Unless ...

I settled myself on the ground beside her.

"*Yaa* A'isha, this is not the first battle to be fought over a misunderstanding. Many wars are fought for this reason. And we cannot undo these errors now. Al-Zubayr is gone. Talha is gone. But I and you, we can begin again. We can make their deaths count for something—"

"Talha?" A'isha's voice rasped. "He's dead?"

I wanted to impale myself, then, for my insensitivity. The hours had been long since the battle, the sleepless night seeming to stretch into eternity, muddling my mind. The terrible news about al-Zubayr had made me forget to inform her about Talha.

I looked down at my folded hands, unable to bear her pleading gaze. She loved Talha yet, I could see that clearly. "I buried him last evening under the thorn tree," I said.

She threw herself down again, sobs wracking her anew, and I could only watch, my touch being unwelcome and my words insufficient. "*Yaa* Talha, forgive me," she said. "I encouraged you to seek the *khalifa* because of my own lust for revenge. Now you are dead, the finest man of all. *Yaa* al-Lah, take me, also! How I wish I were dead! No, death is too good or me. How I wish I had never been born!"

I listened and watched, debating whether I should tell her the truth about her beloved Talha. More than almost any other man, he had been responsible for Uthman's assassination. He had given money to the rebels, enabling them to continue their siege of Uthman's home. He had helped Mohammad and his friends gain access to Uthman's roof. I had always wanted to tell A'isha these things, but I had known she would not believe me. Now, hearing her sobs, I could not bear to cause her more pain. So I kept my knowledge to myself, for her sake.

"A'isha," I said when her tears had finally subsided, "remember what I said before. We cannot correct the errors that have been made, or bring back the lives lost. But we can give meaning to the sacrifice. We can join together, I and you, to do what we have both wanted to do: to return *islam* to its original vision."

Her eyes flashed like daggers. "What does that mean to you, Ali? Power? Money? Status?"

"Refuge for the poor, the orphans, and the weak," I said. "Recognition that we are all created from a single soul. Submission to the One God."

She fell back, her eyes wide. "By al-Lah!" she whispered. "I and you want the same things."

"You speak truly." I gripped the edges of my cushion. "A'isha, work with me. Together, we can make *islam* strong again, and we can prevent Mu'awiyya from seizing the *khalifa*."

A'isha wiped the tears from her eyes with the sleeve of her robe. "I must respectfully refuse."

"But why? We could bring much good to the umma—"

"I'm finished with public life," she said. "I've lost the heart for it." She turned to the corner near her bed and lifted al-Ma'thur in its bejeweled sheath.

"Take it," she said, handing it to me. "This belongs to you now. I will never fight again, al-Lah willing. You, on the other hand, are the *imam*, and you will need it."

I accepted it from her, felt its weight in my hands and arms, and marveled that she could have even lifted the sword, let alone wielded it in battle. Here was the possession I had coveted after Muhammad's death, and that I had resented A'isha for inheriting. Despite all the swords, daggers, and shields he had left to me, this, handed down to him from his father, was the one that mattered—then. Now, though, it felt wrong in my hands, as though it had been shaped for someone else's use.

"I cannot take this." My voice sounded like a tearing cloth. "It is yours, A'isha, 'The Legacy,' left to the Mother of the Believers."

"A mother's task is to give life, not destroy it," she said. "There is no place for swords in my life now, Ali."

Then she told me her plans: to confine herself to the mosque and the courtyard for the rest of her days and nights, and to spend her time in prayer and in passing to others her knowledge of the *qur'an* and the stories of Muhammad's life. "This is my atonement," she said, "to become an exile of sorts—but one that will benefit others, and that will benefit *islam*."

For the first time since I had known A'isha, serenity lived beneath her veil. As she told me her plans, her voice soughed like a morning breeze. Looking at her, I felt as peaceful as if she had laid her hand over my anxious heart.

I stood and bowed. "It will be as you wish, Mother of the Believers. And if you ever need anything, please do not hesitate to ask me for it. Anything."

"There is one thing," she said. "Please, Ali, when you leave this tent, protect my honor. No—increase it. Besides my nephew Abdallah, it is all I have left."

That task was to begin immediately, for when I left A'isha's tent I found a crowd of men, warriors from both sides, waiting to hear my verdict for her. *A flogging, by al-Lah, and I will wield the whip!* one man called. *A woman of her courage deserves to be made a queen, if not the khalifa*, another challenged. I held up my hands to quiet them, deciding how I would shield A'isha from speculation that she had retreated in shame, how I would preserve her honor and, although she had not asked for it, her dignity.

"The Mother of the Believers is regretful about her loss, but, as those who know her can imagine, she remains proud of her role in the battle for what she believed was just," I said. "She also remains proud of those who fought so bravely and so well on her side.

"She has offered to advise me on matters concerning the *khalifa*, and

I have agreed, for I find her wisdom and experience to be incomparable. However, I have asked her—and she has agreed—to remain at her home in Medina, out of the public eye, for the sake of *islam*. We do not need divisiveness or any reminders of it, but unity. In the meantime, I beg you all to leave her in peace, so that she may heal."

At that moment, however, A'isha appeared among us, making her way to Abdallah's tent.

"There she is now!" someone cried. "*Yaa* Mother of the Believers! May al-Lah be with you." He ululated in praise of her, as did I, as did every man among us. As for A'isha, she drew her wrapper more closely about her face and ducked into her nephew's tent. Yet, before she disappeared, her gaze met mine for an instant. In her luminous eyes I beheld intelligence, as always, and gratitude. In my eyes, I am certain, she beheld sadness of a most profound nature. For I sensed, in that moment, that I would never see A'isha again.

A'isha

I was standing in the courtyard under the date-palm tree, reciting the *qur'an*, when Abdallah brought me the news.

"*Afwan*, aunt," he said, breaking into my performance, "please, may I speak with you privately? It's urgent."

The tears brimming in Abdallah's eyes filled my mouth with salt. I turned to the men, women, children, *shaykhs*, *hajjat*, *ansari*, Bedouins, Meccans, Companions of Muhammad, and others filling the courtyard and sitting atop its walls. They had come to hear the words of God spoken from the very first—*In the name of al-Lah*—to the very last—*be they djinn or people*. I barely noted how they frowned when I asked to be excused. With legs that quaked, I led my nephew into my hut, moving, once inside, around the graves of Muhammad, my father, and Umar. Foreboding weighted every step as I recalled my dream from the night before, of snarling dogs sinking their fangs into Ali's throat, filling their mouths with his steaming blood.

"Ali is dead," Abdallah said once we were inside. I began to tremble.

"How did it happen?" I asked, praying it wasn't as my dream had shown. "Please, tell me all you know."

In a faltering voice, Abdallah spoke of the Kharijites, a group of rebels who'd opposed Ali. They had also hated Mu'awiyya, who had proclaimed himself *khalifa* in defiance of Ali. The Kharijites had sent murderers to kill them both, but Mu'awiyya, as lucky as ever, had escaped. Ali, on the other hand, had been stabbed in the mosque at Kufa as he'd prepared to lead the Friday prayer services.

"He died a few moments later, after calling out to God and His Prophet," Abdallah said. "May peace be upon him."

May peace be upon him. After my nephew had gone to tell my sister-wives the news, I wondered if Ali, in death, had managed to find peace at last. His life had been anything but peaceful. As a warrior, he'd volunteered for every caravan raid, every battle, every expedition Muhammad had called, and he'd been renowned for his ferocity and his skills with his double-bladed sword. But most of Ali's battles had had little to do with the sword.

Yaa Ali, how alike we were! As I lay on my bed, tears slid into my hair as I recalled the last time we'd spoken, the pleasure on his face as he'd held that sword in his hands. *Al-Ma'thur*, "The Legacy." I'd felt that same glow when Muhammad had given it to me, the prized possession of his father and his father's father.

I'd been happy to give up the sword. The weight of it, hefted so thoughtfully by Ali that day, had burdened me in ways I hadn't realized. Once it had passed into Ali's hands, my spirit seemed to leap, lightened.

Use it well in the jihad *to come.* Those had been Muhammad's words, uttered on his deathbed, as he'd bequeathed al-Ma'thur to me. He'd been talking about a struggle, and I'd always assumed he referred to the contest for the *khalifa* that had shaken *islam* to its foundations. As I'd stood on that camel, however, I'd realized how the lust for revenge, both mine against Ali and his against me, had poisoned us both, and had tainted *islam*. And as I'd watched the men around me fall, I'd known that this was not the *jihad* of which Muhammad had spoken. This was not the battle he'd wanted me to fight. Hatred and killing were not the legacy Muhammad had intended.

The murmurs and shouts of one hundred Believers, my children, still waiting in the courtyard, pulled me out of my bed and up to my window. My niece, A'isha bint Talha, waved to me; I raised my hand, heavy with grief, and she smiled. Like the wings of a bird, her mouth lifted up at the corners, carrying away my sorrow.

In disabling my camel, Ali had saved my life. He had saved *islam*, also, although he might not have realized it. Here, in my courtyard, was where the future of our faith resided, not on some blood-soaked battlefield or in the *majlis* of scheming politicians. *Khalifat* would come and go, but His words—the holy *qur'an*—and the *hadith*, the stories about Muhammad's life—would live forever. Here, at last, was the *jihad* for which I'd been destined: the struggle to keep *islam* in its pure state ever before the minds and hearts of Believers, as Muhammad had envisioned it, as al-Lah had revealed it.

A knock sounded at my door. Little A'isha, her eyes as green as her father Talha's had been, stood on the other side, smiling, lightening my heart. "*Yaa* Mother of the Believers, we are all waiting," she said. "We are waiting for you."

She reached out her hand and I slipped it into mine. I let her lead me across the grass, to the date-palm tree, where I stood in the shade, closed my eyes, and prayed for the words to come, those beautiful words like honey from my lips to those of my children.

"*Bismillah al-rahmani, al-rahim.*"

"In the name of al-Lah, the most Beneficent, the most Merciful."

May peace be upon us all.

Glossary of Arabic Terms

abi: My father
afwan: Excuse me
ahl al-bayt: "People of the house," or family
ansari: Helpers; the Medina tribes who followed Muhammad
assalaamu aleikum: "Peace be with you"; a greeting
bint: Daughter of
dinar: A gold coin, unit of currency
dirham: A silver coin, unit of currency
djinni: A mythical spirit inhabiting the Earth, with supernatural powers
fitna: Civil war; fighting among Muslims
habib: Beloved
habibi, habibati: My beloved
harim: The inner sanctum where the women of the household reside
hawdaj: A curtained seat atop a camel
hijab: The curtain or veil
hilm: Leadership qualitie
huriya: "Lovely eyed" companions in Paradise
ibn: Son of
islam: Submission (to al-Lah)
Ka'ba (cube): The name for the sacred shrine in Mecca
kema: Desert truffles

khalifa: The successor to Muhammad; the spiritual leader of Sunni Muslims
kunya: Honorary name given to a mother or father
majnun: A crazed man
marhaba, marhabtein: A greeting and its response
miswak: Tree with an astringent quality, whose twigs are use to clean the teeth
muezzin: The person who sounds the call to prayer
qur'an: Recitations; specifically, Muhamad's recitations from al-Lah
raka'at: Bows in the ritual of Muslim prayer
sahib: Friend
samoom: A violent windstorm that darkens the sky with sand
shaykh: An old man
tanbur: A musical instrument, the precursor to the lyre
tharid: A dish of meat and bread, reputed to be Muhammad's favorite
umma: The Muslim community of Believers; also, a mother-land
ummi: My mother
yaa: Loose trans. "hey"; a word used before a person's name to address him or her
wadi: A (usually dry) riverbed
zauba'ah: "Devils," or pillars of sand formed in a samoom